My Wild Irish Rose

Rachel Wilson

JOVE BOOKS, NEW YORK

MY WILD IRISH ROSE

A Jove Book / published by arrangement with
the author

PRINTING HISTORY
Jove edition / December 2000

The Penguin Putnam Inc. World Wide Web site address is
http://www.penguinputnam.com

ISBN: 0-515-12972-0

A JOVE BOOK®
Jove Books are published by The Berkley Publishing Group,
a division of Penguin Putnam Inc.
375 Hudson Street, New York, New York 10014
JOVE and the "J" design
are trademarks belonging to Penguin Putnam Inc.

PRINTED IN THE UNITED STATES OF AMERICA

10 9 8 7 6 5 4 3 2 1

To Joan Young,
without whose help it
never could have been written.

Thanks, Joan!

Prologue

Rose Larkin paused with her teacup halfway to her lips, sure she hadn't heard her aunt, Kathleen Flanagan, correctly.

Her father, Edward O'Malley Larkin, had just been laid to rest in the nearby Irish cemetery, amid a host of other dead immigrant Irishmen. Rose had been trying all day not to cry, with varying degrees of success.

Now she sat in her father's parlor, sipping tea with Aunt Kate, and wishing all the guests at the wake would go home so she could break down in peace. She stared at Aunt Kate, befuddled, tears and sorrow forgotten for the nonce.

Kate, her color heightened considerably, said in a stage whisper, "I mean it, Rose. You're too high-spirited a girl to marry some stuffy fellow and fade into the wallpaper."

Although sixty-five years old, Kate was still a very pretty woman, probably because she'd always had plenty of money. Rose had noticed more than once that money was an important commodity if one hoped to keep a firm grip on one's health and beauty. She feared, given her circumstances, her own looks wouldn't last as long as her aunt's—unless, of course, she married some stuffy fellow and faded into the wallpaper.

Personally, Rose had nothing against tasteful wallpaper. Stuffiness, if accompanied by security, would be far preferable to the haphazard life she'd lived with her father.

She cleared her throat, took a sip of tea, and peeked at the guests. One of them was Guy Foskett, who was as stuffy, secure, and rich as any man of Rose's acquaintance. He'd also been paying attentions to her recently. At present he was pontificating in a corner with the priest who had performed the funeral service. Rose looked back at Kate, and said, "Um . . . I'm not sure I understand what you mean, Kate."

"Yes, you do," Kate said with what was for her unusual force. "You understand exactly what I mean. You're your father's daughter, after all."

Undeniable, although Rose wasn't sure what that had to do with anything. She frowned slightly. She'd loved her father dearly, but she wasn't sure she wanted to be like him. He'd embraced life, women, and horses, and had gambled away most of the money he'd ever made. In the end he'd left Rose nothing but a pile of debts, a salable house, and a heartload of grief.

Even the manner of his death had been interesting. He'd bought a high-spirited horse—no surprise there—which had then stumbled and fallen over onto him, crushing the life out of him.

Rose was now faced with selling everything she'd ever owned in order to settle her father's debts—and with marrying Guy Foskett if he ever asked her. Guy was probably the dullest man on the face of the earth. But nice. He was very nice.

She sighed.

"Um, what does my being my father's daughter have to do with anything?"

Kate put her teacup down in its saucer and put a small, black-gloved hand on Rose's black sleeve. "Everything. You have your entire life ahead of you, Rose. You mustn't make the mistake I made. You mustn't."

Rose was appalled to see tears filling her dear aunt's eyes. "Mistake? What mistake?"

Leaning over and whispering, her expression intense, Kate said, "The mistake of marrying before you've had some adventures."

Adventures? Rose blinked. She couldn't think of a single thing to say.

"Not that I didn't love my Glen with all my heart," Kate continued. "But I never *lived*, dear. I don't want that to happen to you. I know your father left you poorly off, dear, but I've got lots of money."

Rose nodded because it was true. She still couldn't think of anything to say.

"And I intend to use some of it on you."

"You do?" Rose set her own teacup in its saucer, being very careful because her hand had started trembling. She wondered if her sweet aunt, who had always been a tiny bit eccentric, had finally passed some invisible barrier and stumbled into full-blown madness.

"But you've always used it on me, Aunt Kate," Rose said with some embarrassment.

"Nonsense, dear. That was only because your father was—well, not all that stable."

How very, unfortunately, true. "Still, Kate, I don't think you should do any more for me. You've already done too much."

Kate nodded with vigor and purpose. "Nonsense. What else do I have to do with my money?"

Rose could probably come up with several hundred things, but she was too stunned to think of them at the moment. "But . . ."

"No. I'm not willing to see you dwindle into a stuffy, bored housewife who does nothing but cater to her husband's whims while he's off living the high life and probably bedding other men's wives." Kate lifted her chin, defiant in the face of her niece's shock.

Rose opened her mouth, couldn't find a word in it to save her soul, and shut it again.

"Therefore," Kate went on, her words gathering momentum although her volume never rose, "I intend to see you *live*, Rose Margaret Larkin. We've spoken before about a profession for you should you decide you can't abide marrying Guy." She shot a glance in Guy's direction, obviously fearing she might have been overheard. She hadn't been. Guy remained engrossed in listening to himself speak.

Rose nodded, since that, too, was the truth.

"Well, then, I have the perfect career for you! And I plan to see that you achieve it."

"You do? That is—you will?" Rose folded her hands in her lap, unable to think of anything else to do with herself. She did dart a glance around the room, in search of someone who might come to her aid should Kate suddenly fall into a fit. She'd never seen her mild-mannered aunt so excited.

"Yes. I do and I shall." Kate picked up her teacup, sipped, and set it down again with a clink. "I think you should become an ad-vumph-drumph."

Her hand had risen to cover her mouth on the last word, and Rose didn't hear it. "Ahem. I beg your pardon?"

Kate took a deep breath, expanding her bosom to an almost bodice-shattering degree. "I believe," she said distinctly, "in honor of your father, your Irish heritage, and me"—she smiled sweetly, to let Rose know she didn't really mean the last part—"that you should set your sights upon being an ad-vumph-drumph." Again her hand covered her mouth, extinguishing the last word.

Rose licked her lips and tried again. "Um, I didn't hear you, Kate."

Kate expelled a huff of exasperation. "I *said*," she said, "that before you settle down into a life of boredom and tedium, as I did, you should become an adventuress." Her cheeks bloomed pink.

Rose heard her that time. She just didn't believe her ears.

One

"And so, Mr. Costello, that's how we happened to be in Dublin. I don't understand how the inn could have lost our reservations, but I truly appreciate your helping us out in this way. But, ah, could you let me know what your plans are? I'm a little concerned about leaving Aunt Kate at the Coat of Arms."

"My dear Miss Larkin, your aunt is perfectly safe."

"Well . . . I'm sure you're right. You're being very kind to a stranger, Mr. Costello."

The lovely young woman speaking to Everett Costello, the blackest rogue in the city of Dublin and perhaps the whole of Ireland, smiled beguilingly. Cullen O'Banyon frowned. She didn't look like one of Costello's typical ladies of the night. She was too innocent-looking, too pink-cheeked, too wholesome.

Too bloody American.

Good Lord, Costello wasn't going to try to seduce an American, was he? Cullen could hear the cannons of war firing in his head already. Ireland already had enough trouble with the British. It didn't need America against them, too.

The girl had auburn hair, a spectacular figure, and the brightest, bluest eyes Cullen had ever seen. Her manner, if not her appearance, reminded him of his sister Brenda. She was obviously a lady and a thoroughbred, however American she was. Because the girl charmed him, because he didn't trust Costello, and because he knew good and well no woman was safe within a mile of the scoundrel, Cullen sidled closer to the two.

They were standing at the door of the taproom at the Green Boar, the girl apparently a wee bit reluctant to enter the taproom with her escort. Smart girl. Cullen pretended to consult his railway schedule as he listened.

"Trust me, Miss Larkin. Your aunt will be fine at the Coat of Arms. I'll send word and some money to hire a room for her. Of course, if my carriage hadn't lost a spoke, we could return to her tonight, but I fear we'll have to stay here this evening."

She looked doubtful—as well she might. Cullen's lips tightened. The villain! He was planning a base seduction of an obvious innocent. Costello was a devil, and Cullen would bet his best horse that the girl didn't have any idea how much trouble she was in.

"But, Mr. Costello," the girl said, "if you can send word, why can't you send me? I'm sure I don't mind spending the night with Aunt Kate at the Coat of Arms, even if we have to sit in the lobby or in one of those rooms where those men were drinking."

Costello took her arm lightly. An expression of alarm crossed her face. About time, Cullen thought sourly.

"My dear girl, don't you trust me?"

"Y-yes," she said doubtfully. "Of course, I do."

"Then, relax. Let's have a pint in the taproom, and you can tell me all about New York."

"But—" The young woman balked as Costello gently pulled on her arm.

That was enough for Cullen. He knew Costello too well to think he had innocuous plans for this girl. She obviously had no experience with the world, or she'd know it too. Costello aimed to ply her with drink, lure her up to a bedroom, and ravish her, and Cullen—no hero, but a gentleman for all that—wasn't going to let him get away with it.

He turned abruptly and pretended to bump into Costello by accident. "Oh, I say there, Costello. I beg your pardon."

Costello scowled at him. "O'Banyon. What are you doing here?" He didn't sound pleased to see him.

"I had to come to Dublin on business." Cullen removed his hat and smiled at the girl. "I beg your pardon, ma'am. Please forgive my clumsiness."

She smiled back at him. "That's quite all right, sir."

Considering what to do now, Cullen opted for a more-or-less straightforward rescue of a damsel in distress. He turned back to Costello. "I couldn't help but overhear some of your conversation, old fellow. If your carriage has sustained damage, perhaps I might help transport the lady back to where her aunt is. Or, if there are no rooms available at the Coat of Arms, I can send Johnny to fetch her. I'm sure the Green Boar has rooms available."

"Oh, how very kind of you!" the girl cried.

"There's no need for that." Costello, on the other hand, sounded sulky.

Cullen ignored him. "It's not kindness at all, Miss . . . ?" He lifted an eyebrow.

She stuck out a hand and gave him one of her glorious smiles. "Rose Larkin. I'm so pleased to meet you."

He took her hand and bowed over it formally. Formality was second nature to him, a fact he sometimes regretted. Like now, for instance, when he wished he knew how to do a little flirting. "Cullen O'Banyon, Miss Larkin, at your service."

"Really, Mr. O'Banyon, you needn't bother," Costello replied.

"Oh, Mr. Costello, I hope you don't mind. But I truly don't want to leave my aunt alone in Dublin on our first night in Ireland." She took her hand from Cullen's loose grip and held it out to Costello. "Thank you so much for trying to be of help to us. You were so wonderful to my aunt and me."

Cullen stiffened, half expecting Costello to take her

hand and begin dragging her off to consummate his fell purpose. But he merely shook it instead and said in a hard voice, "I'm sure you needn't run off with Mr. O'Banyon, Miss Larkin. I am more than happy to take care of you."

"No doubt," Cullen said dryly. He gave Costello a good glare to let him know that he, Cullen O'Banyon, intended to see Miss Rose Larkin stay as innocent as she appeared to be.

Costello, evidently having decided that attempting to deflower Rose Larkin would be too much trouble that evening, bowed, said, "I see," and stalked away.

Rose watched him go, her expression puzzled. Cullen shook his head, wondering how so naive a young woman could have ended up in Costello's clutches so soon after her arrival in Ireland.

"He was really very nice to us." She didn't sound too sure of herself.

"I'm sure he was." Cullen saw no reason to shatter her credulity with a painful truth. The father of two young boys, Cullen appreciated and even valued innocence in its proper place. Alone in a Dublin inn was, however, not one of those places. "But perhaps we can reunite you with your aunt, Miss Larkin. I did hear you say she was at the Coat of Arms, did I not?"

"Yes, indeed, Mr. O'Banyon. And she's probably frantic with worry. This is so awfully kind of you."

"It is my pleasure, Miss Larkin." He crooked his arm. She placed her little gloved hand on it and gave him such a trusting look that his heart tripped.

She spoke as they started toward the door of the inn. "Mr. Costello was being very nice to us, trying to help and all, but a spoke on his carriage wheel broke." She frowned prettily. "I didn't notice anything wrong with it, but I'm afraid I don't know much about carriages."

She didn't know much about men, either, Cullen thought grimly. Which is exactly what Costello had been counting on. He had to stop himself from dropping Rose's hand, running after Everett Costello, and socking him in the jaw. With an effort, he made himself calm down. "Will you have something to eat before we arrange for your aunt's arrival?"

She paused, then shook her head. "No, thank you, Mr. O'Banyon. I really must see to Aunt Kate."

Cullen beckoned one of the boots, who trotted over immediately. He gave the boy instructions for fetching the aunt, then smiled down at Rose. She only came up to his shoulder, and he felt a sudden surge of protectiveness toward her. "But you are hungry. I can tell." She reminded him of his sons when they were starving, but being polite about it.

She smiled back, and his knees turned to water for an instant before he braced himself. This intense a reaction to a woman was nonsensical, and Cullen knew it. He'd been married for five years, for heaven's sake, and widowed for another five. He was too old and staid to indulge in adolescent flights of emotional exaltation.

"I'm actually terribly hungry. We didn't have time for dinner. There was a mix-up at the inn, and we were trying to solve it when Mr. Costello showed up and asked if he could help us."

Cullen would bet on it. Costello was a rat. He only smiled, however, in response.

"We're from America, you see. New York City. Well, my aunt was from Ireland originally, but she left for America shortly after she married, and that was—oh, mercy, it must be more than forty years ago now."

"I see." She really was charming.

Cullen's groom, Johnny Sullivan, strode up to him and fingered the brim of his cap. "Yessir. You sent for me?"

"Yes. Johnny, will you please take my carriage to the Coat of Arms and fetch a lady named—" He glanced down at Rose.

"Kathleen Flanagan," she supplied.

"Kathleen Flanagan. Mrs. Flanagan?" Again, Cullen looked at Rose, who nodded and smiled.

Johnny swallowed and goggled a bit, although Rose hadn't been paying particular attention to him. So Miss Rose Larkin had a dazzling effect on him as well, did she?

Cullen was even more glad now that he'd rescued her from Costello's clutches. A woman who made such stoical specimens as Johnny Sullivan gulp and goggle shouldn't be allowed anywhere near a swine like Everett Costello.

He said, "Yes. Mrs. Flanagan. Miss Larkin will write a note for you to give her, so that she won't be worried." He turned to Rose. "Is that all right with you, Miss Larkin?"

"You're being so awfully nice to us, Mr. O'Banyon. I truly didn't expect such kindness from strangers." She fished in her little reticule until she found a piece of paper, and then looked around the room, evidently searching out a pen and ink. Cullen thought she was adorable, if way too trusting.

"Here, Miss Larkin. While you write your note, let me secure a private room where we can await your aunt's arrival. I'll also arrange for something to eat."

He'd planned on returning to his horse farm in the country tomorrow, but he decided on the spot that he was going to make sure Miss Rose Larkin and her aunt Kate were safe before he did so. Miss Larkin couldn't be trusted on her own—Costello had proved that already. And with her friendly disposition, the good Lord alone knew what would happen to her without someone to supervise her. Her aunt was obviously no kind of chaperone.

He arranged for a private room, and Rose wrote a note to her aunt. Johnny bowed much more politely than was his wont when he bore the note away. To Cullen, the lad looked as if he were going off to slay dragons for the fair maiden, and he smiled after him. Cullen knew exactly how Johnny felt. He was of a like mind himself.

Rose couldn't account for the feeling of relief that swept over her when she said good-bye to Mr. Costello and accepted Mr. O'Banyon's kind offices. She knew Mr. Costello was a nice man; everyone in Ireland was nice, according to Aunt Kate. But there was something rather large and soothing about Mr. O'Banyon, whereas Mr. Costello had an odd, uncomfortable sort of glitter about him.

She was merely being fanciful; she still hadn't adapted

herself to the notion of leaving her home in America and moving to Ireland to become an adventuress. No matter what Aunt Kate said, pursuing life as an adventuress sounded like an intimidating prospect to Rose.

On the other hand, this was a fairly creditable adventure—the first she'd ever had unless she counted the uneventful ocean voyage from New York to Liverpool—and she wasn't about to belittle it. She sank into a chair and watched Cullen speak to the landlord, relaxing for the first time in hours. In spite of a rather dashing and piratical exterior, Cullen O'Banyon seemed so . . . capable, Rose guessed was the right word.

Why, only look at this room. While Mr. Costello had seemed to think getting a parlor room in which to rest was nigh unto an impossibility, Mr. O'Banyon had managed it with no fuss at all. A peat fire burned merrily in the grate, a small table was set in front of it with four chairs around it, one of which Rose now occupied, and there was a nice, comfortable-looking sofa against the wall. Two wing chairs had been placed alongside the fireplace, and there was a cozy bookshelf behind one of the chairs. It looked as if the room had been readied especially for them and had only been awaiting their arrival.

She thought Cullen O'Banyon was rather like a hero, in truth. And he was amazingly handsome.

He turned and smiled at her, and her heart gave a little flutter. He was such a courteous and gracious man. And astoundingly good-looking. Tall and broad-shouldered, with tanned skin and dark hair, he looked very much like a dashing swashbuckler from the high seas or something, although he didn't act like one. Mr. Costello, who was much smaller and less prepossessing, reminded Rose more of a brigand than Mr. O'Banyon did.

"There," he said, coming back to the table where Rose sat. "Would you care for half a pint to warm you up, Miss Larkin?"

"Half a pint? Half a pint of what?"

He laughed. "It's an expression we use for something to drink."

"Oh, of course." She felt silly. "I'd love to have some hot cocoa. And—and maybe a cinnamon bun."

"Hot chocolate." He looked nonplused for a moment— but only for a moment. "Certainly. I'll tell the landlord." He did, going to the door and stepping outside.

Rose sat at the table, gnawed her nails, and wished she'd traveled more in her life. On the other hand, she was only nineteen. No one could expect a nineteen-year-old to be an experienced woman of the world. Especially if her movements had been constricted by poverty during most of those years.

Mr. O'Banyon returned no more than a minute or two later, smiling serenely. Rose felt better at once. "We should have some hot cocoa and cinnamon buns in a minute or two. I asked for raspberries, too. That should sustain us until your aunt arrives. Then we can have a real meal. I'm sorry you two ladies had such a rocky start to your stay in Ireland."

"Thank you so much, Mr. O'Banyon. I don't know what I'd have done without your help."

"I'm sure you'd have muddled through somehow." He pulled out a chair. "May I join you?"

Surprised that he'd even ask, Rose said, "Of course."

He sat, removed his traveling gloves, and smiled again. Rose knew she must be very hungry because every time he smiled at her, she got light-headed. "Well, now, Miss Larkin, what are your plans? Do you and your aunt intend to conduct a tour of our fair green land?"

"Indeed we do, Mr. O'Banyon. Aunt Kate has told me so much about her homeland that I'm dying to see every inch of it. Eventually. She has a few plans for us first." Her mood darkened when she considered those plans of Kate's, but she chased the darkness away as futile and unprofitable.

"Do you have relations here?"

Rose frowned. "Not any longer. Aunt Kate and my father were the last of their family, I fear."

Cullen nodded politely. He was very polite. "And they left for America in search of a better life. That's happened to us far too often, I fear. As beautiful as Ireland is, and as much as I love her, she and the political struggles that have been waged on her sod for so many centuries have been hard on many of her folks."

"Yes. My father used to tell me stories." Rose shook her head sadly. As feckless and irresponsible as her father had been, she missed him a lot. "He was a wonderful story-teller."

"Aye. So many of our lads are."

Cullen's chuckle was rich and deep and made Rose wish she were a more sophisticated woman of the world. Especially since her companion seemed so suave and debonair. She couldn't think of a thing to say, and tried not to stare at him.

After a moment, he cleared his throat and said, "So are you here for a holiday, Miss Larkin? You and your aunt?"

Rose hesitated. "Not entirely."

"No?" He lifted an eyebrow. He had gorgeous eyes. They reminded Rose of dark, sweet chocolate. No, that was absurd. She was only hungry.

"No. I . . . ah . . . intend to seek employment."

"Employment?" His mouth pursed slightly. "Any particular sort of employment? Are you a governess or teacher, perhaps?"

His lips looked full and soft when he did that, making Rose want to touch them. With hers. Good heavens, what did this mean? Perhaps she was more cut out for the adventuress-ing business than she'd originally believed. Deciding to be brave and take the plunge, she swallowed and blurted out, "No. I plan to become an adventuress, Mr. O'Banyon."

His eyes opened wide for a moment, then he blinked twice. He opened his mouth, shut it, and then said, "How, er, fascinating."

Rose felt herself flush, and wished she'd kept her fat mouth shut. "Good Lord, you must think me an idiot, to blurt it out like that. It's only that my father died recently, and my aunt Kate persuaded me to seek some adventures before I settle into a stuffy life as a matron in New York City."

He stared at her, and her blush got hotter.

"I see."

"I'm sure you don't see at all," she said, vaguely discouraged. "How could you? You're a man."

He tipped his head to one side, as if conceding the point. "There is that, of course."

She eyed him narrowly. Was he laughing at her? No. He looked far too polite to be laughing. "I know it sounds silly, but Aunt Kate always longed for adventure herself, you see, but she was forever the good girl. My father was the one who did things."

"He did things?"

She lifted a hand and shrugged. "Oh, you know. He gambled and traveled and so forth. Men have so much more freedom than women have to do interesting things."

"Undeniable."

"And Aunt Kate always felt rather as though life had passed her by."

"I see."

"But it's not fair at all." Rose held up a hand, this time to forestall a protest from her companion. "Oh, I know what you're going to say."

"I doubt it," he murmured.

The door opened and a waiter backed in, carrying a tray. Cullen rose, took the tray from him, set it on the table, and gave the man a coin. The waiter tugged at his forelock and left the room. Cullen spread the food out. Rose's mouth watered. She was *so* hungry.

"Here you go, Miss Larkin." He set a plate before her bearing a huge cinnamon bun, and poured hot chocolate into a pretty flowered china cup from a matching pot. "Eat up and tell me all about your plans to become an adventuress." He lifted a tankard filled with dark lager to his lips. "I must admit to being completely fascinated."

Rose broke off a piece of bun and popped it into her mouth. She knew she should try to be ladylike, but her stomach had taken to growling, and being ladylike was difficult.

She glanced at Cullen and saw that he was leaning back in his chair with his long legs stretched out in front of him and crossed at the ankles, holding his tankard. He looked as if he belonged here, in front of the fire, relaxing and peering at her with an odd sort of half smile on his gorgeous lips. He looked every inch the dashing, devil-may-care rake. He looked exactly, in fact, like the sort of man she'd dreamed about when Aunt Kate first proposed that she become an adventuress. Rose had thought her aunt, who had always been a little scatterbrained—not to mention romantically inclined—was dreaming. Now she wasn't so sure. She cleared her throat.

"At any rate, with her to chaperone me, Aunt Kate thought it might be exciting to come to Ireland and see if I can do something interesting with my life."

"I should think you're well on your way already."

She laughed softly and ate another bite of bun. "Yes, I suppose I am." She looked up at him and stopped smiling. "But I'll be very glad to have Aunt Kate here with me. I didn't like being separated from her."

"No, I'm sure that's true." He took another sip from his tankard.

"And . . . and . . ." She sucked in a big breath. "And I must admit that I feel much more at ease in your company than I did with Mr. Costello."

"Understandable." His tone was dry. "You're a shrewd judge of character, Miss Larkin."

"I am?" She gazed at him for a moment, but his expression had turned dark, and she didn't quite dare to question him further on the subject. It did, however, sound as if he considered Mr. Costello not quite the gentleman he had proclaimed himself to be. Oh, dear. Actually, she'd never suspected as much, so her judgment of character didn't seem awfully good to her. She sighed and decided there was little she could do about that man.

She chewed and swallowed several bites of her sweet roll, drank some more of the hot chocolate, and smiled at him. "This was a wonderful idea, Mr. O'Banyon. I'm feeling much better already."

"I'm glad of that. Care for a raspberry?" He offered the dish, his strong brown fingers looking out of place holding the delicate silver bowl.

"Thank you." She tried not to think about his hands as she took a berry and popped it into her mouth. "Oh, it's delicious."

He watched her lips for a couple of minutes, then sat up straighter and set his tankard on the table. "So, tell me, Miss Larkin, what exactly do you expect from your life as an adventuress? Are you . . . ah . . . anticipating anything of a . . . well, a romantic nature to occur?"

"A romantic nature?" Rose looked at him blankly for a moment before enlightenment struck and she blushed again. "Oh! You mean do I expect to be introduced to gentlemen?"

He lifted his shoulders in a gesture Rose had always associated more with the French personality than the Irish. "Er, something like that, yes. I mean, I had assumed—before I met you, of course—that your average adventuress generally put herself under the protection of a fellow. Or two. One at a time, of course."

"Of course."

Rose considered his question further. She and Aunt Kate actually had discussed the matter. Kate had been all for it. Rose had been shocked. To be keeping company with a gentleman—in *that* way—without the benefit of marriage was a circumstance Rose had never contemplated in her entire nineteen years. She certainly never believed she'd be talking about the possibility with a man.

Mr. O'Banyon was so kind, though, and so gentlemanly. She couldn't see any reason not to be open with him, especially since he was, at present, acting as her good angel. Perhaps this sort of thing is what Aunt Kate had meant when she'd discussed meeting gentlemen. It seemed a little haphazard to Rose, but she knew so little about the adventuress business.

"I didn't mean to embarrass you, Miss Larkin."

Oh, dear, now he looked uncomfortable. "You didn't embarrass me, Mr. O'Banyon. Not really. In fact, I'm sure being an adventuress is an unusual ambition for a woman."

"Er, yes, especially one who seems so . . . so . . . refined."

Did he really think she was refined? Rose was so pleased, she beamed at him. "Thank you. The headmistress of the school I attended in New York City would be very happy to hear you say so. She feared I would take after my father, you see."

"Is that a fact?" He took another sip of lager and looked as if he were fighting a smile.

Rose didn't think it was funny. In fact, it had been downright embarrassing sometimes. She lowered her gaze and fiddled with the plate that had lately held her cinnamon bun. At present it held only crumbs that she wished she could pick up with a moistened finger—but she wouldn't. That would be too much. "My father was sometimes . . . ah . . . tardy in his payments."

"Ah. Sounds like an Irishman, all right."

Rose sighed. "I fear it was the horses, Mr. O'Banyon."

His eyebrows lifted again. He had *such* splendid eyes. "The horses?"

"Yes. He liked . . ." Bother. She wished she hadn't started talking about her father. She was apt to burst into tears if she thought about him too much. He'd been such a flawed person and yet such a wonderful father. "At any rate, the headmistress tolerated my presence even when his payments were tardy because I wrote prize-winning essays."

"Ah."

"The fact that my essays always won the city-wide competition was the jewel in the crown of St. Martin's Academy." She grinned, glad to have left the dismal subject of her dead father behind for awhile. "That's what she used to say: The jewel in the crown."

She giggled, then sobered again. "She said I probably got my way with words from my father, but that I used them to greater purpose than he ever did." She wished she hadn't remembered that part.

"I think I understand, Miss Larkin," Cullen said softly.

"I loved my father very much, Mr. O'Banyon. He was a delightful man, but he did like to take risks."

"He played the horses, did he?"

She looked up, relieved. He sounded so matter-of-fact about it. The headmistress hadn't been at all matter-of-fact. The headmistress called her father names Rose had been shocked to learn she knew. "I'm afraid he did."

"My dear Miss Larkin, it's nothing to be afraid of. The man wouldn't have been Irish if he didn't like the ponies. I love horses myself."

"You do?" Hmmm. He didn't look like the type of man her father used to be chummy with. Thank heavens. Rose wouldn't have trusted some of those fellows in the same room with a young, presentable female. In fact, she used to lock herself in her room when they showed up in the house.

"I do. In fact, I . . . ah . . . have a lot to do with horses."

"Oh!" Goodness, maybe he was more like her father than he looked. Rose didn't know whether to be pleased or upset. Letting her glance slide, she took note of his well-tailored suit and highly polished boots and took heart. Maybe he was one of those rich milords. If one had enough money, it probably didn't matter how much one bet on the horses. "Well, then," she said doubtfully, "you probably understand."

"I believe I do."

"Anyhow, getting back to your question, my aunt and I discussed it, and we decided that I should probably try to avoid entanglements with any particular gentleman until I ascertain whether or not he is of a high moral fiber."

He swallowed the wrong way and coughed.

"Oh, dear, Mr. O'Banyon, are you all right?" Rose got up and went to pat him on the back.

By the time he had enough breath to say, "I'm fine, thank you, Miss Larkin," a knock had come at the door. It was pushed open from the other side, and Rose looked over Cullen's head to see her aunt Kate Flanagan standing in the open doorway, clutching her reticule, and looking like a dear, pretty, frightened little bird.

Rose rushed to her and gave her an impulsive hug, which her aunt returned with enthusiasm.

TWO

Cullen had never met a less likely adventuress than Miss Rose Larkin in his life. Not that he'd had the opportunity to meet very many before this. He watched the sweet young lady embrace her obviously mentally deficient aunt, and wondered what was going to become of the two of them. With only a mad aunt to guide her in the life of an adventuress, Cullen feared sweet little Rose would have a difficult time of it.

He could understand how a young, vital woman could harbor a thirst for adventure, however. In his secret heart-of-hearts, he even harbored one of his own, although he'd never acted upon it. In fact, when he considered the matter, Miss Rose Larkin had a good deal more spirit in her bones than he possessed. It was a deflating realization.

Here he was, thirty-three years old, the father of two marvelous lads, widowed, and he'd never done anything but go to school, marry, produce heirs, and run the horse farm that had been in his family for generations. The farm provided the best Irish horses in the whole country, as well a fabulous income, but it somehow seemed paltry when he watched Rose and her aunt.

Now *those* two were living. They weren't following the same decorous rules he'd always followed. They were reaching out and grabbing life by the lapels. Granted their first foray into adventuress-ing had landed them in the lap of a black-hearted scoundrel, but Cullen still honored their resourcefulness.

He contemplated their daring enterprise, and his own safe and secure life paled in significance. Oh, he wouldn't give it up. He loved his heritage, the beautiful valley in which he lived, the rolling green hills of his home. He loved his sons with a fervor he hadn't believed himself capable of until he first saw them in their mother's arms.

And his wife . . . Judith. He still missed her. Theirs hadn't been a match born of violent love and unbridled passion, but they'd cherished each other.

Cullen had a feeling that any man who wanted to take Rose Larkin to his bosom would have to persuade her by something more than gentle wooing. For all her obvious intelligence, total ignorance of life, and basic air of breeding, she was a little reckless.

She left off hugging her aunt and turned, a luminous smile on her face, and began tugging the small woman toward him.

Mrs. Flanagan looked perfectly respectable, Cullen thought with some amusement. She didn't appear at all the sort of woman who would persuade her niece to pursue the life of an adventuress. Cullen would wager neither female knew exactly what an adventuress was. Or that the type of man an adventuress generally got entangled with was more like Everett Costello than Cullen O'Banyon.

A swell of protectiveness for these two women rose in his breast. He tried to squash it. He had enough responsibilities; he didn't need two more. Besides, he had a feeling that steering Rose Larkin and Kate Flanagan in a new direction would be akin to trying to harness smoke.

"Mrs. Kate Flanagan, please allow me to introduce you to our kind rescuer, Mr. Cullen O'Banyon."

Cullen took Kate's hand and bowed over it with the exquisite politeness that had been drilled into him from the cradle. "How do you do, Mrs. Flanagan? It's my great pleasure to be of assistance to two such lovely ladies." He could hardly believe he'd said that. It didn't sound like him at all. He'd spent the last few years trying to wean himself away from the formality his mother had favored.

"Oh, Mr. O'Banyon, how very kind you are!" Kate tittered, looked at her expensively gloved hand resting in his, and blushed like a schoolgirl.

Cullen was charmed by her almost as much as he'd been charmed by Rose. These two made quite a remarkable family. "Won't you sit down, Mrs. Flanagan? I've ordered a meal, but the landlord was waiting until you arrived to serve it. You must be very hungry after your ordeal."

As if on cue, waiters appeared with covered dishes and began laying them out on the table. The succulent aroma of roast beef and potatoes kissed Cullen's nostrils. He noticed that Rose lifted her head and sniffed, then swallowed, as if she could hardly wait to chow down.

Kate looked at the preparations, and her eyes gleamed. She was obviously as hungry as her niece. "Thank you so much, Mr. O'Banyon. I must admit I am quite hungry. We were astonished to discover that our letter requesting rooms had been lost at the Coat of Arms, but Rose tells me you've secured rooms for us here. I don't know what we'd have done without you. We'll never be able to thank you sufficiently!"

"It truly nothing, Mrs. Flanagan." Aunt Kate was quite a flutterer. Rose wasn't. Cullen wondered if she'd had to become levelheaded out of self-defense, because her father and aunt had been so capricious. He wouldn't be surprised.

He held out a chair for Kate to sit on, then did the same for Rose. They both smiled at him so warmly that he almost wished he were a different sort of man. If he were more like, say, Everett Costello, he might be inclined to take advantage of these two ladies' innocence. He wouldn't mind having a tasty article like Rose Larkin under his protection—except that such a move would set a deplorable example for his sons, and be unfair to Rose, and he'd never do it. He sighed. Occasionally, being the soul of propriety had its drawbacks.

Rose spoke to her aunt, drawing Cullen's attention. "I told Mr. O'Banyon about our plans, Aunt Kate. I hope you don't mind."

"Oh?" Kate glanced at Cullen, who had taken a seat at the end of the table, and her expressive face fairly bloomed with interest. "What do you think, Mr. O'Banyon? Don't you think our Rose will make a delightful adventuress?"

"Er, of course. She'd be delightful in any occupation."

Rose ducked her head, embarrassed. Kate beamed and patted Rose's hand. "That's exactly what I've been telling her. She's far too lovely and personable to hide her light under a bushel."

"Aunt Kate!" Now Rose looked mortified.

"Nonsense, Rose. It's the truth."

Cullen deemed it prudent to intervene. "And, ah, I take it you consider marriage would be in the nature of hiding her light, Mrs. Flanagan?"

"Oh, not at all, Mr. O'Banyon, but you must know that marriage is the end of any hope a woman has for adventure. At least, that's been my experience."

"I see."

"I married early, you know, and I always regretted not having . . . oh . . . *lived* first. I would hate to see Rose dwindle into a matron without having experienced one or two adventures first."

Made sense to Cullen—after a fashion. He opted for another "I see," and glanced at Rose, who was watching the food as if she feared it would vanish if she looked away.

Aunt Kate frowned prettily. "The only problem is— well, the first problem is—that Dublin seems to have changed so much since I was a girl here. Why, I don't recognize a single thing."

"Ah." Cullen began carving the roast beef.

"So it's difficult to know exactly where to begin, although I have some ideas." She lifted a newspaper. "While I waited to hear from Rose, I looked through the advertisements, and I think I have exactly the right job for Rose to begin with."

"You do?" Rose was evidently surprised.

Kate appeared to be satisfied with her research. "Indeed, I do. I spent my time at that inn doing some research." She took the plate that Cullen handed to her. "Thank you, Mr. O'Banyon."

"You're welcome." Since Rose looked like she might faint from hunger if he didn't hurry up, he lost no time in filling a second plate and offering it to her.

She managed to murmur, "Thank you," before she attacked her potatoes.

Aunt Kate turned to Cullen, popped a green bean into her mouth, chewed and swallowed, and said, "My Rose has a perfectly lovely voice, Mr. O'Banyon."

"Does she?" Cullen could well imagine it.

"Oh, my, yes. And you see here? I've circled this position." She tapped at a column in the newspaper. Sure enough, she'd circled an ad for a singer and dancer at the French Academy. "I've never heard of the French Academy, but it sounds quite respectable."

Then and there, Cullen decided he was going to extend his stay in Dublin beyond merely tomorrow. He'd send a cable to his estate manager, post a message to the boys, and remain here for awhile. If Kate Flanagan thought having Rose secure a job as a singer at the French Academy was a wonderful idea, these two needed looking after.

Respectable, his foot. He generally visited the French Academy during his visits to Dublin, and very often visited one of the dancers after the show was over, but he didn't consider his visits in the light of a respectable activity. Far from it. And they certainly weren't experiences he ever related to his children. "Ah, well, it's not exactly a regular opera house, Mrs. Flanagan."

And not only did he want to protect the two women, Cullen realized as he chewed roast beef, but he was ripe for an escapade himself. He hadn't had an adventure since he was around twelve years old and his father had taken him to Edinburgh. Even that hadn't been much of an adventure; he'd heard so much about the barbarous Scots that he'd been terribly disappointed to learn they were just like

Irishmen, except for their strange accents. Edinburgh was so civilized in spots, it made Dublin look like a backwater.

"No?" Aunt Kate's brow wrinkled momentarily, then cleared. "Well, I don't suppose we have to accept that particular position. I'm sure there will be boundless opportunities for so talented a girl as Rose." She patted Rose's hand again.

Rose had been too busy eating to contribute much to the conversation, although Cullen noticed it embarrassed her to be so highly lauded by her aunt. Now she looked up and said, "My aunt has a somewhat inflated opinion of my talents, Mr. O'Banyon."

"I'm sure she's a superb judge, Miss Larkin," he said gallantly. She offered him a smile, but he could tell she didn't mean it. "At any rate, since my business in Dublin will extend for some few days more, will you allow me to escort you to the French Academy? I'm familiar with the place, and I think two ladies alone could use the services of a gentleman."

He placed special emphasis on the last word, hoping they might take a hint that they shouldn't entrust themselves to any old man who happened along. Like Everett Costello, for example. He didn't want to burst their happy bubble by telling them in so many words that he thought they needed assistance.

Rose, at least, appeared interested, although Kate didn't seem to notice. Cullen sighed, wondering what it would take to get Kate to be sensible.

"Oh, how very nice of you!" Kate exclaimed.

"Please don't go out of your way, Mr. O'Banyon."

Rose sounded as if she were uncomfortable with his offer, which irritated him. She hadn't been so scrupulous before she took up with Everett Costello—at least Cullen presumed she hadn't been.

"It's not out of my way at all, Miss Larkin," he assured her. "In fact, it would be my pleasure." At least it would ease his conscience. If these two were let loose on an unsuspecting Dublin, he wasn't sure who would suffer more: them or Dublin. He'd not lay any wagers.

"Thank you, then," she said, capitulating with a grace that Cullen was becoming aware was second nature to her. "My aunt and I will be forever in your debt."

"Nonsense. I have business in Dublin."

"Business?" Kate looked interested.

"Mr. O'Banyon is interested in horses, Aunt Kate," Rose explained.

"Oh." Kate blinked at Cullen. "You don't look like a horse-mad fellow. Not like my late brother Edward, God rest his soul. But then, if you're so fond of horses and such, I expect you *are* a good deal like him." She frowned slightly.

"Er, yes." For some reason, in spite of his unwillingness to be likened to reckless Rose's feckless father, Cullen discovered he was also unwilling to tell these two fey creatures about himself. His real life sounded so dull compared to the dashing and rakish gambling man they'd made of him.

Rose changed the subject, for which Cullen was extremely grateful. "This is a delicious meal, Mr. O'Banyon. I fear I was rather more hungry than I'd thought. I had believed that cinnamon bun would satisfy me, but guess I needed a real meal."

"I'm certain of it," he said. "So eat up. Then I'm sure the two of you will be happy to be seen to your rooms. You must be very weary after your long journey and the mix-up at the Coat of Arms."

"Yes, I am awfully tired," Kate said. She smothered a yawn behind her hand.

Rose sat up straight and looked Cullen square in the face. "Are you sure you aren't merely being kind to us, Mr. O'Banyon? I'd feel terrible if I thought you were ruining your own plans in order to see to our welfare. Why, you must believe us to be veritable idiots for getting ourselves into this predicament."

Not after meeting Aunt Kate, he didn't. He didn't think anybody could resist Kate's blandishments. At the moment, he thought they were a beguiling and misguided pair of sweethearts. And he anticipated the morrow with much more eagerness than he generally looked forward to days away from his home, his horses, and his boys.

Yes, indeed. This was exactly what he needed to jolt him out of his rut.

When the meal was finished, he had the landlord show the two ladies upstairs to their rooms. Then he betook himself to his own room, composed a cablegram to his estate manager and a letter to William and Ferris, his sons, and opened a window. He sat in his dressing gown and slippers, smoked a cigar, sipped brandy, and contemplated Rose Larkin for almost an hour before he finally went to bed.

He really wanted to get back to the farm and to his boys. He missed them a lot, even though he'd only been gone for a week. Yet he felt an obligation to save those two females from their own folly. They weren't his concern; he told himself that over and over—and he agreed with himself. Yet he couldn't make himself abandon them here, in an alien city in an alien country—because Ireland was alien to the both of them, wherever the dithery Aunt Kate had been born decades earlier.

Cullen sighed. Reckless Rose. The title fitted her. Then he grinned.

He really ought to stop worrying about his business. He'd made a fine transaction here in Dublin and had already cabled his estate manager about it. Everything had been taken care of. He should relax and enjoy himself for a few days. He deserved an adventure. He was becoming too much of a stick-in-the-mud. He was going to turn into a crotchety old man without ever having been a young one if he didn't do something interesting every now and again.

Anyway, Rose and Kate already evidently had cast him in the role of savior. He might as well enjoy it while he could.

Rose sat on the vanity bench, brushed her hair out, and watched in the mirror as her aunt fluttered around the room. Her aunt was a first-class flutterer.

She suspected the room was a good deal better than the

one she and Kate should have had at the Coat of Arms had the inn not lost their reservation. She'd bet it was because Mr. O'Banyon was a wealthy and influential man.

Her imagination featured him on the leads of an ancient castle, his legs braced apart, a black cape flapping around his shoulders in the wind, his dark hair speckled with dew, and his eyes burning with passion. Ready for battle. Oh, my. He was *so* dashing. She tried to concentrate on her hair to take her attention away from the butterflies in her stomach.

"I do declare, Rose, I think we've just had a smallish escapade." Kate was happier than Rose had ever seen her. "And it's the very first one I've ever had in my whole life, barring the ocean voyage from Ireland to America, but that was merely uncomfortable. I was sick the whole time, and your uncle—God rest his soul—hovered over me the entire time and took care of me. It wasn't as if I was alone in the world or had been forced to flee after having taken the fancy of a wicked count who was bent upon kidnapping and ravishing me."

"A wicked count?" Rose laughed.

Kate blushed. "You know what I mean, dear. I think I've been longing for romance my entire life." She folded a black petticoat and stuffed it into her suitcase. "Anyway, we had a first-class stateroom. It's not as if we'd had to book passage in steerage or anything dramatic like that."

"Lucky for you."

"Lucky?" Kate stopped fluttering for a moment and frowned at the back of Rose's head. Rose grinned at her in the mirror. "Oh, you're teasing me, you wicked girl!"

"I'll warrant you'd have been even more uncomfortable if you'd had to be sick in steerage, Aunt Kate. Admit it. Poverty isn't all it's cracked up to be."

Kate blinked once, surprised by Rose's dry tone, then giggled. "Oh, Rose, you must think I'm a perfect goose."

"You know better than that, Kate. I love you very much, and I think you're a wonderful woman and my best friend. Why, if it hadn't been for you, I don't know what I'd have done all those years when Father and I—" She broke off suddenly because she realized she was about to say something not quite kind about her father, and she didn't want to. She and Kate had loved her father, they'd both understood his weaknesses, and it wasn't fair to discuss them now, when he was dead.

"Oh, Rose." Kate rushed up to her and gave her an impulsive hug. "I know your life was difficult. I tried to take the sting out of some of the rough times."

Rose turned on the vanity bench and returned Kate's embrace. "And you did, Aunt Kate. You did. You were our mainstay. Our rock. I don't know what we'd have done without you."

"Thank you, dear."

Kate wiped away a tear that had slid from her eye and followed a crease down her cheek. She had remarkably few wrinkles for a woman her age. Rose hoped she'd look that good when she was Kate's age.

That thought brought her butterflies back. This time they showed up with friends. Bother.

Her aunt, who had a hard time keeping to one topic for very long at a stretch, turned and began flitting around the room again. "But, it really was an adventure, Rose! Why, imagine the inn losing our reservation like that. And then being rescued by two such kind men in one evening!" She gave Rose a teasing look. "It's because you're such a pretty girl. This bodes well for our plans. I'm sure it does."

"Are you?" Rose wasn't the least bit sure about that, although she wasn't unkind enough to burst her sweet aunt's bubble by saying so.

Every time she thought about Cullen O'Banyon, her butterflies stirred up a storm. Every time she thought about Everett Costello, they settled into a cold, lifeless heap. Dead butterflies. Strange.

Tentatively, because she didn't want to distress Kate, she said, "Um, I'm not altogether sure Mr. Costello had our best interests at heart."

Tentative or not, Kate stopped dead, swirled around, and gaped at Rose. "No! You don't say so! Did he do anything horrid to you, Rose? Did he offer any scurrilous suggestions? Did he make advances of an improper nature? Why, if he did, I'll never forgive myself for allowing you to—"

Rose got up and went to her aunt. "Don't be silly, Kate. He was very nice. I just—oh, I don't know." She wished she'd kept her mouth shut, actually. "I didn't feel quite as comfortable with him as with Mr. O'Banyon."

"Oh, Mr. O'Banyon!" Kate pressed her hand over an obviously palpitating heart. "Have you ever seen such a handsome man in your life?"

"Not often. Rose patted her aunt on the back and went over to her bed, where she sat and wished she didn't feel so very odd. She'd had this strange quivering feeling in her stomach ever since Mr. O'Banyon entered into her conversation with Mr. Costello. "But I never once doubted Mr. O'Banyon's sincerity in wanting to help us." As opposed to Mr. Costello, whom she'd began to doubt was truly a gentleman.

"Oh, no!" Kate looked at Rose as if the thought of insincerity on Cullen O'Banyon's part had never entered her head. Which, Rose thought resignedly, it undoubtedly hadn't. Kate was such a warmhearted, open-handed woman; she never suspected guile in others. "Why, he couldn't have been more kind. So urbane, too. And such a gentleman. And so awfully handsome."

"Indeed." Removing her wrapper, Rose flung it at the foot of her bed, then crawled between the sheets. She was tired after her first full day in Ireland with all of its attendant starts and inconveniences.

She wasn't exactly looking forward to applying for a position as a singer and dancer at the French Academy, although it might be fun to experience life as an actress. Most people thought acting a wicked profession, but Rose believed it might be exciting, so long as no one in New York ever heard about it. Still, she had very little experience in acting. She'd sung at school when they'd performed works by Messrs. Gilbert and Sullivan, but Rose wasn't sure that counted.

However, she owed Kate a good deal, so if Kate wanted

her to do this, she'd do it. Surely she could muddle through an audition. And nothing would happen to her as long as she kept her eyes open and her senses alert. Rose had heard tales about certain unscrupulous men taking advantage of young, comely, single ladies. Rose wouldn't allow that to happen to her.

Anyhow, Mr. O'Banyon had told them he'd take them to the French Academy tomorrow, so that would be extra protection.

At the thought of Cullen O'Banyon, her butterflies, which had nearly gone to sleep, rioted. It felt as though they'd called in recruits. She pressed a hand on her stomach and glared at the ceiling.

"Electric lights, Rose!" Kate exclaimed. "Imagine that! I don't believe the Coat of Arms had electric lights."

"No, I believe the lights there were gas." If anything should be able to calm her stomach, it was the pedestrian subject of hotel lighting. Didn't work. Not even electricity was strong enough to vanquish the effect Cullen O'Banyon had on Rose's innards.

She wasn't sure this was a good sign.

Kate plunked herself down on the bed across from Rose. "You know, dear, if it should come to it, I do believe Mr. O'Banyon would be a wonderful protector for you."

Rose sat bolt upright in bed, her butterflies forgotten. "Aunt Kate!" The notion of Cullen O'Banyon wanting her as his mistress wouldn't have occurred to her in a million years. He was too . . . too . . . too . . . something.

Kate held up a placating hand. "I know, I know. How shocking of me. But he seems like such a suave, sophisticated man, and I'm sure he'd make a marvelous protector. And Rose, darling, you really do deserve some excitement in your life. Trust me, dear, if you throw away the opportunity, you'll regret it all your life."

"But . . . but . . ."

"I suppose it is shocking in me to suggest such a thing regarding Mr. O'Banyon." Kate looked troubled.

"I should say so."

"But, it wouldn't be so horrible, really, dear. I mean, it's not as if you were thinking of taking him as a protector in New York, where everyone knows you. This is Ireland. Who would ever know?"

"I would!"

"Of course, you would, dear, but just think about the excitement!"

She gave Rose such a sweet smile, Rose could only swallow, and her brain dried up. With an effort, she managed to blurt out, "But what if I should want to marry later?"

Kate shrugged. Rose watched her, speechless. Kate said, "You must know, Rose, that men very seldom pay any attention to the women they wed after the ceremony is over. Any woman with half an ounce of sense should be able to act the innocent for the six months it generally takes gentlemen to work up the courage to propose."

"But . . . but . . . but . . ."

Kate looked as severe as was possible for her. "Rose, the married state is an important one because women are treated so abominably in the world. But it's not the only state! Why should men have all the fun? It's not fair, and I don't believe you should throw your life away just because men don't think ladies deserve excitement."

Not for the first time since her aunt first proposed their trip to Ireland, Rose couldn't think of a thing to say.

"Why, goodness gracious, child, even if you were to produce a child by such a union, no one need know about it. Except you and me, of course. And we could just say that your dear husband died. I'm sure women have used that story long before either of us were born."

Rose was sure of it, too. She still didn't know what to say.

"Now, I don't advocate such a course of action for every female, Rose dear."

Rose was glad to hear it.

But you're special." Kate gave her a beaming smile. "You're so lovely, dear, and so spirited. It would break my heart to have you marry at your age and dwindle into boredom as I did."

"Oh." It came out a squeak, and Rose cleared her throat.

"I mean," Kate continued. "You know very well that I loved your uncle Glen, and unlike some men, he was always kind to me. He didn't even ignore me most of the time."

"Good heavens." Rose had never thought about marriage in terms of boredom and being ignored. She wished she hadn't been forced into thinking about it in those terms now.

Kate continued, "But for forty years, I wondered how it would have been to be swept off of my feet. To have experienced a grand passion. A romance, Rose. Is one little, tiny romance too much to ask of life?"

Rose stared at her aunt.

"Mind you, I'm sure it must be uncomfortable if one had to live in some sort of exalted state for very long—but don't you think it might be nice to try it? Once?"

"I . . . I . . ."

"Oh, dear, now I've really shocked you, haven't I?"

"A little." Rose nodded. It was the most she could do.

Kate heaved a sigh that was larger than she was. "I suppose it *is* shocking, dear, but I always did think it would be wonderful to be madly and passionately in love. Just once. Just for a little while."

"You weren't madly and passionately in love with Uncle Glen?"

"Well . . ." Kate sighed again. "I loved him very much, of course. But ours wasn't a grand passion. We'd known each other all our lives, and we married when we were quite young. And we had no struggles to overcome, because Glen's maternal grandparents were British. The British are the only rich people in Ireland. They gave him all sorts of money."

Sounded like heaven to Rose. She didn't say so, since she was sure her aunt could never truly comprehend how ghastly living in fear of eviction and starvation was. Kate had helped as much as she could. Since Rose had never revealed her father's gambling losses, Kate wasn't able to help as much as they'd needed. If Rose had been older, she'd have secured employment. She could have worked in one of those clothing factories with the rest of the Irish immigrants. The thought made her shudder. And her father would have hated it. He'd always said his little Rosie was too good to work in a factory.

Anyway, Kate didn't seem to think Rose was too good to give herself to the keeping of a man. To become a man's—Rose gulped audibly—mistress. The very idea scandalized Rose. Although . . .

She knew she was probably wicked, but she didn't think being Mr. Cullen O'Banyon's mistress would be half bad.

No, no, no. Whatever was she thinking? Perhaps she really was like her father. What an unpleasant notion *that* was.

"At any rate, I'm sure we need to get some sleep now," said Kate. "We have an adventure ahead of us tomorrow."

Rose was glad. Her butterflies had kicked up again and we're now waging a mad, scrambling, full-fledged war. "Do you want me to get the light, Kate?"

"No, no, dear. You're already under the covers. I'll turn the knob."

She did, the room went dark, and Rose sank back onto her soft pillow. She went to sleep under the influence of Kate's lurid suggestion and dreamed of Cullen O'Banyon kissing her. Madly. Passionately. Exaltedly.

Three

Cullen held out his arm and assisted Kate Flanagan to alight from his elegant black traveling carriage. The older lady's cheeks were as pink as summer roses this morning, and she was terribly excited. Her enthusiasm for her niece's incipient career as an actress amused Cullen.

Rose herself didn't appear quite so enthusiastic. Her own cheeks were pale, and she seemed edgy and nervous. Cullen gave her what he hoped was an encouraging smile, but the grimace she gave him in return made him doubt its efficacy.

"Buck up, Miss Larkin," he whispered as she stepped down from the carriage, using his arm as a brace.

She shot him an apprehensive glance and whispered back, "I've never really done anything like this before, Mr. O'Banyon."

"Is that so?" He kept his countenance serene. He felt like bursting out laughing at the absurdity of her believing he'd taken her for a hardened woman of the world. Ah, dear goodness. Even if he did miss his sons, he wouldn't have passed this opportunity by for worlds. It was probably the greatest adventure he'd ever have.

"There's no need to be apprehensive," he assured her, *soto voce*. "I'm acquainted with Mr. Nesbitt, the proprietor of the French Academy, and I'm sure he'll treat you with the utmost respect." Cullen planned on seeing to it, actually, but he didn't let that part slip. "He's a nice man."

Patrick Nesbitt ran the best stable of fancy ladies in Dublin, which is how Cullen had become acquainted with him in the first place. Cullen might be a widower, and he might not believe in stocking the home of his children with mistresses and loose women, but he was a man for all that, and he had a man's appetites and needs. He enjoyed slaking them in Dublin when he came to town for business, and he trusted Nesbitt's stock of women. They were all first-class and healthy.

He would, however, murder Nesbitt with his own hands if Nesbitt tried to make Rose Larkin into one of them. The poor girl was only doing the bidding of her sweet-tempered, slightly deranged aunt whom, Cullen gathered, had kept Rose and her father out of trouble quite often in America.

The smile Rose gave him this time made him slightly light-headed, and his gratitude that he'd accompanied the two ladies on this morning's enterprise trebled. They shouldn't be left to their own devices; that much was obvious. Anyone could take advantage of them. His blood still ran cold, his hands bulged into fists, and his murderous instincts surged when he recalled Everett Costello. The next time Cullen saw Costello, he was going to have a good long talk with him. By hand.

Kate was standing on the sidewalk looking up at the tall building that housed the French Academy. Fancy name for a fancy cathouse. She blinked, and Cullen wondered if she was going to lose heart at their enterprise. He could always hope.

"Oh, dear," Kate said. "Do you know where to enter, Mr. O'Banyon? I imagine applicants should go to the back entrance, but I'm not sure how to get there."

So much for faint hope. "It's through this gate, Mrs. Flanagan." He pushed it open and stood aside to let the ladies precede him.

Rose gave him another nervous little smile. He gazed

after her for a moment, and wished he could take all of her burdens onto his shoulders. A young woman like her shouldn't have to seek her fortune in this way. She should have a man to take care of her.

He tried to remember his own dead wife's face, and couldn't quite manage it. Shaking his head, he decided he was merely suffering from some of Rose's contagious anxiety. He led the way to the back entrance of the Academy, and he knocked at the door. A small black man opened the door, and a smile split his face.

"Mr. O'Banyon! What are you doing back here again so soon?"

Damnation. Casting a quick glance at his female companions, Cullen decided they had no idea anything but singing and dancing went on in the French Academy.

He removed his hat and said, "Hello, Julius. I've brought a young lady who's interested in applying for a singing position with Mr. Nesbitt. Is he handy?" If ladies hadn't been present, Cullen would have asked if Nesbitt was awake and stirring, but he thought they might be offended at anyone's lying abed so late into the day, so he didn't. He did, however, repeat, "A *singing* position."

The madness of this situation almost made him laugh again. Since Rose and Kate were looking, big-eyed, at Julius, he tried to convey with his facial expression that Julius should mind his tongue. Julius, a smart fellow, caught on at once.

"Come into the parlor, Mr. O'Banyon. I'll see if Mr. Nesbitt is busy."

Cullen hoped Nesbitt wouldn't have to be hauled away from one of his lady friends in order to visit with Cullen and his own lady friends.

He heard Kate murmur, "I've never seen a black man with an English accent before."

Rose nudged her aunt—Cullen suspected to shut her up—but only said, "Nor have I."

Ah, good. They were in luck. Not long after Cullen and the ladies settled into Nesbitt's back parlor—a gaudy room imminently suitable for the activities generally carried out there—Nesbitt entered the room, looking befuddled. Cullen had never visited the Academy so early in the day before.

"O'Banyon. Good to see you."

Cullen rose and went over to shake Nesbitt's hand. "Good to be back so soon." He winked to let Nesbitt know there was a bit of a charade going on.

"Er, yes. Yes, indeed." Nesbitt stood back and rubbed his hands together. A big, bluff, good-natured man, his paunch was as large as his heart, and his fluffy gray side whiskers gave him the benevolent appearance of a Father Christmas. Nesbitt loved women, wine, and song, pretty much in that order, and he ran the liveliest cathouse in Dublin. He provided all sorts of entertainment there, and Cullen hoped those girls who danced and sang weren't always required to perform other, less savory, jobs.

"So, what have we here, O'Banyon?"

"I'll introduce you." He turned to the ladies. "Mrs. Flanagan and Miss Larkin, please allow me to introduce you to Mr. Patrick Nesbitt, owner of this fine establishment."

Nesbitt executed a creditable bow. Both Rose and Kate rose from the sofa and curtsied charmingly. Cullen shook his head. This whole situation was ludicrous.

As the ladies resumed their places on the sofa, Nesbitt continued, "Julius tells me you've brought a young lady seeking employment." His eyes went round. "Not Miss Larkin, certainly?"

Rose spoke up, surprising Cullen, who'd believed her to be too nervous to take matters into her own hands. "Yes, it is I, Mr. Nesbitt. I've just come from America, and I'm seeking employment as an entertainer."

"Are you now?" Nesbitt hesitated, pulled a fat cigar from his vest pocket, removed the band, and rolled it between his palms. "How interesting."

Cullen didn't like the twinkle in Nesbitt's eye. He said repressively, "Miss Larkin would like to apply for a position as a singer and dancer, Nesbitt. Mrs. Flanagan is her aunt." He thought about adding, "and chaperone," but didn't.

He wasn't surprised to see an expression of perplexity descend upon Nesbitt's face. Women didn't generally come to Nesbitt's place with their aunts in tow. "Oh." He turned to gaze at Cullen. "Oh?"

"Yes." Cullen cleared his throat and held out a hand to Rose. She stood, looking scared and very, very young, and took his hand. "Miss Larkin is a singer. Isn't that right, Miss Larkin?" He gave her a kindly smile.

"Er, yes. Yes, I've had experience as a singer."

Nesbitt, going along with the game, nodded soberly. "In America, I take it."

"Yes. "

"Good, good." Nesbitt glanced at Cullen, then at Kate, then back at Rose. "And, ah, what sorts of things have you done in your career, Miss Larkin? What sorts of venues have you graced?"

Rose's pale cheeks flushed. She sucked in a big breath. Cullen would bet any amount of money that she'd never performed on stage in her life. Leastways, not a stage like the one in the French Academy. She recovered her composure in a flash, though, and he was proud of her.

"I, ah, sang mostly in productions of Gilbert and Sullivan's operettas, Mr. Nesbitt."

Nesbitt nodded sagely. "Aha. That's good. Good. Our girls do one of those numbers here. 'Three Little Maids From School,' don't you know."

Cullen, having seen that particular number, rolled his eyes. Good Lord. He could just imagine Rose Larkin prancing on the stage in one of those so-called maids' costumes. He said nothing.

Rose's aspect brightened. "Oh, yes. I sang that. I was in the chorus a couple of times. Then I sang the role of Mabel in *Pirates of Penzance*."

"Ah." Nesbitt smiled at her. Then he smiled at Kate. When he looked at Cullen, his smile faded, and Cullen clearly saw the plea in his eyes. What was he supposed to do now? Cullen decided to move the proceedings along.

"So, ah, Nesbitt, would you like to hear Miss Larkin sing?"

"She dances beautifully, too," Kate chimed in.

"Does she?" Nesbitt's skepticism was evident.

"Oh, my, yes. Why, Rose is a wonderful dancer."

Cullen would warrant she'd never done the kind of dancing Nesbitt required. He said nothing. Maybe it would be best if Rose's ambitions were nipped in the bud before she had a chance to get into trouble.

What was he thinking? Of course, it would be best! He said, "You may have to wear costumes that are unlike those you wore in America, Miss Larkin. Mr. Nesbitt's clientele is made up of men, and—well, they come prepared to enjoy the whole show. So to speak."

"Oh." Rose's cheeks drained of color again, and she sank down onto the sofa once more.

"Why, of course, they are!" Kate exclaimed. "That's why we're applying here."

"It is?" Nesbitt blinked at Kate, obviously dumbfounded.

Kate's smile was glorious. "But, of course, Mr. Nesbitt. Where else could our dear Rose meet wealthy men?"

Where else, indeed? Cullen nearly choked to death, trying to stifle a spasm of something. He wasn't sure if it was outrage or hilarity.

"Uh . . ." Nesbitt looked helplessly at Cullen, who lifted his eyebrow to let him know he didn't understand it either, but it couldn't be helped. Perceiving no assistance from that source, Nesbitt took a moment to clip the end of his cigar, fetch a match from the mantel, strike it, and light the cigar. Having gained some time that way, he turned back to Rose. "Er, perhaps it would be best if we heard you sing, Miss Larkin. As you suggested."

Rose popped up from the sofa she'd so recently graced with her soft bottom. Cullen shook his head and told himself to stop thinking things like that. Just because women employees did things besides sing in Nesbitt's Academy, it didn't mean they *all* did. He hoped. He'd make sure Rose Larkin never did, that was for certain.

"Yes," she said. "I think I'll be more comfortable once I understand what's expected of me." She smiled at Nesbitt, who blinked back. Cullen was absolutely sure that Nesbitt had never before been faced with the prospect of a Rose Larkin.

Rose suspected she'd have to wear a less-than-modest costume if she secured employment at the French Academy. Oddly enough, the prospect didn't alarm her too much. Actually, the notion of parading around in a low-cut gown with a short hem was sort of titillating. She wouldn't mind riveting the attention of a man like Cullen O'Banyon, for example, with her feminine charms. And how better to do it than to have him see her in all her female flesh? She did have a nice figure, after all.

Good heavens. Wherever had that thought sprung from? She decided she'd better keep her mind on her singing and forget about costumes for the time being.

Mr. Nesbitt first led them into an auditorium of sorts, although the seats weren't arranged auditorium style. Rather, tables had been set around the room with several chairs at each table. The room had been swept and the tables polished, but the air still held the faint scent of old cigar smoke and liquor.

Rose's eyes opened wide. Why, this was a nightclub! She'd heard of a nightclub. There was one in New York City. Perhaps even more than one. Her excitement edged up. This was an unprecedented opportunity, indeed, to be singing in a nightclub.

"Your aunt and Mr. O'Banyon can stay here, Miss Larkin. I'll take you to the wings and introduce you to the pianist."

With a jerky gesture, Rose handed Kate her reticule and then fingered the pins holding her hat in place. If she was going to be auditioning as a nightclub singer, she might as well get into the spirit. "Thank you, Mr. Nesbitt. Here, Aunt Kate." She thrust the hat into Kate's hands and turned to accompany Mr. Nesbitt. Then she remembered her gloves, decided to leave nothing but air between her and the world she hoped to enter, tugged them off, and tossed them onto the table.

She felt incredibly bold and daring when she followed Mr. Nesbitt backstage.

Cullen watched Rose walk away, her lovely bottom swaying in its elegantly tailored suit skirt, and sighed deeply. He didn't know about any of this.

"It was so nice of you to accompany us to Mr. Nesbitt's Academy, Mr. O'Banyon. Without you, I'm sure we never would have been accorded such a fine welcome."

Cullen was sure of it, too. He smiled at Kate. "Has your niece performed in any public arenas before this, Mrs. Flanagan?"

"Rose? Oh, my, yes. Why, her school performances were attended by everyone from the parents of the students to the mayor of New York."

"I see." Cullen resisted the urge to take the sweet little lady by her throat and shake the flummery out of her.

"And then, of course, there were the Fourth of July picnics in Central Park. She sang in the chorus, but it was still a public arena."

"Undeniable."

"She sang most often in church," Kate said, as if admitting to a terrible flaw. She frowned, and two creases appeared in her brow. "I hope she won't select a hymn to sing for Mr. Nesbitt. I don't think it would be appropriate."

"I think you're right."

Kate braced herself with a big breath. Nothing seemed to keep her down for very long, Cullen was interested to note. "But she has a lovely voice, whatever she sings. You'll see." Kate sat back, smug in her evaluation of her niece's talents.

Her smugness was well earned. Rose Larkin had the clearest, purest, loveliest soprano voice Cullen had heard in a very long time. He was tense when she first stepped onto the stage. She looked so small, not to mention terribly demure and out of place in Nesbitt's Academy. And nervous. She was definitely nervous.

She consulted with the piano player, a fellow named Sean O'Day whom Cullen had met several times, and Cullen was interested to note that they seemed to hit it off. He wasn't sure he approved. O'Day was a nice-enough man, but he belonged in this milieu. Rose Larkin didn't.

Then O'Day struck up an introductory series of chords, Rose began belting out "Champagne Charlie," and Cullen was hard-pressed to keep from gawking like a fool. He glanced at Kate, who was smiling up a storm, holding her folded hands in her lap and looking for all the world as if she were watching a favorite grandchild reciting in church.

When the song was over, Kate applauded wildly. Cullen joined her, more sedately. He really, really wasn't sure he approved of this enterprise. Actually, he was pretty sure he didn't approve at all. Nevertheless, when Kate turned her glowing smile upon him, he managed to smile back.

"Isn't she superb?" Kate asked in a grating whisper.

"She is," he admitted truthfully.

They were both silenced by another chord from the piano. Then Rose began to sing "Aura Lee," and Cullen experienced a sudden and unexpected tightening in his chest. His late wife, Judith, had loved that song. This was the first time he'd remembered Judith and music, but now he recalled that she'd enjoyed playing and singing. Her voice had been nothing to compare to Rose Larkin's, but it had been sweet.

He sighed heavily, wishing he hadn't thought about Judith. He always felt sort of guilty when he remembered her. Her death had been a blow to him, but not a crushing one. Cullen believed that if he'd been a proper husband, he should have been overcome and distraught.

It's not as if they hadn't been fond of each other, because they had been. Their union hadn't been one of Kate Flanagan's grand passions, however, and no amount of wishful thinking or gilding of memories could make it into one. He imagined Rose Larkin would encounter a grand passion, if she encountered any passion at all. He envied her that, and felt old all of a sudden.

He heard Kate sniffle, looked at her, saw her wipe her

eyes with a handkerchief, and grinned. He guessed he wasn't the only one for whom "Aura Lee" conjured sentimental memories.

When Rose had finished that one, even Nesbitt applauded. "Can you dance, Miss Larkin?" he asked, sounding truly happy for the first time since Rose Larkin had entered his establishment.

"Dance?" Rose, on the other hand, sounded doubtful.

Nesbitt gestured with his cigar. "Nothing fancy. Just a kick or two. Maybe a twirl?" He made curlicues with his cigar hand, and the smoke corkscrewed up to the ceiling.

Rose thought about it for a moment, then shrugged. "I suppose so." And she took off spinning. Across the stage she went, then back again. Sean O'Day got into the spirit of it on her trip back and began playing "The Man on the Flying Trapeze." Then, in spite of the narrowness of her skirt, Rose did a little dance number that made Cullen smile. She was panting when she finally stopped, and slammed a hand to her heart.

Sean O'Day shouted, "Huzzah!" and clapped loudly.

Rose smiled at him. "I'm not accustomed to singing and dancing in these clothes," she said by way of apology.

"No need to apologize, my dear Miss Larkin," Nesbitt told her, climbing onto the stage. "You were wonderful. I'm sure we can use you."

"Really?" Rose looked both gratified and astounded. She plucked a handkerchief from her skirt pocket and dabbed at her dewy forehead.

"Indeed. Especially if you're a quick study." Nesbitt winked at her.

Cullen's jaw clenched, and he made an effort to unclench it. No need to get angry, he told himself. He'd just take Nesbitt aside before he left and explain a few things to him. And he'd make damned sure he was in the audience every time Rose Larkin performed.

How in the names of Jesus, Mary, and Joseph would he arrange that?

Well, no matter. He'd think of something. Right now he rose from his chair and strode to the stage. "Very good,

Miss Larkin." He pinned Nesbitt with such a glare, the poor fellow blanched and nearly swallowed his cigar. "Why don't you wait with your aunt while I have a chat with Mr. Nesbitt."

Rose nodded. "Certainly." She walked to O'Day and held out her hand. "Thank you so much, Mr. O'Day. You play beautifully."

"My pleasure, Miss Larkin." O'Day winked at her, and Cullen's hands formed fists.

He waited until Rose had descended the three steps and walked to her aunt's table. Then he turned to Nesbitt and tried to make his lips form a smile. From the look on Nesbitt's face, his expression was more like a grimace. Well, no matter.

"As you can see, Patrick, my friend, Miss Larkin is a bit of an innocent."

"Aye." Nesbitt nodded energetically.

"And she doesn't understand what kinds of things are required by *some* of the women who work in the French Academy."

Nesbitt opened his mouth—probably to tell Cullen it wasn't some of the ladies who worked there, but all of them, who were required to do other sorts of work—but, noting the look in Cullen's eyes, he closed it again. "Er, I see."

"Now, I don't expect you to do anything exceptional by way of keeping Miss Larkin safe and sound—and innocent—Patrick, but if I pay you a little extra, I *will* expect you to keep your eye on her—at least at first—and make sure she isn't bothered by rowdy patrons."

"I see." Nesbitt bit on his cigar.

His eyes took on a pleading cast, but Cullen didn't drop his own stern expression. "I mean it, Patrick. She's a baby. A child let loose in the world. I don't want her molested. She's here because her aunt has some crazy idea that she should become an adventuress—"

Nesbitt goggled. "An ad—" He swallowed the rest of his sentence when Cullen raised his hand.

"Yes. An adventuress. It's silly, but there it is."

A light came into Nesbitt's eyes, as if he'd just realized something. "I see what it is. She's a relative of yours from America, is she?"

"Until last night, I didn't know she existed on earth. Or her aunt, either."

"Oh." Nesbitt chewed on that piece of information as he chewed on his cigar. "But she's become something special to you?"

Cullen shook his head. "I only want to make sure nothing happens to her." He put a hand on Nesbitt's shoulder and leaned closer. "For the love of Christ, man, she's a babe in the woods! And her aunt is even worse than she is. I don't want anything to happen to them. Can you help me here, Patrick?"

Nesbitt looked beleaguered. "Aye, I expect I can, but not forever. Have mercy, Cullen O'Banyon. I'm a businessman, not a nanny."

"I know it." Cullen frowned as his gaze slid past Nesbitt and traveled to the two lovely American ladies who had suddenly become such a huge problem in his life.

But that was nonsensical. They weren't his problem. Cullen squared his shoulders. "All right. Just do it for tonight. I'll come and watch, too, to make sure she settles in properly."

"Well . . . Very well. I suppose it'll be all right."

Cullen nodded. "Thank you, Patrick."

"But for how long will this go on? I don't mind a little extra vigilance every now and then, but I won't be able to play nursemaid forever."

"I know, I know. I'll think of something." God alone knew what. Maybe God would help.

Kate's voice came to the two men from the cavernous room behind them. When Cullen turned, the two ladies looked like orphans lost in a sea of tables. "Well?" she asked brightly. "What did you think, Mr. Nesbitt?"

Nesbitt took the cigar out of his mouth, glanced at Cullen, sighed, and said, "I think Miss Larkin is very talented, Mrs. Flanagan. A wonderful singer." He shot Cullen another sideways glance. "Ah, if you'll come back here around noon, I'll introduce you to the other ladies in the chorus, and have Millie—she's the choreographer—teach you a couple of the numbers." Out of the side of his mouth, he muttered, "That all right with you, O'Banyon?"

Cullen smiled. "Fine, Patrick. Thank you."

Four

Cullen took Rose and Kate out for a bite of luncheon, then had his coachman drive Kate back to the inn. Since ladies were not allowed to attend performances at the French Academy, she agreed to stay at the Green Boar, rest, and read while Rose learned the tricks of her new trade. Cullen promised to bring Rose back to her as soon as possible.

"This is awfully nice of you, Mr. O'Banyon. I don't know why you're being so good to us."

"Nonsense, Miss Larkin. I was in Dublin on business, and am more than happy to lend my assistance to two charming ladies who are strangers in our lovely land."

Rose was sitting in the carriage, her hands folded demurely in her lap, and when she smiled at him Cullen's heart did a double somersault. He didn't understand his reaction to her. She was only a girl, and he was a middle-aged widower, for heaven's sake.

Oh, very well, perhaps he wasn't precisely middle-aged, but he was the father of two young boys and had become accustomed to thinking of himself as past the age of schoolboy infatuations. Beyond daydreams. Way too old for romantic notions of adventure and grand passion.

The problem—as his nagging heart reminded him—was that he'd never had any schoolboy infatuations, daydreams, romantical notions, adventures, or grand passions. He'd always been such a sobersided fellow. Serious-minded and mature, he'd eschewed larks and capers as juvenile and beneath him. He'd never once kicked up his heels and behaved in a rash manner.

Now he wished he had something exciting to look back upon. He sighed. Good God, he sounded like Kate Flanagan.

"Well, I think it's very nice of you, whatever you say." Rose looked out the window where the street scene revealed thereby was typical to the city. Women called out the merits of the wares contained in their pushcarts, snatches of songs came from pubs, laborers building a bank swore and bantered with each other. Horses clattered, boys and girls ran alongside their mothers, carrying baskets of fish and fruit. The aroma coming from the baker's was enough to make one's mouth water.

Cullen enjoyed the city as a change of pace, but he treasured his home in the country. The quiet and green solitude of his horse farm was probably the closest to heaven he'd get in this life. He watched Rose as she gazed out at the city, and wondered if she'd ever be satisfied living in the rustic quiet of the country. He doubted it.

"Have you lived in New York City all your life, Miss Larkin?"

She gave a start, as if she'd been lost in her own thoughts, and turned to face him. "Why, yes. My father and I lived there, as did Aunt Kate and Uncle Glen. I often stayed with them when my father was . . . out of town."

He wondered what she'd been going to say before she settled on that quaint phrase, *out of town.* "I see. And do you like the city? Or do you sometimes crave the peace and quiet of the country?"

She hesitated. "I hardly know, to tell you the truth. I only visited the country once that I can remember. And I enjoyed it very much. It was so . . . calm."

Cullen wondered if it was his imagination making him think her expression looked slightly wistful. Probably. "Your school was in the city?"

"Oh, yes." She made a small gesture with her hand. "New York is a wonderful place, but I've always wanted to travel and see the world." She gave him another one of her wonderful smiles. "And now I am. Thanks to Aunt Kate, at least I'm seeing Ireland."

"Indeed." He returned her smile, feeling unaccountably saddened by her answer. "I hope our fair land lives up to your expectations."

"Oh, it already has." Her smile faded. "I only hope I can live up to poor Aunt Kate's expectations."

"Aye? And what exactly are her expectations? She seems a very nice woman to me. Not the critical, hard-to-please type."

"Oh, no, she's an angel! Truly, she's a wonderful woman. She's been the mainstay of my life, really. I barely remember my mother, and Aunt Kate took care of me for—well, she took care of me a lot."

Cullen would bet on it. He'd like to shake Rose's dead father until his teeth rattled. "What is it she wants for you, then? Does she want you to become a world-famous actress? Another Sarah Bernhardt or Eleanora Duse?"

Rose laughed. It sounded like a genuine laugh, and Cullen was pleased. "No. She's not interested in fame. She wants me to have at least one grand romance in my life."

"That's a noble wish," Cullen said with a grin.

"I suppose it is." She smiled faintly. "And I really do think it would be exciting to be a successful adventuress."

"Indeed."

Suddenly, she lifted her chin and stared straight at him. "But I'm not at all sure how to go about it, you see. I mean, I don't know anything about making exciting men fall in love with me, and I'm sure that's what she wants. I truly don't want to fail her, Mr. O'Banyon. She'd be so disappointed if I fell in love with a dull man."

Cullen, startled, sat up straighter. "Uh, yes, I see what you mean. At least, I think I do. Perhaps."

She sighed. "You probably don't." Her smile came out of nowhere and seemed to brighten the day. "You see, Aunt Kate and Uncle Glen were married for eons and eons, and they were very happy together. But they never had a relationship that Kate considered exciting. She seems to think that in order to be truly happy, I need a knight to dash up on a white horse and sweep me off my feet and snatch me away to his castle."

"Ah. I see."

Her giggle washed over him, making his nerve endings tingle.

"Evidently, being swept off of one's feet is one of the requirements of a proper love affair—or a good marriage, of course."

"Of course."

She paused for a moment, glanced out of the window, and then returned her gaze to Cullen. With heightened color in her cheeks, she blurted out, "Have you ever been swept off of your feet, Mr. O'Banyon?"

Hell, no. Cullen bit back the caustic answer. "Ah, I think it's the man who's supposed to do the sweeping, isn't it?" He asked the question lightly.

"I suppose so. But no man would sweep a woman off of her feet if he hadn't first been swept away by passion himself, would he?"

Good point. "I don't suppose so."

"Has that ever happened to you?"

Cullen lifted his eyebrows in a quelling gesture. It generally quelled Ferris and William, anyway.

It apparently had a similar effect on Rose, who turned to stare out of the window again. Her cheeks looked like they were glowing. She was embarrassed by her question, Cullen imagined—as well she should be. Imagine asking a veritable stranger such a thing as whether he'd ever been swept away by passion.

He had a feeling he wouldn't be so indignant if he had a more interesting answer for her. "No, Miss Larkin, I don't believe I've ever been swept away by passion."

Her sigh nearly lifted her off of the carriage seat. "No. I have a feeling Aunt Kate might be mistaken in her notion of love and so forth. She seems to think insecurity makes life exciting. As far as I've been able to determine, insecurity only makes one uncomfortable."

Cullen's indignation collapsed in a rush of sympathy. "I believe you're right about that, Miss Larkin." He felt like saying he was sorry her life had been fraught with so much insecurity, but held his tongue. It was enough—more than enough—that he was getting himself entangled in her present circumstances.

Although, he reminded himself, this *was* rather an adventure. And, since it was so seldom he had an adventure, perhaps he should remember to look upon it in that light.

Rose evidently misinterpreted his smile. "Oh, dear, I'm sorry, Mr. O'Banyon. I didn't mean to sound so ungrateful. I'm sure my family has been wonderful to me. You probably think I'm an unappreciative dimwit."

"Good heavens, no. Such a notion never entered my head. I was . . . ah . . . thinking about something else entirely."

Now why, he wondered, did he hesitate to tell this lovely girl that he'd been thinking about his children? He'd wager she'd be interested to hear about them, and to know his sons led a happy, secure life—directly opposed to what her own had been—on a pretty horse farm in the rolling green Irish countryside.

That was it. Right there. He didn't want her to know how uneventful and pedestrian his life was. He shook his head, amazed at his own silliness.

She didn't believe him. "I knew it! See? You weren't even listening to me. It's because I'm boring. I'll never be able to fulfill Aunt Kate's expectations." She sounded very discouraged. "I beg your pardon, Mr. O'Banyon. I honestly don't know why you're being so nice to my aunt and me. You must consider us awful pests."

He leaned forward and put a hand on hers. She looked shocked. He was a little shocked himself. "That's not true, Miss Larkin. You and your aunt are very interesting to me."

"Interesting? Good heavens, you speak of us as if we're

a couple of lunatics." She frowned. "I suppose we're acting like it."

He couldn't help smiling. "Not at all. I'm finding this a stimulating experience. Am I not to be encouraged to seek adventure too?" That was a good one. He was surprised he'd thought of it.

It worked. Her dimple peeked out and her beautiful smile came, and his heart leaped. "I have a feeling your life is already very eventful, Mr. O'Banyon. I'm sure you don't need the paltry amusement provided by my aunt and me."

"Now *there*," he said with a wink. "You're dead wrong. This is the most excitement I've had in a long time."

"I don't believe that for a second," she said. But she laughed.

Glad the conversation had taken a lighter turn, Cullen lifted his eyebrow again. "Oh? And why not, pray?"

"Because you look so . . . so dashing. Suave. Sophisticated. And you're so at home in the world. You're obviously not a little innocent from America."

"You lived in New York City, Miss Larkin. Surely a young lady who's lived in New York City all of her life isn't exactly a bumpkin."

She sighed. "I suppose not, really, but I certainly do feel like one."

"That's only because you're young." He felt a little tug of melancholy when he said it.

"I'm not all *that* young," she declared stoutly.

He didn't believe it. "And how old is 'not all that young,' pray tell?"

"I'll be twenty years old on my birthday."

"And when will that momentous event occur?"

"On October the twelfth. So, you see, I'm not an infant. I know many young ladies my age who are married and starting families." Her voice had taken on a wistful note.

Cullen cocked his head, wondering why that should be. He didn't ask. "Aye. So do I." He remembered being twenty years old. He'd been as much of a baby as his current traveling companion, although he hadn't known it at the time. He'd been barely twenty-three when he'd become a husband, and Judith had been only eighteen when she'd become his wife. She'd been dead before she was twenty-five.

Lord, he didn't want to start thinking about Judith again. That subject was entirely too depressing—mainly because he could conjure up so few tangible memories of his late wife and marriage. "At any rate, you're far from an ancient, Miss Larkin, no matter what your degree—or lack of—sophistication."

There went her dimple again. Cullen was charmed.

"I suppose you're right." She tilted her head and gazed at him from under her eyelashes. Cullen had a feeling she didn't know how coy and flirtatious the posture appeared. She'd better not do that at Nesbitt's place, or the men drinking there would never believe she was an innocent girl. "How old are you, Mr. O'Banyon?"

Then she blushed, and completely shattered her flirtatious image. Cullen shook his head. No matter how he sliced this one, he always came up with a girl who was barely old enough to be let off of leading strings, much less set loose on an unsuspecting world. Of course, her aunt was every bit as innocent of the world as Rose, and she must be in her sixties. "I'm thirty-three, Miss Larkin. An old man."

"Oh!" Her exclamation came out loud and startled, and she blushed again. "I beg your pardon."

As well she might. Cullen got the impression she was astounded that such an elderly fellow should still be tottering around—and without a cane, yet. His innards gave a cynical twist. "Thirty-three's not so awfully old, Miss Larkin. I'm not yet in my dotage."

She waved a hand in the air. "Of course it's not. I . . . ah . . . was only a little surprised, is all. You seem so young and . . . and . . . well, dashing."

"We dashing fellows age well," he said dryly.

"No doubt."

They were both still laughing when they arrived at the French Academy.

•   •   •

Rose felt a good deal of trepidation when she left Cullen in the huge auditorium and walked by herself to the stage where a woman waited, watching her, hands on hips. The woman didn't look very nice. She looked rather hard and cynical and world-weary, actually. But Mr. Nesbitt was there, and he was smiling, so everything would probably be all right.

Because she felt so out of place, and because she didn't want anyone to know it, she approached the hostile-looking woman with the biggest, friendliest, most American smile she could muster. The woman sniffed. So much for a friendly smile. On the other hand, according to her aunt, a smile never hurt anyone, so Rose turned it on Mr. Nesbitt, who seemed to appreciate it. He took her hand and pumped it vigorously.

"How-de-do, Miss Larkin. Good to see you. Please allow me to introduce you to Miss Mae O'Malley. Mae's our best dancer, and she choreographs the numbers our girls perform."

"Thank you, Mr. Nesbitt." Rose mentally braced herself to confront Mae. She decided to continue being friendly until actively rebuffed, stuck out a hand, smiled, and said, "How do you do, Miss O'Malley. Thank you very much for taking the time to teach me these things."

Mae eyed Rose's hand, then took it grudgingly. She sniffed again. "Aye, well, we'll see."

Not exactly encouraging. Nor was the expression on Mae's face when she eyed Rose's traveling skirt. "Ye'll need to put on looser clothes if y'expect to dance for Nesbitt, girl."

"Oh." Rose felt like a fool. She hadn't given a thought to costuming. "Um, perhaps there's something backstage I can wear?" She hoped she wasn't being entirely idiotic. "I, ah, have never done anything like this before."

Mae's eyes went round in mock surprise. "No! You don't say!"

"Mae," Nesbitt grumbled under his breath.

Mae huffed, chastened by Nesbitt's rebuff. "Come with me, then." She turned and began to stalk away.

Rose hesitated for a moment, looked into the huge room, saw Cullen sitting there resignedly, and made up her mind that she would do everything in her power not to fail in this endeavor. No matter how humiliating the experience was sure to be. She hotfooted it after Mae.

Mae led her to a long dressing room lined with mirrors, tables, and benches. The room was rather untidy, but clean for all that. A long rack containing hanging garments stood at one end. Mae didn't pause until she got to the rack. She yanked a loose-fitting wrapper from the rack, turned, and thrust it at Rose. "Here. I expect ye can wear that."

Rose bit back a stinging rebuke for Mae's rudeness. She said, "Thank you," and looked around for a screen or something to step behind so that she could disrobe and put on the wrapper. There were no screens in the room.

Good Lord. Rose experienced a sensation of dawning horror. Her bleak notion was confirmed by the smirk on Mae's face.

Mae crossed her arms over her chest. "Aye. We ain't much for modesty in this business, *Miss* Larkin. Take them clothes off and get dressed in that wrapper if ye want to learn how to dance. Pretty soon, you'll be taking 'em off onstage, if ye're a success."

Good gracious. Rose swallowed hard. She'd drink poison before she took off her clothes onstage, but she didn't tell Mae that. She merely took the wrapper, turned around, found a chair over which she could lay out her walking skirt, blouse, and matching jacket, and began to remove them. When she glanced over her shoulder, she saw Mae watching her with a grim expression on her face, her arms still crossed, and her foot tapping impatiently.

Rose cleared her throat. "I fear I'm rather a bother to you, Miss O'Malley, and I do apologize. This was my aunt's idea, you see, and I'm trying to please her because she's been my kindest friend all my life."

"Ye're trying to please your auntie, are ye? By takin' to the stage?" Mae sounded incredulous.

Rose didn't blame her, really. She sighed. "Yes. You see, Aunt Kate thinks singing and acting are professions that bring a woman in contact with the exciting side of life."

"Exciting!" If Mae had blurted out "garbage," she couldn't have sounded more astounded. "Well, if she considers being ogled by drunken louts exciting, I expect she's right."

Oh, dear. Put that way, acting and singing sounded terrible. "I . . . ah . . . don't believe she was thinking about the stage along those terms. Exactly."

"No, I expect she wasn't. If you don't mind my saying so, Miss Larkin—"

"Oh, please call me Rose!" She'd blurted it out without thinking, but when she saw the expression on Mae's face softening, she was glad of her impetuosity.

"Then call me Mae."

"Thank you." Rose spoke her thanks humbly.

"Anyway, Rose, I don't think your auntie has thought this out very carefully."

"No, I'm sure she hasn't. How could she? She's been so sheltered all of her life, don't you see. She has no idea, really, what life can be like."

"And you do?"

"Well, I've seen more of it than Aunt Kate, at any rate."

"Humph."

"She believes she missed out on fun and excitement by marrying a wealthy man and living a solidly respectable life for forty-five years."

"Ha." Mae's disgust with such fatuous thinking was patent.

"But I know, because my father and I had such an uncomfortable, unsettled life, that she only thinks such things are romantic because she's never experienced them. If she'd been faced with creditors and no food in the house and being evicted from various flats and expelled from school, she wouldn't think it was exciting at all."

"And you were? Faced with those things, I mean."

Rose was pleased to note that Mae didn't sound as contemptuous as she had earlier. She folded her skirt and placed it carefully over the chair back, sighed, and said,

"Oh, my, yes. Aunt Kate helped us all she could, but I hated to go to her for as much help as we really needed because—well, I thought my father should have been supporting us." She shrugged out of her blouse. "My father was a wonderful man, but looking back on everything now—well, I hate to say it, but I believe he was a bit of a scoundrel."

"He were a man," Mae said, as if that explained everything.

As she folded her blouse, Rose glanced at Mae. "Do you think all men are like that?" After meeting Cullen O'Banyon, she didn't think so.

"Ha! If you have to ask, sweetie, you have a lot to learn."

Rose sighed again. "I know I do. I have a feeling my aunt is wrong about this particular career move."

"I know she is."

Rose contemplated her corset, remembered how out of breath she'd been after doing her tiny little audition dance number for Mr. Nesbitt, threw caution and modesty to the four winds, and removed the wretched thing. She sucked in a huge breath and felt almost free.

Watching her, Mae's face softened further. "It'll be all right, dearie. I know you're not cut out for this life, and I'll keep me eye on you. Maybe your auntie will be satisfied afore too long, and ye can go back home to America and find yourself a nice man and settle down."

"That sounds like heaven, actually." Except that for the last day or so, when Rose thought about marrying and settling down, it wasn't in America, but here, in Ireland. Good gracious, what a fool she was! Disgusted with herself, she slipped the wrapper over her head, tied it, and was shocked to discover it didn't reach past her knees. She looked down at her calves sticking out below the hem, dismayed.

Mae chuckled. "That's nothing, sweetie. Wait till you see the skimpy thing you have to wear in the chorus when ye start dancin' with us."

Oh, dear. "Oh?" Rose contemplated the nature of modesty, decided she was extremely glad she was in a land full of strangers if she had to do this, and squared her shoulders. "I suppose that's just the way it is."

"Aye," said Mae, and she chuckled again. She seemed much friendlier now than she had before. When she led Rose back out to the stage, she even walked next to her. Rose appreciated her change in attitude more than she could say.

When they got to the staging area, she felt terribly self-conscious. No man alive, not even her father, had ever seen her knees before. She feared she was blushing, but since the room was dark, she didn't suppose anyone could see. She dared one tiny peek at the sea of tables in the audience, saw Cullen O'Banyon sitting there, frowning horribly, and decided she'd not look out there again. Perhaps when she was performing in the chorus with other girls, she wouldn't feel so conspicuous.

Nonsense. She'd feel conspicuous no matter where she was, or with whom. This was the most outrageously immodest costume she'd ever been in. And, according to Mae, it was prudish compared to what she'd be prancing around in during actual performances.

Well, no matter. She was here, this was Aunt Kate's dream for her, and Rose wasn't about to disappoint Aunt Kate. She sucked in about a bushel of air and smiled at Mae. "I'm ready."

"Aye, I expect ye are. But we have to wait for Sean O'Day. I imagine he's not feeling his best right now. He never is in the morning."

Rose considered pointing out that it was afternoon, but, thought she'd better not. Perhaps theater folks had a different concept of time than the rest of the mortal world.

Sean O'Day appeared then, straggling out from the other side of the stage wings. Rose had to admit he looked a bit under the weather. She smiled at him, hoping in that way to encourage him to enjoy the day. He grunted in return, and she guessed she wasn't a potent-enough force to vanquish a late night and too much whiskey. At least, she presumed that was his trouble. His appearance reminded her very much of her father's on certain mornings past.

"Give him a minute, dearie," Mae said, her tone a little snide. "He'll give over after a bit. He needs a tankard, is what. I'll fetch it for him."

Mae sauntered off stage right, and Rose was left on the stage alone, wondering how one relatively small human being could feel so ill at ease. She clasped her hands; considered her knees, realized that was the wrong thing to do, because it made her even more nervous, eyed the curtain, saw that it was faded and cheap-looking; glanced at Sean O'Day and received an ill-natured scowl; looked quickly away; caught an outraged stare from Cullen O'Banyon who still sat in what would soon be a room containing an audience filled with men; and decided her best bet would be to turn her back on him and ponder the stage itself. So she did.

There was certainly nothing remarkable about it. A scarred floor stained in patches by who knew what, backed by a red velvet curtain losing its nap in spots, a girl. A girl? Rose gaped at the newcomer, who had just appeared stage left. The two women smiled tentatively at each other.

Thank God, thank God. At least this one looked friendly.

"Hello," said the girl. "I'm Sally, and Mae said I'm to help you learn the 'Three Little Maids from School' number for tomorrow night."

"Thank you very much, Sally. My name's Rose."

Rose was shocked when Sally walked over to her. Why, the girl was even younger than Rose herself! But she didn't look the least bit shy or out of place. Rose wondered how long Sally had been dancing at the French Academy, but didn't feel comfortable asking her right off the bat.

Sally turned toward Sean O'Day, put her hands on her hips, and struck a pose that scandalized Rose. "Start the music, Sean. We don't have all day."

O'Day struck a chord. Sally said, "All right, Rose, first we trip out onto the stage, like this."

Rose tried very hard to concentrate on the lesson. It got easier when Mae came back with a beer for Sean and helped demonstrate the steps because then she could stand beside Sally and imitate her movements as Mae explained the choreography to her. It wasn't awfully difficult, although her nervousness inhibited her a good deal. Then there was the dance itself.

Before long, though, the worst of her trepidation eased, and she found it easier to concentrate. She even forgot about Cullen O'Banyon, sitting there, watching her knees. That is to say, watching the three of them dance. Rose wished she could forget about her wretched knees. Perhaps, in time, wearing these types of costumes would become second nature to her.

When she had to face Cullen O'Banyon after the practice session was over, she decided it would take a lot of time. He was nice to her, though, and she managed to give a fairly accurate report to her aunt, although she left out the salacious details.

The next day's session went well, and Rose was told she'd be expected to take part in the performance that evening. Immediately, her heart leapt into her throat, and it was all she could do to squeak out an appropriate response.

That night, after she had eaten as much of a meal as she could—her stomach was fluttering too much to allow her to do more than nibble at her food—she guessed she was ready. She saw a couple of the other girls gulping strong spirits, and wondered if they did that to numb themselves for the work they had to do.

What a depressing notion. Rose would almost sooner disappoint Kate than take up the bottle. She squeezed her eyes shut and told herself firmly that those weren't the only two options available to her. And if she'd only give herself time, she was sure to come up with one or two others, no matter that she couldn't do so now.

Shaking her head hard, she commanded her nerves to settle and her brain to concentrate on the here and now.

She held up the costume Mae had just handed her, blinking in dismay. "This is it?"

"Aye, that's it, dearie. It ain't much, are it?"

"Er, no."

"After a bit, you won't think nothing of it, ducky. Trust me. It gets to be old hat."

Rose licked her lips. "Good."

Mae laughed. "Here. Wear these, too." She tossed her a pair of fishnet stockings. "And these." Two black garters adorned with bright pink satin roses followed the stockings.

"Mercy," Rose whispered.

By the time she was rigged out in her costume, which showed a good deal more of her body than just her knees— her entire bosom felt as if it was going to pop out if she moved the wrong way—Rose was resigned to her fate. She could do this. She *would* do it. For Kate.

She paused to utter a brief prayer for strength before she, Mae, and Sally pranced out onto the stage. They were supposed to be the three little maids from school. Rose thought cynically that if Gilbert and Sullivan's schoolgirls dressed as the three of them were dressed, they wouldn't be allowed to remain in school because the headmistress would have a spasm and expel them all.

And they certainly weren't going to be maids for long. She was shocked to know she could harbor such a lurid thought.

Five

The music was ear-splittingly loud, and the room was filled with cigar smoke and the aroma of whiskey and beer and rough male voices. Cullen slumped at a table, feeling savage. This was no venue for a sweet, innocent, nineteen-year-old girl from America to be parading herself, and he vilified himself for bringing her here.

Of course, if he hadn't done it, Rose and Kate would have come here on their own, and things would be even worse than they were now. Lord. At the moment, he'd like to shake Kate Flanagan until she rattled and put Rose Larkin over his knee and paddle her rump.

He wished he hadn't thought about Rose's rump. He was seeing entirely too much of it right this minute. Damnation, this was awful!

"I want the one in the middle."

Cullen jerked out of his sullen contemplation of Rose Larkin prancing on the stage, almost naked, with two other females similarly clad—or unclad—and turned to the next table. He eyed the fellow who'd spoken the words, and his hands clenched automatically. He made an effort to relax them.

The one in the middle, needless to say, was Rose Larkin.

Cullen had to admit that she no longer looked innocent and virtuous. Not in that costume she didn't. And she was cavorting around on the stage as if she'd been doing it all her life. His heart twisted, and he wondered if he'd been wrong about her all along.

"I think I'll ask her after the show if she'd care for some company," the man said, his leering gaze fixed on Rose. "You never know. She might be eager for a discreet alliance." His eyebrows waggled, and his companion at the table sniggered.

One of them said, "If she ain't already got a discreet alliance going for her, she ain't the gal she looks like she is."

The first man shrugged and grinned. "Maybe she's ready for a change in protectors, then."

Cullen turned and stared straight at the speaker, who was young—younger than Cullen by a decade, probably—and quite presentable. From his elegant garb and his elegant accent, Cullen pegged him for a British landowner who was slumming in Ireland. Perhaps visiting his various properties, or his parents, or resting up after a debauch somewhere else.

And taking an interest in Rose Larkin. Who, evidently he'd already decided would make a perfectly splendid mistress with whom to pass a few idyllic weeks or months while rusticating in the sticks. Cullen passed a hand over his eyes in an effort to vanquish the haze of red fury that seemed to have suffused the air around him.

This reaction was nonsensical. Rose Larkin wasn't Cullen's concern. If that fellow made her a salacious offer, her aunt, if not Rose herself, would be elated. It would mean money. It would, according to Aunt Kate, mean excitement, adventure, and grand passion.

Having observed one or two affairs of that nature from the outside, Cullen was far from certain about the latter issues. He cleared his throat and leaned over to speak to the young man.

"Er, I believe you're talking about a young woman who's already been taken."

The younger man blinked and glanced at Cullen. "Oh,

really? I must say that comes as a severe disappointment to me, old fellow."

"I'm sorry, but there it is." Cullen smiled to let the fellow know there should be no hard feelings, although he wanted more than anything else to put his hands around the reprobate's throat and squeeze the life out of him.

The man turned in his chair so as to have a better view of the stage. He kept his eye on Rose as he spoke to Cullen. "Are you sure it's a solid connection? Perhaps she's interested in a change of associations."

Prying his teeth apart so that words could pass through them, Cullen said, "No. She's not."

"Oh, I say!" The man, apparently hearing something ferocious in Cullen's tone, turned to look at him. Enlightenment dawned. "Ah, I see. She's yours."

Cullen expected his smile was relatively wolfish. "Yes." He didn't elaborate for fear he'd lose control. He owed it to his sons not to be imprisoned for mayhem or murder.

"I do congratulate you on your impeccable taste, old man. Hope you didn't take offense at my attentions toward your 'ward,' but she's quite a fetching article." The younger man pulled a calling card from his vest pocket. "If you ever tire of her, here's my direction. I'd appreciate a note." He winked, and Cullen decided they'd both be better off if Cullen moved to another table.

The next table was worse. There were three men seated there, and they were all salivating over Rose Larkin. Cullen wanted to bury his head in his hands and groan. He restrained himself, but it was an effort. He did, however, listen carefully.

"I say, isn't she a corker?"

"New here, I'd say."

"Yes. I haven't seen her before, and I've sampled all of Nesbitt's wares." A lascivious chuckle followed this announcement.

When he looked over, Cullen noticed that this particular rake was older than the first one. He was older than

Cullen. Cullen was disgusted that a man so old wanted to take advantage of helpless, innocent females.

Of course, while her female attributes were overtly apparent, the bastard had no way of knowing that Rose was helpless or innocent. Who could, watching her singing and dancing on the stage in so unrestrained a fashion? Cullen realized he was gnashing his teeth, and made himself stop.

"She's something, all right," the old man's companion said. He was old, too, and he was all but slavering. He lifted his pince nez and held them before his eyes in order to better ogle Rose.

"I say, I wouldn't mind making a deposit in that bank," said the third man, chortling evilly.

That was the snapping point for Cullen. He stood up, barely catching his chair before it could crash to the floor behind him. Flattening his hands on the table, he glared straight into the third man's eyes. "That girl, my good man, is my sister, and I'll thank you not to talk about her in that obscene way."

All three men gaped at him. The one with the pince nez snatched them from his nose and glared. "I say, you'd best start taking care of her, then. A fellow can't allow his sister to dance naked in a place like this!"

"She's not naked." Cullen's jaw was so tight, he could scarcely say the words.

"She might as well be," muttered the man who'd made the offensive remark. He looked peevish.

"I wouldn't let any sister of mine work in a place like this," said the first man.

Cullen only growled at him.

He looked startled for a moment, then grinned at Cullen. "She's not your sister, I'll warrant." He gave Cullen a lurid wink.

Because he didn't want to fall prey to an apoplectic fit, Cullen drew himself up and said stiffly, "I don't recommend you pursue the matter, gentlemen," and stalked to the back of the room. There he stood against the wall and fumed until Rose's act was over.

Then he went to the stage door and mounted guard. He

thwarted several men who desired entry to the dancers' dressing room. He didn't know which of the females they'd intended to pursue, but Cullen was taking no chances. None of the men appreciated his chivalry. Cullen was surprised none of them called him out.

When Rose finally appeared, looking pleased with herself, he was exhausted.

"But after the first minute or two, I must admit it was rather fun."

Rose's cheeks bloomed with color, her excitement was palpable, and in spite of his state of near collapse from worry, Cullen was hard-pressed to keep his hands to himself. *She's only a girl,* he told himself. Several times. Unfortunately, she was about the tastiest girl he'd come across in years. Even more unfortunately, the entire male population of Dublin seemed to think so, too.

Which reminded him of all the sordid comments and suggestions he'd heard about her from various men in the audience. He told himself to keep calm.

Her words, however, alarmed him. "You think you'll enjoy singing and dancing at the French Academy indefinitely?"

They were taking tea at a pub near the Academy, Rose being too stimulated to return immediately to the inn and sleep. Cullen understood. Sometimes when the boys had experienced an exciting day, they needed time to settle down. He could even remember a time or two in his own long-vanished youth when he'd been too exhilarated to sleep. It seemed like lifetimes ago.

Rose sipped her tea. Her eyes sparkled like diamonds. His question sobered her slightly. "I'm not sure about that, Mr. O'Banyon." She gazed at him over the rim of her teacup, her expression serious. He wanted to take her chin in his hand and kiss her beautiful lips.

Lord, whatever was the matter with him?

"I mean, it was enjoyable. But, however innocent you think I am—"

"Hunh."

She grinned. "Oh, very well. However innocent you *know* I am, I found the other women who work there somewhat daunting."

Cullen raised his eyebrows. "They were unkind to you?" He had a difficult time featuring anyone being unkind to Rose Larkin, but he'd have a chat with Nesbitt about it if he had to.

"Good heavens, no." Rose appeared startled at the question. "They were very nice. All of them. Even Mae O'Malley. She was a little stiff at first, but she turned out to be very helpful, and awfully sweet." She shrugged, and then frowned. "No, it was that they seemed so . . . so . . . Oh, I don't know. Sad, or something. As if the entertainer's life was hard on them."

"I can imagine," Cullen said dryly.

She shot him a sharp look and said with a touch of chill in her voice, "I know you consider me a fool, Mr. O'Banyon, but I'm doing this for my aunt, and I shall continue to honor her with my compliance. She deserves much more than this from me."

"I don't think you're a fool, Miss Larkin." He didn't say what he considered Kate Flanagan.

"Hmmm."

"And I have a feeling that if your aunt knew the truth about the life she claims to want for you, she'd change her mind and alter her ambitions for you."

Rose scowled at him.

Cullen held his hands up in a gesture of surrender. "Honestly. I don't mean to be unfair, Miss Larkin, and I don't think either of you lack intelligence or . . . or analytical abilities. I may believe that your aunt and you haven't thoroughly considered some of your plans, but I don't think either of you is a fool. Far from it."

Rose eyed him skeptically for a moment, then gave it up. "At any rate, many of the girls are no older than I, yet they seem . . ." She chuffed, as if she were impatient with her paltry vocabulary. "I guess hardened is the proper word, although I don't mean that they're unkind or cruel.

It's more as if life has been very difficult for them, and they've had to toughen up to survive. Or something."

"I'm sure that's true, too. Not too many women seek the acting life on purpose, as you're doing."

"No?" Rose's big blue eyes opened even wider trapping Cullen in their depths. He almost suffocated for an instant before he reminded himself to breathe.

"No," he said gently.

"I suppose you're right." Rose picked up a macaroon, bit into it, and chewed thoughtfully. "And then there are the men."

Cullen's spine went rigid, his fingers tightened on his tankard, and the blood began to course through his veins like stampeding horses. "The men?" he squeezed out between his teeth. If anyone had tried to do anything improper or immoral to Rose Larkin, he'd just have to kill him, is all, and pray that the courts and his sons would understand. He'd believed he'd thwarted any of the men who'd been interested in her before they'd been able to enter the dressing area.

Rose evidently didn't notice any change in his demeanor. She smiled at him, "I'm sure you aren't surprised, but I fear Aunt Kate's idea of a grand passion might not be all that it's cracked up to be."

Expelling a breath and taking another one, while telling himself not to become overwrought—yet—Cullen said, "No, I'm not surprised. But what do you mean?"

Rose heaved a huge sigh. "Most of those poor girls seem to be in the throes of terrible discomfort resulting from love affairs or in some sort of acute misery related to the loves in their lives. I don't think a single one of them has ever been happy in love." She studied her teacup and frowned. "Perhaps what they have isn't really love."

"No?" Now, this was interesting. Although Cullen himself had never taken a mistress, he knew many men who had actresses, singers, or dancers in their keeping. "Why do you suppose that is?"

"Well . . ." Rose turned her head and gazed off into a corner of the pub, as if she couldn't quite meet Cullen's eyes. "Actually, I think it has to do with the girls expecting more than the men in their lives are able to give them."

Now that, to Cullen's way of thinking, was a very mature discovery. "What do you mean?"

"Oh, you know."

"Not really."

She huffed. "Bother. What I *mean* is that those poor girls really want husbands and children and homes and so forth. Security—in a way. But the men they meet in that venue are looking for . . . other things."

"Mistresses," Cullen supplied helpfully, sensing that Rose was too embarrassed to say the word. "Recreation away from the confines of their marriages and family. A mere diversion."

He knew he was right when her blush deepened. "Exactly."

"I see." Since he'd had to forcefully restrain himself from stomping up to the stage, throwing a blanket over Rose, and hauling her bodily out of the French Academy, Cullen felt a little sensitive on this subject. He'd died a thousand deaths when she'd first cavorted out onstage with the other "little maids," with her legs exposed and a good deal of her bosom hanging out.

He muttered, "When a woman shows so much of her body to perfect strangers, Miss Larkin, what do you expect the strangers to think? Don't you believe them to be justified—if only a little bit—in assuming she is interested in a liaison that might be less than what you consider ideal?"

She pressed a hand to her cheek, clearly mortified. "Oh, dear, you must consider me such a simpleton!"

"Not at all," he assured her.

"But, honestly, Mr. O'Banyon, not many of those poor girls had much choice in the matter of careers, you know."

"No?" He lifted his brow politely, waiting for an explanation. He was surprised to see her lips thin, her brow crease, and an expression of frustration—perhaps even anger—invade her face.

"No! Why is it that men always think women are either good or bad, as if we were born with labels on us or something? I can see it now. God's angels standing at the pearly gates with little tags on elastic bands that they slip on the girl babies' toes. This one will be a scullery maid. This one a princess. This one an actress. This one a drunkard."

Since she was upset, Cullen thought it best not to laugh, but the image she'd created amused him. He said nothing, but only sat there, sober as a judge, and let her rant.

Emphasizing her point with her forefinger, with which she poked the table, Rose said, "I'll have you know that most of those girls never started out wanting to parade naked in front of strangers! They're only doing it because they have to make their ways in the world, and that's the only way they *can* do it! It's fortunate they're of an age when they can do that! Otherwise, they'd be perishing on street corners, begging for pennies."

Her voice had risen, and she realized a couple of late-drinking patrons had turned in their chairs to look at her. one of them grinned and winked.

Clearly embarrassed, Rose muttered, "I beg your pardon, Mr. O'Banyon. But truly, there aren't many opportunities in this world for a female who has to earn her bread and shelter. A woman can be a teacher or a nurse if she has the funds to secure an education, I suppose, but if she doesn't like children or blood, those two are out." She paused to glare at him for a moment. "And then there are the poor ones who don't have the opportunity to go to school. Or the ones who aren't clever enough. They deserve suitable work, too. And what about widows? What about *them*? Widows with children can't even be teachers or nurses!"

She was very passionate in her defense of working women and the choices they were forced to make; Cullen had to give her that. She was also angry with him. He didn't like having her angry with him. "I'm sorry, Miss Larkin. I'm sure you're right."

Sitting up straight and putting her cup down with a clink of china, Rose said, "What do you mean, 'you're sure I'm right,' in that superior tone of yours? You know very well I'm right!" She sniffed and her frown got deeper. "No, you probably don't know. You wouldn't know, because you're a man, and a wealthy one, and men have all the power and privileges in this stupid world. Even the ones who don't have your money!"

Cullen blinked, not having anticipated Rose getting huffy about anything, particularly women's rights. "You sound like a suffragist, Miss Larkin." He said it mildly, and with a friendly smile, because he didn't much care what her political leanings were, although he did consider roaring feminists rather off-putting.

"No, I'm not a suffragist, actually, although perhaps I should be. What I care about is women being forced into being the playthings of men. If they could earn a living wage doing respectable work, they wouldn't *have* to become mistresses and so forth. Or wives, either, for that matter."

Good Lord, that put an interesting slant on things. As much as he hated to admit it, Cullen realized she was correct. "I see." He watched her as she fumed and fiddled with her teacup for a moment. "And, er, you don't think that being a wife and mother is a noble profession—profession in the broadest definition of the word, I mean to say."

She lifted her head and glared at him. "Of course, I do. But if there were more opportunities available to women, they wouldn't have to endure horrid situations."

Horrid situations? Good Lord.

"I've seen awful marriages, Mr. O'Banyon, but the women are stuck in them. It's either stick it out or lose her children. Or starve to death because no one will hire a divorcee for anything. Oh, it all just *infuriates* me!"

Rose flung an arm out, almost whacking it on the back of an empty chair. "And even the lucky ones aren't really lucky! Why, just look at my dear aunt Kate! Mind you, her marriage was happy and she never had to worry about money or where her next meal was coming from. But look at her today. She's a wealthy woman who believes life has passed her by! If women were permitted to *do* things, Kate wouldn't be pressing me into fulfilling all of her thwarted dreams for her! She might have been able to fulfill some of her dreams by herself when she was still young enough to enjoy them."

What she said actually made sense. In a way. Cullen wasn't sure that was a good thing. "Er, yes. I think I understand."

"I doubt it," she said sourly. "How could you? You're a man."

Indeed. "Yes. I recall you telling me that before. And I fear I can't deny it."

"Now you're patronizing me," she accused him, her eyes blazing.

"Not at all, I promise you. It's only that I've . . . ah . . . never thought about things in the light you describe. That's the only reason I hesitated."

"Hmmm." She appeared unconvinced.

They sat in silence for several minutes, Rose frowning at the tabletop, Cullen watching her and wishing he could solve all of her problems for her. And then take her to his bed. Thus making of himself the very sort of man she seemed to despise.

Actually, he thought suddenly, he *could* take another wife. Give the boys a mother, as it were. And provide himself with a companion and a partner in his bed. He hadn't thought seriously about remarriage. His first marriage had been pleasant, but not so rapturous that he'd missed it awfully after Judith died.

That sounded terrible, even in thought. Cullen mentally chastised himself. Judith had died far too young, of influenza, and if nothing else, he should at least honor her memory.

If Judith hadn't been precisely a soul mate, that was all right. It was only silly women like Kate Flanagan who dreamed of grand passions and soul mates and so forth. Cullen certainly hadn't experienced a grand passion with Judith—but he hadn't expected one either. He was also sure he'd fallen short of Judith's notions of a grand passion, too, if she'd ever had any.

The truth of his thoughts made him feel suddenly empty inside, and he was irked with himself. He had two little boys who depended on him—he couldn't afford to be indulging in fantasies of love and heart-pounding excitement.

Anyway, even if he did take a new wife, it couldn't be Miss Rose Larkin. Not that he wouldn't like to bed her, but she and her aunt weren't about to set aside their lofty notions of love and passion for anything so dull as a thirty-three-year-old widower with two little boys and a boring horse farm in the Irish countryside. And marriage.

The emptiness in his soul began to ache.

Rose took a deep breath. "I'm so sorry, Mr. O'Banyon. it was offensive and unforgivable of me to take you to task for anything at all, since you've been my kindest friend and benefactor practically since we stepped off the ocean liner."

"Please don't let my small services weigh on you, Miss Larkin. I only did what I wanted to do."

She eyed him slantwise. "I don't believe that for a minute. We've been two troublesome women, and I'm sorry for snapping at you."

"I'm sure you must be exhausted," Cullen offered politely.

"I suppose I *am* a little tired."

"Then let's get you back to the inn. I imagine your aunt is chewing her nails, wondering what's become of you." He smiled at her and held out his arm. She smiled back, and the night seemed brighter. He didn't like thinking she was angry at him.

As Cullen escorted Rose to her hotel room Rose thought hard. If Cullen O'Banyon offered her a position as his mistress, Rose was going to take it.

No, she couldn't do anything so shocking.

But Aunt Kate had as much as told her to become some man's mistress, and Cullen O'Banyon was the most wonderful man Rose had ever met.

But she didn't *want* to be his mistress. She wanted more than that. She wanted everything.

As if a man like Cullen O'Banyon would ever consider

Rose Margaret Larkin, impoverished daughter of an irresponsible gambler and rogue, as anything but a brief,
hopefully pleasant, interlude in his life. He was too sophisticated. Too much the man of the world. He definitely
didn't appear to be the marrying kind—and if he were to
marry, it would be someone suitable. Which wasn't her,
Rose Larkin, impoverished American.

With a dispirited sigh, Rose opened the door to her
hotel room, bade Cullen good night with a handshake and
a smile, agreed to meet him with Kate for luncheon tomorrow, and went inside. Kate had left a candle and a
match on the table beside the door since the electricity in
the hotel was cut off at midnight. Rose fumbled a bit as she
lit the candle. She was depressed, which didn't seem right.

She'd been a smashing success, for heaven's sake. All
the girls said so. Mr. Nesbitt had told her so himself. After
the performance, she'd been quite elated. But her euphoria
had faded as she'd sat in the pub with Cullen and watched
him, and they'd chatted. He was so at ease in the world. So
suave and charming. So far superior to Rose in culture and
elegance. She was surprised he even bothered with such as
she.

She tiptoed to her aunt's bed. Kate was sleeping like a
baby. So much for chewing her nails in anxiety over
Rose's fate at the French Academy.

Rose knew she must be more tired than she'd believed
herself to be when she had to fight tears. As she sat on the
edge of her bed and began to remove her shoes and stockings, she had the thought that she'd been putting on and
taking off clothes all day long—and she was tired of it already. She didn't know how actresses put up with all the
costume changes.

And the men! Rose blushed in the darkness of the room
when she recalled how stimulating it had been to see the
avid expressions on their faces, and to know that, at least
partially, they were lusting after her. Not, of course, that
she was as pretty as Sally. But she could have sworn that
one or two of the men in the audience had been eyeing her

especially. And quite greedily. As if they'd like to take her to bed, at the very least.

She couldn't recall seeing Cullen in the audience, although he must have been there because he'd been waiting for her at the stage door afterward. Had he been thinking lustful thoughts about her? Or—Rose swallowed hard—about one of the other dancers?

All at once her reserves collapsed. Throwing herself onto her bed, she tried to muffle her sobs in her pillow. Thank goodness Kate was a sound sleeper.

Rose felt a little better in the morning, although she did find Aunt Kate's excitement about her premier performance at the French Academy rather trying. She bore it as well as she could, but she had no appetite for the lovely breakfast Kate had had sent up.

"Do drink your tea and tell me all about it, Rose."

Rose did the latter. She even managed to choke down a few sips of tea, but she couldn't face more than a couple of bites of the sausages and toast. Somewhat tentatively, because she'd do anything to keep from hurting Kate's feelings, Rose said, "I'm not altogether sure that singing and dancing in a nightclub is the best way to meet rich men, Aunt Kate."

"No?" Kate stopped her enthusiastic chewing and glanced at Rose, her gaze clouding.

Rose cleared her throat. "That is to say, there were many, many men there last night."

"Do you think they weren't wealthy, dear?" Kate looked disappointed.

"Well," Rose equivocated, "I suspect many of them were quite rich, actually. According to Mae O'Malley, the very nice woman who taught me my routine—"

"Oh, I'm so glad the other ladies were nice to you!" Kate beamed at her, and Rose didn't have the heart to tell her she doubted most of them were ladies—either in the British or in the American sense of the word.

"Er, yes, they were very nice." Rose braced herself with

another sip of tea. "But they didn't seem awfully satisfied with the arrangements they had with their protectors."

"Oh." Kate's face fell. Rose felt guilty. "You mean none of them had a rich protector?"

"Well, I suppose the ones who have protectors are well provided for, but they didn't seem . . . happy, I guess is the word I'm looking for."

"No?" Picking up a piece of toast and slathering it with marmalade, Kate pondered this unwelcome piece of information. "I wonder why that is. I should think it would be terribly exciting to be a rich man's mistress."

Oh, dear. There, in a nutshell, was the crux of her problem, and Rose knew it. Kate longed for a life she'd never experienced, and she'd romanticized it to an exalted degree. Rose, whose life had been perilous from the beginning, only wanted the security Kate took for granted.

She feared there would never be a meeting of minds on this issue. She also feared she might have to hurt her aunt's feelings one of these days. Either that or sacrifice her own virtue and, perhaps, her sanity. Neither option appealed to her.

"Um," she said, "I think perhaps the girls at the French Academy wish their lives weren't quite so unsettled. Sometimes. I got the impression that they might welcome a permanent alliance."

"A permanent alliance?"

"With a nice man."

"A nice man?"

Rose said it baldly. "Marriage."

"Oh." Kate's brow wrinkled. "Well, now, this is distressing news, Rose. I think we should consult Mr. O'Banyon about it." She brightened at the thought. "He's ever so clever, you know."

Rose's heart sank to her shoes. Cullen O'Banyon was indeed clever. He was also rapidly assuming a position as the man of Rose's dreams. She didn't want to burden him with any more of her problems. In spite of his many protests to the contrary, Rose was sure he thought of Kate and her as two troublesome idiots.

"I don't know, Kate . . ."

"Oh, but Rose! He seems so very fond of you. I'm sure he won't mind administering just one more tiny piece of advice." She munched a bite of sausage thoughtfully. "You know, dear, I'm not sure I was entirely prepared for how arduous a chore becoming an adventuress would be."

A faint hope began to burn in Rose's breast. "No?" With luck, maybe Kate would abandon the insane scheme altogether.

"No," affirmed Kate. Then she brightened again. "But you're young and healthy, and I know you can do it!"

Wonderful. Exactly what she wanted to hear. The faint hope smothered and died unborn. Rose tried valiantly to smile at her aunt.

Kate leaned over the table and patted Rose's hand resting on the tablecloth. "And you're so lovely, dear. So very pretty. I know some nice young man will make you a wonderful offer one of these days."

Since Rose knew what sort of offer her aunt was hoping for, she was not gratified.

"Why, perhaps even Mr. O'Banyon might offer to set you up in some luxurious place, Rose. Wouldn't *that* be exciting?" Kate was practically bouncing in her chair, she was so thrilled by the prospect.

Rose, who only last night had all but prayed for such an eventuality, sat unmoved, her heart stony and bleak. The cold light of a new day had thrown a bucket of ice water on that particular notion. In fact, if Cullen O'Banyon asked her to become his mistress, she thought she might collapse from the overwhelming anguish of it all.

She didn't want to be his mistress.

She didn't want to be *any* man's mistress. She wanted to be loved. Unconditionally and forever. She didn't want a temporary liaison based on nothing more than physical pleasures. Not that she had anything against physical pleasures. But she didn't want a relationship based solely on sex. And she didn't want a relationship with just any man. She wanted it to be with a special, extraordinary man.

Unfortunately, she had a feeling Cullen O'Banyon

would do nicely. And if he thought of her as a mere plaything, a female to be used and tossed aside when he got bored, a temporary soft body with which to slake his passions, Rose thought she might very well die. She sighed heavily.

"Whatever is the matter, Rose? Don't you think Mr. O'Banyon would be a kind and generous protector?"

"He already is," Rose said, feeling wretched.

She didn't want to go back to the French Academy. She didn't want to have all those men drooling over her exposed bosom again. It had been slightly stirring at first, but now that she could look back on the experience, she knew she wanted more out of life than the ability to titillate men and to get one of them to seduce her—and paying for the privilege.

Oh, Lord, she wished this Irish adventure were over. She'd had about all the adventures she cared to endure.

As she looked into her aunt's eager eyes and saw her excited expression, she knew good and well she'd never be able to say so to Kate. At least not without considerably more provocation than she'd endured so far.

Perhaps she should pray that she'd fall onstage and break her leg. Or . . . or . . .

Rose heaved a gusty sigh.

This, she thought unhappily, was too big a pickle for her to manage on her own. Perhaps she should talk with Cullen O'Banyon. One more time. That's all. If he had a suggestion as to how she could find a rich man to take care of her, fine.

As long as it wasn't him.

Six

Cullen had no idea how to talk the two Larkin ladies out of their ambition to make Rose into an entertainer, but he aimed to give it his best shot. He had to get back to the farm soon, and he couldn't bear the notion of Rose Larkin prancing about on the stage of the French Academy without him there to protect her from amorous advances.

Of course, she believed she *wanted* amorous advances. At least her aunt did. Gad, this whole thing was turning out to be a nightmare.

He met them in the lobby of the Green Boar at one o'clock, and intended to take them to the best restaurant in Dublin. Food and drink generally went a long way toward softening hearts; perhaps they'd work on his two new friends.

He was unhappy to note that Rose looked pale and tired when she got up from the flowered sofa on which she sat with her aunt. But she gave him one of her pretty smiles, and his heart turned over, and he guessed she wasn't *that* tired. He bowed before the two women. "How do you do today, ladies?"

"We're quite well, Mr. O'Banyon," said Rose. The way she said it made him doubt her words.

"Oh, Mr. O'Banyon!" Kate began with her usual

slightly daft enthusiasm. "Thank you so much for bringing my Rose back to me last night. She told me all about her performance, but you were in the audience. You saw her. Isn't she wonderful?" She clasped her hands and fairly glowed at Rose.

"Her performance was every bit as wonderful as you said it would be, Mrs. Flanagan," Cullen told her gallantly. It was also the truth, although there were some other truths he intended to spare her, mostly because he caught the pleading expression in Rose's eyes.

"Thank you," Rose said, flushing slightly. At least embarrassment added some color to her cheeks.

"You seem a little tired this morning, Miss Larkin. Perhaps you aren't accustomed to the late nights entertainers have to endure regularly."

"I'm certainly not."

Kate blinked at Cullen, as if late nights had never occurred to her. "Oh, my, I didn't realize."

Rose glanced at her aunt, for the first time looking slightly less than imperturbable. "Did you believe night-club singers performed for the luncheon crowd, Aunt Kate?"

Kate turned an unsettled glance upon her niece. She'd obviously never heard anything so acerbic come out of her niece's pretty mouth. "No, dear, of course not. I suppose I never thought about the hours."

"Perhaps we can discuss this over our own luncheon, ladies," Cullen offered diplomatically. He gave his arm to Kate, although he wanted to give it to Rose because she looked as if she could use some support, and the three of them went out to his carriage.

The sky was overcast. It seemed to match Rose's mood. Cullen watched her surreptitiously, noticing that her enthusiasm for her enterprise seemed to have dimmed considerably overnight—unless, of course, she was merely suffering from lack of sleep.

The off chance that she might have been jolted out of her unrealistic expectations of life as an adventuress gave him hope. If she were having second thoughts about singing and dancing at the French Academy, she might be more amenable to a less hazardous career course. After all, he'd be going home soon, and then she wouldn't have a protector in the audience. She'd have to fend off all of those lust-crazed men by herself.

His fingers formed claws on the knob of his cane, and he forced himself to relax. Then he had to unclench his jaw to answer a question Kate had posed.

"Do you have a house in Dublin, Mr. O'Banyon?"

When he forced himself to look at her, she was smiling at him brightly, as usual. "Er, no. I don't own a home in the city."

Kate looked as if this information astounded her, although Cullen couldn't imagine why. After all, he was well-set-up in the world, but he was no British duke or prince or lord with grand estates scattered all over the world. He tried not to resent the surprised expression on Kate's face, although he did resent it, mainly because he imagined his lack of castles in every city gave her one more reason not to look upon him with favor when it came to her niece. He wished he could inject Kate Flanagan with a degree of common sense.

"I see."

Rose turned and gazed at her aunt. "Why did you think Mr. O'Banyon had a home in the city, Aunt Kate? He told us he was only here on business."

Kate flapped a hand in the air. The gesture was vague and suited her fey personality to perfection. "Oh, no particular reason. When I was a girl here, it wasn't unusual for families to have homes in various cities to which they traveled in different seasons."

"It's still not uncommon," Cullen told her, trying with all of his emotional strength not to snarl. "Primarily it's the English who have the homes scattered hither and yon. We Irish aren't as eager to swallow up pieces of the world."

Rose looked as if she was startled by his tart comment. He smiled at her, hoping that would take the sting out of his words. The English and their damned empire—and the way they treated the folks they trampled underfoot—was a very raw sore in Ireland.

"Oh." Kate's mild blue eyes focused on him. He smiled at her, too, although he had to try harder than with Rose to keep the smile friendly. "Do you have a home anywhere else? Other than where your family seat is, of course." She placed emphasis on the *anywhere*, as if she half-expected him to admit to being a wandering rakehell.

He took a deep breath. "Actually, I do own a small hunting box in Yorkshire, on the moors. I inherited it from my mother's family, and I've kept it." He opened his mouth to add, *for the boys,* but he remembered these two ladies didn't know anything about his boys. And he'd never tell them that he'd only kept the hunting box in case the boys had more interest in killing wild animals than he'd ever possessed. Kate would be aghast, he was sure.

"Where's Yorkshire?" Rose wanted to know.

"In northern England," Cullen supplied. It sounded curt, and he took a breath and tried to elaborate without bellowing. "Yorkshire is known as good fox-hunting country, Miss Larkin. A good many gentlemen of my acquaintance have places there." Most of them were Englishmen, but Cullen actually liked one or two of them.

"Oh. They hunt foxes?"

"Yes." He gave her as amiable an expression as he could come up with, and wished he didn't feel so tense. And helpless. He hated feeling helpless.

What he wanted was to be able to tell this girl that her plans were idiotic; that what she really needed to do was find a nice, suitable man, get married, settle down, and raise lots of nice, suitable children. She had no business parading her sexual wares in a public arena in an effort to sell herself to the highest bidder. And all for the sake of her batty aunt, for the love of Christ.

"I knew several of my father's friends in New York who liked to take trips to Maine to hunt moose and deer and so forth, but I don't know anyone who hunted foxes. Are they good to eat?"

Her question made him laugh, and he blessed her for it.

He'd been in a black temper, which was unusual—and uncomfortable—for him. "I don't believe anyone actually eats them, Miss Larkin. They're considered vermin because they kill sheep and chickens. You may have noticed the abundance of sheep in the Irish countryside. I believe fox hunting probably originated among farmers as an entertaining way to get rid of pests."

Rose nodded thoughtfully. "Enterprising of them."

"I think so, too," said Kate "I've always believed in making the best of necessity. I mean, why should one pout about having to fulfill one's responsibilities?"

"Why, indeed?" Cullen said dryly. He doubted that Kate Flanagan had ever *had* to do anything at all except decide which frock to purchase.

"Yes," said Rose. Then she sighed. "I'd like to visit the countryside someday. Dublin is beautiful, but I hear the land is spectacular."

"I think it is," Cullen said.

"Oh, my, it's splendid," Kate said rapturously. "And I'm sure we'll be able to tour the land, dear. We only need to get you established first."

"Of course." Rose turned her head and began staring out of the window once more.

Cullen wished he knew what was going on in her head. If she so much as hinted that she didn't like performing at the French Academy, he was going to propose another line of work to her.

He spent the rest of the ride to the restaurant wracking his brain, trying to think of a suitable job for a nineteen-year-old female who was smart, fairly well educated, came from America, could sing and dance, and who looked like Rose Larkin. Failing that, he decided he could at least aim her in a less perilous direction should the occasion arise.

Rose watched Cullen O'Banyon closely, trying not to be conspicuous about it, as he accompanied them into the tasteful restaurant. He was so much of what she longed for in life. He was so cultivated and sure of himself. Today he was even carrying an exquisite ebony cane with a polished knob at the end, just like one she'd seen in a painting of some duke or other in London. His clothes were splendidly cut, and he wore them with such understated elegance. Even his accent, while definitely Irish, was high-class.

His every gesture bespoke his cultivated background. She smiled up at him as he held a chair for her, and nearly swooned. He looked exactly as she'd always imagined a well-heeled riverboat gambler would look—only more intelligent and much more debonair. He possessed the most dashing good looks she'd ever seen.

She wished he didn't. It would be so much easier to accept his assistance if she didn't always have this terrible urge to fling herself at him and beg him to kiss her silly. Why couldn't a gentleman look like Cullen O'Banyon, be as kind and friendly as he, only be stable and responsible and not apt to gamble on horses and go to nightclubs and consort with low women and so forth? It wouldn't hurt if he'd fall madly in love with her and want to marry her and take her away from her aunt's mad schemes, either.

Perhaps those dashing good looks were only given to gentlemen who were like her father. He'd had rakish good looks, too, yet he'd been totally irresponsible. But very charming and absolutely lovable. It didn't seem fair to her that it should be so, and she wished it wasn't.

Wish for the world, why don't you, Rose? She heaved a big sigh, and was embarrassed.

"I wonder if there's another way to show off my dear Rose's excellent qualities to the finer element among Dublin's gentlemen. Besides singing and dancing at the French Academy, that is to say. I had no idea Rose wouldn't take to the late hours involved in entertaining gentlemen."

"Kate!" Rose was mortified. She was already depressed. She didn't need to be humiliated, too.

Cullen seemed not to mind Kate's indiscreet query. Which was just like him. It was because he was such an elegant man of the world, Rose thought glumly. She'd bet nothing ever ruffled him. With a miserable sigh, she again wished she were like that.

But no. She was a rustic Yankee from America, and she could but gaze wistfully upon the dapper Cullen O'Banyon and wish she could be as worldly-wise as he. She wondered if all adventuresses wished they could settle down and be merely a good wife and mother. Her original niggling fear that she wasn't cut out for this adventuress-ing business had received a big boost last night. Unfortunately.

"I believe you're right, Mrs. Flanagan."

Rose, who had lowered her head to contemplate the lovely luncheon that had just been placed before her—and for which she had no appetite at all because of the miserable future also looming before her—jerked her head up.

Kate said, "Really?"

"Yes. As a matter of fact, I've been giving the matter a good deal of thought."

"You have?" Rose was astonished. And that was putting it mildly. Why should Cullen O'Banyon, of all the magnificent blades in the universe, put any thought at all to her problems? Her eyes burned, she feared she might burst out crying, and she looked down at her lunch again.

"Yes, I have. I don't believe you'd like being on the stage after a while, Miss Larkin."

"You don't?" asked Rose, who didn't like it already.

"You don't?" echoed Kate. "How disappointing."

He nodded. "In fact, Miss Larkin and I spoke briefly about it last evening after her performance."

"You did?" Kate turned to stare at Rose, and Rose read hurt and mild—very mild—reproach in her old blue eyes. Rose suspected it was beyond Kate to experience any emotion more than mildly.

She felt horrible, and turned a murderous scowl upon Cullen. He seemed to catch her meaning immediately, which didn't surprise her. He was perfect; that's all there was to it. The knowledge didn't improve her overall mood any.

"We did. And it isn't that she didn't enjoy her experience on the stage, because she did."

Rose nodded energetically.

"And it isn't that she wasn't good at it. She was. Very."

"Thank you," Rose said in a stifled voice, memories of her naked legs flashing in high kicks making her wish she could sink through the floor.

"I *knew* she would be!" Kate cried.

"Indeed, she was." Cullen gave them both a warm smile. Rose wanted to curl up in it and purr. "However, I believe that if your ambitions are to be achieved, there might be a better venue in which to hunt—er, I mean operate."

"Really?" Kate popped a bite of fish into her mouth and chewed enthusiastically. "What do you suggest?"

"Yes, Mr. O'Banyon. What do you suggest?" Rose's own appetite gave a faint stir of interest and she ate a bite of her fish, too, in anticipation. She had to keep up her strength, no matter what.

"You obviously enjoy music." He tilted his head in Rose's direction.

She nodded. "Yes, I'm very fond of the musical theater."

"How about opera?"

"Opera?" Rose had seldom been to the opera. Opera performances were expensive and, except when Uncle Glen had been unable to attend with Kate and Kate had invited Rose to go with her, Rose hadn't gone. When she and her father had any money, Rose tried to spend it on food and shelter, if she could get at it before her father lost it. "I've, ah, enjoyed the few I've seen." She'd loved them, actually.

"Oh, my, yes. Why, my husband and I used to have a box at the Metropolitan in New York City, Mr. O'Banyon, and Rose used to attend with me sometimes."

Rose nodded again.

"I see. Well, Dublin has a fine opera house, ladies, and the people who attend the opera are generally those with money. It would be my pleasure to escort the both of you to the opera and introduce you to several eligible gentlemen of my acquaintance."

Rose's heart gave a gigantic spasm. He was trying to get rid of her.

Well, of course, he was. *Don't be any more stupid than you have to be, Rose Larkin,* she lectured herself furiously. This was a generosity on his part. He aimed to introduce her to men who would treat her kindly if they decided to take her as a mistress. After all, that was what she was supposed to want.

She still felt like crying. Nevertheless, she knew she couldn't allow her inner turmoil to show, so she placidly took another bite of her luncheon. It tasted like ashes in her mouth.

"What a splendid offer!" Kate's fork clattered onto her plate, and she clasped her hands to her bosom, as if she'd just been presented with the world on a platter. With chocolate sauce and a cherry on top.

Rose wanted to glare at her, and was proud of herself when she managed a serene smile instead. She turned the smile upon Cullen, who was watching her closely. "Thank you, Mr. O'Banyon. But what about the position you begged for me at the French Academy. Mr. Nesbitt was awfully nice to take me on, especially with such short notice. Don't I owe him at least a few more performances?"

"Think nothing of it," he said with a careless wave of a splendidly manicured hand. "I'll speak to Nesbitt after I drop the two of you ladies off at the inn."

Kate unclasped her hands and pressed one of them onto Rose's arm. "Oh, Rose, just wait until you see the opera house. It's so lovely."

"You've been there?" Rose was surprised.

"Actually, no, but I've seen pictures of it. It was built after I left Ireland, but friends have told me about it."

Kate's eyes, which had recently held a touch of hurt, now gleamed with happiness. Rose was glad to see them thus, and recalled all at once how very, very wonderful her aunt Kate had always been to her. Why, if it hadn't been for Kate, Rose would probably have been left an impoverished vagabond. Maybe thrust onto one of those dreadful orphan trains, or forced to work in a factory. She sat up straighter and told herself she was a selfish, ungrateful girl, and that Kate wasn't really asking much of her.

It was ridiculous of her to want moonbeams and orchids and a timeless love—and security. For heaven's sake, the world didn't work that way, and if anyone should know it, it was Rose Larkin. She ought to be profoundly thankful that she had these two nice people looking out for her. Even if she, Kate, and Cullen did seem to desire different things for and of her, they all wanted her to have a good life.

Her mind told her to buck up. Her heart continued to ache. Yet she managed to swallow most of her lunch, and even attempted the trifle Cullen ordered for dessert. She was sure it was all delicious, although she barely tasted any of it.

He dropped them off at their inn after luncheon. He was going back to the French Academy to finagle Rose's way out of performing there again. She felt like a rank deserter.

"Oh, Rose, the opera! Won't we feel grand in Mr. O'Banyon's box?"

"Does he have a box?" Rose asked mildly.

Kate's brow wrinkled. "You know, I'm not sure. I didn't ask him." She paused at the door of the inn, halfway in and halfway out. Fortunately the liveried doorman was well trained and didn't so much as frown at her.

Rose sighed, and appreciated the man's forbearance. She loved Kate more than she could say, but there were times . . .

"No!" Kate said suddenly, making both Rose and the doorman jump a little. "I don't want to waste the afternoon resting in our room."

"Oh. Do you want to go sightseeing?" Rose would love to see more of Dublin than the insides of a couple of inns and nightclubs.

"Sightseeing?" Kate looked at her as if she'd grown two noses. "Good heavens, we have the rest of our lives for sightseeing, Rose. No, indeed." She grabbed Rose by the sleeve of her morning coat. "We're going to shop!"

And shop they did. Kate had outfitted the both of them in New York before they'd boarded the ocean liner, and Rose had considered her wardrobe—larger and more lux-

urious than it had ever been in her life—more than sufficient for a stay in Ireland, if not for the rest of her life.
Kate, however, had other ideas.

It must be nice to have money, Rose thought as Kate
and she entered a discreetly fashionable modiste's shop on
Grafton Street. Her gaze lit on a hat. When she looked at
the price printed in a tiny, elegant hand on a card next to
the hat, she nearly fainted. Fifty guineas! Good Lord.

She wished she were bold enough to take pen and paper
from her reticule and sketch the hat so that she could try to
reproduce it when she got back to New York.

Kate spied the hat, too, and plucked it from its ceramic
form. "Oh, Rose! Look at this. I do believe it's exactly
right for you, dear!" So saying, she unpinned Rose's current hat—a plain but elegant morning number in bleached
straw—and plopped the new confection on Rose's auburn
locks. Then she stood back, clutched her folded hands to
her bosom and beamed at Rose. "It's beautiful, dear.
Splendid. It's perfection. Perfection itself."

"I . . . ah . . . yes, it's lovely." Having no earthly idea
what to do now, Rose turned and looked into a mirror. Her
heart sank when she realized Kate was right. The hat could
have been made for her. How discouraging, when she'd no
more spend fifty guineas on a hat than she would fly to the
moon.

"Oh, milady, I was hoping you would find that hat!"

Rose turned to see a shop girl staring at her, her hands
clutched to her chest much as Kate's were. "You were?"

"The hat is definitely you. I feared some fat blonde lady
would purchase it, and it belongs on the head of such as
you."

"Oh," said Rose, and nearly giggled.

"You're absolutely right." Kate, thrilled to have her
opinion confirmed, tripped over to the shop girl, exchanged a smile with her, and turned to gaze upon Rose
some more.

Their stares made Rose a bit uncomfortable but nevertheless, the hat, of a modified turban shape trimmed with
chiffon, roses, and plumes, was beautiful. And its color

was a muted forest green. Rose looked particularly good in green, probably because of the color of her hair.

Kate sighed rapturously.

The shop girl clucked, as if she couldn't contain her ecstasy.

With a stab of regret, both for the hat and because she knew she was frivolous to want it so badly, Rose lifted her arms and prepared to remove it.

"What are you doing?"

Kate's screech startled Rose, who turned and blinked at her. "I'm taking the hat off, Aunt Kate."

"Ah, but no," the shop girl cried. "You mustn't!"

"No? Why not?" Rose bit her lip to keep the annoyance she felt out of her voice. After all, it wasn't the shop girl's fault that Rose was too poor to buy the hat.

"No," corroborated Kate. "We must buy that hat for you, dear, and we must also find a costume to go with it. What perfection it will be for traveling!"

Rose stared at her aunt. "Ah, are we going to be traveling? I thought you planned to stay in Dublin."

Kate waved that aside. "Not indefinitely. Besides, I have a feeling we're going to be enjoying the countryside soon, dear, and that will be a splendid traveling costume."

Rose finished lifting the hat from her head and gazed at it. It was a lovely hat, but it wasn't a traveling costume. "Um, you think I need to purchase an entire costume? To go with this hat?" She lifted it up as if offering it to Kate as her mind sifted through her clothes. She was sure she already had a gown that would go with it.

"Why, of course!" Kate spoke as if she'd never heard such a silly question.

"I see."

"I have the fabric here, milady," the shop girl offered. "And the patterns."

She obviously scented a big sale and wasn't going to let it pass without pouncing on it. Rose wished she could think of some way to thwart her generous aunt, but knew it only hurt Kate's feelings if she tried to refuse the proffered bounty.

"If you will step this way, madam, it will be my great delight to show you the fabrics and styles." The shop girl bowed graciously.

Kate grabbed Rose's hand and began tugging her along after her as she followed the shop girl. "There, you see, dear? Things have a way of working out, don't they?"

"Do they?" Rose wasn't sure about that. Ever since she'd arrived in Ireland, her life seemed to have begun heading straight downhill.

If she'd never met Cullen O'Banyon would that still be the case? Rose tried to remember life before Cullen. It wasn't so long ago that she and Kate had arrived in Dublin. Only a few days. Their first night here had been interesting. She didn't doubt she'd have thought up some stratagem to get herself away from that awful Everett Costello if he'd proved to be a problem, but there was no denying that Cullen O'Banyon had eased her out of the situation. As he'd been easing her way ever since.

So why was she so depressed about everything?

Because she wanted Cullen O'Banyon to love her, is why, and she knew it. She'd never been any good at pulling the wool over her own eyes. She'd been forced to be sensible, since her father wasn't, and she generally didn't try to call a spade a shovel. Or a silver spoon. She admired Cullen more than she'd admired any other man in her brief acquaintance with men, and she wished he wanted her. As something more than a mistress.

She was a total blithering idiot.

Bother. Why did life have to be so complicated all the time? Rose was positive that lots of other women her age would leap at the chance Kate was now offering her. She'd gone to school with girls who'd have given their eyeteeth to go adventuress-ing. So why did it fall to her lot to fulfill everyone else's dreams? All she wanted was a nice little house and a loving husband. Children. Stability. Was that too much to ask?

Evidently.

Her thoughts dried up when she saw the glorious array of fabrics, fashion plates, dressmakers' dummies, and live models in the large room into which she and Kate had been led.

"Mercy," she whispered.

"Oh, Rose, this is exactly what we need!"

"It is?" Rose didn't think so.

"It is." Kate plainly did.

The shop girl had the two of them sit down on a couple of fancy wrought-iron chairs with delicately flowered cushions, and brought them tea and macaroons. Then, while Rose goggled, she paraded a series of dresses before them, all culled from the modiste's store of ready-made samples, and all geared to complement Rose's hair color, figure, height, and skin tones. She'd never been treated thus. It was an experience to savor, and she tried to do so in spite of the heavy thud of dread that occasionally invaded her heart when she contemplated her future, which, in spite of Kate's enthusiasm, seemed precarious to Rose.

By the time she and Kate got back to the inn, she was exhausted and extremely glad that she'd have time to rest before Cullen was to pick them up and escort them to the evening's entertainment.

She also had a thrill in her heart, of which she was ashamed, because she had a simply smashing new gown to wear to the opera. She could hardly wait to see how Cullen reacted to her in it.

Seven

Since Rose and Kate believed him to be dashing and daring and quite the swashbuckler, Cullen did not stop cold in his tracks and gape at the sight of Rose Larkin all dressed up for the opera, but it was a struggle. He'd never seen anything to match her. She was magnificent.

She appeared to be slightly upset, however. Her cheeks bore a flush of anxiety, and her gaze darted here and there as if she wasn't sure where to look. He walked over to greet her as she descended the hotel's staircase. He heard several gasps behind him, and knew that other hotel guests had spotted her, too. In a reaction he was sure had been spawned by Rose and Kate's misapprehension about his basic character, he felt a strong urge to shoot all the other men in the room who were daring to look upon Rose Larkin with lust. Lord, what a fool he was.

"You look lovely this evening, Miss Larkin."

"Thank you, Mr. O'Banyon." As for him, he was clad in his best evening-out clothes, along with his top hat and ebony walking stick and snowy white cravat. In a bow to the image his two American friends had conjured for him, he'd purchased a small white buttonhole, as well. A flower in his lapel—what was he coming to?

Ah, well, Rose was worth it. She was clad in a beautiful cream-colored gown with a short train. The bodice had been worked in seed pearls, and it fitted her form and coloring to perfection. Cullen wished he could paint; he'd paint a picture of Rose as she was this evening, hang it in his study at home, and look upon it in years to come—and wonder whatever happened to his pretty young American adventuress who didn't know quite how to go about her line of work.

Yet there was definitely something wrong with her. Cullen hadn't known her long, but he'd never seen her ill at ease before now. He held out his arm for her to grip. "Is something the matter, Miss Larkin? You look a trifle peaked." Which was a flat lie. She looked nervous. Her health was obviously, stunningly radiant.

She huffed once. "It's Kate." She sounded cross.

"Your aunt? I trust she's not ill?" He took the cream colored satin cape she was carrying and helped her into it. He wished he could let his hands linger on the silky skin of her shoulders, but he didn't. She might believe him to be a hardened rake, but he wasn't. More's the pity.

"Oh, she's well enough," Rose said. "But she's claiming she's too exhausted to go with us tonight." As if she'd suddenly been stricken with an inspiration, she stopped and looked up at him. "If you'd care to wait until she's no longer feeling so tired, perhaps we can do this another night."

Eager to get out of an evening alone with him, was she? The little minx. Cullen didn't know whether to be amused or insulted. "I'm sure she wouldn't want us to do that, Miss Larkin," he told her gently.

"No," she said, and huffed again. "I'm sure you're right."

The way she said it made Cullen suppose that Rose knew exactly what her aunt's hopes for the evening were. Good old Kate—indisputably a failed romantic—was anticipating a seduction of Rose on his part, or he would be much surprised. It was obvious that Rose didn't share her aunt's ambitions about the matter. He wondered if it was because she didn't care to be seduced by him, if she thought it was too early in the game, or if she were holding out for bigger game.

It was a lowering reflection on his own moral standards to know that he wanted to be considered a rake and a roué by these two women. Actually, at the moment, he wanted to *be* a rake and a roué. His imagination had always been remarkably active, and his mind's eye had no trouble at all picturing how pleasant it would be to rid Miss Larkin of her gorgeous opera gown.

Lord, if he didn't get back to William and Ferris soon, he was liable to suffer a complete moral collapse.

Which might not be a bad idea.

Good God, what was he thinking? Rose Larkin was a virgin or he'd eat his hat, and he certainly didn't want to be seducing virgins. What kind of example would that be for his sons? Cullen loathed the exalted British lords who owned most of the land of his birth and who thought nothing of ravaging both the land and the people on it. He wouldn't allow himself to become like one of them.

Every now and again one's principles really did stand in the way of a good time.

"I'm sure we'll have a lovely evening, although we'll miss Mrs. Flanagan," he said as he led her out to the carriage.

"Yes. Of course."

She didn't believe him. Cullen found himself wondering if she'd shrink away if he sat next to her as they traveled to the opera house. Perhaps her aunt had drilled her on the proper way to accept a gentleman's advances—if dear Kate even knew. Cullen had a feeling Kate's knowledge of the world had been gleaned from romantic novels and pitifully little personal experience.

Perhaps he should try cozying up to Rose, as an experiment, just to see what she would do. He mentally punched himself in the jaw and wished his mind would crawl out of the gutter and remain on a more honorable plane. If Rose Larkin expected to assume the position of adventuress, she'd have to do it with another sort of man than he. Damn.

"Is anything the matter, Mr. O'Banyon?"

Cullen glanced at Rose, who appeared more nervous than ever now that the two of them were alone in his carriage. He smiled at her, thinking she made a truly pathetic adventuress. He wondered how long her innocence would last. "Not a thing, Miss Larkin."

She turned to peer out of the window, but the night was dark and the curtains were drawn, so she didn't have much luck. "I'm sorry Aunt Kate wasn't able to come with us tonight."

"Aye?" There was some devil afoot tonight. Cullen knew it when he felt compelled to add, "Are you afraid to be alone with me, Miss Larkin?" He kept his tone extremely mild.

Mild or not, the glance she shot him was so apprehensive, he nearly laughed.

"Of course not! I'm only sorry because Kate so loves the opera. She and my uncle used to have a box at the Metropolitan, and they went to all the performances there. Why, they saw Nellie Melba and all sorts of wonderful people sing there." She seemed to realize she was chattering and shut her mouth abruptly.

"I see."

A tense silence descended upon the occupants of Cullen's carriage. He lounged on the seat opposite Rose, determined not to allow his natural gentlemanliness to overcome his pose as a rakish man of the world. If Rose Larkin knew how dull his life really was, she'd move on to greener pastures at once. He enjoyed her company too much to let her go yet.

Rose took a deep breath and expelled it in a whoosh. "Anyway, I'm sure I shall enjoy the opera, Mr. O'Banyon."

"In my company."

"In your company." Her dimple peeked at him, and he was charmed. Again.

With the utmost aplomb he assisted Rose from the carriage in front of the opera house, helped her adjust her cape, and took her arm. She placed her small, satin-gloved hand on his arm, and they walked up the steps to the doors.

A sudden wash of possessiveness overtook Cullen. He tried to shake it off, to no avail.

The crowd was grand. Cullen saw several gentlemen of his acquaintance, and leaned over to whisper into Rose's ear. "I believe your aunt expects me to introduce you to eligible fellows here, Miss Larkin."

Her back went rigid. This was a curious reaction by Cullen's way of thinking, unless Rose wasn't as eager as her aunt for her to form an alliance of a nonmarital variety.

"Er, yes, I guess she does."

"Would you like to start now, or would you prefer to wait until the first interval?"

The swift glance she shot him was so full of relief, he smiled. She was definitely not eager to become some man's mistress.

"Oh," she said, waving a hand in the air in so nonchalant a gesture that it might have fooled Cullen if he hadn't seen the expression on her face, "I think I'd rather wait. I, er, want to look at everything first."

"Of course. Perfectly natural."

He led her upstairs to a box he'd borrowed for the evening from a friend of his. Zachary Molloy was a good fellow. He'd actually be perfect for Rose's purposes, except Cullen wasn't about to introduce the two. She needed a slightly more responsible sort than Zachary. Zachary, while good-hearted and generous, was flighty. Rose needed someone older. More refined. Less scatterbrained. Dammit, she needed a husband.

Forcing himself to stay calm despite his riotous thoughts, he escorted her to a chair near the balcony, and watched her eyes brighten as she scanned the array of humanity spread out before her. Zach was a rich man, and he could afford to pay for his box in the best tier at the opera house. From it, one could see the entire audience—and it was a glittery one, indeed.

Glancing at the other boxes, Cullen noted wryly that several theatergoers had their opera glasses trained on Rose. Not all of them were matrons eager for gossip, either. He saw lots of men going goggle-eyed at the sight of her.

Something cynical and savage curled in his chest. Damn them all. Let them find their own mistresses. Cullen would be hanged if he'd give Rose into the keeping of any of them. He'd do his level best to protect her from her aunt's foolishness.

Lord, he'd never get home at this rate.

"You're an object of eager interest, Miss Larkin." He tried to keep the sarcasm from his voice.

She gave a start and blinked at him. "I beg your pardon?"

If the question had come from any other female in the world, Cullen would have chalked it up to disengenuity. He hadn't known Rose Larkin long, but he knew that this reaction on her part was genuine. Nodding at the audience, he said, "Take a look around. People are very interested in you."

She did as he'd suggested, and her cheeks flushed with embarrassment. It might have been pleasure, but Cullen didn't think so. "Good heavens."

"At the worst of times you're an extremely attractive woman, Miss Larkin. This evening, you're ravishing."

She flicked open the fan that hung from her wrist on a satin ribbon and fanned her face furiously. "Nonsense! It's only that I'm new at the opera. And—and I'm with you. They're probably used to seeing you with other people. Other women, I mean." She added, a little bitterly, "I'm sure you have dozens of them."

Far be it from he to spoil her concept of him. "That must be it," he murmured. "Yet, I suspect this kind of attention is exactly what your aunt was hoping would accrue to you."

"Oh." Her blush faded as quickly as it had come. "Of course. I'm sure you're right." Her fan snapped shut and dropped to dangle, unused, at her side. She didn't appear to be particularly gratified that her aunt's wishes for her were coming true.

The curtain opened behind them. Rose looked up

quickly. Cullen frowned to see another of his Dublin associates, Eric Janeworthy, standing there looking like a cat who'd just cornered a fat, succulent canary, and couldn't wait to pounce and devour it. Of all of Cullen's acquaintances, Janeworthy was probably the most like the type of man Kate Flanagan wished had swept her off her feet when she was young.

Janeworthy was an unprincipled sensualist.

Cullen would sooner climb the pyramids of Egypt than introduce Janeworthy to Rose Larkin. And Cullen hated camels.

"Cullen, old man, I didn't know you'd come to Dublin!" Although he spoke to Cullen, Janeworthy leered at Rose.

"Short trip, old fellow. I won't be here for long."

The two men shook hands. Janeworthy didn't linger over the ceremony, but turned immediately to Rose. Cullen scowled at his back and resisted the urge to shove him over the balcony.

"And who is your charming companion, Cullen? You must introduce us."

"Of course." Cullen walked over to Rose, who was offering the interloper a friendly smile. He stood behind her, put a hand protectively on the back of her chair, and said, "Miss Rose Larkin, please allow me to introduce you to one of my associates who lives here in Dublin. Eric Janeworthy, Miss Rose Larkin from New York City." He glowered ferociously at Janeworthy, who ignored him and advanced upon Rose. To Cullen, he looked like a panther stalking a helpless spring lamb.

"New York City? My, my. You've traveled a long way, Miss Larkin." Janeworthy bowed low over Rose's hand.

The bounder was undoubtedly ogling her bosom. Cullen said, "Miss Larkin is a cousin, Janeworthy. From America. She's come to visit Ireland with her aunt, who was unable to join us this evening. Are you attending the opera with your *fiancée* tonight?"

Janeworthy jerked upright. "My fiancée? What are you—"

"I'm afraid the performance is about to begin. And Miss Larkin and I have something to discuss before the lights dim. Don't want to be rude and chatter during the performance, don't you know."

He took Janeworthy's arm and, using great force, hauled him toward the door of the box and out into the hallway. "Keep your eyes to yourself, Janeworthy," he advised in the stern voice he used on his children when they misbehaved. "Miss Larkin is not for the likes of you."

Janeworthy tugged his evening vest down, because it had hiked up when Cullen manhandled him. "My goodness, old fellow, I've never known you to take such a propriety interest in a female. Should we expect an announcement? Of some kind?"

Cullen eyed him darkly—so darkly indeed, that Janeworthy took a startled step backward and put up a hand as if to block a swing. "No, you shouldn't expect an announcement, Janeworthy—of any kind at all—and I advise you to go back to your box and keep your mouth shut about having met Miss Larkin."

Janeworthy smiled. "Ah. She's yours. I see how it is."

"Think what you will," Cullen said forcefully. "But stay away from her."

"All right, all right, Cullen. Sorry she's taken."

He sauntered away. Cullen wished he could speed him on his way with a boot to the tail of his evening coat. This was crazy. He had to talk to Rose. He didn't want to be fending off lecherous fiends like Eric Janeworthy all evening.

Not that Rose would thank him for being gallant, he thought bitterly. Janeworthy was exactly the sort of fellow Kate wanted for her. Rich, promiscuous, and jaunty. Precisely what Rose and Kate thought Cullen was, as a matter of fact.

Damnation, life could get complicated at the drop of a hat, couldn't it?

When he was fairly certain he wouldn't yell at Rose, he returned to the box. She glanced up at him curiously. He walked over and sat in the chair next to her, wondering how to begin saying what he wanted to say.

Rose helped him along. "Er, is Mr. Janeworthy a good friend of yours?"

Cullen glowered at her. "Friend? The man's a cad."

"Oh." Rose sat up straight and started fanning herself again. "I wondered."

"Of course, you did."

She sighed. "Yes, although sometimes it's difficult to tell about people." She frowned slightly. "But if he left his fiancée to come over here to look at me in that unseemly way, he certainly isn't a nice man. The least he could have done is bring her and introduce us."

Fiancée? What was the woman talking about?

Oh, yes. Cullen recalled that it was he who'd given Janeworthy a fiancée. If Janeworthy ever got himself engaged, the world would stop spinning. And the poor girl might as well slit her wrists and get it over with as live with so sorry a specimen of manhood as Janeworthy.

"He's a fortune hunter," he lied with no compunction whatsoever. "You don't want to become involved with anyone like him."

Rose opened her eyes wide, then chuckled. "If he's a fortune hunter, he wouldn't want anything to do with me, since I have no fortune."

Cullen stared at her for a moment, then said, "Yes," deciding not to dismay her by telling her any man would delight in a dalliance with her, whether she had money or not.

"I wish I knew more about the world. It would help if I could spot fortune hunters and other unlikely candidates before I bothered with them."

Cullen had a sudden brilliant idea. "For this evening, Miss Larkin, why don't you allow me to guide you? You may rely upon me to steer you in the right direction. If a gentleman meets your aunt's requirements, I shall nod. If he doesn't, I shall shake my head. That way, you'll know beforehand whether to be particularly charming or not." He almost gagged on the last sentence.

It was worth it, however, when Rose gave him one of

her radiant smiles. "Oh, will you do that? Thank you so much!"

"It will be my very great pleasure, Miss Larkin." It would also ensure that Rose wouldn't meet any eligible candidates this evening. He wished he knew a way to protect her from men like Janeworthy forever. Fortunately, the house went dark at that moment, so Rose didn't see his murderous expression.

During the interval, Cullen felt that, since she'd agreed to take his hints regarding men, it was safe to escort Rose out of the box and guide her to the wine bar in order to partake of a glass of champagne. He kept her close by his side, smiling and nodding at acquaintances.

They were stopped several times on their way by friends of Cullen's parents. He didn't have any qualms about introducing Rose to them, and he was pleased to see that Rose had an easy, gracious style about her. She wasn't forward and she wasn't shy, and her open, friendly manner seemed to charm everyone. Even Mrs. Roundtree, his grandmother's best friend, the highest stickler Cullen had ever met, and a woman who took pleasure in finding fault, smiled at her. Cullen was amazed.

He was less amazed, and infinitely less amused, when Rose's beauty attracted men in swarms. They took one look at her, about-faced, and headed toward her like so many bees toward a field of clover.

In between head shakes, he introduced her to them, one and all. Taking note of his negative signals, Rose always kept her greetings cool and aloof. He was proud of her. And damned glad. He wasn't sure what he'd do if she chose to ignore his shakes and encourage any of them.

Some of them were very nice men, too. He knew he was being less than honest with her. One or two of them might even be good husband material, and Cullen told himself that Rose would probably be very happy if she were to marry a suitable man, no matter what her crazy aunt's ambitions. Yet every time he saw someone of whom he would have approved if, say, his sister were to be in the market for a match, he discovered his head shaking no.

What did this mean? He had a feeling he knew, and he spent the second and third acts of the opera mulling it over. By the time the performance ended, he'd made a decision. It would keep him away from the boys for a while longer, and he regretted that part, but it would be worth it in the end.

Besides, it would give him ample time to not only experience an adventure, but to overcome his strange and uncomfortable obsession with Rose Larkin. He figured he owed it to himself.

Rose was disappointed that none of the gentlemen at the opera were judged by Cullen to be suitable to her purposes. She'd had no idea so many Irishmen were fortune hunters, yet she had no reason to doubt his assessment of them. She kept expecting him to nod—at least once—but he never did.

Nevertheless, she enjoyed the opera. And she felt safe. Safe and secure and protected. She'd seldom felt that way in her life, and she liked it.

She'd been to the Metropolitan Opera in New York City, but this seemed more exciting somehow, probably because it was in a foreign land. It didn't hurt that she was dressed to the nines in a gown the likes of which she'd never dreamed she'd ever own, either. Or that she was accompanied by Cullen O'Banyon, whose dark good looks made her want to swoon every time she looked at him.

To her extreme pleasure and surprise, Cullen insisted they dine after the opera. He took her to the fanciest restaurant she'd ever seen, but she felt not the least bit out of place. For perhaps the first time in her life, she felt as if she belonged.

It was a novel experience for Rose, who had always lived under the cloud of her father's invention of life, which had been crafted of show and contained no substance. They'd always been one step away from being evicted, or of having his kneecaps broken, or having Rose expelled from school because he hadn't paid the bills. Living without constant anxiety over possible calamities was ever so much more comfortable than what she'd known for so many years.

If she could only convince Kate of that. Rose would even settle for a life of spinsterhood if she could do it securely and not live in fear of bankruptcy or worse. Thank God there were no debtors' prisons in America!

"Does Ireland still throw people into debtors' prison if they can't pay their bills?"

Cullen had just helped Rose into her chair at the restaurant. His face held an expression of amused puzzlement when he seated himself. "Debtors' prison? No, not any longer. Thank goodness, I might add. I suppose the most infamous of such was the Fleet, in London, where Charles Dickens's family was housed for a while. Vile place, from all I've heard."

"I'm glad to hear such prisons no longer exist," said Rose with feeling, and she couldn't suppress a shudder.

He cocked his head to one side. When he did that, Rose's insides fluttered. He was such an amazingly handsome man.

"What a curious question, Miss Larkin. Do you have reason to fear debtors' prison?"

"Not any longer," she muttered, and blushed. "Oh, I'm sorry, Mr. O'Banyon. I guess I was thinking about my father. He was a wonderful man. Very funny. And he tried his best. But he wasn't very good with money."

"Yes, I remember you saying that before."

She heaved a happy sigh. "But the poor man is dead, and Aunt Kate is determined that I shall not want for anything, God bless her."

"Yes."

His "yes" didn't sound as pleased as Rose would like. "It's true she's not the most worldly of women, but she's got the best heart of anyone I've ever met, Mr. O'Banyon."

"I'm sure you're right."

"She helped Father and me more times than I can count."

"Yes, I can imagine."

Rose wasn't sure, but she feared she'd painted her father in a bad light. Since she didn't know how to clean up his image for Cullen, she didn't try.

He paused to order a bottle of wine from a white-coated, white-gloved waiter, who looked ever so superior. Rose was glad it fell to Cullen's lot to place their orders, because that stuffy waiter would intimidate the life out of her.

When he was finished with the waiter, Cullen turned back to Rose. "I don't suppose I could prevail upon you to call me Cullen, could I? It seems to me we're past the formal stage of our relationship."

Their relationship? Again, Rose's heart fluttered. Oh, wouldn't that be grand, to have a relationship with Cullen O'Banyon? She told herself to stop being silly. "I'll be happy to call you Cullen if you will, in return, call me Rose."

"Rose."

He lifted his water goblet and offered a mock toast. His smile was gorgeous, his eyes twinkled devilishly, and Rose hyperventilated and nearly fainted dead away. Blast tight corsets! She recovered, and was proud of herself when she was able to lift her own water goblet and return the toast with relative equanimity. "Cullen."

The waiter returned with the bottle of wine. He poured some into a stemmed glass, offered it to Cullen, who swirled it, sniffed it, sipped it, and nodded. Rose was terribly impressed. She'd read of just such scenes in novels, but never thought she'd be witnessing one herself.

The waiter half-filled two glasses, and Cullen lifted one. "I suggest a real toast this time, Rose. To you."

Oh, dear, what was she supposed to say to that? Rose had never been toasted before. She picked up her glass, tilted it slightly at Cullen, and whispered, "And to you."

This had, thus far, been the most romantic night of her life. Actually, it had been the only one. It would be even more so if she cared for the taste of wine. She did her best.

"What would you like to eat, Rose? Are you hungry?"

She was famished, actually, but knew it would be unladylike to say so. Instead, she said, "Why don't you order for me? I'm unsure of what things are called over here." That wasn't really such a stupid thing to say, was it? After all, it was the truth If she hadn't had Kate along with her during her first days in Britain, she'd never have known what a banger was. Or mash. She didn't understand why folks couldn't call things what they were. What was wrong with the words *sausage* and *egg*?

"I'll be delighted to order for the both of us. I'm hungry myself. If you can't eat everything, don't feel compelled to stuff yourself."

Fat chance. Rose was starving.

Lord, she was nervous. There was something about being alone with a man that she'd like to ravish her that did something to her equilibrium.

Thank heavens Cullen was such a man of the world, because he kept them chatting about inconsequential things until their meal arrived. They spoke about the opera, and about Dublin, and about the sights Rose would like to see after she fulfilled Kate's hopes for her—if that ever happened.

After the meal came, Rose concentrated on that. The food was delicious. She tried not to stuff it into her mouth as she wanted to. Fortunately, her tight corset came to her assistance in moderating her food intake. She hated corsets with a passion.

When they were halfway through the second course, Cullen leaned a little forward in his chair. "Rose, I have a proposition for you."

She froze with her fork midway to her mouth, and stared at him. A proposition? Good Lord, this was it. The moment she'd awaited—dreaded—longed for.

She didn't know whether to be happy or to burst into tears, although the sinking feeling in her middle gave her a fair indication. She'd never felt lustful impulses for a man before she'd met Cullen but she still didn't want to be his mistress. She was pretty sure she'd not be able to contain her tears if he made an improper proposal.

Kate, of course, would be thrilled.

She managed a tiny, squeaky, "Oh?"

"Indeed. I hope you won't take it amiss."

She slowly lowered her fork to her plate, wondering how she could have been so hungry only seconds earlier, when now she felt sick.

"Please don't think I doubt your aunt's goodwill in your regard, Rose. I'm sure she has only your best interest at heart."

"Yes," she whispered. "I know she has."

"But it seems to me that she might not quite understand what she's actually asking of you. The consequences, that is to say."

"Oh." She watched him warily. He didn't look like a lust-crazed fiend who only wanted to pounce on her and have his way with her. Her emotions waffled between gratitude and disappointment.

"So, what I propose is that I accompany you for a week or two as you become acquainted with Ireland. Since your aunt hasn't lived here in so many years, she probably doesn't understand how things have changed. If I traveled with the two of you ladies, I could, oh, ease your way, as it were. Help you over the rough spots. By the time you're comfortable with the way things operate here, you won't need my services any longer, and you'll be better able to take care of yourselves."

"Oh." Rose didn't quite grasp what he'd said to her. He hadn't mentioned a thing about unbridled—or even bridled—passion. He hadn't mentioned mistresses. He hadn't mentioned protection—not in the way Aunt Kate meant it, anyway.

He held up a hand, as if he understood her hesitation. "I know your aunt is eager to establish you under the protection of some wealthy gentleman, but I believe you'd be better equipped to make a decision in that regard if you knew more of the in-and-outs of my country. You'd have a broader base of understanding so as to make your selection with greater intelligence and discretion."

That actually made sense. Sort of. "But—but, don't you

have business you must attend to? Can you afford the time to travel with us?"

"To tell you the truth, I've been longing for a little holiday away from business. It would be my great pleasure to take it with two charming ladies."

She didn't know what she was supposed to say. *Yes* sprang to mind, but she wasn't sure she meant it. The deepdown truth was that she wanted Cullen O'Banyon to desire her as a woman—even if she didn't really want to become his mistress.

She licked her lips. "Er, do you mean to say, you only want to travel with us? Um, you don't want . . ."

Good gracious, how embarrassing! How could she ask him if he didn't really want to make mad, passionate love to her?

His smile was a work of art. "No strings attached, Rose."

There was no doubt in her mind that he'd read her unspoken thoughts. She blushed furiously.

He reached over and patted her hand. "Please don't be embarrassed. I feel toward you as I would a sister. And, as much as I respect your aunt, I honestly think the two of you could use a chaperone. At least until you understand the lay of the land."

A sister. Rose wished she were alone so she could beat her fists in her pillow, drum her heels on the floor, and throw a tantrum.

Instead, she smiled serenely. "This is an extremely kind proposition, Cullen. I appreciate it very much, and I'm sure that Kate will, too."

Eight

No strings attached, he'd said. *I feel toward you as I would a sister,* he'd said.

Offhand, Cullen couldn't recall when he'd told a bigger whopper, unless it was when he was a lad and his father had asked him if he'd seen his fishing pole, and he'd said no.

But this time, unlike that other one, his lie had worked. She'd agreed.

Kate had been ecstatic. No surprise there. He and Rose had extended his offer to Kate when he'd returned her to the inn after dinner. Then he'd suggested he take them on a tour of Dublin before they continued their journey to more distant hunting grounds.

"Oh, Cullen! I'd absolutely love to see Dublin. I'd so hoped to do some sight-seeing while we were here."

"We would have gone sight-seeing, dear," Kate said, sounding somewhat distressed. "I merely wanted to see you established first."

Rose hugged her aunt. "I know it, Kate. And I appreciate it, too."

Cullen didn't. He did, however, have a comment he hoped might assuage Kate's bruised feelings. "You know, Mrs. Flanagan, if Rose were to become established under some gentleman's protection, perhaps the gentleman wouldn't care to have her go jauntering off sight-seeing with her aunt. At least, not immediately." He saw the stunned expressions on the two ladies' faces, and murmured, "Merely a suggestion, of course."

"My land, you're right!" Kate looked horrified. "Oh, I'm so glad you pointed that out, Mr. O'Banyon. I never thought about it myself. My goodness, I couldn't tour Ireland on my own, could I? Well, I _could_, of course, but—"

As if she were hoping to ward off a long ramble on her aunt's part, Rose said stoutly, "I'd never desert you, Kate. You know I wouldn't do such a thing."

Kate patted her niece's arm kindly. "I know it, dear, but you shouldn't be sacrificing yourself on my account, for heaven's sake."

Cullen didn't point out that Kate was asking Rose to sacrifice herself for the sake of Kate's fancies.

"No, no. That would never do. I fear my brother forced you into too many sacrifices already." Kate smiled sadly at Rose.

Cullen noticed that Rose flushed slightly. "Nonsense!" But she thought so, too; Cullen could tell.

"At any rate," he said, in an effort to forestall any more discomfort on anybody's part, "why don't we begin tomorrow. I'll pick you up at noon, and if you'll have your bags packed, we can begin our grand tour of the city then. I'll show you all the sights. I believe you'll find them interesting. In spite of her many tragedies, Ireland is a fascinating land."

"It certainly is," Kate affirmed.

As for Rose, she looked so excited, Cullen wouldn't have been awfully surprised if she'd jumped up and down like William and Ferris did in anticipation of a promised surprise.

He left them at the inn, the two of them chatting away happily. He was glad to have occasioned them such glee. He was relatively happy himself. Not only would he have been in a state of severe anxiety over their welfare if he hadn't offered to accompany them, but he'd be forever left in doubt of Rose's fate. He didn't think he could abide not knowing she was alive and well and safe in the world.

This change of plans meant, however, that he would have to stay away from his children even longer. He wished he could visit them before starting on his journey with Rose and Kate, but there was no logistical way to accomplish that, so he promised himself he'd write them a long letter before going to bed.

Before he could even see his own bed that evening, Cullen had one more errand to run. He'd already visited Patrick Nesbitt once this day, but they had parted on less than amicable terms. Since then, Cullen had visited his bank and drawn a largish draft in Nesbitt's name. He could afford it, and it was worth the expense to keep Nesbitt as a friend. After all, one could never have too many friends, whereas even one enemy was too many.

When he entered the French Academy, three women were going through the steps and music to "Three Little Maids From School." None of them looked as good as Rose had. Small wonder Nesbitt hadn't been pleased when Cullen told him Rose wasn't coming back for a second performance.

"Dash it, man," Nesbitt had said, glowering fiercely. "I've already spent a good deal of time and money on the chit."

Cullen had refrained from planting a facer on Nesbitt's chin for calling Rose a chit.

"And the audience loved her. Most of these men have come back tonight, hoping to get another glimpse of her."

Cullen hadn't taken a pistol and shot up the room full of lecherous men, either, as his inclinations had prompted him to do. He'd merely offered to pay Nesbitt a goodly sum in an effort to make up for the inconvenience to which Nesbitt had been put. Nesbitt had been mollified. He'd even grumbled his thanks.

This evening, after a few inquiries, Cullen found Nesbitt standing in a corner watching his girls perform. He didn't appear to be particularly cheery. Cullen hoped the bank draft he carried would alter the man's demeanor.

It did. Nesbitt squinted at the draft, then relaxed. "I say, this is generous, old man."

Cullen could have told him that Rose was worth every penny of that draft and a good deal more besides, but he suspected Nesbitt would only laugh at him and call him a besotted fool. Which, he thought gloomily, he was.

He could pretend all he chose that he only wanted to assure himself of Rose's welfare—and he did. Her welfare, however, was only part of his problem. He didn't want to leave her; that was the primary problem. Every time he considered going back to the farm, his heart lit up when he thought about William and Ferris—and then went completely black when he thought about never seeing Rose again.

Well, he might not be able to put off their separation forever, but he could postpone it, and he aimed to do so. With luck, by the time they'd traveled together for a couple of weeks, they'd be heartily sick of each other.

He didn't believe it for a minute.

Rose was so happy, she felt near to bursting. Oh, she knew her happiness wouldn't last. How could it, with the prospect of becoming the plaything of some rich stranger staring her in the face? Yet she was ever so glad to be able to remain in Cullen's company for a little while longer.

"And we're going to see Dublin, Aunt Kate! And perhaps even more of Ireland! This is so thrilling."

"Yes, indeedy, Rose. I'm quite glad of it." Kate glanced sheepishly at Rose. "You must believe me to be a terribly selfish old woman, Rose, not to have understood how very much you wanted to see the wonders of Ireland. After all, I was born here, but you've never seen it. I do apologize."

Rose rushed over to her aunt and embraced her warmly. "Don't be ridiculous, Kate! You've always been my best and kindest friend. For my whole life, you were the one who was always there, no matter what happened."

"And no matter what foolishness your father got up to," Kate said grimly. "I know, dear. I used to despair of him— and you, too. I can admit it now, although I never would have done so while dear Edward was alive, but I wanted to thrash him sometimes for the careless way he saw to your welfare. And that of your poor mother, God rest her soul."

Rose's eyes suddenly filled with tears, and she dashed them away impatiently. She'd cried over her mother and father quite enough. She still loved them. She'd always love them, but they were dead, and she was alive, and she was going to see Ireland! In the company of Cullen O'Banyon. Her heart skipped, then raced crazily. She wished she could get over these intense feelings about him.

As if she ever could. Rose had a feeling that, no matter what her ultimate fate, and no matter how many rich and/or kindhearted protectors she picked up in her lifetime, she'd always consider Cullen O'Banyon the man of her dreams. What a depressing thought.

Nevertheless, she was bubbling with excitement when he came to pick them up in his carriage. He'd told them to pack their belongings because he intended that they would stay at another, grander hotel that night, in another part of the city. Rose was looking forward to it.

"First of all, I want to show you the Liffey," Cullen told them when they were settled in the carriage.

"The Liffey?" Rose asked. "Oh, you mean the river?"

"Yes. Our river. It runs through Dublin, and there are a number of lovely and historic bridges crossing it."

Kate clasped her hands. "Oh, yes! I recall Ha'penny Bridge. My father used to positively rant and rave about having to pay the toll whenever we came to town." She giggled like a schoolgirl at the recollection.

Rose smiled at her aunt, glad to see she was enjoying herself. "Why is it called Ha'penny Bridge? That seems an odd name for a bridge."

"Its true name is the Wellington Bridge," Cullen told her. "Named for the famous Irish-born Duke of Wellington. Folks have called it Ha'penny Bridge for decades because of the toll charged for crossing it."

"I see."

"And we're coming to it now."

Rose was glad they were in Cullen's roomy carriage,

because both she and Kate were able to sit beside a window. Although she knew it wasn't exactly ladylike behavior on her part, she leaned out of the window and craned her neck. She was excessively happy she'd done so when the most gorgeous bridge she'd ever seen hove into sight, arching across the most gorgeous river she'd ever seen in her life.

"Oh, my goodness! It's spectacular. And look at that blue, blue water!"

"Isn't it beautiful, Rose?"

Kate's words sounded suspiciously thick. Rose quickly drew her head back inside the carriage and found her aunt with a hankie pressed to her drippy eyes.

Kate gave her a shaky smile. "I'm sorry, dear. There's no fool like an old one, I suppose. I was only wishing your uncle Glen could be here with us now. He so loved the land of his birth."

"Oh, Kate!" Rose hugged her aunt hard, and all the unkind things she'd been thinking about Kate and adventuressing flew right out of her head. Kate was an angel, and Rose knew it.

She glanced up to find Cullen watching them with a curious expression on his face. Rose couldn't put an emotion to the expression, although melancholy came close—but that didn't seem right. Why should Cullen O'Banyon observe the two of them with sadness?

Kate straightened and Rose thrust thoughts of Cullen aside. Or she tried to. Unfortunately, she could never quite banish them entirely.

"I do beg your pardon, Mr. O'Banyon," Kate said, after blowing her nose. "Please forgive a foolish old woman a moment of weakness."

"Not at all," murmured Cullen. "I quite understand. I'm sure I'd feel the same way were I to leave my homeland for years and then return without the person I'd most loved in my life with me."

Kate beamed at him. Her eyes were still moist. "That's it exactly! Thank you for understanding, Mr. O'Banyon. And you, too, Rose." She pressed Rose's hand. "Now, you take a good gander at that magnificent bridge, dear. There are a dozen more of them crossing the Liffey, and they're all wonderfully pretty."

"A dozen! Mercy sakes!" Rose scooted over to the window again.

"Well, about a dozen. I don't know exactly, but there are a whole lot of them."

"And if you approve, we can go to evening mass at Saint Patrick's Cathedral," Cullen suggested in a subdued tone. He didn't know how the two ladies felt about church services, but if they were Irish they were probably Catholic. Anyway, *he* had no objection to church services, and after all, they *were* in Dublin. He figured a trip to Saint Pat's was a required element of a stay in the great city.

"How wonderful! I'd love to do that."

Rose's expression of delight was genuine; Cullen could tell. He was pleased to have put it there.

"I haven't been to a church service since we left New York City," she continued. "We went to the chapel on the ship, but it wasn't the same. Oh, and in Saint Patrick's Cathedral. I've heard about it all my life."

If Cullen had entertained any doubts about this hare-brained scheme of his to tour Ireland with these two women, Rose's tone of absolute joy vanquished them. With a sigh, he settled back against the comfortable squabs in his carriage, determined to play tour guide. If luck was with him, he might also discover flaws in Rose Larkin that would end his senseless infatuation with her. He wished he believed in luck.

Their day proved an exhausting one. They crossed Ha'penny Bridge, visited Dublin Castle, the Custom House, and made a trip down O'Connell Street. Rose's eyes were huge the whole time.

"This is so fascinating. Why, in America everything is so new compared to this."

Cullen chuckled. "I suppose a hundred years or so is young compared to some of our relics. There's a church near Oxford, in England, that's been in use for nearly a thousand years."

"A thousand years," Rose whispered, awed.

Prompted by her fascination to provide more interesting information, he said, "And Saint Patrick's Cathedral itself was built in the twelfth century."

"Mercy!"

"They say it was built on the spot where Saint Patrick himself baptized Christians in the fifth century."

"My goodness."

"Wait until you get out in the countryside, Rose," Kate put in. "There are places that have been inhabited since before Christ was born."

Rose gazed about her with wonder. Cullen wanted to lift her in his arms and kiss her madly. She was such a darling. So much for finding something *not* to like about her . . .

Rose was so tired she could hardly stay awake through supper, although she did her best.

"This was such a wonderful day, Cullen. I can't thank you enough for taking us under your wing." To the devil with wings. Rose eyed his broad shoulders and experienced a mad wish to see his naked arms. She hoped the improper desire was merely her exhaustion making itself known, but feared it wasn't.

"Yes, Mr. O'Banyon. I must say I've never seen the city in such an interesting way." Kate was tired too. She even had to smother a yawn, which was unlike her. She was usually too proper to yawn. Tonight she'd struggled to stay awake through evening mass, however, so Rose knew how worn out she must be.

"Believe me, ladies, the pleasure was all mine."

He looked a little wistful, though, and Rose wondered suddenly if he were harboring a secret heartache. She'd been so involved in her own problems—er, that is to say, her own plans—recently, that she hadn't given a thought to anyone else. She felt selfish and inconsiderate now.

Clearing her throat, she determined to behave in a more openhearted manner toward this man who was being such a blessing to her and her aunt, and she aimed to start now.

"Don't you have family, Cullen? Isn't there anyone who misses you as you gallivant all over Ireland with us?"

His eyebrows rose, giving him the same masterful expression that Rose had seen before once or twice on his handsome features. It was an intimidating expression, and she didn't much like it.

"Don't tell me you're tired of my company already, Rose."

"Good heavens, no!"

"Oh, my goodness, Mr. O'Banyon!" Kate shrilled. "I'm certain dear Rose didn't mean it in that way."

"No, I didn't." Because she was so tired, Rose allowed his misunderstanding to hurt her feelings. She sniffed, and then felt silly. She was behaving like a spoiled child, and she decided to thrust her personal megrims aside and try again. "What I meant was that I can't imagine a man like you not having someone to miss him when he's away from home for weeks at a time."

Gracious, did that express it any better? Rose feared it didn't when Cullen's eyebrows went up again in that imperious way. She wished she'd kept her fat mouth shut. Feeling a little desperate, she blurted out, "I mean, I can't believe you don't have a wife. Or a family. Or something. Someone who misses you."

Cullen tilted his head. Now he looked as if he not only considered her rude and forward, but probably a lunatic as well. If Rose were alone, she'd forget the whole thing, climb up to her room, crawl into bed, and go to sleep. Since she was sitting at dinner in a fine restaurant with Cullen O'Banyon and her aunt, she wasn't able to exercise that pleasant option.

She chuffed loudly. "I'm saying this all wrong, I know, but I can't believe you've never married. And, if you're married, doesn't your wife miss you terribly? I'm sure I would."

Hearing herself, she felt her cheeks ignite. Fiddlesticks! Her tongue was totally ungovernable tonight. It must be because she was so tired. She was no good to anyone when she was completely exhausted.

"You'd miss me, would you?"

Cullen's voice had gone soft, and to Rose it sounded as if he were speaking only to her; as if Kate didn't exist. What did this mean? She had no idea.

"Yes. I—I would." *So there,* she thought, and knew she was being childish.

"Thank you, Rose." He spoke in a more solid tone, and it broke the spell his prior question had woven around her.

Thank heaven! Rose breathed deeply, as though her insides had been starved for lack of air for a minute. "You're welcome."

Cullen took a sip of wine before he spoke again. Rose decided she'd done enough damage for one evening and she'd let someone else talk from now on—preferably someone who wasn't too weary to think before he or she spoke.

"Actually, I was married ten years ago."

Rose almost dropped her wineglass. She managed to avoid that catastrophe, but her hand was shaking when she replaced the glass on the table. "You were?" Her voice squeaked a little.

"Oh, my!" said Kate, as if she were shocked.

Rose was shocked, too, but she wouldn't say so. Even as her heart ached painfully, she told herself that this is what adventuresses got out of life: married men.

She really didn't think she could stand this much longer.

"Yes. Ten years ago. I was married in Saint Patrick's Cathedral, right here in Dublin." He looked down at his dinner plate, which was empty now. "My wife's name was Judith. She died."

Rose expelled the huge breath she'd been holding. She knew she was wicked to experience such profound relief to hear that Cullen's wife had died. He must have loved her terribly. But because she knew she should, she said, "I'm so sorry, Cullen. How awful it must have been for you."

"Well, she's been dead for five years now, so I've had a good deal of time to get over the worst of it, I suppose."

Kate made a noise that might have been a sniffle. Rose reached for her hand and squeezed it. "I'm sure one never really gets over the loss of a loved one. I know I still miss my mother, and she's been dead for more than ten years. And I'll always miss my father."

"With all his faults," sighed Kate. "Yet he was a good man, in spite of them all. And I do believe I shall mourn my dear Glennie forever." She let loose with another mournful sigh and one more sniffle.

"At any rate," Cullen continued, as if he wished the subject closed, "I've been keeping in touch with those who are particularly involved in my life and business by cable-gram, and I've written letters."

He smiled at her and Rose, who was very close to tears herself, was glad his expression had softened. She vowed to make sure she got enough sleep for as long as she was traveling in Cullen's company, because it would never do to fall apart inside every time she got the least little bit over-tired.

She saw his smile fade and braced herself. Then she realized he was aiming his gaze over her shoulder. He frowned. Then he smiled again, but it looked forced.

Obviously, someone was approaching their table whom Cullen knew—and didn't much like. Although she wasn't sure of the proper etiquette under the circumstances, Rose glanced over her shoulder and saw a very stout, elderly man, leaning heavily on a cane, trudging toward them. He was also leering in a most impolite way, and Rose was unnerved.

"You're about to see one of the antiquities of Ireland, ladies," Cullen muttered under his breath. "Brace yourselves."

"Oh, my!" said Kate, then tittered softly when she glanced around and saw the elderly man.

Rose silently blessed Cullen for a saint. His dry comment, uttered soto voce and with an accompanying wink, vanquished her blue-devils better than any of her stern lectures to herself had done. She folded her napkin and placed it on the table as her aunt Kate had taught her was proper. Then she folded her hands properly, too, and waited.

"Cullen O'Banyon, you old sod!"

Not only was he old and stout, but he'd also been drinking heavily or Rose missed her guess. Rose recognized the symptoms in his red nose, ruddy cheeks, and slurred words. The good Lord knew, she'd seen the same symptoms in her father and his cronies often enough. She disliked strong spirits intensely because of it, too.

She banished the thought as disrespectful and turned to smile at the newcomer. She was embarrassed when he waggled his bushy eyebrows at her.

"Good evening, Captain," Cullen said. He didn't sound cheerful. "Please allow me to introduce you to some friends of mine who are visiting from America."

"America! My, my, you're expanding your horizons, boy!" The captain winked at Cullen and ogled Rose some more.

She didn't appreciate it, and felt her smile tighten. Nevertheless, she'd been taught polite behavior—even if the captain seemed to have forgotten it.

Cullen rose and gestured at the fat, sloppy man. "Mrs. Flanagan and Miss Larkin, please allow me to introduce you to Captain Averill Poindexter. Captain Poindexter, Kate Flanagan and Rose Larkin. Mrs. Flanagan left Ireland some years hence, and has returned for a visit. She's brought her niece, Miss Larkin, with her to see the sights."

The captain bowed. Rose heard something creaking, and wondered if he was wearing a corset, too. He appeared to be a thoroughly unpleasant man, and she'd be happy to discover that he was vain enough to wear whalebone as well.

"Ladies, it is my very great pleasure." He winked at Rose, which she found offensive, and grinned at Kate. "You're from Ireland originally, are you?"

Kate waved her hand in the air, flustered. "Indeed, sir. My husband and I left these shores over forty years ago."

"I see. Yes, it does seem as though most of Ireland's best patriots now live in America. Odd how things like that happen, isn't it?"

His voice had a bite to it, and Rose didn't quite understand the words, but she didn't like them at all. She sat up straight.

Cullen muttered, "It's not odd in the least if one knows our history, Captain."

"Ha!" Captain Poindexter cast a supercilious glance at Cullen. "We British have always done well with barbarians."

Rose thought that was a downright horrible thing for the man to say, even though she still wasn't sure what he was talking about. Even so, she spoke up, her voice firm. "Our Irish heritage aside, I believe my aunt and I both consider ourselves citizens of the United States now, Captain Poindexter."

The captain put his head back and roared much more loudly than Rose's comment, however tartly rendered, deserved. Rose was dismayed by her own shabby behavior. She turned to glance at Cullen and found him rolling his eyes in disgust. She hoped it wasn't meant for her.

Kate whispered, "Oh, my," in a worried little voice.

"Yes, well, Captain, it's good to see you. Shall I give my regards to Mrs. Clapton?"

The captain seemed to sober instantly. His eyebrows dipped until he was glowering at Cullen. "And what exactly do you mean by that?"

Cullen shrugged and pasted on an innocent expression. "Why, only that you and she seemed to be getting on well when last you met."

"Nonsense! You're out of your mind, boy. Never thought you was a lunatic." The captain stomped away as quickly as his girth and condition would allow.

Rose watched him go, relieved.

Kate whispered, "Oh, my," again.

Cullen said, "I beg your pardon, ladies. I'm not fond of Captain Poindexter, and I fear it might have showed."

"Yes," Rose said. "It did. And I, for one, don't blame you. What an unpleasant man he is."

"But rich," Cullen said softly.

Rose turned her head abruptly and stared at him. Could he possibly be implying . . .

Cullen, noting her expression, gave her a lopsided, cynical-looking smile. "Oh, my, yes. He's rich as Croesus. Most of the rich men in Ireland are Englishmen, you know, Rose. He looked rather intrigued by you. I'm sure he'd be interested if you'd given him any indication that you might consider him as a likely candidate in your quest for a protector."

Rose pressed a hand to her throat, feeling almost physically ill. "Good heavens."

"Oh, no," said Kate, her voice having taken on a firm tone at last. "No, indeed, Mr. O'Banyon. We shan't be seeking anyone of that sort for our Rose. I can't imagine how you could consider that awful man appropriate." She shook her head. "No, indeed. Not appropriate at all."

Thank God. Thank God. Rose bowed her head and offered a silent prayer to her Maker for this deliverance, however temporary it might be.

Her mood was sour when she crawled into bed in the expensive hotel at which she and Kate stayed at that night.

Nine

Cullen felt a little mean about Poindexter. He also felt a good deal of satisfaction, and knew it did him no credit. But he'd seen the look of horror on Rose's face when he'd suggested Poindexter as a suitable protector, and he'd been glad of it.

Foolish, reckless Rose, to believe she could have her pick of the rich men in Ireland and not have to choose from—or fend off—the Poindexters of the land. Who did she think had the money in Ireland, anyway?

Cullen knew himself to be an unusual Irishman, and an incredibly fortunate one. He was one of the few landowners among the native Irish of his homeland, and one of the even fewer who had any money.

Most of Ireland's wealth resided in England, and the land was tenanted by the poor Irish who seldom if ever saw their absentee landlords. The situation was a bad one, and often festered into eruptions of violence. It was some kind of miracle that Cullen and his family had been so little touched by the trouble. He thanked God daily for his family's reprieve.

The British domination of Ireland was a fact of life here that most Irishmen deplored, and most of the rest of the world didn't even know about. Cullen was doubly fortunate because he not only had a fair degree of wealth, but he also had the respect of his fellow Irishmen. That combination didn't happen often.

The next day he and the ladies continued their tour of Dublin, taking in many of the sights they hadn't had time for the day before. He aimed to take them in the general direction of his horse farm in County Clare when they left the city. Perhaps he could sneak away once or twice and visit the boys. His heart seemed to have a hole in it from missing them.

Nevertheless, he had little trouble in concentrating on his duties as a tour guide when he was with Rose. Her company assuaged both his guilt and his loneliness to a degree he didn't consider quite proper.

When he told Johnny Sullivan, his coachman, that their plans had changed yet again and that they'd be taking a small tour of the Irish countryside, Johnny had looked at him askance. He was too good a servant to ask any questions or to protest, but Cullen felt a little silly about this strange compulsion of his to remain in Rose Larkin's company. He was sure Johnny guessed the reason for his change in plans.

He had a discouraged feeling about this whole affair. Only it wasn't an affair, which made him feel even more discouraged sometimes. He told himself to stop thinking and enjoy himself—and he almost succeeded sometimes.

Rose had never seen anything to equal the lush, rolling green landscape that passed outside of the coach's window. She felt as if she'd entered some kind of enchanted land, emerald green and otherworldly. She wouldn't have been too much surprised if a band of fairies should appear suddenly on a hilltop, or a leprechaun. She almost understood the flights of fancy her father's mind had taken. If one grew up in this amazing land, one had to believe in magic. Anything more pedestrian than magic didn't belong here.

When she managed to wrest her gaze away from the wonders revealing themselves on the outside of the carriage, she saw that Cullen was watching her, a soft half smile on his lips. She smiled back. "It's ever so lovely, Cullen. I'm awfully grateful to you for taking the time to accompany us."

"I wouldn't have missed the opportunity for worlds, Rose." He sounded as if he meant it, and Rose was embarrassed. She turned to stare out of the window again.

"I'd forgotten how green it all is," murmured Kate, as if she, too, were lost in reverence.

"We'll be getting to Mellifont Abbey soon," Cullen said with a sigh.

Rose looked at him again, wondering what the sigh was for. She hadn't a clue. "Mellifont Abbey? Sounds fascinating."

"It was the first Cistercian monastery to be built in Ireland. Sometime in the twelfth century, I believe."

No more than an hour later, they arrived at Mellifont Abbey. Rose was nearly overwhelmed by the beauty and antiquity of the old building. It looked like something out of a fairy tale, and the green of the countryside seemed to be creeping up on it. She stared, speechless, for what seemed like forever.

After several minutes, Cullen said softly, "It almost look as if the great green earth is trying to take it back again, doesn't it?"

"Yes. It does." She wished she could convey how much she appreciated him putting into words what she'd been feeling. She didn't dare, for fear she'd give away other feelings as well; feelings that were better left unexpressed.

After another moment or two of silence, Cullen said, "It would be out of our way, but I've just been overcome by a strong urge to show you and Kate Monasterboice in County Louth. I can't offhand think of a better example of the blending of the Celtic and the Christian."

"Oh!" Kate cried, patently delighted. "I went there once with my grandmother. It's special, Rose. You'll enjoy it."

The Celts. Rose had studied the Celts in school. She'd

never even dared to dream about seeing anything genuinely Celtic. She turned toward Cullen. "I should love to see it!"

Impulsively, she reached out a hand, but stopped herself before she could touch him. He looked down at her, an odd expression on his face, and Rose told herself sternly that she must always, always watch herself in Cullen's presence. Her feelings for him were getting too strong, and if she didn't watch it, she'd do something foolish and abandoned and make him despise her. She didn't think she could stand that.

They spent the night in an inn, and headed out the next morning in the opposite direction.

Two wonderful, fascinating days later, they reached County Louth and Monasterboice. Cullen secured them rooms at a beautiful country inn, where the landlord and landlady seemed especially jolly and good natured, and Rose knew for a fact that she'd never have such a glorious holiday again; not if she lived to be a hundred.

Early the next morning, Cullen had his coachman drive Kate to the ruins of the old monastery founded by St. Boethius in the sixth century. Rose was thrilled when he rented horses for her and himself to ride. Kate preferred the comfort of the carriage, but Rose craved the open air and exercise of a horseback ride.

"I haven't ridden for so long! I'll probably be sore as blazes tomorrow."

He smiled one of his wonderful smiles. "If you get too tired, you can always finish the ride with your aunt in the carriage."

She laughed with pure, unadulterated joy. "Not on your life! I'm going to enjoy this ride!"

With her face to the sun and the wind whipping at her skirts, she felt akin to one of her Irish ancestors, galloping across the green, unsullied countryside in pursuit of— what? A pot of gold, perhaps, at the end of the rainbow. She sucked in a lungful of clean, cool air, and expelled it in an exuberant whoosh.

"Did you used to ride with your father?"

When she turned in her saddle, she saw Cullen watching her with a half smile on his face. He looked as if he were happy to be riding, too.

"Oh, yes. I believe the most fun we ever had together was when he'd take me riding. He knew so many horse people. We seldom owned horses—at least never for very long—but he loved them, and his love transferred itself to me."

"I see." Cullen eyed his mount with disfavor. "I fear these two are rather sluggish beasts, but I thought it might be nice to travel in the fresh air. I'm not fond of extended rides in closed carriages."

"I'm not, either. Although I would like to take a train trip someday."

"Aye? And where would you like to go in your train?"

"Oh, to the West! To see Tombstone and Santa Fe and Abilene, and all of those other wild Western places." She laughed, knowing how foolish she must sound.

"You have a romantic heart, Rose Larkin."

She heaved a big sigh. "Yes, I suppose I do. Although my romantic notions don't seem to be akin to the ones Kate has." She wished she hadn't said that aloud.

"No?"

"Oh, but it's such a glorious day, and this is so much fun, I don't want to talk about disagreements today!"

She spurred her nag on. Cullen was right; it was a sluggish animal. Yet it was a horse, and it responded to her sure touch. Her father had taught her horsemanship well. He might not have been good for much, but he had certainly known horses.

That's an unkind thought, Rose Larkin. You should be ashamed of yourself. She knew her stern words were right, but she couldn't drum up much shame that morning. The day was too fine, the company too congenial, and she was *riding.* She vowed to herself that she wouldn't think another unpleasant thought all day long, but would savor this day. And Cullen O'Banyon's company.

They chatted about inconsequential things for the rest of the way to Monasterboice. Cullen helped her dismount and held her arm for a few minutes afterwards, until she got her rubbery legs under control.

"Mercy, I'd forgotten how one's limbs can go numb after one rides for a few miles!"

"Indeed," said Cullen, although he seemed to be having no trouble at all making the transition from horseback to solid earth.

She was disappointed when he let her arm go, even though she'd told him she was able to walk again.

"Here, Rose and Kate. Please allow me to lead the way. The brambles are thick along the pathway."

So he cleared the way for them—as he'd been doing ever since their arrival in Dublin—and Rose and Kate followed, looking around avidly. Everything was green. Rose, who grew up in New York City, where there was a fair bit of green, had still never seen anything like this.

She gasped when he led them to the three enormous crosses that were all that was left of the monastery.

"Sixth century," he said. "I believe this monastery was the first one ever that served as a foundation for both men and women. All of its predecessors had been intended for men only."

"Goodness sakes." Rose stared at the huge cross covered with intricate carvings depicting scenes from the Old and New Testaments, and felt awe swell in her bosom. "I've never even imagined anything like this."

Aunt Kate crossed herself. "I'd forgotten how wonderful Ireland is."

"The sixth century! I can hardly take it in." Rose still couldn't wrest her gaze away from that cross.

"It's truly wonderful," Kate said reverently. "In spite of its poverty and want, Ireland is so beautiful, and so full of—well, holiness."

"Aye, that it is," agreed Cullen.

His voice sounded odd, and when Rose turned to see why, she discovered him staring at the cross, too, and with a look of longing on his face. She didn't understand, but she felt suddenly lonely for him. All sorts of emotions rose in her breast, and she had a sudden mad urge to unburden

herself, to tell Cullen all of her most fervent and private secrets and yearnings.

She was going mad. It must be all the ancient stones and
greenery and the Irish magic in the air. Her Irish heritage
coming out in her. She'd always suspected her father was
slightly touched; perhaps she was, too.

But no. Her father had merely been irresponsible. There
was nothing intrinsically crazy about irresponsibility. She
sighed deeply, and consigned her inner turmoil to perdition.

"Is anything the matter, Rose?"

Cullen's soft, lilting voice nudged her out of her contemplation of possible incipient madness and other black
musings. She turned to him and smiled. "No. Nothing.
This is the most wonderful trip I've ever undertaken in my
life."

His smile looked slightly rueful. "You've not lived for
very many years yet, Rose. I'm sure there will be many
more wonderful trips in your future."

For some reason, his words stabbed at Rose's heart and
made her eyes prickle. She turned away quickly so he
couldn't see. How foolish she was being!

He walked up and took her elbow. There was nothing in
the gesture but friendship, but Rose's skin burned where he
touched her. When she looked up into his eyes, her gaze
got trapped there for a moment, and her heart fluttered.
Was his gaze particularly warm today? Did it tell her she
was someone special to him?

Of course not. She mentally shook herself out of her
fanciful daydream. Her recovered honesty didn't help,
however, in that she still wished she could lay her head on
his broad shoulder and feel his arms around her.

Idiot. She was an idiot.

But the notion of becoming his mistress was beginning
to sound not quite so awful to her. If that was all she could
ever have of him, at least it would be something.

*For heaven's sake, Rose Larkin, he looks upon you as a
sister. He told you so.*

That reminder was so gloomy it almost spoiled her enjoyment of the wonders of Monasterboice. Nothing could quite do that, however, and they ended their visit in high good spirits.

"I know a little inn not far off where there's always a good deal of music and dancing, ladies. If you'd like to accompany me there, I believe you'd enjoy it. You haven't heard any of the country lads playing yet, Rose. I'm sure you'd appreciate the music. It's special, Irish music."

"Oh, my, yes!" Kate affirmed. "My ma and da used to take me to the local pub, where we'd all sing and dance and listen to the music."

"They took you to a pub?" Rose couldn't quite hide her astonishment. She'd never heard Kate refer to her parents as her "ma and da," either. The Irish was coming out in her aunt with a vengeance. Rose thought it was rather sweet.

"Irish pubs are nothing like our saloons in America, dear," Kate told her earnestly. "They're neighborhood gathering places. Everyone goes. And they bring their children and their dogs. And everyone has a grand old time."

"Aye, it's so, Rose. Often the local pub will be the social hub of a village."

Rose couldn't imagine it. "I can't wait to see it."

"So you shall."

Cullen seemed pleased, and that made Rose even more eager to accompany him to his country inn. Where mothers and fathers and children and dogs all gathered. Dogs, for heaven's sake! She laughed, just thinking about it.

Before she even set foot inside the inn, she knew Cullen was right. From the stable lads who ran out to secure their horses and take care of the carriage, to the smell of the peaty smoke pouring out of the chimney, to the gay laughter within, Rose thought this was a practically perfect place.

Cullen entered and held the door for them, and Rose saw a sight she'd only envisioned whilst reading fairy tales. "Oh, it's perfect!" she cried before she could stop her unruly tongue.

"Glad you think so," Cullen said. She heard the smile in his voice.

They ate a lunch at the pub and listened to various patrons play and sing. One of the men played the violin, another plucked a small harp—an Irish harp, according to Cullen—and Rose felt as though she'd entered another world. It was a world she wished she could remain in, because it seemed so free from worry and other people's ambitions.

Which was, of course, silly. This was Ireland. Ireland had been the scene of bloody strife for centuries. Even today, violent outbreaks were commonplace. She sighed, wishing it weren't so.

"So, if you're sure you don't mind, Rose?"

Rose started, suddenly becoming aware that her aunt had been speaking to her. "I beg your pardon?" She blinked, and wondered if she'd dozed off. But no. She'd only been lost in the music and her own thoughts. "I'm sorry, Kate, I was in a fog."

Kate laughed. "I know, dear. Ireland does that to people. But if you don't mind, I believe I'll go back to our inn now. I'm rather weary."

Immediately, Rose felt contrite. She sprang from her chair. "Oh, Kate, I'm so sorry! I shouldn't be dragging you all over the place, sight-seeing with me. I'm being terribly unfair to you!"

"Nonsense!" Kate looked as stern as she could, which wasn't very. "You're here on my whim, Rose, and I'm not going to allow you to sacrifice your fun for an old woman. Mr. O'Banyon has kindly said his coachman will see me back to the inn. I'm sure you two young people will be happy on your horses." She shuddered, as if the notion of riding a horse horrified her.

Rose eyed her dubiously. "I'll be more than happy to go back with you, Kate."

"I won't hear of it!" Rose was astonished when her aunt stamped her little foot. "You're having a wonderful time. I can tell you're enjoying yourself, dear, and I refuse to interfere. Just sit yourself down and enjoy the music some more." She waved a hand in the vague direction of the chair Rose had lately vacated. "Mr. O'Banyon says we're not far from our other inn, and I'll just lie down and take a nap while the two of you finish up your sight-seeing."

"Well . . ." Rose glanced doubtfully at Cullen, who didn't help at all, but kept his countenance as bland and unemotional as a pond. She looked at the pub, and felt longing tug at her heart. "All right. Thank you, Kate." She bent and deposited a kiss on her aunt's plump cheek. "I am enjoying this. Very much."

Kate beamed at her. "Of course, you are, child. This is your heritage. It's high time you learned that the Irish are not all like your father, God rest his soul."

She was right. Put that way, Rose didn't feel so guilty about staying here. She glanced again at Cullen and decided there was another reason to be happy she was staying. It would be rather thrilling to ride back to their inn with Cullen, without Kate's chaperonage. Rose felt almost wicked for a second, before she remembered that Cullen was every inch a gentleman and one, moreover, who thought of her as a sister. Ah, well. Such was life. It never *quite* seemed to live up to one's hopes and dreams.

On the other hand, as she'd had nineteen years to learn, often one's hopes and dreams were nonsensical. Just take a gander at Kate's, for instance.

Stop it, she commanded herself. She was supposed to be enjoying herself, not contemplating her gloomy future.

Cullen went outside with Kate, and Rose's attention returned to the fellow who was singing.

"The lad's got a fine voice, don't he?"

Startled, Rose sat bolt upright and turned to see who'd spoken to her. A handsome man sat next to her, where Kate had been, and he was grinning at her in a very friendly—indeed, almost forward—way. She didn't know what to do, but decided to be polite.

"Yes, he has a beautiful voice. And the music is lovely, too."

"Aye, that's a good old tune, that is."

She didn't know if she was supposed to say anything, so she opted not to.

The fellow said, "Me name's Carlos Behan, lovie. Will you honor me with your own name?"

Lovie? Kate blinked at the man. He didn't look as if he intended to ravish her. He looked really merely friendly. "Er, my name is Rose. Rose Larkin."

"Rose. A lovely name for a lovely colleen."

"Thank you."

"Let me stand you to a pint, m'dear. It's lonely I am to be drinkin' alone."

"Alone?" Rose peered around the room, which looked full of people to her.

Behan flattened a hand over his heart. "Alone in here, m'love. All, all alone. As you are."

"As I am?" She'd been alone for all of thirty seconds so far. Rose suddenly understood what was happening. Good Lord above, the man was a masher!

How utterly exciting. Rose had never had a gentleman—or, rather, a man who wasn't a gentleman—push his attentions on her before this. If she'd been really alone, she might have been alarmed, but since she knew assistance was right outside, she wasn't afraid. Rather, she smiled at the man. "I believe I prefer tea, but thank you."

"Tea?" His eyebrows went up, and he looked as if the very word offended him. "Good God, sweetheart, what kind of Irishwoman are you?"

"The American kind, I'm afraid," Rose said apologetically.

"American!" Behan nodded wisely. "I thought you had a strange way of pronouncin' our language."

Rose giggled. "I suppose I do."

"But here now, lovie. Let's have a song for ye." He signaled to the man playing the violin. "Here, Seamus. Play Yankee Doodle for our fair lady friend here. She's from the United States, visitin' the land her parents sprung from, or I'll be much surprised."

"You needn't be surprised," Rose told him, oddly happy

with the attention. "They were from Ireland, all right. County Cork."

"Ah, County Cork," murmured Behan, as if that explained everything.

When Cullen reentered the inn after seeing to Kate's deposition in the carriage and giving Johnny Sullivan instructions, he wasn't altogether surprised to find Rose surrounded by a swarm of men and singing up a storm. Damnation, he couldn't leave the woman alone for a minute. She had a wonderful voice, and she had a friendly nature, and she looked right at home, except that her clothes were fine, she was clean and well-fed, and she lacked the hungry, exhausted look so many of Cullen's countrymen possessed.

That fellow was sitting awfully close to her. Cullen did not approve, although he understood the compulsion that probably drove the man to boldness. Rose Larkin had that effect on men. The good Lord knew, she most certainly had that effect on him. He leaned against the wall of the inn and told himself it was irrational to want to rush up there, grab the fellow by the scruff of his neck, and heave him into the fire.

Rose caught sight of him and waved merrily. He sighed and walked over to join the group gathered around her. Hopefully, he wouldn't be forced to engage in fisticuffs with any of Rose's admirers when they realized she wasn't free for the taking.

But to his relief nothing happened and instead he actually had a splendid time. He hadn't relaxed, let his hair down, laughed, and joked with a bunch of fellows in a country inn for years. He wasn't sure, but he thought he was having almost as good a time as Rose.

Even the fellow who'd been sitting so close to Rose, whom Cullen learned was Carlos Behan, gave over his spot near her with good grace. Evidently Behan thought Cullen and Rose were married or engaged or something. That was all right with Cullen. If people thought they were united in some holy bond, they'd be less apt to try to take advantage of Rose. At least, he hoped so.

In the meantime, he decided to enjoy himself. He sang so much his throat was raw, and he laughed so hard his cheeks ached, and he met so many jolly fellows that if he didn't keep abreast of the news, he'd never have guessed that his country was in the throes of political turmoil. Thank God for the Irish soul. Nothing could keep an Irishman down for long.

However, having all that fun made them late in getting away. Cullen eyed the sky as they stepped outside, noting that it had become sullen and overcast in the hours they'd played indoors, and got a little worried. "It looks like it might rain."

"Really?" Rose, her cheeks as pink as her name, gazed at the sky, too. "I don't think it will before we get back. Do you?"

Cullen's gaze went over their two chubby horses, and he grimaced. "If it does start raining, these two beasts won't be any too quick in getting us back to your aunt. They're more apt to flounder in the mud."

Rose thought for a second, then announced, "Let's try it. If we get wet, water never hurt anyone."

"Spoken like a true adventurer," Cullen said dryly.

He helped Rose into her saddle, allowing his hands to linger on her waist a little longer than necessary, and letting his arm snake partway around her before he forced himself to pull away. He was, after all, only human. Rose smiled down at him, and he almost hauled her back off the horse and into his arms. He stepped quickly away so as to thwart his ungentlemanly urges.

"If it rains on us, it will only add to the day's adventures," she told him gaily.

He contemplated that as he mounted, then grinned. "Good. Then let's be off, my lady, and we'll try to outrun the storm."

They were both laughing as they started back to the inn.

Ten

They'd ridden for about a half hour and had another hour's ride in front of them when the sky opened up and poured buckets of rain down onto them. As Cullen had predicted, the horses were slowed considerably by the muck in the road. The thunder and lightning made a spectacular display in the heavens, although Rose would have appreciated it more if she'd been watching from the window of a snug house.

"I think we'd be better off if we stopped at a farmhouse, Rose," Cullen called over the pounding rain.

A tremendous crack of thunder rendered her response inaudible even to her own ears, so she tried again. "Do you see one?"

"No, but I think I see a lane up ahead."

Rose squinted into the downpour. She couldn't see a thing but water. She said, "Oh."

He laughed at her skepticism. "It probably leads to a farm or a cottage. If we're lucky, the owners will be kindly disposed toward weary, waterlogged travelers."

She thought about it, then grinned. "I'm game if you are." This was the most exciting adventure she'd ever had. It was ever so much more fun than the escapades she used to have with her father, most of which consisted of dodg-

ing tradesmen and debt collectors. And it beat the tar out
of dancing naked in front of a bunch of drunken men. Besides, she was having this adventure with Cullen, and she
had a feeling she'd enjoy almost anything if she could do
it with him.

He smiled back, and sure enough, in a minute, he turned
into a small lane that Rose hadn't even seen until he
pointed it out. They rode for what seemed like forever, the
horses going slower and ever slower as the mud thickened
and the water soaked them.

"Are you sure this road leads somewhere?" she asked at
last.

"Oh, aye. All roads lead somewhere."

He laughed again, and she couldn't help but join in. He
had a wonderful laugh. And he was being so good about
this. Any other man would have been in a temper; Rose
was sure of it.

"Ah-ha! I'm right. See over there? Lights. As they're
high off the ground, I suspect they're in windows. Unless,
of course, the banshees are out."

"Banshees? Good heavens!" Soaked to the skin and really very uncomfortable, Rose began laughing so hard she
nearly slid from her saddle. Of course, that might have
been because the leather was slick with rainwater.

The lightning was coming closer. They saw a pitchfork-
shaped bolt hit the ground not more than a hundred yards
away from them, and heard the ear-splitting sound of its
accompanying thunder almost simultaneously. They were
finding shelter none too soon.

"Here," Cullen shouted over the noise of the storm.
"Let me help you down."

"What are you going to do?"

"I'll see if they'll let us in, and then take the horses to
the barn—if there is one." He glanced around, but the rain
was pounding down so hard, he had to give up looking for
a barn. Instead, he took Rose's hand when she had dismounted and ran to the door of what looked to Rose like it
might be a sweet cottage if she could only see it.

"They'll probably think we're a couple of gypsy

vagabonds," Cullen said, even as he prepared to knock on the door.

Rose looked up at him. "Try to look noble."

"Noble?" He laughed.

"Well, if you look noble, they won't think you're a gypsy."

"If I look too noble, they'll probably take me for an English landlord and shoot me."

"Good heavens!" Rose hoped to goodness he was joking about that.

She didn't have a chance to ask, because even before Cullen stopped rapping on the door, it swung open. A plump, middle-aged woman stood there, looking astonished. She pressed a hand to her large, soft bosom. "My precious Lord in heaven, what're the two o' you doin' out on a night like this?" She stepped back, and beckoned them to enter. Rose smiled at her gratefully.

"We were visiting Monasterboice and got caught in the deluge on our way back to the inn." Cullen looked around, obviously trying to find a place to stand so he wouldn't drip onto her floor, but she clucked and gestured him forward.

"Don't you worry about this floor, sir. It's been dripped on for more than a hundred year now."

"Thank you." Cullen grinned at her.

"Went to Monasterboice, did ye? Them crosses is wonderful things. Do you have cattle to put up?"

"Yes, thanks. Two horses we rented for the day."

"Let me call Charlie. He'll help you put them away." She turned and called up a well-worn wooden staircase. "Charlie. Help this fine gentleman to put up his horses in the barn!"

Charlie, who was about ten years old, must have been lurking close by—probably watching the excitement, Rose judged—because he appeared instantly, tripping lightly down the stairs. "I'll do it," he said, game for anything.

"I'll help you, Charlie," Cullen said. "I'm already wet to the bone. A little more water won't hurt me."

Rose was interested to note that his tone of voice for

Charlie was warm and friendly, and obviously intended to put the small boy at ease. Was he used to being around children? It seemed unlikely, given that he was a practiced rake. He bore no resemblance whatever to the sort of easy-going fellow who'd have had much to do with children. Perhaps he was naturally good with them. She sighed inside, thinking this was all she needed: to find out that Cullen O'Banyon's large, gloriously masculine form masked yet another perfection.

She watched the two males brave the out of doors again, and gave a start when the woman spoke to her. She'd forgotten all about her in her contemplation of Cullen's many sterling qualities.

"But here, dearie, step this way, and I'll get ye a towel to wipe yourself dry with." She led Rose into a cozy parlor.

"Oh, my, this is so warm. I hadn't realized how cold I was." Rose stood in front of the fire and started shivering in reaction to the heat.

"Aye, you're wet clean through, dearie. Just you stand there for a minute, and I'll get you something to warm your insides, and that'll help warm your outsides. I hate to leave you alone in here, but I was in the middle of doing something in the kitchen when the two o' ye knocked."

"Oh, please, I don't want to be a bother to you."

The woman tutted. "Nonsense. It'll only take me a few moments."

The woman and Cullen, with Charlie in tow, reappeared at the same time, a short while later.

"Get on upstairs wi' you, Charlie. It's time for you to be in your bed."

"Aye, ma." Charlie looked as if he'd been visited by a good angel. He gave Cullen such a brilliant smile that Rose couldn't help but smile, too. Jerking a nod at Cullen he said, "Thank'ee, sir. Thank'ee very much."

"Did you give the lad something?" The woman frowned at Cullen, who held up his hands in all innocence. She smiled and shook her head at him.

Rose, taking it in, thought it remarkable how easily

Cullen seemed to have made friends of these people. Her father had been like that. It must be another Irish characteristic.

"Ye're lady's icy cold, boyo. Ye'd better warm her up."

Rose shot Cullen a look over her shoulder. He eyed her back, slid a glance at the matron, who was smiling at them with motherly satisfaction, and went to put his arms around Rose.

"I think we'd better pretend, Rose," he whispered in her ear. "She'll probably kick us out if she discovers we aren't married."

Pretending she was Cullen's wife was all right with Rose. In fact, it would be the perfect capper to a practically perfect day. Or it would be if they really *were* married.

Once again she commanded herself not to be ridiculous. She and Cullen hardly knew each other. For all Rose knew, Cullen O'Banyon had terrible flaws that would render him a ghastly husband.

She didn't believe it for a second.

The woman, who had left the room, bustled back in, holding linen towels out toward Cullen and Rose. "Me daughter Bridget is upstairs fixin' a bed for the two o' you," the woman continued. "Ye'll not be traveling farther on this night."

A bed for the two of them? Rose looked at Cullen, appalled. He looked a trifle appalled himself, but said, "Er, thank you very much, Mrs.—I fear I've failed to introduce my, ah, wife and myself, ma'am. Please allow me to do that."

Rose stifled a groan when he took his arms from around her and stepped over to accept the towels. He handed one to Rose and began toweling himself off. "We are Rose and Cullen O'Banyon, and we truly appreciate your hospitality."

"Oh, aye. 'Tis nothing, Mr. O'Banyon. And I'm Mrs. O'Doyle. My husband Tom has gone to Ennis, where his da was took fair sick." She eyed the two of them shrewdly. "But surely you're the O'Banyon of the fine horses."

Rose looked quickly at Cullen and was surprised to per-

ceive that he didn't look pleased. O'Banyon of the fine
horses? She told herself to ask Cullen about it soon, although she wasn't sure she really wanted to know. If
everyone in Ireland knew about Cullen and the horses, he
must be as bad a gambler as her father—worse, perhaps,
although that seemed scarcely possible.

"Aye, Mrs. O'Doyle, I am that one."

"And the two o' ye haven't been married long, either, or
we'd have heard about it," said Mrs. O'Doyle with a sly
wink. "I'll warrant ye was on your marriage holiday when
ye got caught in the downpour."

"It was something like that, all right," Cullen said. To
Rose, he sounded as though he appreciated the handy excuse.

"Well, this mayn't be what ye're used to, Mr.
O'Banyon, but we have us a cozy home, Tom and me, and
I'm proud to share it wi' ye tonight."

"Thank you," Cullen said.

"Thank you very much," Rose expanded.

"Aye, you're as pretty as your name, dearie," Mrs.
O'Doyle said. "Now, if you think you can walk, let me
take you upstairs. We'll get you out of those terrible wet
clothes. My Bridget will lend you a dress for the evening.
You're about of a size, you and Bridget. Ah, here she is
now." From the tone of satisfaction in Mrs. O'Doyle's
voice, Rose judged Bridget to be a good daughter.

She was certainly a pretty thing. Probably fifteen or six-
teen, she had honey-colored hair, a smattering of freckles,
and rosy cheeks. Rose smiled at her, and Bridget dipped a
curtsy.

"How d'ye do?"

"Bridget, this here's Mr. and Mrs. O'Banyon. Mr.
O'Banyon's the horse man, you know."

"Oh, aye!" Bridget appeared impressed.

"And Mrs. O'Banyon—"

"Oh, please call me Rose," Rose cried, feeling uncomfortable with her new, adopted, false title, although she
wished she deserved it.

Mrs. O'Doyle looked shocked, although Bridget didn't seem to find anything unusual in Rose's request.

"But surely, you're from America," Bridget said.

"Yes, I am. New York City."

Obviously impressed, Bridget said, "Me uncle Charlie's in New York. Me brother Charlie was named for him. He's my da's brother, don't you see."

"Aye," said Mrs. O'Doyle darkly. "Most of our kin's in America one way or 'tother." She shook her head in clear disapproval of such defections.

"Come this way, Rose," said Bridget, ignoring her mother's tart comment. "I'll take you upstairs."

"Thank you, Bridget."

Rose followed Bridget up the stairs., As soon as they were out of her mother's sight, Bridget turned abruptly and said, "Oh, Rose, d'ye mind if I ask you about America? I so want to go there one day."

"You do?" Rose didn't think she'd want to leave such a pretty little house and such a nice mother. It was a further indication that folks all had different goals in life. All Rose herself wanted was some peace and security. Yet everywhere she looked, she seemed to find people who wanted to experience uncertainty and peril. She'd had enough of both to last her several lifetimes.

Nevertheless, she regaled Bridget with tales of New York City as the girl helped her out of her wet garments and handed her a big, comfortable wrapper.

"Ye'll not get into that corset again this night, Rose, so ye might as well wrap up in that. It'll be more comfortable, and I'm sure your man's seen you in less."

Bridget blushed hotly. So did Rose. Then both of them laughed.

"You've got lovely hair, ma'am, but you'd better brush it out so it will dry. If it dries like that, you'll have tangles for a month."

"You're right. Thank you very much." She took the hairbrush Bridget handed her. Then she removed her soaked hat and looked ruefully at the feather drooping and dripping therefrom. "That poor bird will never fly again."

Bridget shook her head. "I fear not." She giggled.

Rose did likewise as she removed pins from her hair and brushed it out. Kate had paid to have Rose's hair cut and styled before she left New York, and she was glad for it now. If her hair were still as long as it had been before her father died, she'd never get the tangles out. Now it fell to her shoulders, curling a little at the ends as it always had, and she thought it might dry before the night was out.

"Thank heaven for haircuts," she murmured, contemplating the nature of hair. Kate was always fussing about her own thin locks. Rose wished she could lend some of her tresses to her aunt, who needed them. Rose herself didn't need as much hair as she had. Yet another inequity life had flung at her.

"I'll fix it for you after it dries, if you like," Bridget offered. "I like working with hair."

"Really? I don't much like fixing my hair in the morning. It takes time, and it never looks right."

"I do hair for lots of the ladies in the neighborhood. And I'm good at it, if I do say so meself." Bridget lifted her chin. Rose imagined she was used to her mother scolding her for boasting—even such a mild boast as that.

"You ought to move to the city. You could make a fortune as a lady's maid."

"Aye, I'd like that, truly. My ma would tan me good if I suggested it." Bridget glowered as she picked up Rose's pins. "But I'd rather be a lady's maid than a farmer's wife."

"Are those your only two options?" Rose asked, interested.

"I fear they are." When the girl looked up from where she'd piled the pins, Rose thought her eyes looked too old. "I'm Irish. There's naught for the Irish to do but what the English let us do."

"So I've come to understand. My father used to tell me stories." Thinking about them now, Rose realized that, although her father had made her laugh as he'd regaled her with his tales, the stories themselves weren't funny. In fact, with Edward Larkin's jolly interpolations taken away, some of them were downright frightful. "I know so little about my Irish heritage," she murmured, and was sorry for her ignorance.

"Well, if you stay here for very long, my da will come back, and then you'll know more than you ever wanted to."

"My goodness, your father sounds just like mine!"

They were both still laughing when they returned to the parlor to find Cullen standing in front of the fireplace stripped of his coat and boots. Rose's breath caught when she observed his skintight breeches, wet and clinging to his muscular thighs, and his white shirt plastered to his chest and arms. The man had muscles. He was built along more impressive lines than Rose had believed he'd be. After all, her father had been slightly built. Rose had assumed that men who spent most of their time playing the horses didn't exercise enough to build up muscles.

Then again, Cullen had proved himself to be an excellent horseman; perhaps he rode horses regularly as well as gambled on them. She didn't have time to entertain the notion, because Cullen turned and smiled at the two women.

"You look much more comfortable now, Rose."

"I am. So do you." She eyed his legs and flushed. She hoped he'd chalk it up to the heat of the fire. "Although you're still wet."

"Yes. I fear I'll have to dry myself by the fire, because there's no britches to fit me in the house."

"No," agreed Bridget, also staring at Cullen's physique. "Me da's too stout, and me brother's too small."

She blushed furiously and dashed out of the room. Cullen smiled after the girl. Rose laughed, and decided to try to act calm and collected. It was difficult, since she wanted to run her hands over Cullen's body, outlined so scandalously in those wet breeches and shirt.

"I think Bridget finds you attractive," she said with a smile that she hoped looked at least a little bit sophisticated.

"You think that?" He appeared startled.

"I think that," she said, trying to imitate his lovely, lyrical accent. She walked up and stood next to him, leaning over some and fanning her hair out so that the heat from the fire could dry it.

"What do you know," he mused. "And does Rose find me attractive, as well?"

His voice had gone soft and low, and it sent shivers of warmth through Rose. She glanced up through a waterfall of hair. He was watching her with one of those beautiful half smiles on his lips. They always made her a little weak in the knees. Tonight, she very nearly fainted dead away in the fire under the influence of it.

Because it was the truth and because she felt bold and daring, being stuck here with him this way, and because everyone in the household assumed they were man and wife, she said, "Yes, I do. Very."

She heard his quick intake of breath, and his soft, "Rose—"

"Cullen."

She had lifted a hand to his when Mrs. O'Doyle entered the room with a clatter of dishes and a thud of heavy foot-falls. Rose quickly stepped aside and tried to pretend that she hadn't nearly succumbed to the lust of her flesh with Cullen O'Banyon, the man of her dreams. Merciful heavens, whatever were they going to do tonight when they had, she presumed, to sleep in the same room?

"I've brung you some good hot soup and tea, dearies, and some of our good soda bread."

"Sounds delicious," said Rose. Her voice, she was sorry to note, sounded thin and a little shaky.

"Thank you, Mrs. O'Doyle. You're a jewel."

"Aye, that I am," the woman said with a laugh. "A flaw-less emerald from the Emerald Isle."

Cullen chuckled, and Rose offered a rather weak laugh as well.

"Before ye eat, would you like me to put your hair up, Mrs. O'Banyon?"

Rose glanced up from the food to find Bridget standing nervously in the doorway, looking as if she couldn't wait to prove herself to a woman who might be able to help her find a good position as a lady's maid. Rose sighed, and wished she really were the woman Bridget thought she was.

"Thank you, Bridget. That would be very nice of you." Because she figured it couldn't hurt—after all, perhaps Cullen knew how to secure positions for young girls who aspired to be ladies' maids—she said to him, "Bridget is hoping to become a lady's maid one of these days."

"Oh, aye? And where would you like to do this work, Bridget?"

Bridget, uncomfortable about being spoken of by these two people whom, Rose understood, she considered above her—if she only knew—muttered, "Oh, anywhere, I reckon. I don't know."

"I see. Perhaps there's more call for that sort of thing in the city."

Bridget frowned slightly. "Oh, aye, I know it, but me ma and da would die sooner than see me go to Dublin or London. They fear I'd come to grief." She sounded bitter about the edicts of her parents.

"They may be right there," Cullen said. Rose shot him a look of reproof. He saw it and shook his head. "There's many a pitfall in the big city when a lad or a lass is unprepared. 'Twould be better to secure a position before you travel anywhere."

"I suppose so." The girl heaved a large sigh. "But I'd like to know how I'm supposed to do that, livin' out here on the farm and all. Nobody's going to hire the likes of me, who's never been anywhere."

"Well, now, that might not be true," Cullen said judiciously after he'd downed a spoonful of soup. "I'll take your name and direction and see if there's something I might be able to do for you."

Bridget had been carefully brushing Rose's hair into two equal masses, parted in the middle. When she took in Cullen's offer, she dropped the hair, the hairbrush, and her unhappy demeanor. "Oh, Mr. O'Banyon! Would you do that? For me?"

"It's the least I can do, Bridget, after accepting your kind hospitality."

"Indeed," concurred Rose. "He—that is, we'll be happy to look out for something for you."

"Oh, ma'am. Oh, sir! I don't know what to say!"

"Say thank you and keep brushing," her mother told her, standing in the doorway and looking cross. "You haven't done a thing to earn their help yet."

"She's doing very well with my hair, and she was kind enough to offer me something dry to wear," Rose said, leaping to Bridget's defense.

Bridget, red in the face with embarrassment over her mother's censure, picked up the hairbrush and set to work again. "I'll—I'll be happy to do anything to learn. I'll work hard. I'll be glad to be an under maid or anything. Anything!"

"I'm sure you're a very hardworking girl, Bridget," said Rose in a soothing tone.

Mrs. O'Doyle sniffed. "She's a sight better at fixin' hair than she is at cooking." She sat in a rocking chair near the fire and reached into a basket set next to her chair, withdrawing a sturdy sock with a hole in its toe. She stuck the sock on a darning egg and set to work with a needle and thread. "'Tis a scandal, her cooking."

Bridget muttered, "Ma!" under her breath and colored prettily.

Cullen laughed softly, but was too busy eating to say anything.

Rose said, "I suppose each of us has a calling." She said it uncertainly because so far in her life, she'd failed to discover what her own calling was, or if she even had one. Thus far, she'd made a dreadful adventuress. The notion was fairly depressing, and she decided she didn't need to think about it now. She added, "You're doing a very nice job with my hair, Bridget. I'm sure you'd be a wonder at a hair salon or as a lady's maid."

"A hair salon," Bridget said dreamily. "Just like in the fine magazines."

Rose hadn't seen any fine magazines lying around, and she doubted if Bridget's mother allowed her daughter to spend good money on their purchase, but she decided she could do the child a charitable turn after she left the O'Doyles' home. Although her own supply of money was scanty, perhaps she could discover some fashion magazine that was distributed in Ireland and get the girl a subscription. Bridget deserved at least that. And Rose had no doubt that Cullen would honor his promise to the girl and would try to find her a suitable job somewhere.

Maybe some good would come of this unplanned detour due to rain. Her thoughts turned to Kate. "Oh, dear, I hope Aunt Kate won't be worried about us." She glanced at Cullen and began to gnaw her lower lip.

He looked up from his soup bowl. "We'll set off first thing in the morning, Rose. I'm sure she'll understand how we were delayed by the weather."

"You've got your auntie along with you on your wedding trip?" Mrs. O'Doyle peered at them narrowly.

Rose improvised quickly. "She's from America. She came over to Ireland with me, you see, and she wanted to see the land of her birth before she returned to New York."

"Ah." Mrs. O'Doyle seemed to accept her glib answer. Through with the no-longer-holey sock, she folded it and placed it on the hearth. Reaching into the basket again, this time she plucked out a cardigan. "I don't know how your brother can get holes in his things like he does. You'd think the lad walked on his elbows." She held up the offending garment, and Rose saw that the sleeves were worn at the elbows.

"Pisht, ma, that cardigan's went through seven people before it even got to Steven. He's not hard on his clothes; it's only his clothes that have seen lots of wear."

Mrs. O'Doyle sniffed, as if she didn't believe a word of it, and that as far as she was concerned, clothes should last for as many people as they were required to serve.

Rose, who'd always been poor but who'd never had to share with siblings or other relatives, was amazed at how some families were forced to make do. In spite of her father's irresponsibility, at least she'd been the only one to suffer. Although she feared it might be considered a sin by some people, she gave a little prayer of thanks that her parents hadn't had more children. It would have been terrible if she'd had to watch brothers and sisters suffer the hunger pangs and terrible doubts she'd endured for the sake of her father's whims.

Good heavens, what an unkind thought. She'd have an entire volume of sins to confess the next time she went to confession. How discouraging. She wondered where her next confession would take place, and if the priest who heard her would be genial old Father Robert back home in New York, or some Irish priest whom she'd not met yet. She also wondered if priests were able to absolve adventuresses of their many sins.

A sudden wash of homesickness attacked her, catching her unawares. Her breath snagged in her chest.

"Oh, dear, did I pull?" Bridget sounded horrified.

"No, no. Not at all. I just had a thought, is all."

"Well, I hope the rest of your night's thoughts will be happier than that one." Mrs. O'Doyle laughed.

Rose joined in, although her heart felt funny. Heavy.

Bridget made her hair look lovely—a waste when all she was going to do was sleep on it—but Rose didn't mind. "Thank you very much, Bridget."

Bridget bobbed a curtsy and blushed.

"Very well done," agreed Cullen. He smiled at the girl, who was so overwhelmed by the magnanimity of her new-found friends that she pleaded exhaustion and fled up the stairs to her bed.

Mrs. O'Doyle sighed as she worked on her Charlie's cardigan. "The girl's got fanciful notions, Mr. and Mrs. O'Banyon."

"She's very talented," murmured Rose. She hurried to the soup, for she was very hungry. The bread was delicious. Rose had sampled Irish soda bread a lot since she'd been in the land of her ancestors, but she'd never had it so well made. And the soup was tasty, too.

Against Mrs. O'Doyle's strong objections, she helped clean up the dishes after she and Cullen had eaten. It stood to reason that Mrs. O'Doyle would not think Rose capable of doing anything—after all, she was supposed to be Mrs.

Cullen O'Banyon. But Rose knew better. She was all too accustomed to hard work, so she overrode the kindhearted woman's objections, and was quite tired by the time Mrs. O'Doyle led her and Cullen upstairs to bed.

Her heart hammered like a woodpecker when she saw the small room with the commensurately small bed.

"Sleep tight, dearies," Mrs. O'Doyle advised. She left them with a candle, and a cheery wave.

Rose felt small, alone, inadequate, entirely too innocent, and really quite frightened.

Eleven

Cullen took note of the bed, covered with a pretty flowered quilt that he imagined Mrs. O'Doyle or Mrs. O'Doyle's mother or grandmother had made from scraps of old clothes. Nothing was ever discarded in an Irish family, not even in a relatively well-to-do one like the O'Doyles. Life was precarious here for those born of the land.

He walked to the window, drew the curtain back, and peered outside. The rain had slackened slightly, but it was still coming down. The ground would be as soggy as a marsh unless the drenching stopped soon and the sun came up hot and early on the morrow. No matter how slushy traveling was sure to be, however, he had to get Rose back to her aunt. If they didn't make it tomorrow, he feared he'd lose control of himself. He'd sooner die than fall into Kate Flanagan's scheme for Rose's future. Her downfall, was more like it.

He turned to find Rose standing by the door, fiddling nervously with the ribbons of her wrapper. He could read the thoughts on her face as clearly as if they'd been painted on her forehead. He sighed, knowing it was going to be a long night, and probably not a very restful one.

"Don't be afraid, Rose. I'll not take advantage of you because we're caught in a misunderstanding."

He saw her swallow. Some kind of adventuress she was. This is exactly the sort of situation she was supposed to have been seeking, wasn't it? If he were the sort of man she thought he was, he'd pounce on the opportunity. The good Lord knew he desired her. He wanted her more than he could recall ever wanting another woman. More than he'd ever desired poor Judith, God forgive him.

"I'm not afraid," she said in a voice that shook in spite of the effort she put into keeping it steady.

Fearing it might be a big mistake, Cullen held out a hand to her. "Come here, Rose. I'll tuck you in. I'll sleep—" Where? Glancing around the room, he saw a likely chair. "Over there." He pointed at the chair.

"You can't sleep on a chair." She hadn't drawn near to take his hand.

"Of course I can. I'll turn the chair and draw it near to that chest against the wall, and I'll have me a fine bed."

"I'm smaller than you and won't be so uncomfortable sleeping on the chair, Cullen. Let me take it. I've caused you enough trouble."

He shook his head and smiled at her. "And what sort of gentleman would that make me, Rose? I'll not have you sleeping on chairs when there's a bed handy."

From her quick exhalation of breath, Cullen judged her to be laboring under pique as well as nervousness. He was sorry to see her in such a condition. Now why, he wondered bitterly, had she not experienced this much trepidation at the notion of dancing in front of a roomful of lusty men? He was only one lusty man, and he knew he was less of a menace to her than most of the other men in his relative financial and social position. Not many fellows of his acquaintance would balk at bedding the lovely Rose.

Not that he wanted to balk. He wanted her so badly, he all but ached for her. It had been so long since he'd felt an emotional tie with a woman. He'd cared for Judith, but he hadn't felt akin to her, as he did to Rose. They made no sense, his feelings for Rose.

And she wanted nothing to do with a solid family man

with so dull a prospect to offer her as a horse farm and two little motherless boys. He let his hand drop to his side.

"Cullen, this isn't fair. I'm the one who's dragged you into my silly affairs. You shouldn't have to spend an uncomfortable night because of me."

He took a deep breath and said, "The truth of the matter is that I expect to spend an uncomfortable night no matter where I sleep, Rose. You might as well be comfortable." If he hadn't been so alert to her presence, he'd never have blurted out the truth that way. He wished he hadn't when she looked puzzled.

"Oh, dear, are you so very wet and miserable? Perhaps you can wrap yourself in a blanket or—or that quilt on the bed."

He huffed impatiently. "It's not wet breeches that will make me uncomfortable this night, Rose."

"No? I—I guess I don't understand."

"Of course, you don't. How could you?"

It was the expression of faint bewilderment on her face that finally made Cullen's reserve snap. He strode to her and grabbed her by the shoulders. "For the love of Christ, girl, don't you think I want to bed you? Don't you think I've been holding myself back since the night we met? You think you want to become an abandoned adventuress, but you don't know what you're talking about."

She blinked up at him, shocked. He was ashamed of himself, but he couldn't seem to stop. He shook her lightly. "You're no more than a babe in the woods, Rose Larkin. A babe in a big, bad world that's full of wolves and tigers. A man of the sort you think you want would devour you and spit out the pieces. And your auntie's no better than you are. If anything she's worse, because she's old enough to know better."

"I'm old enough," she said in a voice that wasn't very loud. She cleared her throat and seemed to gather her reserves of dignity and defiance together. "I'm plenty old enough to seek my fortune in the world."

Cullen peered down at her and shook his head. She was scowling up at him in a way that told him she had no idea how many perils the world held for a beautiful young lady with no masculine protectors. "Is that so?"

"Yes."

With his heart pounding as he considered what might have happened to Rose if he hadn't discovered her and Aunt Kate in Dublin, Cullen said, "Try to get away from me then."

"I beg your pardon?" This, spoken with faint surprise.

"I said, try to get away from me. Go ahead. Try."

She pulled at her shoulders. They didn't budge, and she stopped pulling.

"I mean it, Rose. Really try. Do your best."

"I don't understand, Cullen."

He nodded soberly. "Exactly. And I'm a person who only has your best interests at heart. But try again. Go on, Rose. Do your best."

"Oh, for heaven's sake!" But she did as he'd commanded. She tried to step away from him, but he held on easily, preventing her escape. She tried to pry his fingers from her upper arms and couldn't do it. "Cullen," she said, exasperated.

"Do you see yet what I'm trying to tell you? If you can't even escape from me, how do you think you could get away from a real villain? I'm only a pretend one, but there are lots of the genuine article out there."

"That's not fair, Cullen! I'm not stupid." She was starting to get angry.

"It is fair. If you'll think for a minute, you'll agree with me. I won't be able to travel with you forever. I might not be along the next time you run into a rogue like Everett Costello, whose primary aim in life is deflowering virgins because he's rich and unscrupulous enough to think it's jolly sport."

"Cullen!" She was shocked.

"I'm sorry, Rose, but it's the truth. I know Costello. You don't. It's to your credit that you believe the best of your fellow man, but it's not very sensible."

She huffed indignantly. "All right. You made your point. Now let me go."

He didn't want to let her go. He wanted to know how her life turned out. He wanted to be part of it. He wanted to love her, damn it. He wanted to take her home with him and install her in his house, and make her his wife.

And he couldn't say so. She'd laugh in his face.

Instead, he loosened his grip on her shoulders, slid his arms around her, and lowered his face to hers. His lips covered hers in a kiss so sweet, it nearly made his knees buckle. He wanted to devour her. To kiss her until they were both senseless, then carry her to his bed and make slow, precious love to her. He wanted to teach her that, while the rest of the world harbored dangers galore, she would always be safe with him.

Since he couldn't tell her all of those things, he tried to show her.

She gasped in surprise. For ten seconds she was stiff in his embrace, then her lips softened, her posture lost its tense rigidity, and she seemed to melt against him. Cullen knew he should pull away, but was too far gone to stop. His body was screaming for her, and his tongue sought her lips and plunged between them. He felt her arms go around him, clutching tightly, as if she feared she'd fall if he let her go. As if he'd do anything so stupid.

He allowed his right hand to go wandering. Her body was wonderful. It reminded Cullen of paintings by old masters he'd seen in galleries. Hers was an ideal of femininity. Soft and rounded and wonderful, and Cullen wished he could lay it bare to the air and to his eyes and feast on it for the rest of the night. He wanted to lose himself in her womanly flesh and forget his ordinary life and his everyday responsibilities. Only for this night. Just one night. Was that too much to ask?

His hand found the opening in the front of her wrapper and he pushed the fabric gently aside. She no longer wore her corset and Cullen found her lush breasts. Lord, Lord, she was wonderful. Her nipples had pebbled already, and he longed to taste them, to lick them and nip them, and feast upon them. He thought he might die if he wasn't able to slake his lust soon.

She made a soft little female sound, like the mew of a kitten, and Cullen realized her hands had begun to wander, too. They traveled up his arms and pressed the muscles of his shoulders. His stiff sex throbbed, and he pressed it against the softness of her belly. She was probably too innocent even to know what it was, but Lord, he wanted her.

And if he took her, he'd be worse than Everett Costello. He'd be a cad. A louse. A bad man. A man who didn't deserve the blessings God had granted him, and who was violating his own moral code and every single one of the principles he was trying to instill in his sons.

With a groan of frustration, he tore himself away from her. He was panting like a racehorse, and as aroused as he'd ever been in his life.

She looked befuddled, as if she wasn't sure what had happened to her. His lips tightened, and a sense of ill-usage washed over him. Why should she be confused? This is what she wanted, wasn't it?

He was being irrational, and he knew it. With a soft curse, he turned. Out of the corner of his eye, he saw her wobble on legs that had evidently gone rubbery. He walked to the window, pulled back the curtain, and stared into the night.

Damnation, what an ass he was! He shouldn't have touched her. It was his own damned fault for being weak. He was older than she by more than a decade. He'd been married and widowed and knew what was what. He was a respectable landowner and farmer and father. He had no business succumbing to his lustful urges, especially with a foolish American virgin who's head had been filled full of romantical trash by a silly aunt.

This wasn't her fault. He told himself that at least a hundred times in the minute or two he stood there, seething and frustrated and wishing he were home in his snug little farm with his two darling boys, and had never met Rose Larkin or her crackbrained aunt.

"C-Cullen?"

He shut his eyes and stifled a groan. Lord, he didn't want to talk now. He wanted her to go away. Just go away.

But, of course, she wouldn't do that. Couldn't. This was all his fault, and he had to face it. He turned, sucked in a deep breath, tried not to stare at her disordered hair and her beautiful body, which she was attempting to cover with her wrapper again. Her hands shook. He could see them tremble from where he stood.

He couldn't think of a single thing to say to her, and didn't try to. If she wanted to talk, let her talk. He was beyond speech at the moment. Maybe she could think of some way to diffuse the situation. He snorted internally, knowing that if anyone was responsible for clearing the air, it was he. Yet he couldn't make himself do it. Not yet.

"Cullen?" she said again.

He nodded curtly, unwilling even to open his mouth for fear he'd shout at her. He couldn't recall a time he'd been so angry, confused, and thwarted.

She finished covering herself and held out a hand. He looked at her hand and noticed that it no longer shook. What the hell did she want him to do? Shake hands? He wasn't bloody apt to do that, now, was he? What a silly little girl she was.

"Cullen, I—I wouldn't mind . . ." She licked her lips. "I mean, if you want to—well—you know. The bed and all. I mean—well, I wouldn't mind."

"*What?*" He couldn't credit his ears.

She flushed, embarrassed. "I mean . . . well, I guess this is what Aunt Kate was hoping for me. A—a grand passion and all that."

Cullen's eyes closed, his hands clenched, and he murmured, "Jesus," under his breath. A grand passion. He couldn't stand it. "Go to bed, Rose." He pushed the words out through gritted teeth, and opened his eyes to slits. Her lower lip had started to tremble. Damn.

"Um, what I meant was that . . . well . . ." She shrugged, and the wrapper slid down, revealing her left shoulder in all its creamy soft beauty. Cullen shut his eyes again.

She went on, "What I meant is that I really ought to

learn about these things. Don't you think? I mean, I think Kate thinks so."

"Kate's a madwoman."

"She's not!"

He turned his back on her. He didn't trust himself facing her. Not with her standing there, disheveled, her wrapper all but falling off of her, nearly naked, thoroughly kissed. "She's either a madwoman or she's stupid."

"That's not fair." Rose's voice hitched in the middle.

"It's the truth. Go to bed, Rose."

"I—I think I'd rather have you teach me those things than anyone else." Her voice had sunk to a whisper now.

"Go . . . to . . . bed." If she offered herself to him again, he knew he'd not be able to hold back from accepting the invitation, and then he'd be worse than the lowest sod.

After several moments that fairly crackled with tension, he heard her pad to the bed, and heard the ticking crackle as she lowered herself onto it. He pictured her in his mind's eye. She probably wouldn't take the wrapper off yet, but would keep it on while she crawled under the covers. Little Miss Modesty, the adventuress-in-training. Not a cynical man by nature, Cullen nevertheless felt a cynical twisting in his guts.

"It's because you don't want me, isn't it?"

Her voice was so small, Cullen barely heard it. When her words registered, he whirled around and goggled at her. She was sitting against the headboard, the pretty quilt pulled up to her chin. Tears stood in her eyes. She looked truly pathetic.

"Now you're the madwoman. Or stupid," he said gruffly.

"I'm not. I wish you'd explain it to me, Cullen. I don't understand."

"No, I'm sure you don't." In order to understand, she'd have to know a lot more about life and men than she did. She'd also have to know him, and he didn't want her to. She'd leave him then, and he had an unhappy feeling that he'd die if she left him.

It was beginning to look to Cullen as if knowing Rose

Larkin was going to scar him for life. It was a very forlorn realization.

That night in Mrs. O'Doyle's cozy cottage was one of the most miserable Rose had ever endured. And she'd endured plenty of miserable nights; nights when her father and his friends had loudly caroused outside her room, nights when she feared the debt collectors would come pounding at the door any second, nights when she was sure she faced expulsion from her school the next morning. This was worse.

Cullen didn't want her. He didn't even like her. What's more, she'd made a dithering fool of herself by as much as flinging herself at his feet and begging him to teach her the pleasures of the flesh.

And he'd refused. He'd rejected her out of hand. After kissing her to within an inch of her life, so that she'd felt things she'd only dreamed of feeling in her most fanciful flights of longing.

There was no reason that Cullen, who was a seasoned man of the world, would have refused the offer of her body unless he found her unappealing. What a ghastly thought. He looked upon her as he would a sister; he'd told her so, and she'd conveniently forgotten his warning. Lord, she was stupid. He was right about that.

Her throat ached and her eyes stung with the effort she was putting in to forcing herself not to cry. She wouldn't give him the satisfaction of knowing how much his refusal of her had hurt. Men. She'd never felt a grand passion before, but she was feeling one now. For Cullen O'Banyon.

Small wonder the women at the French Academy had seemed so unhappy, if this is what they had to endure. It was humiliating to have one's entire self repudiated when it was offered so freely. She didn't even expect him to marry her or anything. She didn't even expect him to set her up as his mistress. She only wanted crumbs from him, and he was unwilling to give her that much. She'd never been so ashamed in her life.

Her father had taught her a lot about embarrassment and abasement, but she'd always stood somewhat aloof from his follies. This was her very own. She owned every degrading moment of this travesty. She'd created it. All by herself.

Cullen had been generous to a fault. He'd always behaved like a perfect gentleman—well, until he'd kissed her, but that was Rose's fault. Her hand crept to her face, and she touched her lips with her fingers, wondering if she'd ever forget the way he'd kissed her.

What was she thinking? Of course, she'd never forget. She didn't even want to forget the physical sensations he'd drawn from her.

She sighed heavily, then wished she hadn't. She didn't want Cullen to know how deeply his rejection had crushed her. About the only thing she had left to call her own was a modicum of pride, and she needed that to keep herself from falling apart.

Perhaps one day she'd forget the terrible emotional toll this experience had exacted from her and recall only the pleasant physical sensations.

An emotional toll. Just like Wellington Bridge.

Wonderful. From this night onward, she'd forever think of herself as Ha'penny Rose. What a dreadful thought.

She turned over and buried her face in the lumpy pillow the hospitable O'Doyles had provided. She realized that she hadn't heard Cullen stirring, and she perked up her ears. He wasn't going to stand there, glowering into the dark all night, was he? Rose didn't think she could stand that. But she hadn't heard him fix the chair to sleep in.

Sleeping in a chair. Along with humiliation and grief, Rose welcomed guilt inside for a visit. He hadn't turned down the lamp either. When she slitted her eyes open—she didn't want to open them wide, because she couldn't bear to see Cullen again—the room was still light.

She got to worrying. Cullen was such a totally nice man. She couldn't bear the thought of him refusing even the comfort of a chair because she was a fool. Worry gnawed at her, making her stomach churn and her head begin to ache.

After what seemed like an eternity, Rose couldn't stand

it any longer. She turned over in bed, trying not to make too much noise on the tick mattress, and opened her eyes. Cullen stood by the window, holding the curtain back, staring out into the pitchy night. Rose noticed that the rain had stopped.

Well, now what? Should she ask him if he planned to stand there all night? What business was it of hers? Actually, it was her business in a way, because she was in the bed. He should be here instead of her.

Lord, she wished she hadn't gotten herself embroiled in this pickle. She could have refused Aunt Kate. She *should* have done so. She'd known better than to set off on this harebrained trip. She was no more fit to be an adventuress than Kate was herself.

But it was fruitless to contemplate the should-haves of life. She cleared her throat.

"Cullen, aren't you going to . . . sleep?" She'd been about to ask if he wasn't going to bed, but she caught herself before making that particular blunder. Chalk one up for Rose. It was a pitifully small score when stacked next to the thousand mistakes she'd made.

Without turning around, he asked, "Does the light bother you?"

"No! No, I just . . . didn't want you to . . . lose sleep. That's all." She wished she hadn't spoken.

"I'll fix a bed for myself in a minute."

His tone was cool and detached, and it renewed Rose's urge to burst into tears. She'd ruined everything. With her foolish impetuosity, she'd spoiled the easy friendship between them, and it would take a miracle to get it back. Even if they did, it would never be the same. Her head pounded in time to the aching of her heart, and she turned over, pulled the quilt up, and shut her eyes.

Eventually, she slept.

Rose looked pale and shaky in the morning. Cullen eyed her keenly, and didn't like the pallor of her cheeks and the dark rings under her eyes. He should be horsewhipped for what he'd done to her.

But there was no time for self-recriminations. They had to playact through breakfast in the O'Doyles' big, warm kitchen, and then they had to slog back to the inn where Kate was probably pulling her hair out in anxiety over Rose's welfare.

Cullen aimed to see that they all rested for the remainder of this day. Rose obviously had not slept any better than he had last night, and she needed rest. He did, too, for that matter. Kate could be hanged. This was all her fault to begin with.

He knew he was being irrational, and cursed his fuddled brain. It was exhaustion making him want to blame Kate for his own mistakes. Kate might be a misguided romantic, but she hadn't made Cullen lose control of himself. He'd done that all on his own. And now he'd ruined everything.

"You look tired, Rose. Are you feeling well?"

She gave him a wan smile. "I have a little headache, is all. I'll be fine."

He frowned. She looked decidedly peaked. "Are you sure?"

"Oh, yes. I didn't sleep very much last night, and I always get somewhat headachy and so forth when I lose sleep." She gave a game little laugh. "I promised myself that I'd get sufficient sleep on this trip with Kate, because I know how I get when I don't rest."

He nodded, but he didn't like it. He told himself not to be an ass. She knew herself better than he'd ever know her, to his everlasting misfortune, and she had no reason to lie about a headache.

They got through breakfast with the voluble Mrs. O'Doyle, Bridget, and Charlie talking for all of them. It was a good thing, too, because he didn't feel up to cheerful chatter, and Rose, for all she tried valiantly, looked ill.

He and Charlie saddled the rental horses after breakfast, and Rose kissed Bridget and Mrs. O'Doyle farewell. Cullen heard her promise Bridget that she'd get in touch with her should she find any opportunities for her. She'd probably do it, too. Rose was an honest woman, for all that she had her head stuffed with nonsense. Cullen admired her for the quality; it was one he prized.

That being the case, he decided he ought to practice a little honesty this morning himself. After he'd helped Rose to mount, they'd waved a last farewell to the O'Doyles, and they'd been riding for about a half hour, Cullen spoke.

"We should talk about what happened last night, Rose."

Her head bowed for no more than an instant before her back straightened, and her chin lifted. "If you don't care to, that's all right, Cullen. I'm sorry I made such a fool of myself."

She'd made a fool of herself? Cullen stared at her. "No, no, Rose. It was my fault. It was all my fault."

"Nonsense." She sounded cross. "You're right about me. I'm a silly little innocent with her head in the clouds. I'm surprised you put up with me, quite frankly."

He didn't like this. While he agreed with her in her assessment of herself, she made it sound like a condemnation, and he hadn't meant it as one. It wasn't her fault she was innocent. Nineteen-year-old girls were supposed to be innocent, for the love of God. They weren't supposed to aspire to become a man's mistress.

"What I meant was that you're too good for the life you're trying to achieve, Rose," he said, trying to make his tone mild. He wanted to pound the truth into her, by force if necessary.

She heaved a huge sigh. "No, I'm not." She sounded quite sure of herself.

Cullen shook his head and decided he'd have to think some more before he could bring up this subject again. He was obviously saying the wrong things this morning. Not surprising, that, but discouraging.

They rode on in silence, Cullen sneaking peeks at Rose from time to time. Her color had improved slightly, probably because the sun was out this morning. The air was crisp, but the weather had cleared and it was a perfect, fine day. It was the kind of day in which he loved to ride for miles and miles. He'd be enchanted to do so in Rose's company under other circumstances. A momentary vision

of Rose, William, Ferris, and himself riding the hills sur-
rounding his farm made his heart squeeze. His boys would
love Rose as much as he did, for a certainty.

Jesus, Mary, and Joseph, where had that thought sprung
from? Wherever it had, it had better get back there and
stay. Cullen couldn't afford to allow adolescent fantasies to
spoil his notion of reality.

He was startled when Rose spoke.

"I wanted to leave some money for the O'Doyles, but I
didn't have any."

Cullen heard the regret in her voice. "I tucked a ten-
pound note under the dresser scarf. I didn't want to embarrass them by handing it to them."

She turned her head and gave him a glowing smile.
"Oh, thank you! I'm so glad you did."

Knocked slightly silly by her sudden change in aspect,
Cullen only nodded.

"I do plan to look for work for Bridget, too. Once
I'm . . . settled somewhere."

"That's good of you."

"Is it?" She'd reverted to looking sad.

Cullen wished he could wave a magic wand and make
everything wonderful for her. "I think so."

"I know what it's like to long for things that seem so far
away from you that they're not achievable in this lifetime.
I'd hate to think of Bridget dreaming forever—you know,
getting old under the influence of her dreams, and always
believing that life had passed her by. That's sad."

"Aye." Actually, Cullen was horrified by her words. She
was too damned young, and pretty, to be having such notions. She had her whole life ahead of her, and he could see
no reason she should pine away and long for things she
couldn't have. Hell, he'd give her the world and the moon
and the stars if he could.

"I wish I could do more for her."

"I have a feeling she'd be ecstatic even to know you remember she lives on this green earth. We Irish aren't accustomed to folks caring about us, I fear."

"That's very sad."

Cullen was appalled to see the glitter of tears in her eyes. She stubbornly swallowed them, but his resolution to see her rest redoubled.

They made their muddy way into the inn yard not more than forty-five minutes after that. Kate had been pacing in the lobby, and saw them out of the window when they rode in. She dashed outdoors to greet them, with a flutter of exclamations and questions on her lips.

Cullen explained what had happened to them, and Kate took Rose under her wing. Both of them agreed that rest and recuperation was the logical course to follow that day. He left them at the door of their room after promising to have luncheon sent up.

When he walked down the hallway to his own room, he was looking forward to getting out of the breeches and shirt he'd slept in. His anticipation of the rest of his trip with Rose and Kate wasn't so sanguine.

Twelve

"I can't account for it, really," said Rose. Then she sneezed violently.

"It was getting caught in that confounded rainstorm," grumbled Cullen.

"I'm sure you'll be all right, dear. Your health is generally splendid." Kate smiled at them both.

"True. And I don't really feel bad. Just a little sneezy." Rose acknowledged her aunt's words, but she didn't like the gleam in Kate's eye. Nor was she comforted by the knowledge that Kate, in spite of Rose's denial, assumed that she and Cullen were now lovers.

If it had been up to Rose, they would be. The truth was very distressing, and it made her head throb like a drum. Another truth was that she really felt quite dreadful. She couldn't recall ever feeling so weak and dizzy. But she'd die sooner than spoil this trip for Kate or acknowledge her weakness to Cullen, who'd already been put to too much trouble on her account.

She watched him now as he walked ahead of them toward the entrance to Kilkenny Castle. The castle was an impressive place, and Rose was sure she'd enjoy seeing it—if only she didn't feel so poorly.

They'd been caught in the rain three days ago. There

was no reason for her to be sickening now. Annoyed with herself for coming down with whatever this was, she refused to give in to it, but trod stolidly on with her aunt in tow, Cullen leading the way—as usual. She was beginning to harbor terribly guilty thoughts about Cullen. She and Kate were nothing but a burden to him; she knew it in her bones. Maybe that's why her bones seemed to be aching.

Bother! She had to stop thinking about it. That was the ticket. *Stop thinking and enjoy the castle, Rose Larkin,* she lectured herself. *You're an American, and you've never seen a castle before.*

"Isn't this fascinating, Rose," Kate whispered. "Imagine. A real castle."

"Exactly what I was just thinking," Rose told her with a smile.

"Aye. We have some lovely English castles here in Ireland."

Rose blinked, a little startled at the caustic tone of Cullen's voice. "Um, is it only the English who built castles here?"

"Of course."

That was all. He didn't elaborate. Rose sighed and wished she could think of a cogent question to ask. He seemed almost short-tempered today, and she couldn't account for it.

He stopped so suddenly that she nearly bumped into him, then he whirled around. "Are you sure you're well enough to be tramping around in a damp castle, Rose? You look like you're about to drop."

Kate, alarmed by Cullen's observation, took a step back, put a palm to her cheek, and stared at Rose as if she'd never seen her before. "Do you really think so?"

Irked, Rose snapped, "Nonsense. I'm fine. It's only a little sniffle." She sneezed again, and hoped to heaven she was right. It didn't feel like a little sniffle. Her chest was tight, her head ached, and her joints felt as if somebody had gone at them with a hammer and nails.

To her astonishment, Cullen yanked off a glove and pressed a hand to her forehead. He did it so fast, she was caught off guard, and stumbled back a pace. He had an awful frown on his face. "You feel warm to me."

She felt warm to herself, too, and she ached, and she felt sick, but she would be boiled in oil before she admitted it. If she got sick, she'd spoil everything, and she wouldn't do that. She couldn't. She was already a problem for everybody, not to mention a ridiculously wanton lunatic whom even Cullen didn't want. To everything else, the urge to cry assailed her, and her temper snapped.

"I wish you'd stop harping on my health! I'm perfectly fine, and I want to see Kilkenny Castle. The guidebook says it dates from the twelfth century and was built by the Normans!" She glared at Cullen. "You said it was only the English who built castle in Ireland."

His lips pinched together and he looked more peeved than Rose had seen him. "I beg your pardon. I should have said only conquering imperialists built castles in Ireland. I shall try to be more precise in future."

"You needn't be sarcastic," Rose muttered.

Kate said, "Oh, dear, please don't quarrel."

Cullen huffed, turned, and started off once more, his long strides eating up much more land than Rose and Kate could cover without hustling. So they hustled.

"Interfering, nosy beast," Rose grumbled under her breath. She didn't mean it. She still felt like crying.

"I beg your pardon, dear?"

And that was another thing. Kate, as sweet as she was and as much as Rose loved her, never knew what was going on. It was as if she went through life with blinders on. Today Rose considered the trait intensely annoying. She said, "Nothing, Kate. I was just talking to myself."

"Oh, my, you'd better not start talking to yourself, dear. I'm sure Mr. O'Banyon wouldn't like it, and you really should try to behave well for him. Now that . . . well, you know." She smiled beatifically, and Rose stifled an unkind urge to smack her silly.

Lord, she must be honestly and truly sick if she was harboring violent urges toward Kate. She vowed to keep her mouth shut and her eyes open and not say another word unless it was an exclamation of awe over the beauties to be unfolded before them in Kilkenny Castle.

She kept her word to herself better than she'd expected to. About an hour into their tour of the castle, when they were on the grounds and Kate was oohing and ahhing about the glories of the Irish countryside, Rose involuntarily gave up the battle against the illness that was trying to lay her low, and fainted dead away.

Kate stared at Rose's immobile form crumpled on the ground, pressed a hand to her cheek, and whispered, "Oh, my goodness!"

A woman who had been standing nearby uttered a stifled scream. "She isn't contagious, is she?"

Cullen, who had watched in consternation as Rose collapsed to the ground, had already reached her body. As he knelt beside her, he glared at the woman. "Of course, she's not contagious. She's merely suffering from exhaustion." He pressed his hand to her forehead. She was burning up. "Damnation. The little fool."

With one fluid movement, he lifted her in his arms and began striding purposefully toward the area where they'd left his carriage. He hoped to God Johnny hadn't stepped off to take a pint. Without even looking to see that Kate followed his instructions, he growled, "Follow me, Mrs. Flanagan. We've got to get her in bed."

"Oh, dear. Oh, dear. Oh, my dear good gracious sakes." Kate kept up a steady stream of frightened ejaculations as she pattered after Cullen, running to keep up.

When they were away from the other people touring the castle, Cullen said, "I knew she was sick. Why didn't she say something? We should have stayed at that inn until she was well. I knew she didn't feel good. Damnation!"

"I'm sure she'll be well in a short while, Mr. O'Banyon. Rose has always had a sturdy constitution."

Cullen swiveled his head and scowled at Kate, who seemed to shrivel under his overt anger. He didn't care. Rose was sick. She was sick, and he was to blame because he dragged her out in a rainstorm on horseback, and the little idiot hadn't admitted it. He should have forced her to rest.

But no. He hadn't. And her crackbrained aunt had tried to assure them all that Rose was merely suffering from a sniffle and that they shouldn't break their trip. Damn her to perdition! This was all *her* fault. She's the one who'd dragged Rose over to Ireland to fulfill her idiotic schemes. She's the one who'd pushed Rose to do too much.

What if she had influenza? What if it went into her lungs? What if she got pneumonia?

God, what if she died? People died from those things. Cullen's heart stopped for a minute before it took off racing like one of his horses at the Derby.

"She won't die," he said to himself.

"I beg your pardon?" Kate was panting by this time.

He'd almost forgotten she was there. As much as he resented what she'd done to Rose, he wouldn't be unkind to her. Rose would never forgive him if he was mean to Kate. "I said, I'll call in a doctor as soon as we get her to the inn."

"Oh. Thank you so much."

Kate appeared puzzled, probably because what he said just then didn't sound like what he'd said before. That didn't matter. Kate was so fuddled to begin with, she'd soon forget the discrepancy.

"Sir!"

Thank God! Johnny hadn't strayed far away from the carriage. He'd been chatting with a couple of other young men, probably drivers of other rich men's carriages. As soon as Johnny saw Cullen with Rose in his arms, he bolted away from his chums and loped toward the carriage.

"Miss Larkin has fallen ill, Johnny. We need to get her back to the inn as soon as possible, and then fetch a sawbones for her."

"Yes, sir!"

The boy didn't linger over hitching the team. He was a good lad, Johnny. He deserved a rise in salary, and Cullen would see that he got it.

"She's probably wrapped up as tight as a drum in

whalebone and stays," Cullen grumbled after he lifted
Rose into the carriage and scrambled in after her. He even
forgot to assist Kate to enter, but Johnny, bless his soul, did
that for him, so it didn't matter, except that he'd been rude.
He didn't care.

Kate colored. Cullen, impatient with maidenly airs and
graces, snapped, "If she's laced up too tightly, she won't be
able to get enough air." He sucked in a peck of air, closed
his eyes, prayed for patience, and opened his eyes again. "I
beg your pardon, Mrs. Flanagan, but do you know if Rose
laces her stays very tightly?" Sudden inspiration made him
add, "My wife used to do that, and the doctor told her it
was bad for her health."

Oh, Lord, Judith had died of influenza. If he lost Rose,
too, Cullen wasn't sure he could bear it.

He wouldn't think about that now.

His explanation of why he'd asked his shocking question seemed to have soothed Kate. "Oh, I don't think Rose
laces her stays very tightly. I know she doesn't like wearing tight things."

"Good." That was something, anyway. "I think I'll
loosen the buttons at her throat. Maybe it will make respi-
ration easier. Her breathing seems rather heavy."

Lord, lord, she was gurgling. He could hear the fluid
in her respiratory passages. With shaking fingers, he un-
buttoned the collar buttons at her throat. Because he
couldn't help himself, he lifted her onto his lap and
wrapped his arms around her. He expected Kate to
protest, but she didn't. She only looked worried.

"Do you think she's really very ill, Mr. O'Banyon?"
Kate asked after the carriage had jolted into motion and
they'd been on the road for several minutes.

It took him a second's contemplation before he decided
on the truth. "Yes. People don't faint from little colds, Mrs.
Flanagan. She's burning with fever, I can hear her breath
coming through some kind of fluid blocking the passages,
and I'm afraid she's very ill."

He feared she had influenza. Like Judith. He couldn't

believe this was happening again. It couldn't be. They weren't even married, for the love of God.

"Oh, dear."

Cullen shot a suspicious glance at Kate, but she looked genuinely worried. Perhaps she'd always been merely flighty, and wasn't at ease in expressing her anxiety. Cullen hoped so, because if she planned on treating this like a minor inconvenience, he'd have something to say about it. He planned to make sure Rose had the finest medical help available. What's more, he wouldn't stand for a relapse.

Oh, Lord, what could he do about it? If God decided it was Rose's time to go, Cullen couldn't do a dashed thing.

He hated feeling helpless.

After a few more jolting miles, Rose's eyelids fluttered, and her eyes opened. She appeared surprised to find herself on Cullen's lap and struggled for a second before weariness claimed her, and she sank back against his chest. "Wh—what happened?" Her voice was getting hoarse, and she coughed after asking her question. It was a croupy, wheezy cough, and it made Cullen's insides cramp.

This was Judith all over again.

Kate leaned over and patted Rose's limp hand. "You fainted, dear. Mr. O'Banyon says you're ill."

Rose blinked muzzily. "I fainted?"

"Yes. And you were an idiot not to tell us you were really sick. A little sniffle, you said. You confounded little fool!"

Cullen felt like a beast when tears dripped from Rose's eyes. He wiped them with his own fingers. "I'm sorry, Rose. I didn't mean to scold you."

She sniffed miserably. "I didn't want to spoil everyone's fun." She sounded pitiful, like a sick child.

Which is exactly what she was, Cullen thought savagely. She was a child. She had no business trying to protect the adults in her life. "Our fun will be spoiled a good deal more if you should take a lung ailment and die."

"Oh!" Kate cried. "Oh, Mr. O'Banyon, please don't say things like that!"

Rose sniffled again.

Cullen muttered, "I'm sorry. But I'm worried about you, Rose, and I don't think it was very smart of you to fib about being sick. My wife died after a bout with influenza, and I know how bad it can be."

"Good heavens," Kate whispered, horrified.

"Stop it!" Rose whacked him on the chest. She was weak, and the slap was feeble, but Cullen was again ashamed of himself.

"Sorry," he grumbled, even though he wasn't. He was furious at both of these women. Kate for being an idiot. Rose for making him fall in love with her—and then getting sick.

"You should be," Rose murmured thickly.

He pressed her head to his shoulder. She was as hot as a live coal. "Try to sleep, Rose. You can scold me later."

She said, "Good, I will," and complied with his request. She was asleep again when the carriage reached the inn.

By the time Johnny had fetched a physician—Cullen told Johnny to give the man any amount of money to compensate him for possible inconvenience—Rose's fever was sky-high, her breathing was labored and croupy, and she was as white as the sheets upon which she lay. Except for the hectic flush of fever on her cheeks.

Cullen himself had disrobed her, ignoring Kate's protests about the impropriety of such an action. "For the love of God," Cullen had snapped, "you already think we're lovers. If we were, I'd have seen her naked countless times by now."

"Oh! Oh, Mr. O'Banyon, I forgot." Kate collapsed into a chair and stared at him, aghast.

Cullen gritted his teeth. It aggravated him that Kate should believe him to be the kind of man she was seeking for Rose. In truth, he was the kind of man Kate *should* be seeking for Rose, although neither Kate nor Rose knew it. They should be seeking a husband for her; a man who would cherish and protect her forever; a man like him.

Then he sat on the edge of Rose's bed—ignoring shocked looks from the landlady and her daughter, a highly respectable pair who tottered out of the room making the sign of the cross—and held Rose's hand. In spite of the terror gripping him, he spoke soothingly to her, in case she could hear. He feared she was beyond hearing, although he refused to give up hope for her renewed health.

"You're going to be fine, Rose. Hang on, love. The doctor's coming, and he'll fix you right up."

Liar, liar, his conscience screamed at him. He tried to ignore it as he had the landlady and her daughter. He tried to ignore the fact that people succumbed to illness every day, and neither he nor Rose were immune to the troubles that plagued the rest of humanity. Regardless of his money or how important he was.

Please don't let her die, God. I swear I'll build a chapel at the farm if you let her live. I'll donate new carpeting and a new communion service to the village church. Please don't let her die.

Bargaining with God was a new low in Cullen's experience. He'd always believed that God expected a body to live a good life daily. Waiting for a crisis before assuming the role of a moral individual was waiting too long. Last-minute wrangling when one's life or loved ones were in peril didn't appeal to Cullen in the least. On more than one occasion, he'd entertained the cynical thought that, were he God, he'd tell folks who tried to strike bargains that they were on their own.

He hoped to whatever saints were in heaven that God was of a more liberal turn of mind than he himself was. Compassionate. Wasn't God supposed to be compassionate? If He was compassionate, surely He'd cure Rose. A merciful God wouldn't take Rose away from her loving aunt. Or from Cullen O'Banyon, whom she had no idea loved her madly.

Holding her hand to his cheek, he bowed his head and for a moment allowed his tears to fall. He didn't cry for long. Somebody had to be strong for Rose. He knew good and well that Kate, however much she cherished her niece, wouldn't be.

A fierce fit of coughing served to snap his gloomy

thoughts to attention. Quickly and carefully, he lifted Rose so that she wouldn't choke on the thick phlegm her coughing produced. She collapsed again after the fit passed, limp as a rag, not having opened her eyes once. Cullen very nearly gave in to his anguish.

Fortunately for all of them, the physician arrived just as he settled Rose back onto her sweat-soaked pillows. A soft knock came at the door an agonizing hour after they'd arrived at the inn. Kate had succumbed to silent tears and hang-wringing. Cullen was beyond all that. His jaw ached from being set so hard, his head throbbed, and his heart felt as if it were being squeezed by a giant's fist. He turned, startled, toward the door and saw it being pushed open.

"What have we here?" came a bluff, hearty voice from the doorway.

Kate squeaked and jumped to her feet, her handkerchief pressed to her damp cheeks. She uttered a soft, "Oh!"

Without releasing Rose's hand, Cullen got to his feet. "Are you the doctor?" He saw Johnny, looking distressed, standing behind the large man, so his question was answered even before the doctor spoke.

"Aye, that I am. And I hear we have a very sick lady here." He strode forward, shifting his black bag to his left hand, and held out his right for Cullen to shake.

Although he had to relinquish Rose's hand to do so, Cullen shook the doctor's hand. "Cullen O'Banyon, Doctor."

"O'Banyon? The horse O'Banyon, by any chance?"

Cullen's jaw tightened for a second before he said, "Yes."

The doctor nodded briskly. "Malachai Swift, Mr. O'Banyon. Pleased to meet you." He went to the bedside and looked down at Rose, frowning. "Can you tell me something about this lovely thing and the progression of this sickness? She's ill—very ill, I'd say."

"Yes. She's very sick, Doctor. It sounds like it's in her lungs, and her breathing is rough."

"Yes, I hear it." The big man set his bag on the chair lately occupied by Cullen, snapped it open, and withdrew a stethoscope. "Tell me about the onset, if you will." He didn't wait for Cullen's compliance before pushing the folds of the bodice of Rose's nightgown aside and pressing the instrument to her chest—Cullen winced for Rose's sake, although she made no move of protest, nor gave any indication that she knew the doctor was even there. Dr. Swift continued to frown as he listened to Rose's labored breathing and Cullen's explanation.

"It started when we got caught in a rainstorm," Cullen began. He proceeded to take the doctor through their adventures, from the storm to Rose's collapse at Kilkenny Castle. "She said it was only a sniffle. I wanted her to rest, but she wouldn't hear of it."

A wail from Kate made both men turn to look at her. "It's all my fault," she cried, weeping copiously. "She didn't want to spoil my trip, you see, and I didn't want her to feel guilty by resting. I knew I should have made her rest, but I didn't because I was afraid she'd take it amiss, and now look. She's so sick, and it's all my fault!" She went off into a paroxysm of grief.

Cullen was surprised to hear that Kate understood the situation so well. He hadn't given her enough credit for perception, he guessed. Here he'd been thinking she was totally oblivious to Rose's distress. Well, no matter. He'd apologize later if such a course of action still seemed warranted. If Rose died, he wasn't sure he'd be able even to speak to Kate.

"Pisht," said Dr. Swift gruffly. "'Tisn't your fault, and 'tisn't mine, 'tisn't God's, and 'tisn't the poor child's. It's fate, is what it is. If you're Irish, you ought to be acquainted with fate by this time."

Kate's muffled sobs came to Cullen and the doctor in reply. Cullen sighed. "What do you think, Dr. Swift? Can you do anything for her?"

The doctor didn't reply immediately. He finished probing various parts of Rose's anatomy while Cullen stood by in agony, wanting to shout at the man to answer him. That was his irrational emotional turmoil demanding answers, however, and he wouldn't succumb to anger and frustra-

tion at this point. Rose needed him. It wouldn't help her if
he alienated the doctor.

Dr. Swift went to the wash basin, poured water from the
pitcher into it, and scrubbed his hands before he spoke. By
the time he turned to look at Cullen, Cullen was about
ready to tear his hair out.

"She's in bad shape, Mr. O'Banyon," Dr. Swift said.
Then he gave a quick, apologetic grin and added, "But you
already knew that."

"Yes," Cullen croaked.

Kate sobbed more loudly.

"The influenza has taken a firm hold on her constitution. It's in her chest, but I can't tell if it's gone into pneumonia yet."

Cullen's heart gave a hard, painful spasm. He whispered, "Pneumonia?" It was practically a death sentence.

Kate's sobs got louder still, and she moaned.

"She's a young, strong girl, though." Dr. Swift stopped
short, as something occurred to him. "Is she your wife, Mr.
O'Banyon? I hadn't heard you'd remarried."

Jesus, Mary, and Joseph, did the whole of Ireland know
his life's story? Tamping the anger threatening to flare up
in his breast, Cullen said, "I haven't. Rose Larkin is my fiancée"

He lied. So what? Anything, even falsehoods, were
proper if they would help Rose. Dr. Swift didn't look like
the type who'd refuse to help a lady in distress, even if her
mode of travel through Ireland was unusual, but Cullen
didn't plan to take any chances.

"Ah. I see."

"And this is Mrs. Kate Flanagan, Miss Larkin's aunt.
They're both from New York City."

"Ah."

Kate sniffled and said, "I came from Ireland forty-five
years ago, Dr. Swift. This was supposed to be a happy trip
to show Rose the land where her father and I came from."
She subsided into noisy weeping again.

"I see." The doctor looked as if he'd like to say more—
offer sympathy, perhaps—but he didn't.

Cullen was glad. He didn't think he could stand it at that moment. It was hard enough to keep himself together already. "Can you do anything for her? If you need anything—medications, help, anything at all—just let me know, and I'll get it for you. Money isn't an object in her treatment."

"Lucky for you."

Dr. Swift's voice didn't sound as dry as his words might indicate. Cullen eyed him sharply, but detected nothing but honest concern on his ruddy face. "Yes, I'm much more fortunate than the majority of my countrymen."

His acknowledgement of the truth seemed to please the doctor. He nodded. "We may need some supplies, although I'm not sure at this point."

Cullen's heart leaped out of his boots, where it had lain cold and lumpy when it wasn't aching. "So you *can* help her?" He almost didn't dare hope too hard for fear he'd die if Rose did.

"Oh, aye. I can apply mustard plasters to keep the phlegm loose in her chest. She'll have to be watched—"

"Can you stay to monitor her? I'll pay you anything."

"Steady, lad. You won't do your sweetheart any good if you lose your mind, you know."

Again swallowing his anger, Cullen muttered, "Right. You're right, of course." He ran his fingers through his hair and wished he were magic so he could merely wave his hand and cure Rose.

Dr. Swift fished around in his black bag. His tone was sympathetic when he spoke again. "I understand, Mr. O'Banyon. And I'm sorry you have to see your sweetheart in such a state."

Cullen muttered some noise he hoped sounded appreciative. His nerves were jumping and skipping, his heart and head both throbbed, and he wanted to scream his rage and anxiety to the skies.

"I'll send for a nurse—"

"I can watch her," Cullen broke in. He didn't care to have some unknown nurse to watch his Rose. "I don't want strangers to frighten her."

The doctor straightened, took a step, and gripped Cullen's shoulder. "Calm down, lad. She's in no fit state to be worried about strangers, and you won't be any help to her if you collapse from exhaustion."

"But—"

"I can watch her, too," came thickly from Kate. She stood on shaky legs and teetered to the doctor. "Please. I feel so at fault for her being ill. Please say I may nurse her."

The doctor smiled. "You can both nurse her, but I'm going to fetch a professional anyway. The woman I have in mind is experienced, efficient, and about the best nurse in these parts. He name is Heloise McGinty, and she'll take no nonsense from nervous aides, so you'd both better re-sign yourselves to doing what she tells you to without fuss-ing." He chuckled.

Cullen saw no reason for levity. However, he acknowl-edged that, as long as he was allowed to stay in the room with Rose, it probably was a good idea to get a trained nurse. He nodded his assent.

"Good." The doctor rubbed his hands together briskly. "Now, I'm going to administer a dose of quinine if she can swallow it. Mr. O'Banyon, I want you to lift her head and shoulders. The quinine will help the fever, if we're lucky. I'll see if I can secure some salicylic powders, which I've heard from others are efficacious in reducing fevers. Then you—" He pointed to Kate. "—can fetch some cold water and clean rags. The two of you will have to take turns putting cold damp cloths on her forehead. We've got to get the fever down. We also have to keep her upper body ele-vated to a higher point than her legs so her chest can get rid of the phlegm that's hindering her breathing."

His matter-of-fact assumption of responsibilities made Cullen feel better. It apparently had the same effect on Kate, because she stopped sniffling, squared her shoulders, and said, "I'll get one of the maids to help me until the nurse arrives."

"Hire her to help even after the nurse arrives," Cullen

said to Kate's back. "Secure all the help you can. Money is no object."

"Very well." Kate appeared quite firm of purpose as she strode out the door.

"Good, good." The doctor smiled after her. His smile left as soon as the door shut behind Kate's bustled rear, and he turned to Cullen, whose heart fell back into his boots.

"What?" he demanded. "What is it?"

"It's bad, is what it is," said Dr. Swift without mincing matters. "She's got a terrible fever, and the accumulation of fluids in her chest is at a dangerous level. You're stronger, both physically and mentally, than Miss Larkin's aunt or I miss my guess, and you'll have to lift her when she coughs and be sure her aunt doesn't go to sleep on the job. Your lady will probably alternate between fever and chills, so you'll have to be prepared to switch from cold compresses to warm blankets when the changes occur."

Cullen had been nodding ever since the doctor started speaking. "Isn't there some other medicine she can take?"

"Ah, lad, there's so little modern medicine can do for these cases. Perhaps if the lass was in her own New York City, or if she'd taken ill in London, there'd be more by way of modern medications available to her, but you know as well as I do that Ireland's languishing in the Dark Ages, God love her."

"Yes." Feeling considerably grimmer about the perils of being an Irishman in Ireland than he generally did, Cullen walked to Rose's bedside. "Can you give her the quinine now, Dr. Swift? The sooner we start trying to get her fever down, the better she'll be, I suppose."

"I suppose." Dr. Swift smiled and held up a bottle of powder. "I've already got it here, lad."

"Thanks." The serene, good-natured efficiency of Dr. Swift made Cullen grateful to Johnny for finding him. "You'll come often to monitor her progress, won't you?"

"Of course, I will. And I have a feeling that what with you and her aunt standing by her and praying over her— for the good Lord responds to prayers, you know, in spite of the way He's allowing his creature Irishmen to suffer—she'll pull through."

Cullen shut his eyes and stood still for a moment, too moved to speak. He was very thankful to the good doctor for his words. "Yes," he said. "Prayers. We've both been praying."

Dr. Swift clapped him on the back. "I'm sure you have." He stirred some of the powder into a glass of water. "I wish medicine didn't need so much of the good Lord's help sometimes, but progress is being made all the time. They've discovered the cause of consumption. It's a bacillus."

Cullen didn't care about the cause of consumption. Nevertheless, he nodded agreeably because he'd do anything to keep from offending what seemed to him to be the only hope Rose had. "What about those powders you talked about? What were they?"

"Salicylic powders. I think I can scare some up if we're all lucky."

"Hmmm. Good," Cullen murmured distractedly.

Dr. Swift smiled at him. Cullen detected a world of sympathy in his face. "All right. We're ready here. Lift her shoulders, lad, and I'll see how much of this we can get down her."

As gentle as he tried to be, jarring Rose precipitated another racking spasm of coughs. It hurt Cullen to watch and listen and to be unable to take the burden of this sickness from her. He gently wiped the involuntary tears from her cheeks and the phlegm from her lips and realized he had tears in his own eyes when he gazed at Dr. Swift, who stood by with the medicine glass in his hand. The doctor gave him a nod laced with understanding and sat next to Rose on the bed.

Very carefully, drip by drop, he spooned medicine into her mouth. She was so weak that it was difficult for her to swallow, so he rubbed her throat to promote a swallowing response. Cullen's arms were aching by the time the glass was empty, but he didn't even notice until he'd tenderly laid her back against her pillows. Then he built the pillows up so that her chest was elevated.

"Is that right, Doctor?"

"Right as rain, lad. I'm leaving another dose here for you to give her in two hours."

"Won't we have the other medicine by then?"

"I don't know, lad. If we don't, remember: Two hours."

"Two hours. Right."

Dr. Swift frowned at Rose as he packed his black bag. "If her chest begins to tighten, we'll try mustard plasters."

Cullen took out the pocket watch he'd inherited from his maternal grandmother. Lord, a lot of time had gone by since they'd brought Rose here. He passed a hand over his eyes, and was startled when he felt the doctor's hand on his shoulder again.

"Buck up, lad. I know you'll do everything you can for her. I'll be praying for her, too. And for you."

"Thank you." Cullen's voice was thick.

Thirteen

Nurse McGinty arrived at the inn sometime after Dr. Swift left, and took over Rose's room like a general capturing a battlefield. Cullen didn't begrudge her air of command; in fact, he appreciated it, since it seemed to indicate that the nurse knew what she was doing.

He found it a torment, though, watching Rose waver between fever and chills, life and death. In the hours after Nurse McGinty arrived, Cullen stayed by Rose's side, in spite of knowing the nurse wished him to perdition more often than she'd ever be likely to admit.

"You're not doing her any good, Mr. O'Banyon," she said in her most severe tone—which was very severe, indeed, and reminded Cullen of the nuns at school. "And you're not doing me any good, either, with all your fussing and stamping about."

"I'm staying," Cullen said stubbornly. "I can't leave. I'd go mad, wondering and worrying."

"If you must remain in the room, at least stay out of my way."

"Yes, ma'am."

Nurse McGinty shot him a skeptical glance, but he was too worried about Rose to be sarcastic. He honestly tried to stay out of her way. Of course, every time she left

Rose's side, he took her place and had to be shooed away again, but he didn't consider that as being in the way. He considered it a condition necessary to maintaining his own sanity. He didn't like to think about Rose possibly dying, but he did, every waking minute. He wasn't sure what would happen to him if she died. He wasn't sure he could stand it.

Kate was not so stubborn. Nurse McGinty managed to cow Kate without more than a steely glance every now and then. Even Kate, however, ventured to tiptoe to Rose's bedside whenever the nurse left the room.

She laid a cool, damp cloth on Rose's forehead. Cullen handed her the old one, which was now hot from Rose's fever. "What do you think, Mr. O'Banyon?" Kate whispered. "Does she seem any better to you?"

Cullen swallowed the curt *no* that immediately leaped to his tongue. Poor Kate didn't deserve his anger, no matter how much Cullen's baser self wanted to blame her for everything. "I'm not sure," he equivocated. "I wish we could get some of those powders the doctor told us about."

As if on cue, the door opened and Dr. Swift walked in, closely followed by Nurse McGinty, whose very walk, accompanied by crisp rustlings from her white uniform, proclaimed her efficiency. Cullen rose to face the doctor, praying he had some miracle in his black bag.

"Salicylic powders!" the doctor proclaimed, holding up a brown vial that looked as if it contained white powder.

Cullen's heart jumped. "Thank God," he whispered.

Kate murmured, "What kind of powders?"

"Salicylic," said Nurse McGinty, frowning at Kate, who scurried back to the corner she'd staked out for herself during the nurse's occupation of the room.

Kate said, "Oh."

Cullen was more enthusiastic. "Wonderful. How do you administer them?"

"Stir them into water and try to get them down her throat," Dr. Swift said, proceeding to act on his own advice. "They taste pretty bad, but I don't think she's in any condition to complain."

Cullen feared the doctor was right.

Nurse McGinty stood back, folded her hands at her waist, and waited, with an austere expression on her face, for the doctor to finish. She scowled once at Cullen, but gave it up when he scowled back and didn't relinquish his position at Rose's bedside.

"I'll lift her for you, Doctor," he said, giving Nurse McGinty a good glare to prevent her from trying to usurp his authority. She merely sniffed.

"Fine, fine," Dr. Swift said. "We'll have to work quickly, because the powders tend to settle fast. Lift her up, lad, and I'll keep stirring."

Cullen did as he was told. Rose still felt as though she might ignite any second, she was so hot, and the fresh nightgown Kate had put on her was now as wet as the old one. Cullen's insides cramped with fear for her. "She's hot as a firecracker."

"This will help," Nurse McGinty said, sounding as sure of herself as she usually did, which was quite.

"Aye, they're said to," Dr. Swift confirmed.

Cullen almost took heart from the words of these two medical professionals. His insides still ached from Rose's latest coughing spasm, precipitated when he'd lifted her. She was weakening, and it had been almost too much of an effort for her even to cough. Her eyes hadn't opened, she'd moaned pathetically, and he feared she might drown in her own fluids if she didn't regain some strength soon. He prayed hard as the doctor spooned the medicated water into her mouth and it dribbled down her throat.

"They smell vile," Cullen murmured.

Nurse McGinty humphed, as if she didn't think Cullen should be complaining about anything so trivial as a bad smell.

"Aye, they do. I don't expect all of God's miracles smell as foul, but you can't expect everything to be served up in a tidy little pellet, now, can you?" He chuckled softly.

Cullen expected not, but was too occupied in holding Rose to comment. *Please, God, let them work. Please, God.* His heart and mind kept up a chant of prayer as, slowly but surely, the salicylic-powder-laced water trickled down Rose's throat.

When the last of the medicine had been administered, Cullen laid Rose back against the pillows and ran his hand through his hair. "How long do they take?"

"I don't know, Mr. O'Banyon. I've never used them before. This is the first time I've been able to find them."

"Good God." Cullen was appalled.

"There is no standard dosage set as yet, Mr. O'Banyon," the doctor continued. "I gave her as much as I think will do some good, but not enough to kill her."

From her corner in the room, Kate gasped.

"To *kill* her?" Horrified, Cullen stared down at Rose. "Good God, man, do you mean to say too much can be lethal?"

"So they say." Dr. Swift sounded unconcerned.

Nurse McGinty said, "For heaven's sake, Mr. O'Banyon, do you really believe Dr. Swift would do anything to hurt the woman? If her fever doesn't go down, she's going to die anyway, and this is the only medicine we have these days that's universally acknowledged to reduce fever."

Kate began sobbing.

Cullen's gaze flew wildly between the nurse and the doctor. "You sound as if this is the last resort."

The doctor and the nurse exchanged a somber glance. Cullen felt his heart sink. "It *is* a last resort, isn't it?"

For a second or two, neither professional spoke. Then Dr. Swift put a comforting hand on Cullen's shoulder. "Take heart, lad. We should see results soon."

Far from soothed, Cullen sat on Rose's bed and took up her hand. "Mrs. Flanagan, her nightgown is soaked through. Can you get another one for her?" His voice shook. He heard Kate get to her feet.

"Of course, I can." Kate's voice shook, too.

Yet it wasn't more than thirty minutes later, when

Cullen, who had been praying to a God he wasn't sure he believed in, passed a hand over Rose's forehead and thought he detected a slight lessening of the heat radiating therefrom. He sat up straight and scrutinized Rose's face closely. He pressed a hand to her forehead and then to her cheek and then to her chest.

"My God," he whispered. "I think they're working."

Nurse McGinty, who had been folding towels and putting Dr. Swift's prescription medication bottles in a tidy row on the dresser, turned abruptly. Kate, who was on her knees with her hands folded on the chair, praying, looked up.

"Let me see." Nurse McGinty abandoned her bottles and towels and strode to the bed. She bumped Cullen ruthlessly aside.

Kate struggled to her feet and tiptoed over, willing to risk a scolding from Nurse McGinty in order to ascertain the truth of Cullen's statement.

Cullen held his breath. It left him in a whoosh when the nurse said, "I do believe the miracle drug is working its miracle."

Then she smiled. She *smiled*. It was the first smile Cullen had seen on her face. He caught Kate when her knees gave out and she might have fallen. Then the two of them proceeded to make fools of themselves by crying, right in front of the nurse, who sniffed in disapproval of such an undisciplined display of emotion.

Rose wasn't out of the woods yet, however. Her lungs continued to fill with fluid regularly, and Cullen had to lift her in order to assist her to cough it out. The salicylic powders seemed to strengthen her, though—the doctor said it was because reducing the fever reduced her lethargy—and she seemed to have less and less difficulty as the days passed by.

For three days, Cullen and Kate worried together, neither one of them leaving Rose's side. More than once, Nurse McGinty found Cullen sitting beside Rose's bed, his arms folded, his head resting on them in an exhausted slumber, and had to roust him from the floor so she could do her work. She disapproved mightily, but Cullen didn't care. He wasn't going to abandon Rose in her hour of need.

He did, however, send a cablegram to MacNeill, his estate manager, telling him that he was again delayed on the road. He felt guilty about having been gone from his home and his sons for three whole weeks. He'd never been away from them for so long before. But he would have felt guilty if he'd left Rose's side, too, so he merely resigned himself to feeling guilty and stayed at the inn.

Rose opened her eyes and recognized him on the fourth day in her sickbed. Cullen hadn't meant to fall asleep in the chair he had positioned by her bed but the exhaustion had finally claimed him. Kate, who had made up a bed for herself in the parlor next door, was sleeping there. She had performed yeoman's service in assisting with nursing Rose, and Cullen had revised his overall opinion of her considerably.

"Cullen?"

Into Cullen's dreams a raspy voice intruded. It took him a moment of trying to assimilate the voice into his dream, which featured horses and his sons, before he realized it didn't belong there. Then his head snapped up so fast he nearly broke his neck, and he gaped at the patient. "Rose?" He didn't dare believe she was actually coherent and speaking.

"Cullen? What . . . where are we? I . . . don't seem to recall."

"Oh, God, Rose, you're talking!"

She frowned weakly. "Of course, I'm talking."

"No. No, Rose, you don't understand. You've been sick."

Still frowning, Rose seemed to be puzzling his comment out in her head. Her brow cleared. "Oh, yes, I remember. I got sick at Kilkenny Castle, didn't I." She flushed. "Good heavens, I remember. I fainted. How embarrassing."

"Don't even think about that now, dar . . . Rose. You've been terribly ill. You almost died." He practically choked on the words. He couldn't bear to imagine Rose dying, yet he'd been imagining nothing else for days now.

"Dear God." Her flush faded into the pallor Cullen had become accustomed to seeing on her cheeks during the last horror-filled week. "I hope I wasn't too much trouble."

Cullen's nerves danced and fluttered. It was all he could do to be rational and carry out this conversation. He wanted to set off fireworks and holler from rooftops. She was going to live!

He tried to sound firm. "For God's sake, don't worry about that now. You're getting better, and that's what's important at this point."

"Kate?" She lifted a hand, but seemed to have no strength left to keep it lifted. It flopped to the covers, and Cullen took it up. He wanted to kiss it, but didn't dare. She was still his wild, Irish Rose, the would-be adventuress, and he didn't want to jeopardize any fragile bond between them by pushing his attentions upon her. He was going to do something more to the point later. Right now, he wouldn't risk worrying her.

"She's asleep. She's been helping to nurse you."

"Oh."

"Along with the Gorgon."

"The Gorgon?" Rose blinked.

It hurt Cullen to see her eyes so lifeless and dull. But she'd get better now. She *had* to get better now. "Nurse McGinty. She's . . . very efficient."

"I see."

He almost broke down and confessed his love when she smiled at his euphemistic explanation of Nurse McGinty's steely quality. He didn't do it. He feared he'd ruin everything if he admitted his emotional state at this point.

Perhaps when she was stronger . . . But perhaps not. He needed to think this through carefully. She had ambitions, however foolish they seemed to him. From what he'd gathered, she aimed to fulfill her aunt's whim. She didn't want a man like him. She wanted grand passion and excitement and adventures. It was a depressing acknowledgement, although he had difficulty feeling glum now that Rose seemed on the road to recovery.

But he'd had a revelation during her illness. Or perhaps he'd merely stopped trying to lie to himself. He loved her. When he feared he was going to lose her—really and forever—it had become clear to him that Rose Larkin was precious to him. So precious that the notion of her slipping away had terrified him.

He wasn't sure what, if anything, he could do to keep her in his life, but he aimed to do some very thorough thinking on the matter.

Rose couldn't recall ever being so weak. When she first regained consciousness, she was so lethargic that it took every ounce of her energy to sit up and eat a tiny bit of soup. Her strength improved gradually until, by the end of the second week of her recovery, she was actually able to stand, albeit with help and a good deal of difficulty.

She clutched Cullen's arm while Kate uttered incoherent murmurs of worry and encouragement at her back.

Her legs felt as if the bones had been removed and replaced with jellied aspic. Her breathing came in short, labored gasps that hurt her lungs and didn't seem to provide enough air to fuel her body. Since her lungs had lately been infected and filled with fluid, Dr. Swift told her any pain and shortness of breath she experienced at first was only to be expected, and she shouldn't worry about it. She worried anyway.

"I've never been so sick," she whispered. She hadn't intended to whisper; she was too weak to speak more loudly.

"I'm sure that's so." Cullen's voice, on the other hand, carried a bracing quality that Rose didn't fully appreciate.

She expected an anxious father might speak to a child in just such a tone if the child were recuperating from a near-fatal illness. The knowledge didn't lighten her heart. She wanted to hear Cullen speak in other tones to her; low, soothing, *loving* tones.

She wanted, however, to thank him for his concern, as Kate had told her how very kind he'd been, but couldn't because her energy and breath were occupied in clinging tightly to his arm and attempting to put one foot in front of the other and trying to remain upright. She'd already fainted once in front of him. She'd be nailed to a stake before she'd do it again.

That night, Cullen left her and Kate together and went to his own room. Rose fought hard to keep from crying when the door shut behind him.

Kate patted her hand. "How do you feel, dear?"

Poor Kate. Rose appreciated the dear little old lady very much. She was still so concerned about Rose's welfare that she bore the appearance of a clock that had been wound too tightly. Rose almost expected her to burst from tension, and the nerves in her body to fly around the room like clock springs and bounce off the walls.

Making a valiant effort, she managed to smile at her aunt. "I'm feeling much better, Kate. Thank you so much for your help during these past few, er—how many days *has* it been?" Lord, she'd lost track of time. Her eyes closed, and she forced them open. She felt so awful. In spite of herself, her eyes drifted shut again. It seemed pitiful that even her eyelid muscles should be so out of condition after such a short little period of illness.

"It's been a little more than two weeks, dear. For one of those weeks, we hardly expected you to pull through. Mr. O'Banyon never left your side once."

Rose's eyes popped open on their own. "Really?" She hardly dared believe it.

Kate smiled sweetly. "Indeed, Rose. I believe he cares for you very much."

Not bloody likely. Rose was shocked by her own linguistic selection; she must have learned more from the girls at the French Academy than dance steps. She muttered, "I'm sure he's a very kind man, Kate. He's demonstrated it more than once."

"It was more than kindness, Rose. He was frightened for your life. We both were."

"I'm sorry to have put you through such a time, Kate. Believe me, I'd rather not have done it." Rose managed another weak smile.

"Don't be silly, Rose. Mr. O'Banyon even bullied Nurse McGinty, and that took a good deal of courage."

Rose had met Nurse McGinty soon after her fever had broken and thus her smile felt less forced than it had before. "That was kind of him, too."

"And Dr. Swift very nearly despaired of Mr. O'Banyon's own health because he was constantly by your bedside. I can't count the times I entered your room and found him slumped on the floor with his poor head resting on his folded arms at the edge of your bed. It was as if his noble heart and body had finally forced him to sleep in spite of himself."

How romantically dramatic. If Rose didn't know Kate to be the possessor of an exalted soul, she might have been more pleased by the recounting of this strange behavior on Cullen's part. As it was, she expected he'd felt morally responsible for her welfare. In other words, he was a truly noble man, and one who wouldn't abandon a friend in need.

Well, she supposed, being his friend was better than nothing. Far better.

That night, after taking supper with Cullen and Kate from trays brought in by the landlady and her daughter, Rose discovered that her hair had begun to fall out. She stared at the hairbrush in her hand in horror. "Oh, no!"

Kate, who had been peering into the mirror and slathering on night cream, swiveled the vanity stool around and peered at Rose. "What is it, dear?" She looked a fright.

Rose hardly noticed her aunt's odd appearance and fearful tone. As hard as she tried to be strong, she couldn't prevent the tears from puddling in her eyes and dripping down her cheeks. She pulled the hairs out of the bristles and gave her hair another sweep of the brush, only to draw it away, again full of long auburn hairs. She wailed, "No!"

Kate jumped up and scuttled to the bed, alarmed. "What? Oh, Rose, what's the matter?"

"My—my hair! My hair is falling out!"

Kate stared at her for a moment. "I beg your pardon?"

Rose shook the hairbrush in her aunt's face. "My hair is falling out! I can't bear it!"

"Mercy!" Kate frowned at the hairbrush, glanced once more at Rose, who was beyond reason by this time, and rushed out of the room night cream and all, closing the door with a sharp bang behind her.

Rose had never been vain of her looks. She knew she was relatively pretty, but she also knew that looks, in the overall scheme of things, meant little. One needed only to look at her father if one were in doubt of that basic principle of life. Edward Larkin been handsome as the devil, and he'd been virtually worthless as a man. If it hadn't been for her beloved aunt Kate, Rose and he probably would have starved to death.

However, the fact that her one real beauty, her hair, now seemed to be deserting her—in great huge brush-fulls, moreover—was the last straw on this particular camel's back. She hurled the hairbrush as far as her weakened arm could hurl it—not far. It bounced to the braided rug beside her bed and lay there, a mute witness to her misery. Then she buried her head in her pillow, and sobbed her heart out.

She heard the door open, but couldn't control her tears. She was *so* weak, and she'd been *so* sick, and she loved Cullen O'Banyon *so* much—and he thought of her as a pesky sister—and she simply couldn't take one little more thing.

"All right, what do we have here?"

The voice belonged to Nurse McGinty, and she sounded as indomitable and dictatorial as ever. Rose wasn't sure she could bear Nurse McGinty at this point, either. She was too distraught to answer the brusque question.

"It's her hair," Kate whispered. "She brushed it, and some of it came out."

It wasn't just *some* of it. Rose wished she had enough

strength to scream at her silly aunt. It was a *lot* of it. And it was her *hair*! Her *hair* was falling out!

Brisk footsteps neared the bed. "All right, Miss Larkin. There's no need for this fit."

A fit, was it? Furious, Rose rolled over—she'd have leaped out of the bed and pummeled Nurse McGinty if she'd had her strength—and glared up at her. The nurse was blurry around the edges through the film of her tears.

The steel-nerved nurse shook her head. Then—Rose could hardly believe her eyes. Perhaps it was only the blur making her think it—Nurse McGinty's severe expression softened. She tutted softly.

"Aye, you've had a high fever, child, and it lasted for too long. This often happens after a person sustains a prolonged and high fever. The body's hair seems to lose its grip on the scalp and thins out."

Rose wouldn't have believed herself capable of the wail that escaped her if she hadn't heard it with her own ears. She even managed a few feeble thumps on her pillow.

Kate began crying. Rose felt guilty about that, but she couldn't seem to control herself.

"Here now, lovie," Nurse McGinty said—it was the first time she'd ever used an endearment in Rose's experience of her. "There's no need to carry on so. Your hair will grow back again, and losing your hair is a far better fate than losing your life, which we feared would happen."

Rose didn't care. Cullen was going to see her bald! She couldn't say it.

The door burst open. Rose heard Kate and Nurse McGinty swirl around in alarm.

"What was that cry? Good God, what happened?"

It was Cullen. This was all Rose needed to crown the ignominy of her disgrace. She wailed again. She heard Cullen's heavy footsteps rushing to her bed, and felt the bed sink when he sat next to her. "Rose! What is it, Rose? Good God, what happened?" He lifted her into his arms, and she wept onto his strong, broad shoulder. His arms held her tightly, and she wished she could stay in them forever.

"It's her hair." Kate sobbed out her explanation.

Rose wasn't altogether surprised to hear Cullen snap, "What does her hair have to do with anything? Is she in pain? Is she suffering a relapse? What's going on?"

"It's no relapse." Nurse McGinty had recovered her stern efficiency of voice. "The poor child's hair is falling out. I have a notion she hadn't expected it and it frightened her, and now she's pitching a fit."

"Her *hair* is falling out?" Cullen sounded even more puzzled than he had when he first entered the room. "Why is her hair falling out?"

"It's the fever, Mr. O'Banyon," Nurse McGinty explained. "This often happens after a person suffers a severe illness with a prolonged high fever."

"Oh."

Rose tried to cling to him when he gently disengaged her arms and pressed her down on her pillows. He cupped her cheek with his hand and brushed tears from her face. She knew she looked a sight with her red eyes and blotchy skin, but at least she wasn't bald as well—yet. The knowledge that she soon would be made her sob again. She couldn't stop crying for the life of her.

"It will grow back again." Nurse McGinty was losing patience with her; Rose could hear it in her voice, and it made her cry harder.

Good heavens, whatever was the matter with her? She hadn't cried this much since her father died. It must be that her defenses were down, what with the strength having been sapped out of her body by the influenza or whatever it was. With a great effort, she pushed out some words. "It . . . it was the . . . the . . . the last straw."

Cullen's chuckle infuriated her. She tried to pound on him as she'd recently pounded on her pillow, but he caught her fist in his big hand and lifted it to his lips. Rose was so shocked, her tears choked to a stop. She stared at him, blinking furiously. He was kissing her hand! With her eyes swollen and her cheeks a blotchy mess and her going bald, he was kissing her hand. She didn't know what to make of it.

"It's all right, Rose," he said gently. "I know you've been through a terrible ordeal. And it must make you feel horrid to know that some of your hair is falling out. But it will grow back again. Nurse McGinty said so, and she'd never lie. The world would stop spinning if Nurse McGinty ever told a lie."

Nurse McGinty snorted her censure.

"But—but I'll be bald," Rose stammered, her words still thick with tears. "I'll be—*ugly*!" Another wail accompanied the last word.

She resented Cullen's shoulder-shaking laughter with a passion. At least her anger dried the last of her tears. She glowered up at Cullen while he tried to compose himself.

"It's not funny." She sounded like a spoiled child, knew it, hated herself for it, and couldn't help it to save her life.

"Of . . . of course not." It sounded as if Cullen were speaking while driving over a corrugated road, his voice shook so hard. Rose resented that, too.

"It's terrible, Rose," Kate ventured weakly. "But you've always had such lovely hair, and I'm sure it will still look good, even if you lose some of it."

Rose couldn't suppress a shudder. "I'll be bald," she said flatly, unwilling to contemplate any less drastic scenario for the time being.

"Nonsense," said Nurse McGinty. "I doubt sincerely that you'll lose all of your hair, Miss Larkin. Generally a body's hair gets thin for a while and then gradually grows back. You should be glad for your life, not whining about losing a few strands of hair."

The very last thing Rose cared to entertain at the moment was a sensible thought. She transferred her glower from Cullen to Nurse McGinty. "Thank you." Her voice was like ice. "I shall bear that in mind."

Kate gasped.

Nurse McGinty huffed.

Cullen burst out laughing again. Rose glared at him until he stopped. Then she said, "I'm sure you'd look fine bald, Mr. O'Banyon, but I don't believe I shall. I don't want to look ugly—I already feel horrid."

"Rose," he said when he could control his voice, "you'd look beautiful bald. As long as you're breathing, you'll always be beautiful to me."

Kate sniffled.

Nurse McGinty huffed again.

Rose gaped at him, flabbergasted.

Fourteen

Rose was over her crying fit the following morning, but she was still mighty unhappy about losing her hair. Every time she ran the brush through it, more strands came out on the bristles. She knew she should stop brushing it, but she couldn't seem to help herself.

The landlady's daughter had prepared a hot bath for her, and she'd soaked for a long time, using some of Kate's rose-scented bath salts. She was now clad in a pretty new powder blue dressing gown that Kate had bought for her, and was sitting in front of the vanity mirror, brushing her hair out. Literally.

Glumly, she hoped Nurse McGinty had been right about hair growing back after a person was over a severe illness. Rose didn't fancy having to wear hats for the rest of her life. Or wigs. Lord, Lord, she was too young to have to wear wigs and switches and so forth.

"Bother."

She knew she was being silly, that she should be grateful that she was alive, but it was hard to acknowledge that when her hair was falling out. She still felt so weak and helpless—without feeling completely ugly.

Small comfort.

She'd brushed the tangles out and was gathering her strength to stand when a tap came at the door.

After heaving an enormous sigh, Rose said, "Come in," in a dispirited voice.

"Are you up and about?" came through the door.

Every time she heard Cullen's voice, her heart jumped to her throat. She wished it wouldn't. She was having enough trouble with her body without one of its organs behaving in so irrational a manner. "More or less." That wasn't very polite. She tried again. "Yes. Please come in, Cullen." *I'll be ecstatic to see you.* She didn't tell him that part, since she was sure he'd not be pleased to hear it.

The door opened, and there he was, smiling and holding a huge box. Rose blinked at him and at the box.

"I brought you something."

"Thank you." Rose remained seated because she didn't think her legs would hold her. She felt like crying again. He was *so* kind, and *so* thoughtful. Why couldn't Kate want a man like Cullen O'Banyon for her?

Actually, she guessed Kate *did* want a man like Cullen O'Banyon for her, although not in the way Rose wanted him. In fact, Kate thought Rose already had him. It was Cullen who didn't want Rose.

Fiddlesticks. She wished her thoughts would take a more cheerful turn. She never used to be maudlin like this. Of course, she never used to be recovering from a near-fatal illness or suffering from a hopeless love, either. She decided to give herself a break and smiled at Cullen.

"May I open it?" That worked pretty well. She even sounded almost excited, so she decided to try again. "It's such a large box."

"Kate and I went out together this morning. She picked them out."

"Oh, Cullen, you shouldn't have." It was trite, but she meant it. She already owed him too much.

"Nonsense. It was a pleasure. Kate is quite the shopper, isn't she?"

"Shopping is her greatest pleasure in life," Rose told him with a genuine laugh. She was surprised to hear it.

She'd had enough time to compose herself, and she believed she'd be able to stand without teetering or falling over, so she did, then walked to the chair beside the bed. Cullen toted the huge box over and set it on the bed.

Kate entered the room at that moment, bearing a tray laden with tea things. "Oh, Rose! Just wait until you see what Mr. O'Banyon got for you! He was so kind! So thoughtful!"

"Nonsense," Cullen said again, this time sounding embarrassed. "Kate picked everything out. I only went along with her."

"And he paid for everything, Rose. He wouldn't let me pay for a single thing."

Rose felt awful. "You shouldn't have let him do that, Kate."

"Oh, you silly girl! Of course, it's all right, what with your arrangement and all."

Cullen and Rose exchanged a glance and for the first time since before she got sick, Rose felt herself blush. She glanced down, unable to meet his gaze, and stared at her hands. Her fingers looked gaunt; she must have lost a good deal of weight during her illness. With a sigh, she guessed she might as well lose weight. Why should her hair be the only thing to desert her?

"Don't be silly, either of you," Cullen said with something of a chill to his voice. "Here, Rose. Please open this. It's a gift, because I enjoy giving gifts, and if you don't accept it, I shall be very unhappy with you."

There he was, treating her like a troublesome little sister again. Well, she imagined he meant what he'd said about being unhappy if she didn't accept his gift. He was like that—a genuine gentleman. She sighed again. "Thank you very much, Cullen. I'm sure I shall love it."

"Open it and see."

She did love it. It was an entire ensemble, including a basque in a creamy color and a brown-and-cream striped skirt to go with it. The colors were perfect for her. And the hat . . .

Rose's eyes filled with tears when she saw the hat. It

was beautiful, and it looked as if it had been specifically designed for a woman with the problem she was experiencing now. Nobody would ever be able to tell that she had thin—or no—hair when she was wearing this gorgeous creation with its wide brim and sweeping ostrich plumes. She put it on and smiled at Cullen. "Thank you so much."

"I don't want you wearing that gown yet," Cullen told her sternly. "Dr. Swift says you need to rest for another few days before you venture outside, but Kate thought you'd feel more the thing if you had a new ensemble to wear when you do go out of doors again."

"Thank you," she said once more. The words were supremely inadequate to express what she was feeling, but she didn't have any others. She turned to Kate, who was beaming at her, her hands folded at her waist. "Thank you, Kate. You're both too good to me."

"Don't be silly," Cullen said.

"Nonsense, Rose," Kate said. "Mr. O'Banyon said he wants only the very best for you during your recuperation. He even proposed a—oh!"

Kate looked stricken, from which Rose deduced she'd been about to let a secret cat out of a secret bag. She saw Cullen roll his eyes in mock disgust, then smile. Rose guessed it wasn't so terribly secret a cat.

"He proposed what?" she asked, wishing he'd offer her a proposal of another kind than she expected this one was.

"Oh, Mr. O'Banyon, I'm so sorry!"

Because Kate seemed genuinely distressed, Rose said, "I'm sure Mr. O'Banyon isn't angry with you, Kate."

"Of course I'm not," Cullen said gallantly.

He smiled such a lovely, sweet smile at Kate, that Rose had to swallow. Oh, dear, she hoped her strength would come back soon, because this wanting to burst into tears every time she felt the tiniest bit of emotion was wearing in the extreme.

Kate sniffled. "Well, I *am* sorry, Mr. O'Banyon. There's just no trusting me with a secret. Ask Rose, if you don't believe me, although I expect you do by this time, since I let your secret out."

Hoping to prompt an explanation out of one of them, Rose murmured, "Not completely."

Kate stopped twittering and blinked at her. Cullen chuckled. "That's true. So, shall I ask her, Kate, or would you like to be the one?"

"Oh, please, Mr. O'Banyon, you must ask her. It's your surprise, after all."

"I wish somebody would tell me," Rose said, feeling tired and short-tempered in spite of herself. She wanted to crawl back in bed and cry for awhile, and then sleep for a year or so. For about the nine hundredth time, she wished she were completely recovered.

"I don't suppose I ever mentioned two little boys that are of my acquaintance, did I?"

"No, no you did not," said Rose, a sense of unease settling over her. What was Cullen talking about? Did he have sons that were from his first marriage? He didn't look the sort of fellow who'd befriend small children. He looked like a sophisticated man who'd leave the rearing of children to others. For the first time she wondered if his marriage had produced any offspring, but didn't have the heart to ask, because the notion made her jealous. How foolish of her. How could she forget? The mere fact that Cullen knew and liked two little boys had astonished Rose.

"Well, those two little boys live in the country."

"Oh?" So what? Rose wanted to ask. She knew she was being churlish.

"What I suggest," Cullen said at last, "is that you and Mrs. Flanagan accompany me to the home of those two little boys. It's a beautiful farm in the picturesque Irish countryside. It's peaceful and conducive to rest and recuperation. I propose we go there as soon as you're well enough to travel. Dr. Swift said it won't be much longer now, and the farm is very quiet. Dr. Swift said you need to take extremely good care of yourself and rest as much as possible for several more weeks."

His smile looked quite wistful to Rose, although she acknowledged herself to be unable to form sound opinions at the moment. "A farm in the country?" A farm in the country sounded lovely, actually. She wouldn't have credited the stylish and sophisticated Cullen O'Banyon to have much association with farmers.

"A horse farm, it is, in County Clare. It's a pretty place, all green rolling hills and good Irish horses."

Horses again. Rose was interested, though. At least he wasn't offering to take her to a racetrack. She thought she might appreciate horses in a meadow or something. And the Irish countryside that she had seen had been beautiful.

"It sounds restful."

His face clouded. "If you don't want to go . . ."

"Oh, no! I'd love to. Truly, Cullen, I'd be delighted to visit a horse farm. I—it sounds wonderful, actually."

"It's not very exciting." Obviously, he didn't believe her.

Not very exciting sounded heavenly to Rose. "I think I've had my fill of excitement for a while." She hadn't intended her voice to sound as sarcastic as it did when it hit the air.

He took up her hand. "Are you sure, Rose? I don't want to bore you to death."

Lord, if he only knew. The only thing she'd ever wanted in her entire life was the boredom of security—if a body could equate security with boredom. "Don't be silly, Cullen. If I experienced any more excitement at this point, I'd probably fall over in a heap at your feet, and I'm sure you're tired of me doing that." She smiled at him, hoping her expression conveyed her sincerity. "I'd *love* to go to a horse farm for a visit."

He sucked in a breath and let it out in what sounded very much like a sigh of relief. Rose was sure she was mistaken about that.

"Good." He stood up. Rose was disappointed. "Then it's settled. I'll send a cablegram to the estate manager."

"The estate manager?" Rose glanced up at him. "Whose farm is it?"

For the briefest second, Cullen appeared annoyed with himself. "Actually, the farm has been in my family for a number of years. Around three hundred, actually."

"My goodness." Rose was impressed. She wanted to ask more questions, but Cullen seemed to have withdrawn slightly.

"County Clare," Kate whispered dreamily. "I remember it well."

"Yes. Well it sounds lovely. I'll have a grand time, I'm sure."

Kate, who had nearly recovered her composure, clasped her hands to her bosom. "Oh, Rose, just wait until you see County Clare. It's absolutely beautiful!"

"It is that, indeed," Cullen supplied.

"I'm sure of it."

At the end of another five days, Dr. Swift gave his approval for Rose to take a relatively lengthy journey. Nurse McGinty's lips were pinched tight when he rendered his verdict after listening to Rose's lungs, checking her throat, taking her temperature, and asking her about a thousand questions.

"I suppose you're fit to travel, young lady, but don't overdo it."

"I don't think I could overdo anything, even if I tried, actually."

Especially since she now had to wear a hat everywhere she went. Rose had never much liked hats, at least not on an everyday, all-day basis. They were an imperative part of her wardrobe these days, however, unless she wanted to get a sunburn on her scalp every time she set foot out of doors. It was very discouraging.

She felt like asking Dr. Swift when she could expect her hair to grow back, but didn't since she'd asked that same question every day for a week, and his answer never changed. It was always, "In time," and it was always accompanied with a laugh that Rose didn't appreciate.

Nurse McGinty sniffed. "Foolishness," she snapped. "Taking such a trip after being so ill."

"Tut, tut, Mrs. McGinty. A rest in the country is exactly what this doctor orders. I'm sure Miss Larkin and Mrs.

Flanagan will enjoy it. Mr. O'Banyon will take care of them."

Yes, thought Rose. He's good at that. Her heart squeezed.

"And," the doctor continued, "it's sure to be quiet and peaceful in the country, so you can get your strength back in a relaxed atmosphere."

Cullen, who had been standing by the door, muttered, "It's crammed full of peace and quiet, actually."

He sounded wry, and Rose's heart squeezed again. She wished he and she wanted the same things out of life. But they didn't. She craved peace and quiet. He was a rake and a ladies' man. At least, he looked like one. It was true, he hadn't seemed to want *her*, but that was merely a matter of taste.

And she'd better not dwell on it, or she'd cry and disgrace herself. Again.

Dr. Swift gave her shoulder a gentle pat. "The roses will be back in those pretty cheeks in no time with a dose of good country air."

Now there was something to look forward to. Rose sighed and managed what she expected was a sickly smile.

The next morning, after the landlady's daughter had helped Kate pack their bags—Cullen wouldn't allow Rose to so much as pick up a fallen stocking, claiming she needed to rest—the ladies set out for County Clare in Cullen's luxurious, roomy traveling carriage. Rose was clad in her pretty new cream-and-brown traveling ensemble, including her hat, and she felt almost—but not quite—human.

Cullen had padded the already well-cushioned seat with pillows and blankets for Rose's traveling comfort. Until she met Cullen, the only mode of transportation Rose had ever endured was shank's mare, except for the ship and train with Kate. This was ever so much more comfortable than walking.

Rose was flabbergasted when Nurse McGinty had to press a handkerchief to her eyes to catch the tears. When Kate noticed the nurse's emotional reaction to their departure, she began crying too, and so did the landlady and the landlady's daughter. Because she couldn't help herself, Rose joined them, and it was a watery farewell they all bade to one another.

"Thank you!" she called, waving a handkerchief out the window. "I'll write and tell you how things are going!"

Nurse McGinty nodded and sniffed. "I'll write, too!"

Kate was too overcome for words.

Cullen watched stoically, and Rose loved him even more than she had before for bearing with a herd of weeping women without so much as a peeved expression on his face.

Sitting on the bench opposite Rose and Kate and taking note of Rose's pallor, thinness, and appearance of lassitude, Cullen felt his heart ache. He wouldn't show his worry, though. Not by so much as a frown. Dr. Swift had warned him that Rose's condition remained frail, and that anxiety would be almost worse for her than another drenching rainstorm.

Therefore, he kept up a stream of travelogue as the carriage rumbled out of town and into the countryside. It would take them three days of easy traveling to reach his farm, and he was fully willing for it to take another three if it would aid in Rose's recovery. He'd give pretty much anything he owned to see the sparkle return to her lovely eyes and the bloom to her cheeks.

He still hadn't decided exactly how to win Rose's affections. If she insisted on becoming a man's mistress—his mistress—he wasn't sure he could do it. Yet if that's what she wanted, he wasn't sure he could let her go. It was a quandary, and one he was unfit to conquer at the moment. All he knew was that he loved her. Fearing for her life had cleared up any doubt in his mind about that. Everything else would just have to wait.

Neither of the ladies seemed to be paying much attention to his lecture on Irish history and the beauties to be found in this part of the country, so he subsided after a while and passed the time by watching Rose out of the corner of his eye. He didn't want to appear to be keeping an eagle-eye on her, but he was still so worried about her that his insides hurt.

They'd been rolling along for upwards of an hour in silence, with Rose and Kate gazing in what seemed like rapt attention to the passing scenery, when at last Rose spoke.

They'd left all signs of the big city of Kilkenny behind them. "This is such beautiful country."

Cullen was pleased that she seemed to be taking an interest in the landscape. "Aye, Ireland's famous for its beautiful countryside." He smiled so as to assure her that he was feeling chipper and that she could depend on him if she needed his strength.

Her own smile in return seemed tepid. He tried harder. "Tomorrow or the next day, we'll be traveling through some countryside that's considerably more hilly than this. You'll begin to see more sheep on the hillsides, as well as horses. We might even see some cattle, although we Irish raise more sheep and horses than we do cattle."

"I see."

Gad, *I see?* That was it? Cullen could have roared in frustration.

"Oh, look, Rose!" Kate grabbed Rose's arm and pointed.

Cullen blessed Kate for a saint when the expression on Rose's face changed from one of stoic endurance to one of faint interest. He looked, too. There in the distance, he saw what Kate had been pointing out to Rose: the ruins of Jerpoint Abbey.

"That's an old Cistercian abbey, ladies," he said in his helpful tour-guide's voice.

"An abbey," Rose whispered, as if she'd never seen anything so wonderful—which he knew she had, since he'd taken her to a couple of them already.

Kate shook her head, as if in wonder. "Isn't it marvelous, Rose?"

Rose nodded.

Cullen eyed the two women curiously for a moment before he figured out where their awe had sprung from. They were from America. Of course. He'd forgotten for a moment how relatively young their homeland was. Anything over a century old in the new world was a marvel, he supposed. Here, ruins were an everyday part of life. In truth, the Irish people might be considered ruins of a once-proud race.

He was getting gloomy, and he told himself to snap out of it. Soon he would be able to embrace William and Ferris again, and that was something joyful to look forward to. Of course, he supposed he'd have to pretend they weren't his sons.

No, that was stupid. One of these days Rose would certainly uncover the unexciting, dull, non-dashing truth about him. And it wasn't fair to ask his sons to pretend they weren't his. Cullen was more proud of his boys than he was of anything else on earth, including his prize-winning horses.

With a sigh, he decided to solve all of his problems later. With luck, they'd solve themselves, and he wouldn't even have to think about them. Not that he had but one problem, and that was undoubtedly hopeless. He was in love with a woman who believed him to be something other than what he was, and who believed she wanted something other than what was good for her.

Moreover, she'd probably reject him out of hand once she discovered the truth. She'd only thrown herself at him at the inn because she thought he was rich and a rakehell.

Jesus, Mary, and Joseph, the fixes one could get oneself in to without the slightest intention. He'd been merely attempting to extract an innocent girl from the clutches of a beast when he'd met Rose. He'd not intended to fall in love with her.

Life cherished its little jokes, he reckoned. Small wonder the Irish were such a cynical lot.

"This countryside is so beautiful, Cullen. I wonder that you ever want to leave it to travel to the city."

Cullen's head jerked up. Had Rose said that? He squinted at her, detected the meditative expression on her face, and decided her evident craving for peace and quiet was the result of her illness. "I expect life in the country gets tiresome to one who yearns for excitement," he said in as noncommittal a voice as he could drum up.

"Yes," said Kate with a sigh. "But excitement can get tiresome after a while, too."

Had she really said that? Kate, the one who wanted Rose to become an adventuress? Kate, the power behind the throne, as it were? He wondered if he should clean out his ears. "Perhaps." He didn't want to say anything that might put either lady off. Rose would find out soon enough that he was a fraud; he didn't want to rush the inevitable.

Anyhow, they were probably both merely seeking a period of rejuvenation after an ordeal. As soon as Rose got her health back in full, she'd want to be off and seeking men and adventures again. The truth made Cullen's stomach cramp for a moment. When he had to bid her a final farewell, he was certain his heart would go with her.

But no. That was romantic nonsense. He'd always have plenty of love left for his sons.

The love he felt for the boys was different, though, and as much as Cullen tried to buck up his spirits, they didn't seem to want to be bolstered. He decided to try to dispel his gloomy mood with chatter. "When you're feeling better, Rose, you might enjoy visiting that old abbey. There are some wonderful carvings there. You can get an idea of how life was lived in the Middle Ages."

Rose pulled back the curtain to get a better look at the old ruins. She seemed honestly fascinated, and Cullen was pleased. "It's difficult to imagine people living on this land for so many hundreds of years—thousands of years, I suppose, rather."

"Yes. My father used to tell me so many tales." Kate's voice had a nostalgic tinge to it. "All about monks and priests and how they used to tease the English. In the stories, the Irish always won the frays. I suppose that's how all folk stories are."

Cullen's smile didn't have to be forced this time. "Aye. We Irish are a proud lot."

"It all seems terribly sad to me," murmured Rose. "I

suppose that's why so many natives of Ireland move to the United States, because they don't perceive any opportunities here."

"Exactly," said Cullen. "All of God's creatures crave freedom, I imagine. I consider myself very fortunate."

"Yes, you're very lucky."

He was appalled to see Rose lift a hand and brush tears away. Before he thought to stop himself, he leaned toward her and took up her hand. "Rose! What is it? Are you feeling ill?"

Damnation! He wasn't supposed to make her anxious. Cullen gave himself a hard mental backhand upside the head.

She sniffled and gave him a weak smile. "Not at all, Cullen. I think I'm simply being silly. I find I'm very emotional these days. A leftover weakness from the influenza, I imagine."

Cullen let go of her hand, sat back against the soft squabs of the carriage, and cleared his throat. "I imagine you're right."

"Dr. Swift said you'd be feeling poorly for a while," Kate put in, although she, too, appeared uneasy.

"Please," said Rose. "Don't pay any attention to my whims. I'm sure I'll be fine. I feel quite well, actually. I've felt well for several days now."

He didn't believe her. She sure as the devil didn't look well. Lifting his walking stick, he poked the top of the carriage, then leaned out. "Johnny, will you pull up for a bit? I think the ladies need to rearrange themselves."

"Oh, please, no," Rose cried. "Please don't stop on my account."

"Nonsense!" He hadn't meant to sound so crabby, and sucked in a deep breath to calm himself. She didn't need for him to fall apart. She needed rest and relaxation, not temper tantrums on his part. "Dr. Swift told me that we need to take frequent stops along the way. It's not good for you to be jolted around for any length of time."

"Jolted around?" Rose's eyes opened wide. "For

heaven's sake, Cullen, we're traveling in the lap of luxury. There's no jolting involved."

"True, true," Kate murmured, smiling at Cullen.

"Nevertheless, we're taking a rest. It's probably lunchtime, anyhow, and the landlady packed us a fine lunch. We'll just spread a blanket out on the grass under a tree and dine *al fresco*."

Rose expelled what sounded like a soulful sigh. "Very well. I hate being an invalid."

"I'm sure you do, but it won't last forever." At any rate, Cullen prayed it wouldn't. Dr. Swift had told him that such dreadful illnesses as the one Rose had lived through sometimes had lasting effects. Indeed, such infections as scarlet fever and rheumatic fever and so forth could weaken a person's heart forever. Why, Rose might die in a year or two from what she'd been through if he didn't take good care of her.

Damnation, he had to stop thinking like that. He helped Kate out of the carriage, and then lifted Rose down without even attempting to assist her, a maneuver that evidently surprised her, because she reached for his shoulders and gave a tiny gasp. He wished he could simply take her in his arms, lie down with her on the blanket, and let her sleep in his arms until she was well again.

Silly Cullen.

The break from traveling did her a world of good, though. Cullen, watching her like a hawk, was pleased when she ate a piece of cold chicken and some grapes. Kate pressed some bread and butter on her, and she managed to eat that, too.

"I do believe my appetite is returning," Rose said at one point.

"It's the country air," Kate told her, sounding sure of herself. "It perks a body right up. It's always so bracing."

"That must be it." Rose gave her aunt such a sweet smile that Cullen had to look away from it. He could imagine a motherly Rose looking at her newborn baby with that same sweet love.

Lord, he was losing his mind. She didn't want sweetness and motherhood. She wanted adventure and rich men lavishing jewels and money on her.

Rose did not demur when after they'd eaten and climbed back inside the carriage Cullen and Kate suggested she try to sleep. Nor did she demur when Cullen suggested she prop a pillow against his shoulder and lean on him. In fact, he could have sworn she flushed a little bit and looked shyly pleased.

He was definitely losing his mind.

Fifteen

Rose didn't let on at first when she woke up from her nap. The carriage was so well-sprung, and she was so comfortable—pressed up against Cullen with his arm was so blissfully around her—that she didn't want the moment to end.

This is exactly what she'd wish for if she were allowed to have a wish come true. Those people one read about in fairy tales were so foolish, to want money and castles and jewels and so forth. All Rose wanted was Cullen and peace. It'd be nice to have Kate too, because Rose loved her very much, in spite of her sometimes odd notions, and wouldn't want to lose track of her. Children. She wanted children.

Oh, very well, she wanted it all.

Ridiculous Rose.

"Are you awake?"

Cullen's soft question provoked a sigh from her. She didn't want the moment to end. Nevertheless, she was probably squashing him and ruining his coat, and she didn't want to annoy him above all things. She sat up and rubbed her eyes. "I think so."

"You had a fine nap, Rose," Kate said, sending her one of her beaming smiles.

Rose smiled back. "I must have. It feels as though I've been asleep for a hundred years, like Rip Van Winkle."

Kate giggled. Cullen smiled. Rose wondered if he'd ever heard the American story of Rip Van Winkle. She also felt guilty. "Did your poor arm go to sleep with my weight pressed against it, Cullen?"

"Not at all. You haven't enough weight to squash a bug, my dear. We'll fatten you up, though, once we get to the farm. Some good thick cream on your porridge. Fat rashers of bacon, good stewed mutton, a little bubble and squeak, and some mash and country ham will do the trick."

"Yes," said Rose, suddenly depressed. "I'm sure you're right."

He was treating her like a sister again. Well, that's the way he thought of her. She might as well get used to it.

Three days later, when the carriage crested the hill overlooking the pristine glory of Cullen's home, his heart swelled with love for this land of his. And his boys, whom he'd soon have in his arms again.

Glancing at Rose and Kate, he expanded his love to include the two of them. Not that Rose didn't already occupy a place of honor in his heart, more's the pity. She still looked pale and tired, but he took heart from the faint color that had returned to her cheeks during their long journey.

He'd taken it slowly, cognizant the whole time of Dr. Swift's warning about not letting Rose tire herself too much. She'd been a compliant patient, too, which worried him. When he'd first met her, her spirits had been bubbly with youth and vigor as well as the joy and excitement of life. He hoped to see her thus again one day—if she stayed with him long enough. His insides gave a spasm, and he commanded himself to stop dwelling on what might happen in the future: first he needed to take care of the here and now.

"This is the most beautiful place I've ever seen."

Rose's soft voice filtered through his thoughts, and when he realized what she'd said, he turned to peer at her. "You mean Ireland?"

She nodded. "Ireland is beautiful, all of it that I've seen, but this particular place is wonderful. It's—it's almost like magic."

"You mean this valley?" Cullen didn't quite dare believe his ears.

"Yes." Rose heaved a huge sigh. "I'd like to stay here forever and ever."

"It *is* glorious," Kate added. "It's like something out of a fairy tale."

Cullen took heart. Maybe Rose wouldn't tire of his home soon if she considered it so beautiful. "I'm glad you like it. This is where we're going to be staying."

Rose's head jerked around and she stared at him, her eyes wide. "Here? In this gorgeous valley? In that charming place?" She gestured at his home, which was a large country house, but nowhere near as grand as some of the castles and English estates they'd visited during their tour of the land. "You *own* all that?"

"Yes, indeed. It's a horse farm, and it's home to two little boys, William and Ferris. Charming lads. I trust they'll be well behaved and that they don't annoy you too much, Rose."

"Two little boys," Rose breathed. "How wonderful for them to be able to grow up here."

"It's ever so much nicer to grow up in the country than in the big, noisy, dirty city," said Kate, still staring out the window.

"It sounds like heaven to me," Rose murmured.

Well, now, this was a pleasant turn of events, and one Cullen hadn't anticipated. He smiled, pleased that their initial impression of his home was a favorable one. Because he genuinely wanted to know, he asked, "Do you enjoy being around children, Rose? The boys who live here are sturdy lads and generally not a nuisance, although they're a lively pair." They were as close to perfection as two boys could get in his not-so-impartial opinion, but he spared her that.

"I love children," she said. "I'd like to have dozens of my own one day."

"Is that so?" Hmmm. Wanting to have scores of children didn't exactly square with Cullen's impression of what adventuresses generally craved out of life. Perhaps he'd misjudged Rose.

But no. She was thinking of life down the road. After she'd experienced a few of the exciting escapades she sought.

Again she nodded. "Yes. And to be able to rear them in a place like this would be as close to perfection as I expect child-rearing could get. Oh!" She sat up straighter and leaned out the open carriage window. "Look at all those beautiful horses!"

"Aye, they're a grand sight," Cullen said, swelling with pride and satisfaction. He did have a wonderful home, and he was glad that Rose recognized the fine quality of his horses. His herd was the best in Ireland, if he did say so himself. Cresting that hill and looking out over his valley always made his heart sing.

"I'm so glad we're staying here!" Rose impulsively took Cullen's hand. He jerked a little bit, involuntarily, and when she looked up, he got trapped by her eyes. Damnation, but he wished he could shake her silly notions out of her head. He wanted to make her want to stay here. With him. Forever. He wondered what it would take to make her alter her plans.

Recognizing the futility of idle daydreams, he squeezed her hand gently. "I'm glad you're looking forward to it." He'd try to figure out a way to win her love later. Right now he needed to get her settled. Although she was better, she still needed a good deal of rest.

She swallowed, an odd expression on her face, and withdrew her hand from his. "I can't thank you enough for coming to our rescue and for seeing me through my illness and for bringing us here. This is so wonderful of you."

She started crying, and Cullen was horrified. "Here now, Rose. Don't cry. Please." He whipped his own fresh handkerchief out of his pocket and pressed it into her hand.

She mopped her cheeks and sniffled. "I beg your pardon. I fear my emotions are still very poorly contained. I'm sure I'll be able to hold them back better once I recover some more of my strength."

Kate, who had begun patting Rose's knee, also had tears in her eyes. "Oh, Rose, I'm so dreadfully sorry you've had to endure this awful hardship."

"Hardship?" Rose managed a watery chuckle. "Merciful heavens, if all of the poor people in the world who got sick were as well cared-for as I've been, there'd be no hardships left. I fear we'd all go soft."

Cullen appreciated her spunk, but he knew better. While it was true she'd been given medical attention and had experienced fine nursing during her illness, she'd nearly died, and that was a hardship. He hoped never to have to see either of his sons in a like situation.

Speaking of his sons . . . He lifted his walking stick and rapped on the roof of the carriage. Leaning out, he said, "Johnny, do you see anyone from the farm yet?" He'd cabled Ben MacNeill to be on the lookout and to ride out with a horse for him as soon as he saw the carriage cresting the hill.

"Aye, Mr. O'Banyon. It looks like Mr. MacNeill, and he's got another horse with him."

"Good." Satisfaction filled Cullen. He was truly blessed. Not only did he have a lovely home and sufficient income in a country where most of his fellow natives were impoverished, but his staff was absolutely reliable. Turning to the ladies, he said, "I cabled to Mr. Ben MacNeill, the manager of this estate, that we'd be coming. As soon as he draws abreast of the carriage, I'll get out and go on ahead of you. I want to make sure everything is in readiness for your visit."

"My goodness, how thoughtful," said Kate.

"Are you sure you don't mind us descending on you, Cullen?" Rose looked worried.

"I'm thrilled to have you under my roof, Rose." And there was a truth if he'd ever told one.

"Truly?"

"Absolutely."

Cullen didn't wait around to elaborate. As soon as the

carriage had halted, he was out of it and shaking Ben Mac-Neill by the hand.

"How are you, Mr. O'Banyon? We've all missed you here."

"Aye, and I've missed all of you, too. Let me introduce you to the two ladies who will be stopping at the farm for a while, Ben."

He performed introductions, and was pleased to see that Rose and Kate's egalitarian American attitudes had extended across the ocean. He'd never yet met an American who truly understood the distinctions in rank that were so important to the English. He liked them for it, too. Both ladies were as gracious to Ben as if they were being introduced to a duke. Actually, Ben was a prince among estate agents, so he deserved their consideration.

The two men rode back to the house a few minutes later. It was good to be in the saddle again. Cullen lifted his face to the sun and felt the clean country air chase his doubts away. Rose would learn his true identity one of these days, no matter what, and he'd face it then. Perhaps by that time she'd have come to care for him as he cared for her. In the meantime, he could hardly wait to see his boys again.

They were waiting for him on the large porch of his house. Cullen had been contemplating asking the boys to lie and say they weren't his sons, but the notion dried up and blew away as soon as he saw them. Lord God in heaven, he loved those boys. He'd no more deny them than he would deny the existence of Christ. He was ashamed of himself for even thinking of drawing them into his lies. As soon as they caught sight of him, the boys raced down the porch steps and bounded over to him.

"Father! Father!" William, the elder, cried.

Ferris wasn't far behind. Only six, he was a mere year younger than William and didn't let that single year get in his way. Cullen was overjoyed to see his sons. They were both as sturdy as he remembered, and appeared healthy and fit.

Blond and blue-eyed, they looked very much like Judith, who had been as fair as Cullen was dark. His heart twinged slightly as he recalled the years of his marriage. He so seldom thought about them now.

He was laughing by the time he'd dismounted, and he swept both boys up into his arms and kissed them soundly. "And how are the two of you?" He gave them another smacking kiss each and lowered them to the sod—the good Irish sod he loved so well. "You've been eating well, I see. I can hardly lift the two of you."

"Margaret made us eat everything on our plates," Ferris said, grinning at his father and climbing up his leg.

"Good for Margaret." Margaret O'Malley was the boys' nurse, and she was as bighearted and as stern as any woman alive. She'd reared Cullen and his sister, and she was doing the same for his boys, and Cullen cherished her as he would a blood relative.

"And, sir, wait until you see Bonnie's foal," William said. "He's a beauty. Got a perfect white star right there." William pointed to his forehead.

"Ah, so Bonnie had herself a wee colt, did she?" Cullen was happy to hear it. And, since he trusted William's opinion about horses nearly as much as he trusted Ben's, he expected she'd produced a fine foal.

Taking a son's hand in each of his, Cullen walked up the porch steps and decided he was a truly lucky man. Whatever happened with Rose in the long run, his blessings abounded. He'd try his best to dwell upon them and not worry about a future he couldn't control.

As soon as they reached the house, he saw his staff lined up, grinning almost as happily as his sons. Aye, he was blessed in truth. He greeted his staff and then allowed William and Ferris to drag him into the kitchen where Margaret sat with a cup of tea and the cook. Both ladies had been with his family for decades, and he greeted them as the old friends they were. He patiently endured Margaret's scolding for having been away for so long. Then he embarrassed both women by kissing them on their soft, wrinkled cheeks and withdrawing from his pocket a small gift for each of them. He'd been carrying the thing around since before he met up with Rose and Kate.

Leaving the women in a dither of happy surprise, he took his sons into the parlor. "We've got some guests coming in a moment, William and Ferris, in the traveling carriage. There's a lady named Mrs. Flanagan. She's been traveling through Ireland with her niece, Miss Larkin. Miss Larkin took sick in Kilkenny."

"Bad sick?" Ferris wanted to know. He understood that his mother had died of being bad sick, and Cullen knew the notion of illness troubled him.

Cullen ruffled Ferris's fair hair. "Aye, she was bad sick, but she's getting better. The doctor told her it would be good to spend some time recuperating in the country, so I invited both ladies to stop with us for a while."

"Are they old ladies?" William asked, his blue eyes solemn.

William had always been the more serious of the two lads. Cullen expected his constant air of sobriety had something to do with his having been a little older than Ferris when he'd lost his mother.

"Mrs. Flanagan is about as old as Margaret, William. Miss Larkin is much younger."

"Is she as old as you?"

Cullen experienced another sudden pang in the area of his heart. "No, son. She's younger than I."

"Is she going to be our mother?"

Ferris's question caught Cullen completely off guard. He even jumped a little. "What kind of a question is that?"

The little boy shrugged. "I only wondered."

"You'd best not wonder about such things, lads." Cullen kept his voice kind. "And Miss Larkin has been gravely ill, so I don't want the two of you pestering her."

"We won't," William said staunchly.

"I'm sure you won't." Cullen, mindful of the brevity of childhood, drew both of his children onto his knees and nuzzled their necks. Ferris giggled. William squirmed, embarrassed. It wouldn't be long, Cullen knew, before neither lad would stand for such tenderness from their father. He sighed, feeling a vague sort of regret that he couldn't put a name to.

"I hear the carriage!" Ferris cried suddenly.

Both boys scrambled down from his lap.

Cullen grinned, thrusting aside his unsettled mood. The boys always got excited when visitors came. Life in the country was a quiet affair. The most exciting thing that ever seemed to happen was a trip to the nearby village of Kennebone to go to church or the weekly market. The boys loved the market. Cullen expected Rose would like it, too. When he'd visited New York City several years before, he'd been surprised to learn that folks there bought their goods in department stores these days.

He sighed. Ireland was probably behind the times, but he loved her and hoped she wouldn't change too soon. Except here, in his own home, into which he wished he could install an American lass.

Cullen took himself to task for both of those notions. Rose was a lovely young lady recovering from a serious illness. He had no right to love her. And Ireland was Ireland, behind the times or not.

Since William and Ferris were already racing to see which lad could reach the carriage first, Cullen was laughing by the time he descended the porch steps and walked over to greet Rose and her aunt.

Rose, leaning out of the carriage, had never seen such beautiful children. "Why, they look like little angels," she murmured to her aunt.

"Oh, Rose, they're darlings."

"How old do you suppose they are?" Rose had been feeling rather tired and gloomy, but she perked up at the sight of the boys, who were now jostling each other in an attempt to be first in line to greet the visitors.

"I don't know much about children," Kate admitted thoughtfully. "But they look small."

"Yes. I imagine their mother is terribly proud of them." Tears filled her eyes, and she cursed the wretched influenza that had left her so weepy and weak. With a glance away from the boys and around the yard, she decided that, if any place could be conducive to renewed health, this was it. When she looked at the boys again, Cullen had joined them. He smiled a welcome, and she returned his smile with a warm one of her own.

Rose climbed down from the carriage, using Cullen's arm as a brace. She recalled vividly the days not long since when she'd only used men's arms as a polite formality. Now she needed the support of Cullen's strong arm, and she wished she didn't, no matter how much she liked touching him.

"Oh, Cullen, this is so lovely. Thank you for bringing us here." She transferred her smile to the two beautiful boys. "And who are these fine lads?"

Cullen grinned broadly at the boys. Rose thought he might look upon his own children in that way, and her heart thumped heavily.

"The older one here is William. William, make your bow to Miss Larkin, if you will."

William executed a formal bow that seemed much at odds with his winning smile and sparkling eyes. "How do you do, Miss Larkin?"

"I'm quite well, thank you, William." Rose reached out to shake William's hand. The boy flushed slightly, but seemed pleased that she should be treating him in such a grown-up manner.

Ferris piped up, "But we thought you were sick." Then he, too, blushed, even more hotly than his brother.

Rose laughed. Cullen frowned at the boy. "Miss Larkin, this disreputable scamp is Ferris. You must beg Miss Larkin's pardon, Ferris. It's not polite to comment about a person's health before you've even been introduced."

Ferris, his cheeks burning, bowed as formally as his brother had. "I beg your pardon, Miss Larkin."

Rose held out her hand for Ferris, too. The boy shook it, still looking embarrassed. "It's quite all right, Ferris," Rose said. "I'm sure Mr. O'Banyon told you that my aunt and I were coming here because I've been ill. But I'm getting much better, and I do thank you for your concern."

A bright smile broke across Ferris's face. "That's right, ma'am. It's 'cause I was concerned."

"I'm sure that's so."

Rose knelt in front of the boys. "William and Ferris, thank you very much for letting me come to your home. It's beautiful here."

Ferris's eyes were even brighter than his brother's. "Is it more beautiful here than it is in New York?"

"Indeed it is. At least, it's prettier here than where I come from, which is New York City. New York City is big and dirty and full of congestion."

"Congestion? I thought that's what you got when you were sick."

Rose laughed softly as she stood up. On an impulse, she reached to hold Ferris's hand. He obliged without any hesitation at all. William, while appearing interested, hung back a bit. "Congestion is exactly what you get when you're sick. I had a terrible case of congestion a couple of weeks ago. The kind of congestion that New York has is the kind that's caused by too many people and too many wagons and carts and horses and carriages, all trying to take up the same spaces in the street."

"Oh." Ferris nodded, as if he appreciated this bit of information being so freely imparted. "We don't have that here."

"I can see you don't." Rose sighed as she glanced around once more. She wished she could paint this, or photograph it in color—as if there were such a thing possible—or something, and keep the image with her always.

"William and Ferris," Cullen said behind them, and the boys both turned their attention to him. So did Rose, and she found him standing next to her aunt, looking tall and elegant and at home in these surroundings, as he seemed to be at home everywhere he went. "I want to introduce you to Miss Larkin's aunt. Mrs. Flanagan, please allow me to introduce you to William and Ferris O'Banyon."

O'Banyon? Rose glanced in surprise from Cullen to the boys and back again. They didn't look alike. Perhaps they were related by marriage. She didn't feel comfortable asking at this point. Perhaps later, after she and Kate had settled in, the topic would come up on its own.

Both boys bowed for Kate, as they'd done for Rose. Rose was charmed.

So, evidently, was Kate. She beamed down upon the boys. "It's such a pleasure to meet you, William and Ferris. Mr. O'Banyon has been so kind to invite us to your home. I trust we won't be a bother."

"Oh, no, ma'am!" cried Ferris, as if he'd never heard anything so outrageous.

"No, ma'am," concurred William. "We like for people to visit."

Cullen chuckled. "There. You see, ladies? Out of the mouths of babes."

Neither William nor Ferris looked as if they enjoyed being called babes, but neither boy protested.

As what seemed to Rose to be an army of servants piled out of the house to unload the carriage, Cullen led her and Kate inside the house. She looked around the shiny-floored entryway with interest. She loved these old manor houses. She supposed the Vanderbilts, Roosevelts, and Morgans had homes to compare back home in the United States, but Rose and her father had always lived in flats. Generally cold, uncomfortable, often unpaid-for flats. This looked like heaven to her

The floors gleamed as if someone buffed them daily, and there were lovely Persian rugs scattered here and there. A big Chinese urn held a collection of umbrellas, and a polished-oak hat-and-coat rack stood beside the Chinese urn.

A long, wide, curving staircase that split halfway up and separated into two sets of stairs led to the upper floor. A wooden banister gleamed in the sunlight pouring through curtained windows. She imagined William and Ferris sliding down that banister, shrieking with glee. Paintings hung on the walls—paintings of horses and the countryside and boys frolicking with a host of wagging spaniels. The whole effect was oddly cozy. Cozy on a grand scale, one might say. Rose loved it already.

"What a beautiful place, Cullen."

"It's been in the family for a long time," he said. "Which is very unusual in Ireland."

"Yes. I recollect you saying something about three hundred years. And now it's come down to you." Rose eyed him curiously.

He appeared disconcerted for a moment, but recovered quickly. "Aye. William and Ferris and I feel privileged to have such a place in the family."

"I see." That didn't exactly explain everything, although it did go a ways toward accounting for why he'd thought of bringing her here to recuperate. "Well, the house is wonderful."

"Glad you like it."

"Oh, I do."

"Why don't you give Charles your coats and hats and come with me into the parlor."

Charles, who looked like he was the butler—or perhaps a footman; Rose had no experience with servants—solemnly took the ladies' things. After shedding their outerwear, they meekly followed Cullen into another beautiful room, redolent of furniture polish, beautiful old rugs, delightful paintings, and charming lamps. Rose eyed everything with absolute appreciation. This was her idea of gracious living. She wished she could achieve something remotely similar to it one day.

A servant entered, bearing a tray covered with tea things, little sandwiches, and small iced cakes. Although Rose didn't feel very hungry, she knew she should eat, and this whole country culture fascinated her. She'd eat those little sandwiches just to find out what country Irish people took for tea.

"Would you like to pour, Mrs. Flanagan?" Cullen asked politely.

"I haven't been asked that since my darling Glennie died!" Kate exclaimed. "I'd almost forgotten. We've gone so far from tradition in the United States, Mr. O'Banyon."

Rose blinked at her aunt, not having considered pouring tea in the light of a tradition. But it was, she guessed. In all the British novels she read, people were always taking tea. She sighed, wishing she knew more about her ancestry.

"Will William and Ferris be joining us?" she asked, mostly because she liked the boys and wanted to get to know them better.

"No. They have lessons in the afternoon. They only came out to meet the two of you because this is a special occasion. You'll see more of them this evening. They'll come down before dinner."

"They won't dine with us?" Rose paused with the little sandwich she'd selected halfway to her mouth.

"Not tonight. Generally, they dine with the family, but when there are guests, they eat in the nursery."

Rose didn't like that idea at all. "We're putting everyone to a great deal of bother, Cullen. I don't want to disrupt the running of the household."

"Don't be silly, Rose. If you truly want to dine with a couple of little hooligans, William and Ferris will be more than happy to take dinner with us tomorrow." He smiled one of his lovely smiles. "I've found that taking meals with two little boys isn't necessarily an inspiring experience, although it can be lively."

"Oh, but they seem like such fine boys," Kate said, handing Cullen a cup of tea. "And so handsome."

"Yes, they do seem like fine boys. Very polite. And Kate's right about their being handsome. I expect they look a good deal like their parents." She was fishing, and she could tell Cullen knew it.

He said, "They look almost exactly like their mother, Rose."

"Oh." She chewed her sandwich, which seemed to be made with cream cheese and olives. It didn't sound to her as if Cullen intended to entertain questions about the children. She glanced at him, but saw that his eyes had gone cool. She guessed she'd better not pry.

Anyway, she had no business prying. If Cullen O'Banyon chose not to tell her about his private life, it was because he didn't want her in it. And, while the idea didn't make her feel very good, she could understand and appreciate his caution.

With a sigh, she rose from the chair she'd taken and walked to the window, where she looked out over the emerald-green countryside. "It looks magical out there," she murmured, awed by the glory of the scene spread before her. "And those horses look as if they might sprout wings and fly off any minute."

Her father had been wont to rhapsodize about the enchanted Irish countryside, but Rose had stopped believing a word he said after she hit the ripe old age of five or so. It seemed something of a pity now that he should have been so unreliable that even a loving daughter had stopped believing him. She sighed again.

"It is lovely, isn't it, Rose?"

Rose turned to discover that Kate had joined her at the window. The older woman looked as if she were experiencing deep emotions. Rose understood. If she'd had to leave this magnificent country and not return for nearly half a century, she was sure she'd be emotional too. In truth, she felt emotional right this minute.

"I'm glad you appreciate the scenery," Cullen said.

Rose realized he'd walked to the window, too, and turned to smile at him. "It's truly wonderful, Cullen. I'm so grateful to you for bringing us here." Even if he didn't want them in his life permanently.

"Are you?"

His eyes held an odd, faintly quizzical light. Rose didn't understand. He looked as if he wished he could ask her something and didn't quite dare.

Which was patently ridiculous. Cullen O'Banyon would never hesitate to ask a question if he had one. And he'd never hesitate to grab anything he wanted out of life. He didn't want Rose. He'd made that clear.

She silently screamed at herself to stop doing that. She was here to recuperate. She wasn't here to sink into some dramatic, romantic decline like that idiotic female in *Sense and Sensibility*. Rose had always detested that girl. Rose was stronger than that. Rose wouldn't allow herself to pine away because her love life wasn't as she wished it were. She intended to live her life in spite of disappointments.

Losing Cullen O'Banyon from her life would be a bitter disappointment indeed, she acknowledged, but it—it wouldn't kill her.

Would it?

Actually, she feared it might.

Oh, God, please help me. She felt suddenly helpless and alone and overwhelmed by life.

She mentally gave herself a good shake. They'd come here so she could convalesce. And because of Cullen's kindness, she was in this perfectly astonishing country manor house in a spectacularly beautiful country, and she'd blasted well enjoy herself.

At least she would do her very best to rest, eat well, and recover her health. She owed that to Kate and Cullen and Dr. Swift and Nurse McGinty. And to herself. She needed to think of herself sometimes, she guessed.

She nodded firmly, turned, and headed back to the sandwiches.

Sixteen

Rose had never been around small children, except when she was one. She'd always cherished the optimistic notion that she and children would take to each other right off if they ever had the opportunity. Therefore, she was looking forward to getting better acquainted with William and Ferris. She could practice on them, as it were. She awoke the morning after her arrival eager to see the sights—and the boys.

As much as she appreciated this opportunity, however, she wasn't sure what to do when, as soon as she'd descended the staircase, the two boys greeted her with an invitation to accompany them to the nearby lake to go fishing. She'd never been fishing, either.

They looked as if they'd been up for hours, although, according to the pretty flowered clock she'd glanced at before leaving the bedroom assigned to her, it wasn't past eight o'clock.

"You're going fishing?" Rose asked, stalling. Where was Cullen? Where was Kate? Where was anybody who knew what to do with children?

"We've got lots of bait here," Ferris said, holding out a tin for her observation.

The tin was filled to overflowing with wriggling, squiggling worms. Rose, who hadn't known what to expect of "bait," took a startled step backward. Ferris grinned up at her with big, innocent blue eyes, and she acquitted him of deliberately trying to disconcert her. Nevertheless, she wasn't sure she wanted to go fishing if it involved those worms.

"Ladies don't like worms, Ferris," William said severely. "Don't you know anything?"

Ferris, abashed but undaunted, glowered at his brother. "Some of them do. Miss Larkin does." He turned back to Rose and asked hopefully, "You do like worms, don't you, Miss Larkin?"

"Well, ah, I've never actually had much to do with worms, Ferris. I'm sure they're, ah, fine, useful examples of God's handiwork." Mercy, she was babbling like an idiot. Perhaps she didn't get along with children after all. The notion saddened her.

"I'll bait your hook for you," William offered grandly. He gave Ferris a superior glance.

Ferris resented it. "I can bait her hook! You don't have to do it."

"He's just a little boy, Miss Larkin," William explained. "He doesn't understand that you're a lady and that ladies don't like to touch worms."

"I do, too!"

"Do not."

"Do too!"

"Don't!"

"Do!"

Oh, dear. Her first day at the farm, and already she'd provoked a spat. Rose stared at the children in dismay. She would have liked to reach out to them—but she wasn't sure if that was the right thing to do.

The argument grew in volume as Rose watched, wishing she knew what to do. What would Kate do? Well, that was no help. Kate would probably stand still and stare at the children, press her hands to her cheeks, and wait for someone to rescue her. Maybe cry. Rose wouldn't cry.

"Do!"

"Don't!"

"Stop it!" Rose blurted suddenly, shocking herself.

She shocked the boys, too. They stopped yelling at each other and gaped at her. She cleared her throat. "There's no need to argue," she said with what she hoped was an understanding smile. "The truth is that I grew up in the city and don't know anything at all about worms or fishing. I could use your help, actually, but I haven't eaten breakfast yet. Do you suppose we can go fishing after breakfast?"

Oh, Lord, would a delay spoil the sport? Perhaps one had to get at the fish before the day was very old. She backpedaled furiously. "That is to say, if you can wait. If you can't, perhaps I can go with you another day. The doctor has told me I shouldn't skip meals, and I believe I probably should take breakfast before I go outside."

"You certainly should," came a deep voice at her back. Rose's insides lit up as if somebody had turned on an electric lamp in her middle. Cullen. She turned and smiled at him as he descended the staircase, frowning at the boys. "What in the name of heaven are the two of you up to? You look like ragamuffins. What have you been doing?"

"Digging for worms in the garden," Ferris said, again holding his can out, this time for Cullen's inspection. "We thought Miss Larkin would like to go fishing with us."

"I'll bait her hook," William said, somewhat sullenly. He cast his brother an irritated frown.

"I can do it," Ferris countered.

"I will."

"I will."

"No."

"Yes."

Rose felt her eyes widen. Did this sort of thing go on constantly? She glanced at Cullen and saw him frowning at the boys. He reached out and grabbed the scruffs of two dirty necks. His action silenced the boys at once. They peeked guiltily up at him.

"That's enough of that," Cullen said with stern finality. "These are fine manners to show to a guest in your house. I'm ashamed of both of you."

Ferris hung his head. William looked defiant for a second, then must have agreed with Cullen because he shot an embarrassed glance at Rose. She smiled at him to let him know she liked him anyway.

Cullen turned to Rose. "Please apologize to Miss Larkin, William and Ferris. If she agrees to go fishing with you later, after she's had some breakfast, I'll go along to make sure nothing of this nature happens again."

"Oh, will you, sir?" Ferris brightened up immediately.

"Thank you, sir!" William said.

Rose was surprised at the expression of remorse on Cullen's face when he smiled at the boys. "Of course, I will. You know I like to go fishing with you." Then, ignoring their dirt, he hugged them both.

Rose, watching, got choked up and had to swallow several times and blink her eyes furiously. She hoped this urge to cry every time she witnessed a family scene would go away soon.

"Thank you!" they chorused together.

Cullen released them and gently cuffed two dirty ears. "But you have to wash up. I'm surprised Nurse let you come in the house looking like that. There's mud all over the floor."

Both boys glanced at the floor.

William said, "Whoops."

Ferris said, "I'll get a broom."

"I think you'll need a wet rag."

"Right, sir. I'll go get a wet rag."

"Very well. And while you're at it, you'd probably better let Nurse know what you've been up to."

From the guilty glance the boys exchanged, Rose deduced they'd managed to pull a fast one on Nurse. She was surprised that Cullen should have guessed at such a circumstance. Perhaps he remembered from his own childhood. Or perhaps he spent a lot of time here and had been through this sort of thing before.

The boys dashed off, Ferris's worms bouncing around in their tin. One of them bounced out of the can and he stooped and picked it up. When Cullen glanced once more at Rose, she must have been grimacing, because he laughed.

"You're not a fan of worms, Miss Larkin?"

She jumped. She hadn't realized she'd been making a face. "Oh, I beg your pardon. I—it's just that—well, I never had the opportunity to go fishing when I was growing up."

"Your father didn't ever let you go fishing with him?"

"The only thing my father liked to do was go to the track. He took me to the races sometimes, when he couldn't find anything else to do with me."

Cullen lifted an eyebrow, but Rose didn't feel up to talking about her father. She couldn't help but envy William and Ferris though.

Cullen didn't know whether to be pleased or not that Ferris seemed so taken with Rose. After all, she was going to depart from his young life soon, and he'd already experienced too many losses. If he became attached to Rose, it would hurt him when she left.

On the other hand, he wasn't sure what to make of William, who seemed rather standoffish with Rose. Cullen guessed he understood. After all, William vaguely remembered Judith; had undoubtedly put her on a pedestal, perhaps with a halo. He probably feared Cullen would marry Rose and felt some jealousy.

Cullen knew better than to thrust a new mother on his boys and expect them to accept her immediately, but how could one tell a small child so and have him understand? He couldn't, and Cullen knew it. Perhaps bringing Rose here hadn't been such a brilliant idea after all.

But she seemed to be enjoying herself. He listened to her talking to his children, and his heart went mushy.

"Ewww, I don't want to stick it on the hook!" she cried.

"That's because you're a *girl*!" Ferris crowed, as if being a girl was worse than being a worm.

Cullen could hardly believe his ears when he heard Rose blow a raspberry in response. He laughed in spite of himself. Rose heard him, turned to look, realized what she'd done, and blushed. She was probably the most adorable female Cullen had ever met in his life—and he wished he hadn't.

But no. That wasn't true. He'd always be glad he'd met Rose. What was it that poet had said once, "It's better to have loved and lost than never to have loved at all"? Something like that. He'd have to think about that one after Rose was gone and see how he liked it. He had a feeling he wouldn't agree with the poet. At least not right away.

"All right, now what do I do with it?" Rose was holding the wormy line way out, so it wouldn't brush against her skirt.

"The worm won't hurt you, Miss Larkin," William said, sounding faintly disgusted that she should be queasy about worms.

"I suppose you're right, William. They're awfully ugly, though."

William said, "Hmph."

Cullen was glad that Rose didn't seem to resent William's stuffy attitude toward her. Perhaps she understood how it was with children, even though she had no way of knowing these two had lost their mother. Or maybe she did know it. For all Cullen knew, the boys' nurse had filled her head with all of the family gossip. He sighed, hoping she hadn't.

"Do you want to join us, Cullen?" Rose called.

Cullen, sitting back at his ease against the trunk of a huge old oak, shook his head. "No, thanks. I'll just wait here and rescue the first person who falls in."

Ferris giggled. Rose thinned her lips, and for a second, Cullen thought she might blow another raspberry, this time at him. She didn't, but she did give a big, haughty sniff. William said nothing.

Rose and the children caught a total of eleven fish among them. The first time Rose felt a tug on her line, she squealed, then said, "Oh, I beg your pardon, but I think something's caught on my line."

"It's probably a fish," William told her in his don't-be-a-ninny voice.

Rose pretended not to notice his attitude. Instead, she sounded delighted when she exclaimed, "Oh, do you really think so?"

William shrugged.

Ferris said, "Pull it in slowly, Miss Larkin. If you jerk the line, the fish might fall off."

She did as Ferris instructed, and by George, it wasn't long before Rose had caught a fish. She looked as happy as if she'd conquered an invading army.

William and Ferris showed her how to get the fishhook out of its mouth and place it in a net suspended in the water so the fish wouldn't get away and wouldn't spoil. By the time the eleventh fish had been caught and Rose was looking fagged, she had the hang of fishing. She even baited her own hook the last two times before she cast the line inexpertly into the water.

With a sigh, Cullen lifted himself to his feet. It had been pleasant, sitting there, doing nothing, listening to Rose and his children and dreaming about things that couldn't be. He wished this scene weren't temporary, but could be a part of his life forever. He walked over to the trio, who were chattering together as if they'd known each other for eons. "It's time for the intrepid fishermen to go home for lunch."

Rose turned. Although she was obviously weary, she looked disappointed. "Is it really? What time is it?"

Cullen took out his pocket watch and glanced at it. "It is almost one o'clock, and these two have to get cleaned up before they take their lunch. Nurse would faint dead away if they dined looking like that."

Ferris looked down at himself as if he didn't see anything amiss. William, the sobersided, responsible one, pulled his line out of the water and began preparing to leave the lake.

"Here, Rose, let me take care of your pole for you," Cullen offered.

"Very well, but I want to watch how you do it so I'll know the next time. I can't have people doing everything for me, now can I?"

Cullen didn't know why not. Most ladies of his acquaintance took being waited on as a privilege of their mere existence. One more instance in which Rose had proven herself different from the majority of her fellow females. He had so hoped he'd discover terrible flaws in her. He hadn't, more's the pity.

William, Ferris, Cullen, and Rose took the creel full of fish to the kitchen, where the cook was waiting for them. The old lady brightened when she saw the basket. "Oh, what a good haul you have there!"

"There's lots of them," Ferris said proudly.

"Aye, there are."

Even William looked as if he were pleased with himself.

"The boys were nice enough to teach me how to bait a hook, too," said Rose.

The old lady's eyes twinkled. "Oh, aye? And I expect that was just to your liking."

Rose nodded. "Indeed, it was."

Both ladies laughed, and Cullen's heart seemed to expand in his chest like a balloon being blown up.

He was encouraged when he walked Rose to the back sitting room and found Kate in a tête-à-tête with Nurse. The two women were deep into an exchange of personal confidences and both were knitting up a storm.

Kate looked up and smiled when he and Rose entered the room. "What have you been doing, Rose? Your cheeks are blooming with color."

"Are they really?" Rose went to a mirror hanging over the fireplace.

Cullen could have concurred with Kate's assessment, but he let Rose discover the truth for herself. She peered into the mirror and straightened, smiling.

"By George, there *is* color back in them. Fishing must be good for one's health."

"Oh, my goodness," Kate cried. "Have you really been fishing? I haven't gone fishing since I was a little girl in County Cork."

"Fishing's good for the soul," Nurse pronounced. She'd

taken to making pronouncements in that stern voice, Cullen knew, because that's the way she got information across to her charges. He recalled that same inflection from when he'd been a boy.

One thing about Ireland, he guessed, was that nothing ever seemed to change. Not like in America, which was new and growing and constantly changing. Small wonder Rose wouldn't be satisfied with his dull life. She was from a vigorous country that, from all accounts, was expanding by leaps and bounds in all directions. A painting of the farm Cullen had found in one of the attics, done by one of his ancestors in the late 1700's, depicted the same farm, the same grass—it looked like the same horses, even. A hundred years, and nothing had changed, not even the fences.

"Are those two hellions in the washroom, Mr. Cullen?" Nurse gave him a severe look, as if any misbehavior on the boys' part was his fault.

"Aye, they are, Nurse," he said meekly, and noticed that Rose was looking at him oddly. Small wonder, if she still thought he was a rakehell.

He sighed, wishing all pretense was over between them. But then she'd be gone. There was no easy way out of this one, he decided, and felt sad for a moment before he pulled himself together.

"It's a good thing." Nurse sniffed, packed her knitting into a basket sitting next to her chair, and rose. "I'll go see they wash behind their ears and put on clean clothes.

On an impulse, Cullen said, "They can join us for luncheon if they want to."

Nurse eyed him keenly, her old eyes sharp as flints. "This is setting a precedent." It sounded as if she didn't approve.

"It's only because we have visitors, Nurse," Cullen said gently, and knew he was lying. He wanted his children to love Rose as much as he did. Worse, he wanted her to love them.

He shook himself. "Tell them it's just for today, if you will. Because they were kind enough to teach Miss Larkin to catch the fish we'll be dining on at luncheon."

"Very well." Nurse stalked off, not reconciled, but unwilling to argue in front of guests.

Cullen silently blessed the presence of Rose and Kate, because the feisty old woman was generally not so complacent. He supposed it was because she used to change his nappies when he was a baby. One simply couldn't expect the respect one wanted from a person who'd seen him helpless, naked, and firstborn, dash it.

"I'll go upstairs for a moment, too," Kate said, suiting her action to her words. "I should wash up before luncheon." She bustled out after Nurse.

"I'd better go upstairs and wash, too. I have mud all over the hem of my gown." Rose had lifted her skirt and was gazing at it with a worried frown.

"Just set it out over a chair. Molly will clean it for you."

She dropped her skirt and blurted out, "Oh, I don't want to be any trouble, Cullen. I can do it."

He went to her and took her hand. He had a feeling he might be courting trouble, but he gazed deeply into her eyes. "Rose, the people who work in this house are hired to do certain things. Molly's job is to see to the ladies who stop in the house. At the moment, that means you and Kate. You don't want her to be without a job, do you?"

She flushed. "I—it's only that I've never had servants, you see."

"I never would have guessed." He wished he hadn't said that when her lips tightened. He lowered his voice. "I didn't mean that to belittle you, Rose. Please accept the hospitality of this house. I want you to be comfortable and to recover your health. This isn't America. We aren't a nation of aggressive, independent people. We're either servants or lords. I'm fortunate to be among the latter, to a degree, and I'd appreciate it if you'd accept it and let Molly do her job."

"Do you visit here often?"

He hesitated. "Yes. As often as I can."

She dropped her gaze. "All right. Thank you. And I'll thank Molly, too. Or is that courtesy unacceptable to the lord of the manor?"

Damnation, how could he make such a muddle of a simple explanation? Frustrated, Cullen nudged Rose's chin up. "Please, Rose. Don't be angry with me. I didn't mean to embarrass you. And certainly you can thank Molly. Servants appreciate civility as much as the rest of us."

He saw her swallow, and saw her eyes seem to darken. Damn. He knew he was only asking for trouble, but he couldn't seem to help himself. He was going to kiss her.

Rose's lips parted a little bit and Cullen touched them with his own in a caress as soft as eiderdown. A tiny mew escaped her, and she clutched his sleeve as if she were fighting for her balance. He helped her by slipping his arms around her.

She fit into his arms as if she'd been crafted for them. He'd been sort of hoping to discover that the first time they'd kissed had been an anomaly, but no such luck. She was perfect.

"Oh, Cullen," she whispered when his lips left hers to graze her throat.

She was warm from the sun, and as soft as a ripe peach. Her skin was heaven. Cullen could smell the faint aroma of the soap she'd used this morning, heated by the sun and as delicate as a cloud. He murmured, "Rose," and wanted to say more, but didn't know what. *I love you* sprang to mind, but he didn't say it. *Please don't leave me* also crossed his mind, but he didn't dare make such a request.

He was becoming aroused and didn't want to frighten her, so he reluctantly stopped kissing her and only held her close. "You need to rest after lunch, Rose. Remember what Dr. Swift said." His voice, he realized, was hoarse. No surprise there. He wanted to rip her clothes off and ravish her.

"Yes," she whispered. "Thank you."

He felt his heart hammering in his chest like a bass drum, and was sure she could hear it, since he'd pressed her head to his chest on that very spot. He felt her breasts against him, and closed his eyes, bitter longings burning in him.

He feared he'd never see those beautiful breasts again, never feel them, never taste them. He feared he was cursed to love and lose. At this point, he knew good and well that idiot poet was wrong.

Unless—damn it all, if Rose wasn't worth fighting for, what was? Cullen didn't fancy loving and losing, dash it. In that moment, when time seemed suspended and Rose nestled against his chest like a gift from God, he made a decision.

He was going to fight to keep this woman in his life.

Rose didn't know for sure, but she sensed a sudden shift in the atmosphere. She didn't understand it. It was probably another result of her recent illness, but she all at once felt as if she'd die if Cullen let her go.

Nevertheless, she knew she had to clean up. After all, luncheon threatened. From the odd, almost electric sensation pulsing in the air, Rose thought something more momentous than a mere meal should ensue.

But that only happened in fairy tales and romantic novels. She felt a bitter twist in her heart, but said with fair equanimity, "I'd better go upstairs, Cullen."

He let her go, and when he looked down at her, something new seemed to be burning in his eyes. He only said, "Yes. Yes, go on upstairs." He turned and left her standing there.

Rose watched him go and swallowed again. Good Lord, what did it all mean? Would he have kissed her in that tender way if he didn't care for her, at least a little bit?

With a heavy heart, she ascended the stairs. It was all she could do to adopt a cheerful attitude for Kate, but she felt better for it after they'd both washed up and went down to luncheon.

The first person she saw when she entered the dining room was Ferris, who looked as if he'd been scrubbed with a wire-bristled brush. "Oh, you're so clean!" she exclaimed, then wished she hadn't.

Ferris grinned, not at all chagrined, from which Rose deduced she wasn't the first person to comment upon his altered appearance. "Nurse made me," he told her happily. "She said I'd get no pudding if I didn't clean up."

"You're a very handsome boy, Ferris." Rose saw William sitting woodenly across from his brother, frowning. Poor William. Rose didn't know his story, but she guessed at part of his problem. "And so are you, William," she said, giving him her most friendly smile.

"Thank you," he mumbled.

Rose felt a slight heaviness in her heart. William had seemed to be warming up to her for a while as they fished. Evidently the soap and water that had cleansed his body had gone a ways toward removing any good feelings toward her that had sprouted.

Well, it was only her first day here. She didn't know how long Cullen would allow her and Kate to remain, but perhaps she could make friends with William yet.

A servant brought soup, a light, clear broth that Rose thought was delicious. Then came the fish. Rose had always sort of liked fish, but this tasted better than any fish she'd ever tasted before. "Oh, my, is this what we caught?"

"Aye, it is," Cullen assured her.

"It's wonderful."

"Indeed, it is," Kate agreed. "I remember fish tasting this good when I was a girl, but I haven't eaten any since that was so good, until now."

"It's better when it's fresh-caught," said Cullen.

"It certainly is." Rose purposefully thrust aside thoughts of winning William's trust, Ferris's smiling face, Kate's desires for how Rose should live her life, and even how much she loved Cullen, in favor of devouring her luncheon. She hadn't been this hungry for weeks.

Seventeen

The flowered clock on the mantel said the hour was one-thirty. An hour and a half after midnight. Rose sighed heavily. It must have been the long nap she'd taken after lunch that was preventing her from sleeping now. And she was sick of lying in bed, pondering her problems.

"Bother. I'll just go downstairs and find a book to read."

With that, she swung out of the bed, shoved her feet into her slippers, grabbed her satin wrapper, took up her bedside candle, and crept out of her room. She didn't want to awaken anyone else.

The household was as silent as the grave as she softly walked down the hallway to the stairs and descended the long, wide, curving staircase. At the foot of the stairs, she paused, orienting herself to the unaccustomed house.

Where was the library? Cullen had shown it to her when he'd given Rose and Kate a tour of the house. And he'd said that both ladies were welcome to read anything they desired. Rose had seen a shelf filled with older novels, and she knew she'd find something of interest to her there.

Ah, yes, there it was. The second door on the left. She padded softly to the door and pushed it open.

Cullen swirled around, startled, thus startling Rose, who jerked her arm, spilling candle wax on the carpet.

"Oh, dear, I'm so sorry." Immediately, she stooped to clean it up, only to realize she had nothing with which to do so. She glanced up. "Do you have a paper, Cullen? I need to clean up this wax."

"The wax won't do any harm, Rose. That rug's had worse spilled on it."

"It won't do any good, either."

Cullen brought her a scrap of paper, and she cleaned up the wax. "I fear someone might have to go over this with blotting paper and a hot iron."

"That can be done tomorrow."

He sounded testy. Rose, uncomfortable at having discovered him and now being alone with him in the library, got slowly to her feet. "I didn't mean to disturb you. I couldn't sleep and—"

"You couldn't sleep?" His brow creased with concern. "Why not? Do you feel ill? You're supposed to rest."

She sighed. "No. I mean, no, I don't feel ill. And yes, I need to rest, but I rested so much this afternoon that I can't seem to sleep now. I only came downstairs to fetch a book."

He came closer and pressed a hand to her forehead. "You don't feel hot."

His hand on her bare skin made her feel hot inside, however cool she felt outside. She took a step back, trying to get away from it since his nearness was making her feel funny. "I'm fine." It came out with a snap, and she felt foolish. "That is, I can't sleep is all that's wrong with me. I'm fine. Really."

Cullen cleared his throat. "Rose . . ."

"Yes?" Wonderful. Her hand was beginning to shake from nervousness. Why did this man have such an odd effect on her? Was it because she loved him? Was it because she wanted him to ravish her? She suspected the truth lay somewhere between the two, and also suspected that it did her no credit. She was supposed to be a lady. Ladies weren't supposed to want to experience things of a sexual nature.

But Kate wanted her to be an adventuress, and adventuresses, whatever else one might say about them, were rarely ladies.

Bother. She was losing her mind.

Cullen repeated, "Rose."

She opened her mouth, but nothing came out.

He took the candle holder from her trembling hand, set it on a nearby table, growled, "Damnation," and took her in his arms.

Rose felt a surge of fear and love and something else that she very much feared was lust engulf her. "Please don't stop this time, Cullen," she whispered, and was surprised that she didn't feel guilty afterwards.

"I probably won't be able to stop, damn it," Cullen muttered against her lips.

Oh, good. Rose feared there for a minute that he'd develop scruples again. "I don't want you to stop." She hoped to encourage him in that way.

"God, I can't believe this."

He didn't sound happy. Rose didn't know much about this sort of thing, but she'd assumed men were always happy to accept carnal favors from women. That's what Kate had told her when they'd discussed the matter in several embarrassing, but quite interesting, discussions. And her limited experience of observing her father with various ladies hadn't done anything to disabuse Rose of Kate's opinion.

"It's what I want," she murmured. "Truly, I do, Cullen."

"You don't know what you want," he said bitterly.

"That isn't fair. I do, too, know what I want. I want you." There. She'd said it. "I'd rather learn from you than from anyone else."

"Learn?" His voice held a strange mixture of irritation and despair.

Rose didn't understand. "Yes. I want to learn these things from you."

His hands hadn't been still, but had untied the satin belt at her waist even as his lips had been roaming over her cheeks and chin and throat. Rose felt the strangest, hottest sensations wash over her. Everywhere his mouth touched her, little fires ignited, and a hot liquid pressure was build-ing low in her belly. Lust. It must be lust.

Then suddenly, with a faint but forceful curse, he pushed himself away from her. He dropped his head into his upturned hand, covering his face.

She licked her lips. "What is it, Cullen? Did I do some-thing wrong?"

"No."

Groping in the dark, she whispered, "Um, is it because I have no experience?" Perhaps, as a man of the world with a good deal of experience himself, he didn't fancy con-sorting with virgins. Rose had heard hints of such things from her father's circle of friends. They'd been a set of very loose men, in her opinion, but perhaps Cullen shared their views.

"No, Rose. Get your book and go to bed now."

"But, Cullen—"

He lifted his head and said sharply, "Rose if you don't leave me now, I can't vouch for my behavior."

Whatever did that mean? "But I want to understand. I don't know why you want me to go."

He passed a hand over his eyes. "God save me, I don't, so please go."

It was happening again. Rose felt her lower lip trem-ble and clamped her teeth on it. She wouldn't cry. She wouldn't let him get away with not explaining his reluc-tance to bed her, either. "I want to know why you refuse to—to take me to your bed, Cullen. Is it because you find me unappealing? Please tell me the truth. I can't stand not knowing."

His head had jerked up during her last little speech, and he stared at her in overt incredulity. "Unappealing? Are you out of your mind?"

"Maybe. I don't think so. I don't know."

"I don't believe this."

She took a couple of tentative steps forward. "What? What don't you believe? For the love of heaven, *tell* me!" She was getting angry now. "I want you to make love to me, Cullen. What's wrong with that?"

Actually, she supposed there were several things wrong with it, but she wasn't entertaining reason at the moment. She wanted to know why Cullen kept rejecting her.

"What's *wrong* with it?"

"You needn't shout. I only want to know."

"For the love of Christ, Rose, look at you! You're a beautiful, vibrant young woman with your whole life ahead of you. Your idiotic aunt has talked you into a ridiculous course of action, and you deserve better than that!"

Rose drew herself up straight. She was angry by this time. "Kate is not idiotic. She only wants the best for me. She's always been wonderful to me."

"And you think being an adventuress is best for you?"

Feeling frustrated and helpless, Rose lifted her hands and let them drop. "Well—Oh, I don't know." She didn't want to say this, but something compelled her to go on. "My father wouldn't—couldn't—I don't know—provide for us. If it hadn't been for Aunt Kate, I'd have been working in a factory by this time, or—or even on the streets. She paid my school bills, and school was the only thing that saved me, that taught me there was more to life than bleak streets, cold-water flats, and running from debt collectors.

"At first, Kate would give Father the money for school, and sometimes he'd pay the bills and sometimes he'd gamble the money away before he got to the school. She—she's the one who took me to museums and to the opera and things like that. She taught me about whatever refinement I possess today. Otherwise, I'd have had no experience at all of life's finer things."

She had to brush away an angry tear or two. She hated confessing all of this. "Perhaps Aunt Kate and I don't share goals for my life that are entirely compatible with each other, but I shan't let her down. She literally saved my life. She's been better to me than anyone else in my whole life, and she deserves my acquiescence in this matter."

He walked over and stared down at her not unkindly. "I suppose I can understand your feeling indebted to her, but you're talking about your *life*, Rose. What's more, you're talking about it as if it were a plaything. A toy for your aunt Kate to manipulate as if you were a doll."

She'd recently thought the same thing, actually, but she'd not admit it now. "That's not fair. I just told you how it was. I owe Kate my life, and I'm paying her back."

"That's crazy, Rose."

She couldn't explain it any better. If he didn't understand, she didn't feel up to trying to make him. "All of that still doesn't explain to me why you don't want to make love to me." She had to know.

"Believe me, Rose, I *want* to make love to you."

She was beginning to feel bewildered, as if they were traversing around and around in one of those wheels children built for pet rats. She threw out her hands. "I don't understand! *Tell* me! Please!"

"Damnation."

Rose uttered a tiny shriek of surprise as Cullen swept her up in his arms and carried her to the sofa against the wall.

"All right, Rose, all right."

Cullen's whole body was trembling by the time he'd carried Rose to the sofa and set her down. He was furious. Furious at Rose. Furious at Kate. Furious at himself. Yet, when he gazed at her and saw her lying there, wide-eyed, staring up at him, obviously not having a clue as to what to do now, his heart hitched and his anger seemed to evaporate. He loved her so much.

He didn't want her as his mistress. He wanted her in his life forever and ever, until death parted them. He wanted her to become his wife.

Damn Kate Flanagan to perdition. Cullen couldn't bear the notion of Rose sacrificing her life to some foolish old lady's whim.

But what then? If she wouldn't be his wife because of Kate's insanity, could he bear to part with her?

No. By God, he couldn't. If the only way he could have her was as his mistress, he'd take her as his mistress. To hell with his pride and honor.

He ripped off his jacket and flung it over a chair. His shirt and belt followed. Rose's eyes couldn't get any bigger, but he saw the pupils dilate when he began on his trouser buttons. Recalling that the door wasn't locked, he swirled around and walked over to it.

Evidently, Rose misunderstood his purpose, because he heard a rustling from the sofa and her voice, desperate, calling, "Cullen, wait!"

He threw the bolt and turned again, and her words choked off, she gripped the edges of her nightgown together at her throat, and stared at him.

"I'll not leave you, Rose." His voice had gentled; he couldn't help it. He loved her too much to be angry any longer, and he'd told her the truth: He'd never leave her.

It hurt his heart that she was selling herself so cheaply. An adventuress! God save us all. She was too beautiful. Too young. Too sweet.

He went back to the sofa, finishing with his trouser buttons. Then he sat next to her, surprising a gasp from her, removed his shoes and stockings. He turned and stared down into her huge, huge eyes. He didn't want to hurt her.

"Are you still sure, Rose?"

She swallowed. "I'm still sure, Cullen," she said in the smallest voice he'd ever heard from her.

With an inarticulate sound, he lay beside her on the sofa and carefully helped her pull the nightgown over her head. His hands stilled and he could only stare at her. She stared back, and he detected fear and eagerness in her expression.

He tenderly brushed a stray lock of hair behind her ear. "You're beautiful, Rose. You're perfect all over."

She blushed and tried to cover her breasts, but he took her wrists and brought her hands to his lips.

"Don't hide from me, Rose. You're lovely, and you ought to be told so." He kissed the backs of her hands and turned them over to brush kisses on her palms. Her fingers curled.

"Thank you," she whispered.

He left off caressing her body with his gaze and gazed at her face. She didn't look quite so frightened, and her eyes were huge. If he didn't already know they were as blue as a robin's egg, he'd have believed them to be much darker.

"You know, Rose, you don't have to do everything Kate tells you to do. I understand that she helped you out in life, but your life belongs to you."

"I know, Cullen."

"And you still think you want to be an adventuress?" He held his breath when she shut her eyes and sucked in a breath that sounded like it hurt.

"I—I don't think so."

His heart soared until she rushed on.

"But I will. I owe Kate." Her eyes opened, and he read the sincerity in them. "It's the truth, Cullen. She really did save my life."

For a second more, he hesitated. Then he gave up. He was only a man, and a man could only restrain himself so much. Besides, she claimed to want this. The good Lord knew, he wanted it. With a low moan, he stretched out beside her on the sofa and began a thorough, tactile survey of the body he'd been lusting after for so many weeks.

She gasped.

"Don't be afraid, Rose. This probably won't hurt much."

Gad, what was the matter with him? *This probably won't hurt much.* What kind of thing was that to say to a sensitive, eager young virgin? It seemed that every word that came out of his mouth when Rose was around was wrong. Cullen kissed her deeply, hoping to wipe away his inapt phrasing by showing her, without words, how much he loved and desired her.

"I know you won't hurt me, Cullen."

He could hardly believe she'd said that. Yet when he lifted his head from the breast he'd been kissing, he saw the trust in her eyes. They were frightened eyes, still, but trusting for all that. Lord love him, what had he ever done to deserve this much pain and pleasure? And why did they have to visit him in one sweet package?

"Thank you." Her trust humbled him, and he resumed

his tour of her body with renewed gentleness. He'd never felt such fine, silky skin. And her breasts had responded to his touch instantly, their dusky nipples pebbling and standing to attention. He gave it to them, licking and suckling. He took her nipple in his teeth and tugged gently. She gave a little mew as he did the same thing to the other one.

Her hips had begun to lift slightly in the beginning rhythms of love. She probably didn't even know it, but Cullen noticed, and his arousal throbbed in response. His hand caressed its way to the soft, downy curls at the apex of her thighs and cupped her there. A soft cry escaped her.

"Are you frightened, Rose?"

"No. No, of course not."

"Liar," he whispered almost desperately. With a swoop, he moved his hand and lowered his head between her thighs. Let her learn everything.

She cried out again, but Cullen couldn't tell if it was from fear or pleasure. She tasted like the sweetest honey, and as his tongue caressed her most secret treasure, her hips lifted in response.

"Oh, Cullen!"

She was getting close; he could tell.. He continued working on her with his tongue and mouth, loving her as thoroughly as he was able.

"Oh, my!"

He glanced up and saw that she'd shoved the back of her hand in her mouth and was biting it. Probably afraid of what was happening to her, Cullen imagined. He kept it up until she uttered a shriek that was stifled by her hand and her body convulsed under his tongue's assault.

It was glorious to watch. And he was ready. More than ready. About to burst. Before she'd recovered her composure, he'd positioned himself over her, guided his sex to her maiden's treasure, and gently but firmly pushed fully into her.

With a sharp gasp, she went still. So did he. His eyes were shut tight and for a moment he didn't know if he was going to be able to perform after all. If she moved even a little bit, he was going to lose control and spill into her be-

fore he was ready. He didn't want to do that to his wonderful, reckless Rose.

With a massive effort, he managed to control his cli-
max. Only then did he open his eyes and look down at her.
"Did that hurt, Rose? Are you all right?" he asked softly.
Something cynical twisted in Cullen's chest as he watched
her peering up at him, trusting, believing in him. Him, of
all people. Rose was no longer a virgin. He'd dishonored
her, the woman he loved. He could hardly believe it of
himself.

She had to swallow again before she spoke. "A—a little."

He gave one jerky nod. "It will never hurt again."

"But—but the first part was, er, really quite wonderful."

In spite of his tumbling emotions, Cullen smiled.
"Good. I wanted it to be really quite wonderful."

"I—well, I didn't know how it would be."

"No, really?"

He could have kicked himself when she turned her head
away. Damn him, why was he teasing her now, of all inap-
propriate times?

The pressure to complete this act was beginning to
gnaw at him until he finally couldn't stop from moving in
her. She turned her head to look up at him again, startled,
and he saw tears in her eyes.

"I'm sorry, Rose. It's too late to turn back now."

"I know it," she whispered. "I'm glad."

This was it. Love and desire surged in Cullen's body.
He moved gently at first, then more rapidly, until with one
last lunge and a hoarse cry, he let himself go, and his seed
spurted out of his body and into hers.

Oh, God, why couldn't she be his? Really and truly his?
To have and to hold, forever, in holy wedlock? When the
last of his shudders ceased, he lowered himself on the
couch, rolled her body onto his, and shut his eyes as he
wrapped his arms around her.

He didn't know how long they lay there, wrapped
around each other, silent except for their harsh panting.

What had he done? Jesus, Mary, and Joseph, what had

he done? He wasn't the sort of man who did things like this.

Like hell he wasn't. He'd just done it, hadn't he?

Of course, if Rose were a normal woman, he'd demand that she marry him. That's what he'd like to do.

But she'd only refuse him. She wanted to fulfill her aunt's ambitions and be an adventuress. To experience what Kate saw as excitement. Cullen couldn't offer Rose excitement. He could only offer her his love, his life, his sons, and all of his earthly possessions.

His thoughts were as black as the night sky outside when Rose's soft voice filtered through them, sprinkling light on his pain-darkened places.

"Cullen?"

With a deep sigh, he opened his eyes. He had to face her again someday; might as well get it over with. "Yes, Rose?"

"Thank you."

Thank you? "For what?" There was an edge in those two words, and Cullen wished he'd minded his tongue more carefully.

"For being you, and for—for making it wonderful."

He couldn't speak for a moment, and she blinked up at him. Cullen knew he had to say something. "I enjoyed it, too. Very much." She deserved that from him. She deserved much more from him, actually, but he feared she wouldn't accept it.

The ghost of a smile played on her lips. "Did you really? I mean, really?"

He stared at her, flabbergasted. "You mean you couldn't tell?"

She shook her head and sat up. "I've . . . never had the experience before, if you recall."

Of course. He nodded, unable to think of words appropriate to the situation.

"And . . . well you seemed so reluctant. I didn't think you really wanted me, you see. I thought you were only being nice."

"You thought I was only being nice." Lord. With a

mighty effort—his muscles felt like jelly—Cullen pushed himself off of the sofa and stood beside it. He stared down at Rose, whose modesty had evidently flown out the window, because she gazed up at him with frank curiosity, allowing herself to study his body—all of it.

"You, ah, are a very handsome man, Cullen." She flushed a little. "I mean, your body is nice, and all. Plus, you *are* very handsome."

"Thank you."

She sucked in air. "And you're nice, too. Very nice, and I appreciate everything you've done for me. Including tonight."

He felt his lips tighten and couldn't seem to make himself move. Her own body was rosy with love, and he could see where his whiskery chin had scraped her precious skin. He wanted to caress those places, to kiss them, to apologize for hurting her. "Um, do you feel all right, Rose? I mean, are you sore?"

She looked down her body, and Cullen imagined her assessing the damage to her maidenhead. There was no repairing it now. "I'm a little tender, but not sore." She looked up at him again and managed a smile. "In fact, the experience was so amazing that I hardly noticed the pain."

"Good." Good Lord above, what was he supposed to do now? He couldn't merely walk away from the scene of her debauch, particularly since he'd been her debaucher. What an immoral ass he was.

Rose glanced away from him, peering nervously around the room. "Um, I don't suppose you'd like to, well, you know . . ."

He was beginning to feel a little foolish, standing there, naked, staring at her gorgeous body and wishing he could make love to her again. And again and again and again. But instead he walked to the chair where he'd thrown his clothes and grabbed his trousers. "No, Rose, I don't know. Please tell me."

Pausing with one leg in his trousers, Cullen mentally chided himself for sounding cold and aloof. Lord in heaven, he'd just ruined the woman, and now he was acting like a scoundrel. He tried again, his voice more tender this time. "That is to say, no, I don't know what you mean. Will you please explain it to me?"

He heard her swallow. "Um, well, you know, Kate and I set out on this trip in order for me to come under the protection of a man, Cullen. Um, I don't know if you do those sorts of things, but . . ." Her words trailed off.

When Cullen peered over his shoulder, he saw she still wasn't able to look at him. She was also blushing all over. How fascinating. Her entire body glowed with embarrassment.

He wanted to stomp over to the sofa, take her in his arms and demand that she marry him. He bowed his head and shook it, feeling bereft and incompetent.

"You want me to take you as my mistress, is that it?"

"Well—yes." He heard her take another deep breath. "If you'd like to, that is. I . . . ah . . . don't really know about this adventuress-ing business, but I do owe it to Kate to do as she wants me to do. And . . . well . . . I like you so very well. I thought that if you would be willing to—that is, if you . . ."

"Yes, Rose. I would be honored if you would be my mistress." There. He'd said it. He'd violated her. He'd violated himself. And all for the sake of a batty old woman who had no idea of how the world worked.

He thought again, almost desperately, *God save us all.*

"Oh, thank you, Cullen!"

She gave him such a smile that he decided *to hell with it*, removed his shirt, shoved off his trousers, and went back to join her on the sofa.

Eighteen

Rose had never felt so exhilarated as she did the morning after her deflowering. Oh, certainly, she was a little sore, but overall, she felt better than she had since before she'd fallen victim to the influenza.

Cullen had become her protector! She hugged herself all the way downstairs. When she'd begun this mad journey with Kate, she'd never imagined a man like Cullen actually wanting her. At least for a little while.

Some of her happiness dimmed, but she told herself to snap out of it. She had achieved a goal, and she was glad. Glad. Happy, even.

"Good morning, Rose. You're looking healthier every day."

Rose smiled at her aunt, who was passing the foot of the staircase with William and Ferris. William glanced at her and turned away, his face set. Ferris ran up the stairs to greet her and accompany her the rest of the way down.

"We're taking Mrs. Flanagan out to the stables, Miss Larkin, to see Bonnie's new foal. Want to see her, too?"

"I'd love to."

Rose discovered herself glancing around and realized she was trying to catch a glimpse of Cullen. Scolding herself for being a ninny—after all, she was now under his protection; surely she needn't be constantly in his company—she repeated, "I'd love to see Bonnie's new foal."

William was scuffing the toe of his shoe on the hall runner, looking impatient. Feeling expansive and full of love this morning, Rose smiled at him. "Good morning, William."

He heaved a sigh. "Good morning, Miss Larkin." If he'd tried to sound perfunctory, he couldn't have done a better job.

Undaunted, Rose took her place beside him as the four of them started walking again. Ferris skipped ahead to open the front door and held it for his brother and the two ladies. William, having been drilled, Rose presumed, in polite behavior, bowed and allowed the ladies to pass out of the house before him. Rose had a suspicion he didn't want her there at all, although he didn't seem to resent Kate in the same way he resented her.

"The stables are down that way," Ferris told them, and pointed.

"Ah, yes, I see." Rose glanced around. "It's so beautiful here. You boys must love growing up in the country like this."

"We want to stay here," William stated.

Rose glanced down at him. "I'm sure you do. And I'm sure you shall."

"Hmmm."

"Oh, Rose!" Kate exclaimed. "Smell that wonderful fresh air. It's so delightful here, compared to New York City, isn't it?"

Actually, at the moment, Rose smelled horse manure, but she discovered she didn't mind the smell in the least. She agreed with her aunt and turned her attention back to William. "Does Bonnie's foal have a name, William?"

He shrugged. Slightly put off, Rose decided to remain friendly and see what happened. She liked both of these boys very well, and wished William could warm up to her.

Not, of course, that it made any difference in the long run. The reality of that struck her suddenly, and Rose faltered in her steps for a moment.

"What's the matter, Rose? Are you too tired? Do you need to rest for a moment?" Kate asked solicitously. She hurried up to her niece.

"Oh, no, I'm fine." Rose took a deep breath and smiled at Kate. "I, ah, just wanted to look around a little more and take it all in—it's all so different here. Let's go to the stables." She started striding on her way again.

Oh, dear, it really *didn't* matter if William ever warmed up to her, did it? She and Cullen would be moving on, and she might never see William again, depending on Cullen's relationship to these children and whether he tired of her soon. Being brutally honest with herself, she acknowledged that, although she'd never thought about it before, she supposed gentlemen didn't usually take their mistresses with them on family visits. Her heart gave a tremendous spasm.

With bitter understanding gnawing at her, Rose made her way to the stables. They were extensive, and she said so.

"This is a horse farm," William said, as if she should have known that. "We have to have extensive stables."

"Of course."

Ferris took off running toward a fenced-in pasture nearby. "There he is!"

He pointed at a gangly baby horse wobbling next to a beautiful bay mare in the middle of the pasture. Cullen was there, smiling and talking animatedly with a man in a soft gray cap. Rose's heart turned over. She loved him so much. For a moment, she had a vision of herself and Cullen, married, with William and Ferris their own children, here, residing on this magnificent and peaceful place.

Foolish, foolish Rose.

Before she could allow her nonsensical fantasies to color the present moment—which was, after all, splendid—Rose lifted an arm to wave at him. He waved back and strode toward them.

"Good morning, Rose. Good morning, Mrs. Flanagan."

At least he smiled at her, which took some of the chill from her heart. His smile could melt ice.

Cullen winked at the boys. "Want to come and see this new baby?"

"Oh, yes!" Ferris had scrambled up the fence and dropped to the other side in two seconds flat.

"Yes, please." William, the more sedate of the two, took longer climbing the fence.

With another warm glance at Rose, Cullen said, "We'll lure the mother and her colt over to the fence, so you can get acquainted."

"Thank you."

Kate clutched her hands to her bosom. "Oh, I've never seen anything so perfectly charming in my life!"

Rose watched Cullen walk back to the mare and her foal with the boys, Ferris skipping merrily at his side, William looking up and speaking with his usual sobersided deliberation. They looked as if they belonged together, and Rose wondered all at once if they did. Were those two beautiful children Cullen O'Banyon's sons?

She pressed a hand to her aching heart and stared hard at the trio. She heard the man with the soft cap say something, saw Cullen laugh his wonderful laugh, saw the boys laughing too, and she knew.

This was not only Cullen's farm, but those were his sons. He hadn't wanted her to know, because he didn't want her to stay here, cluttering up his life, for any longer than she could bring pleasure to him.

Her knees gave out, and she had to grab the fence and hold tight to keep from sinking to her knees. She wouldn't cry. She wouldn't.

"Are you sure you're all right, Rose?"

Kate was watching her in grave concern, and Rose commanded herself to get her emotions under control. This was the life of an adventuress. She'd achieved Kate's goal. This was part of it. It would be her fate to watch from the outside as the life she longed for—husband, home, family, children, love—was lived by others.

It took her a moment before she was certain her voice wouldn't break, but she managed to say at last, "I'm fine, Kate. Thank you. I . . . tripped over something."

Both ladies glanced at the grass beneath their feet. Rose had heard people jest about tripping over blades of grass, but she herself had always been relatively graceful. Until now. Now she wanted to fling herself on that green, green grass and cry her eyes out.

"Are you sure? You look a little pale, dear."

"I'm fine." Noticing Kate's startled expression—the two words had popped out somewhat crisply, Rose added, "Thank you for your concern."

Then, suddenly, her reserve snapped. "No, I'm not all right, Kate."

"No?" Kate's eyes went huge. "Oh, dear, Rose, do you need to sit down?"

"No." Rose eyed her aunt with a new understanding—and she didn't like what she saw; not in Kate and not in herself. "You'll be pleased to know that the deed has been done, Kate. I am now officially Cullen's mistress."

Kate blinked at her. Her mouth opened and shut several times, reminding Rose of one of the fishes she'd recently caught. She felt cold inside. Cold and miserable, and as if she'd thrown away something precious. She might have fought for and won Cullen's love. She might have thought for herself instead of allowing Kate to think for her. Rose, after all, was much stronger of character than Kate.

But no. She'd allowed herself to fall in with Kate's nonsensical tales of adventure and grand passion and had come to Ireland with Kate, searching for Kate's dream. Kate's dream.

It wasn't Rose's dream, and it looked now as if it was going to break Rose's heart. She'd agreed to the scheme without ever considering her temperament or the cost such a life would exact from her. She should have known herself better. She *had* known herself better, and she'd chosen to ignore her essential nature and character. She was no more cut out for seduction and adventure than a kitten was cut out to stalk big game.

"I . . . don't think I understand, dear," Kate stammered at last. "I . . . ah . . . thought you'd already achieved a, well, an understanding."

Rose sighed. "Never mind. We'll talk about it later."

"Of course." Kate continued to watch her uncertainly for a few minutes. She could never keep a thought too long in her mind, however, and was soon smiling happily.

With a heaviness in her spirit much at odds with the elation she'd felt earlier in the morning, Rose rested her arms on the top of the fence and watched Cullen and the boys—his sons, she knew for certain—and the man in the soft cap deal with the mare and her foal.

The scene was one of breathtaking tranquility that Rose would have sold her soul to be a part of. Cullen was in his shirtsleeves, which were rolled up to mid-forearm, tight riding breeches, and a jaunty hat. He looked wonderful—strong and masculine and proficient. He belonged here. He appeared as much at home here as the man in the cap.

Which made sense, since it *was* his home. Oh, Lord, what had she done?

The wistful longing inside her hurt so much, she almost cried out in pain.

After they got back to the house, Kate showed no hint of remembering what Rose had told her. Rose didn't have the heart to go into it again.

She was becoming more like her aunt—and her father—every day, and she wished it wasn't so.

After dinner, Cullen went looking for Rose. She'd been rather quiet all day, but he hadn't had the opportunity to talk to her. He hoped she wasn't feeling poorly after last night.

He knocked softly at her door. "Rose?"

The door opened, but he didn't see Rose. Somewhat puzzled, he went in and discovered her behind the door, as if she were hiding. "Rose?"

"Good evening, Cullen." She tried to smile at him, with poor success.

He was more puzzled. Nudging her chin up a little, he asked gently, "Are you all right, Rose?" He didn't know if he was afraid she was having second thoughts about this agreement of theirs, or if he hoped she was, but he felt compelled to ask. "Is, ah, anything the matter? If you'd like me to leave, I will."

He clamped an iron hand on his heart that balked at the thought of leaving her alone any more than he had to. If this was all Rose was willing to give him, he'd take it, God save him, if it meant spending eternity in hell.

"I want you to stay," she said hastily, as if she were afraid he'd bolt. If she only knew.

He breathed a sigh of relief. "Good. I'm glad." At least, he thought he was.

"Um, but—well, I'd like to ask you something. If you don't mind."

She was nervous, fiddling with the ribbons of her wrapper. Her hair was down, and the soft candlelight in the room made it gleam with copper and gold.

"Yes? Please, Rose, ask away." Offhand, he couldn't think of anything she could ask that he'd not answer. The brief hope that she'd ask him to marry her visited him, but he didn't allow it to stay. He knew better.

"Um, well . . ." She walked to the window, pulled the curtain aside, and glanced outside. She didn't linger, but dropped the curtain and went to the fireplace. She didn't look at him.

"Go ahead, Rose," he urged gently. "What's the matter?"

She turned quickly. "Nothing's the matter, Cullen. Truly. You've been so wonderful, that nothing could possibly—"

He cut her off, unwilling to hear what she'd been going to say. He was no knight in shining armor, as she thought him to be. He was a cad. "Right. So, please, ask your question."

She sucked in a huge breath that lifted her breasts and made her nipples press against the satin fabric of her robe. He watched avidly. She had a gorgeous body, and he couldn't imagine ever being truly sorry he'd had the pleasure of knowing it intimately.

"I was, ah, watching you with William and Ferris earlier this morning, you know, and—"

"And?" he prompted, wondering what she was leading to. A jot of fear that she'd discovered his boring secret was banished before it had the chance to grow. He was who he was, and he couldn't put off her discovery of who that was forever.

"Well—are William and Ferris your children?"

Even though he'd half-expected the question, Cullen was surprised. Briefly, he thought about lying and decided he wouldn't. It was stupid to persist in this charade. The risk of her learning the truth from a member of his house-hold, or from one of the boys, grew as the days passed. He said simply, "Yes."

She turned away, but he thought he detected the sheen of tears in her eyes before she did so. He didn't understand, and walked over to put his hands on her shoulders. "What is it, Rose? Are you sorry to discover I'm not the rogue you believed me to be, but am in reality a tedious family man with a horse farm?"

In spite of her evident unhappiness, a choked laugh es-caped her. "Good heavens, no! But—oh, I don't know. I thought you were a—a sporting-mad man. A gambling man. Like my father."

Not bloody likely. Cullen would slay anyone who com-pared him to Rose's father. "I'm not like your father, Rose." He kept his tone mild because he knew Rose had loved and honored her father, however little the man had deserved such devotion from his beautiful daughter.

"No, I suppose not."

They were quiet for a minute or two. Cullen wondered what Rose was thinking, but was afraid that if he asked she'd tell him.

Rose spoke into the silence. "I had supposed, when peo-ple kept asking you if you were Mr. O'Banyon of the horses, that you were a famous sportsman or something."

"Not I."

"I didn't realize the whole world knew about your horses—that you *bred* them."

"We've got a reputation as breeding the world's best Irish horseflesh here on the farm, and we're proud of it."

"Of course. You must be very proud of it." She peered up at him. "I'm glad to know your reputation wasn't made because of your famous losses at the track."

Cullen chuckled. "No. I'm too prudent to wager wildly, although I do place a wee bet from time to time. If I don't believe in my horses, why should anyone else?"

"Good question." She turned, directly into his arms, and he held her tightly. "I think it's wonderful that this place is yours, Cullen. And William and Ferris are beautiful children. You must be very proud of them."

"I am." Having Rose in his arms rather distracted him from the serious conversation he and she were conducting. Hoping to distract her, too, he kissed her deeply and thoroughly. He didn't know about Rose, but by the time he pulled away, he was fully aroused and eager to continue lovemaking.

Fortunately for him, Rose appeared happy to forego hearing the humdrum details of Cullen's life. He appreciated her responsiveness to his touch more than he could say.

His heart gave a hard spasm when he recalled her chosen career, and he reminded himself that there was still a chance for her to come to her senses. Nothing was set in stone.

Rose had never been very good at deceiving herself, but she aimed at least to pretend. Perhaps, if she tried hard enough, she could pretend she and Cullen were married, that they lived here on this gorgeous farm, and that those two little boys were hers and Cullen's.

Fortunately, she enjoyed Cullen's caresses so much, she soon forgot all about pretense or deception or the lack of marital ties between them. She mimicked the movement of his hands with her own, running her fingers all over his body. She wanted to feel him, memorize every detail of his body while she still could.

Rose was delighted to discover that Cullen had dark hair on his body. The hair thrilled Rose, who'd only caught brief glimpses of men's body hair before in her life. She'd never dreamed, for instance, that a man's entire chest could be sprinkled with tightly curling hairs, or that the trail of chest hair narrowed beneath his rib cage until it became a thin dark line pointing directly to his sex. At the moment, Cullen's sex was thrusting, stark and straight, from a nest of dusky curls.

Because she was curious and sensed he wouldn't mind, Rose tentatively put her hand around his erect shaft. His quick intake of breath startled her, but when she glanced at his face, she realized his gasp had been one of pleasure. Good.

She remembered in thrilling detail what he'd done to her the night before with his tongue. He'd driven her almost to distraction, the way he'd licked and suckled her until she'd been engulfed by pleasure. She wondered if a woman could provoke the same response in a man by licking and sucking his shaft. The notion shamed and embarrassed her for a few seconds, but she was driven by a need she could not deny.

"Holy mother of God," Cullen whispered when Rose's tongue flicked out to caress his sex.

She hoped she hadn't done something wrong. When she looked, he seemed to be in some sort of ecstasy and, since he didn't draw away from her, she settled in to experiment further. She held him lightly in her hands and thoroughly tasted every inch of him. There was a tiny slit at the end of his sex, and she tasted that, too.

This was the most exciting experience of Rose's life. And the fact that she was experiencing it with Cullen made it supremely special. She was sure that she'd never be this much in love again.

But such thoughts meant sadness, and Rose refused to let them spoil this glorious moment. Instead, she continued to concentrate on what she was doing.

"Are you sore, Rose," asked Cullen in something of a croak.

She was, a little, but she'd never say so. "Not at all."

"Good." He sounded relieved.

Because she was intensely curious, she asked, "Am I doing this right, Cullen?"

"You couldn't be doing it any better," he gasped. "In fact, you'd better stop now, or else I might not be able to hold back much longer."

Puzzled, Rose lifted her head. Cullen drew her to him and kissed her thoroughly, then lowered her onto the bed and entered her with a swift stroke. Rose was thrilled.

She was even more thrilled when, a very few seconds later, she felt what she recognized as the prelude to sexual satisfaction. Release came to her in a rush, and startled a cry from her. Then it seemed that every muscle in her body contracted, and she went over the edge into some kind of madness that dazed and elated her. Cullen joined her in release at that moment, and Rose couldn't recall when she'd felt more at peace with the world.

Her feelings of peace and tranquility didn't last long.

The summer weather remained beautiful. Flowers bloomed in the carefully tended beds around the house, and birds sang from the treetops. Rose had never beheld such a glorious sky as floated over the horse farm. In New York, factory smoke and the stench of too many people crowded into too small a space often made the air terrible to breathe. Not here. Here, every breath was a pleasure.

And the countryside! Rose was sure she'd never tire of it, if she was given three lifetimes to enjoy it. She loved living here. She loved Cullen. She loved Cullen's children. Even the servants became like family to Rose, who'd never had a servant.

The days on Cullen's farm went by in a steady stream of calm and joy, and the more joy Rose felt at the prospect of being part of it, the more the pain of ultimately having to give it up hurt. This was no way to go through life—anticipating the dismal hour of parting. She ought to enjoy the here and now.

That's what a *real* adventuress would do; she was sure of it.

Which made her more certain than ever that she wasn't a real adventuress. She wanted to tell Kate, but held back.

And she'd never tell Cullen. The notion of Cullen thinking she'd tricked him under false pretenses into a relationship he hadn't wanted—after all, she'd practically had to rope and tie him and drag him into her bed—and ultimately hating her was too horrible to contemplate.

Yet she found it more and more difficult to be merry as the days and weeks passed. Even the knowledge that William was warming up to her didn't cheer her, although she put all of her energy into faking it.

Her health was almost back to its full vigor. Cullen taught her more than she ever dreamed about horseback riding, an activity she enjoyed immensely. She wondered why her father had always found more satisfaction in betting on these animals than in riding them. She simply could not understand why her father hadn't been able to find the same joy as she did when riding a horse.

Unfortunately, Kate had managed to end up with a smattering of her brother's odd, excitement-seeking nature. Enough of a smattering to ruin Rose's life.

"Stop it!" She wouldn't blame her problems on Kate. Her life was hers to live and, therefore, it was her responsibility. Solely. She hated that she was so small-minded and petty that she kept trying to thrust the blame for her present circumstances onto Kate.

"Beg pardon?"

Blast. Rose forgot that she was riding with Cullen. She turned her head to smile at him, and nearly fainted from the impact of his smile. Oh, how she'd misjudged him! How stupid she'd been!

"I'm sorry, Cullen. My mind was wandering onto an unhealthy path, and I was telling it to stop."

"I see." His dark eyes twinkled like stars, and Rose went light-headed for an instant. "You know, they say that people who talk to themselves are daft, Rose. Or they're being visited by the wee folk."

She laughed. "I'm sure that's it. It's the wee folk." She adored listening to Cullen's staff of servants spin their country tales. She'd always understood the Irish were a fey, creative people; now she knew it was true.

Cullen kept watching her, and Rose's smile faded. "What? What's wrong. Do I have dirt on my nose?"

He grinned. "No. Your nose is as lovely as ever. I was only wondering if you're enjoying your stay at the farm. I know it's not very exciting here."

"Oh, I *am* enjoying my stay. Absolutely. It's exactly what the doctor ordered."

"He did, indeed."

"And I feel ever so much better."

"Good. I'm glad."

Yet Rose got the feeling that he was troubled. She hoped to heaven he wasn't tired of her already. She knew she'd been an idiot—again—about Cullen by throwing herself at him the way she'd done. If he'd ever been motivated to work up the inclination to ask her to marry him, he wouldn't do it now. She'd given him her favors, such as they were, in the fulfillment of a misguided scheme. She'd heard often enough that men never married what they could get for free.

"What do you want out of life, Rose?"

Rose had been so involved in her own miserable thoughts that Cullen's sudden question startled her into jerking her horse's reins. "I beg your pardon?"

"I asked you what you wanted out of life. And don't tell me what Kate wants for you, please. I've heard that enough already."

Rose glanced over to find him studying her shrewdly. She sensed he wouldn't be put off by half-truths this time. She said, "I, ah, am not sure."

He shook his head. "I don't believe you, Rose. What do you want out of life. Really. Ultimately."

"Ultimately?" That put a different light on things. If she could create fantasies about what she'd *really* like out of life—one day, far in the future—perhaps she could find the truth in her somewhere. "Well, I think I'd like a place like this someday. You know, calm. Peaceful. Pretty."

"Really. That's interesting."

"Do you think so?"

"Yes. Very interesting. It makes me wonder why you're settling for so much less."

His words surprised her, and she glanced at him sharply. "I've told you—"

"Yes, I know." He expelled a gust of breath. "You're fulfilling your aunt's dreams."

"I'm happy, Cullen. I . . . enjoy our relationship."

He nodded. "That's something, I suppose."

Rose pondered his enigmatic words, wondering if he'd explain himself. He didn't, but she kept thinking about them. Settling for less.

Lord, she was a genuinely fallen woman. Kate would be thrilled. Rose felt a fierce urge to cry.

Now that she knew Cullen was basically a family man with a nice farm, two beautiful boys, and a household staff that all but worshiped at his feet, she wished she'd never told him about wanting to be an adventuress.

Pain gnawed at her heart. She was so incredibly stupid. Her judgment was every bit as faulty as Kate's. Actually, it was worse than Kate's, because Rose had known starting out on this mad plan that it was a mad plan. Kate hadn't. Kate had thought she'd be doing Rose a favor by thrusting her into a man's arms without the benefit of marriage.

Neither one of them had bothered to consider Rose's basic character, however, and now her essential nature was being violated every time she made love with Cullen. Not that she didn't enjoy the act. She did. Very much.

But she wanted the act with the institution, and it was far too late for that. She sighed, and saw Cullen turn to eye her again. She managed a smile for his benefit, and he smiled back.

She wondered if she'd ever get over loving Cullen O'Banyon. For the rest of their ride together she alternately hoped she would and that she wouldn't.

Rose stopped on the threshold of the bedroom parlor and gaped at her aunt. "Kate! Whatever is the matter?" She ran over to Kate, who had been quietly crying into her handkerchief.

Kate, looking tiny and bereft, scrunched as she was into the corner of the sofa, started, and looked guiltily up at Rose. "Oh, dear, I thought you were still out riding with Mr. O'Banyon."

"We just returned. But what is it, Kate? Are you ill?"

Oh, Lord, Rose might as well shoot herself and get it over with if Kate had caught the influenza from her. She, Rose Larkin, was a walking disaster on the face of the earth and shouldn't be allowed to contaminate it. She gave herself a hard mental shake and told herself to stop being melodramatic.

Kate sniffled miserably. "No, I'm not sick, Rose. But thank you for asking."

Rose sank down onto the sofa next to her aunt and took Kate's hand in both of hers. "What's wrong, Kate? Please tell me."

Kate's gray curls bounced when she shook her head. "It's nothing, dear, really."

Rose heaved an exasperated sigh. "It's not nothing. Please tell me."

Kate turned her head away and stared off into space. "You'll believe me to have run mad," she murmured.

That was a possibility. Nevertheless, Rose persisted. "Nonsense," she said bracingly. "I know you too well to think you've gone crazy."

Kate sucked in a huge breath and expelled it. "Well, *I* think I've run mad, then, which is just as bad."

"If you'll tell me about it, perhaps we can sort it out together, Kate. I know you're not crazy. But you are unhappy about something, and I hate to see you this way. You know what you're always telling me: A burden shared is a burden halved. Please let me share your burden."

"Oh, Rose, it's too foolish."

Perhaps. Rose said, "Nonsense! Just tell me, if you please, and quit stalling."

Kate's lower lip trembled, and she had to catch more tears with her handkerchief. "It's all my fault."

"What's your fault?"

Kate flung an arm out in a despairing gesture. "Everything!"

Comprehensive, but unenlightening. "Everything what?"

"Oh, you know."

"No, I don't."

Kate sat silent for so long that Rose began to believe she wasn't going to tell her what the problem was. Then she heaved another sigh and blurted it out.

"I've been all wrong about your career, Rose, and I know it. What's more, I know *you* know it, only you're too kind to hate me for it. It took me until now to understand how unhappy you were, and realize the cause of your unhappiness. At first I couldn't figure it out. And then it . . . it dawned on me. And, oh, Rose! I was such a fool!" Kate turned and, with her eyes streaming, confessed. "You're not me, Rose. You're you, and you're a beautiful young woman who deserves happiness. Your *own* happiness, with whatever that entails. You'll never find it pursuing my youthful dreams. Now that I think about it, my dreams were idiotic. Stupid. I had no idea."

She stopped to blow her nose. Rose was too stunned to speak. Kate went on. "You see, dear, I loved my Glennie. He was a wonderful man. And I loved my home in America. I don't know what got me to thinking I'd missed out on something."

Rose didn't either. She still couldn't talk.

"You need a home and a family and a husband who loves you," Kate resumed. "Mr. O'Banyon is exactly the man for you, and this is exactly the life for you, and now I've gone and ruined everything for you by pushing you into having an affair with him rather than demanding marriage. I'm sure he would have married you. It's all my fault for pushing you into my plan for becoming an adventuress. You're no more fit to be an adventuress than I was. Oh, Rose, if it hadn't been for my darling Glennie, I'd never have left County Cork! It was he who showed me the world and gave me my happiness."

Rose was dumbstruck. Even when Kate threw herself into her arms and sobbed out puddles of woe onto her shoulder, she couldn't think of anything to say.

Unfortunately, Kate was right.

Nineteen

"Oh, Kate," breathed Rose when at last she could speak.

"I've ruined your life, dear, and all because of my own misguided fancies about the adventuring life."

Rose tried to deny it, but the words stuck in her throat. Yet she knew Kate wasn't altogether at fault. "I could have said no. I should have understood myself better."

Kate's head began shaking back and forth, spreading the tears out on Rose's shoulder. "No. You thought you owed it to me. You're too kind. Too obliging. Too eager to please. Too willing to sacrifice yourself for your family."

Good Lord, she wasn't all *that* nice. In order to be that nice, a woman would have to be a mouse, and Rose didn't care to think of herself as a mouse. "Don't be silly," she said in an attempt to brace up her aunt's deflated spirits. Since her own spirits could hardly sink lower, she feared the attempt would not prosper, and she was right.

"No. First it was your father, and then it was me. Your father was unfit to have a child, Rose. You know it as well as I do, yet we've tried to protect his memory. No father should need to be protected by his children. He was very much at fault, dear. And then *I*, the person who should have been looking out for your welfare, *I* dragged you into my harebrained scheme! We must have some inherited taint in our blood."

"Well, now, Kate—"

"No, Rose! It's the truth! It's because, with Glennie and your father both gone, I saw that you and I were alone in the world, and all the old romantic notions I'd had when I was young and pretty rushed back to me. I thought to myself, '*Rose* is young and lovely. *Rose* should have some romantic adventures, as I always wanted to do.'" Kate stopped to blow her nose, which was now bright red, once more. "I was such a fool not to realize that those romantic adventures happened in *books*! They don't happen in real life!"

"Well, I'm sure some of them do. I imagine. That is, I expect some people have them." Rose wasn't sure she should have spoken, since she wasn't doing awfully well. She tried to elaborate. "I mean, I believe this adventure with Mr. O'Banyon has been rather romantic." Even if it meant her life was ruined. She couldn't say that aloud, not even if she was a bit miffed at Kate's too-late understanding of the situation.

Kate wailed out a terrible noise, making Rose want to cover her ears. Perhaps it was wailing women who first gave the Irish the notion of banshees.

"But it's all *wrong*!" Kate cried. "It's all wrong! You should be marrying the man, not be in his keeping." She flung herself away from Rose and onto a pile of small pillows arranged on the sofa. "This is going to end miserably, and it's all my fault. I know you'll never be able to forgive me, Rose. Not when you understand the damage my meddling has caused."

Rose understood it already, more's the pity. Still, Rose Larkin was in charge of her life, not Kate Flanagan, and if Rose had been too weak-willed to handle the controls, this mess was primarily her fault, not Kate's.

She tried to make Kate understand. For an hour the two women went round and round, Kate blaming herself for ruining Rose's life, Rose denying that Kate was totally at fault. For the first time, she was willing to allocate some of the blame to Kate, but not the majority. Rose herself was an adult, independent, American woman, and if she'd had enough gumption to defy the aunt who'd saved her life, her own life's happiness wouldn't now be in jeopardy. She'd also never have met Cullen O'Banyon. Taken all together, she figured her own weakness and Kate's canceled each other out.

She couldn't come up with any convincing proofs that her life hadn't been ruined, however. She couldn't make herself tell a fib that large.

Eventually, exhaustion and the necessity of dressing for dinner broke up their conversation.

In her bedroom, Rose peered at herself in the mirror and sighed. "I'll never get my eyes unpuffed in time for dinner." She tried, though, by lying down for ten minutes with a damp cloth across them. It didn't work. At the moment, nothing in her life seemed to be working.

She was sorry to see that Kate appeared even worse for wear than she did when the two ladies met in the hallway, descended the staircase, and made their way into the parlor, where it was customary to await the summons to dinner.

Cullen paced his library, trying to decide whether to confess his love to Rose and ask her to marry him now, or to leave things as they were. If he proposed, she might well leave him, which would break his heart sooner rather than later. Since her leaving would of a certainty break his heart, he felt no need to hurry the inevitable. And she might learn to love him yet if he didn't rush her.

On the other hand, he'd either seen or imagined he'd seen indications that she might not be completely averse to the notion of marrying him. Therefore, she might accept his offer of marriage, thus making him the happiest man alive.

A knock at the door told him that William and Ferris wanted in. They always came to the library before dinner in order to collect him and accompany him to the parlor.

Cullen didn't need the reminder, but his sons cherished the tradition.

He opened the door and was proud of the smile he achieved. "Enter my sanctuary, boys." He reached down and hugged them both, and was happy to perceive that their small arms around his shoulders had the ability to soothe him still, in spite of the mess his life was in.

"Oh, Da, we saw a fox on the hill today," Ferris blurted out, excited, as he wriggled out of his father's clasp.

"A fox, eh?" Cullen sighed and let William go, too. Foxes were a plague among farmers, including Cullen, who raised a few sheep along with his horses.

"Yes!" Ferris was all but jumping up and down with glee.

"Aye? Well, perhaps we'll have to set out with guns one of these days. It probably has a burrow somewhere, and will be after lambs to feed its pups."

Ferris's eyes lit up. Cullen hoped that didn't betoken a bloodthirsty personality. No, he was sure it didn't. Ferris loved the farm, too. He no more wanted foxes eating his sheep than Cullen did.

"It might have been a cat," William said in an obvious attempt to daunt his younger brother.

"It wasn't!" cried Ferris, offended.

William shrugged. "Might have been."

"Must have been a big cat if it was a cat," Cullen observed in an effort to mediate.

He wished they didn't fight so much. He had a feeling that, somehow or other, William had come to associate Ferris's birth with the loss of his mother. Ferris's birth had nothing to do with Judith's illness, but William had been too young to understand such a fine point when she'd died. He watched his sons, and his heart ached.

Would Rose ever be able to take Judith's place in their affections—providing she'd even consider it, of course? Ferris would be easy to sell on the concept of a new mother, especially one as genial and warmhearted as Rose. William was another matter. But not a hopeless one. He'd seen signs.

Lord, why did he keep thinking of Rose in terms of marriage? For all he knew, she still wanted nothing to do with the institution of marriage.

In an effort to banish his fruitless mental wanderings, he held out both hands to the boys. "Come, William and Ferris. Time to go to the parlor. We'll see if the ladies are there."

William shrugged again and took his father's right hand.

Ferris said, "Oh, I hope Miss Larkin is there, Da! I want to tell her about the fox. Maybe she'll ride out with me tomorrow and look for it." He took his father's left hand.

Cullen smiled, feeling gloomy in the face of the lad's happiness. If—when—Rose left, would Ferris turn sullen, like William?

He'd been wrong to bring her here. He knew it now, but it was too late. Way, way too late.

William opened the door, and Cullen entered the parlor. He stopped short, and Ferris almost barreled into him in his hurry to pass him and rush to Rose. Good God, she looked as if she'd been crying for hours and hours. What was the matter?

"Miss Larkin! Miss Larkin!"

Rose, who had appeared rather startled to see Cullen, although why she should was a mystery to him, smiled for Ferris. "Mr. O'Banyon! Mr. O'Banyon!" she said, laughing, and Ferris ran into her arms. She lifted him up and balanced him on her hip as if she'd been doing it all her life.

Cullen had to fight an urge to turn on his heel and leave the room. He couldn't stand much more of this.

"I saw a fox on the hill today!"

"It was a cat," said William with a sneer.

"Was not!"

"Was too."

Cullen said sharply, "That's enough, boys. Please allow Ferris to finish his story for Miss Larkin's sake, William." He was sorry for his stern tone when he saw William flush, bow stiffly, and walk over to peruse the globe perched in a corner on an oaken stand.

"What color was it?" Rose asked.

"Red, like a fox," said Ferris.

"And did it have a big, fluffy tail?"

"The biggest! And it ran like a fox."

"Well, then, I'm willing to believe it was a fox." Rose turned to where William seemed to be studying the continent of Africa. "Although from a distance, it might well have looked like a large cat."

William lifted his shoulders as if he were trying to deflect Rose's attempt to humor him. Cullen saw Rose sigh and return her attention to Ferris.

He eyed her with no little concern. She truly looked as if she'd been weeping. So did Kate, who sat on the sofa, staring blankly out the window and idly fiddling with tassels on a pillow. He wondered what had happened to put both ladies in a state. He feared he knew, and his insides knotted up and took to aching.

Rose allowed Ferris to chatter for a few minutes, until he'd finished his story about the wonderful sighting of a fox. Then she said, "Will you excuse me for a moment, Ferris? I think I shall take a glass of sherry to my aunt."

"Oh, let me!" cried Ferris.

Rose smiled at him. He was such a darling. "Thank you, sweetheart, but I need to tell Kate something."

"All right." Sunny-natured Ferris smiled engagingly.

"Thank you. You're a very obliging young man, Ferris, and very polite. I think you're a fine lad."

Ferris all but glowed under Rose's praise. She went to the small piecrust table in the corner where the sherry and glasses were, poured a little for herself and a little for Kate, and turned. Cullen was there, looking down at her.

"What's the matter, Rose? Is something wrong?"

She shook her head. "No. Not really." She must look awful if Cullen was asking her that. "But I should like to talk to you after dinner, if I may."

"Of course."

She was dismayed when he gave her a formal bow and

walked away. Oh, dear, did he suspect the secret of her heart?

Of course, he didn't. Rose gave herself a mental shake and took a glass of sherry to Kate, who took it listlessly. Then Rose went to the globe where William still stood, looking alone and lonely. He was still eyeing Africa as if he wished he could be transported there somehow and dropped in the middle of one of the white spots, where nobody had ever been before. He knew she was standing behind him. She could tell because his body tensed. She hated knowing she'd come between William and his peace of mind.

"I've always been curious about those big, blank spaces on the globe," Rose said softly. "I like to read Sir Richard Burton's stories about his trips to the Orient and Africa."

For a moment, she thought William wouldn't respond, but his training in civility came to his assistance. "Aye. Me, too."

"Oh, have you read Sir Richard Burton's books?" They were somewhat risqué for a young boy, but Rose didn't think that should matter. The accounts of Burton's adventures were fascinating and very informative.

"My da won't let me read Burton's books, but I've read lots of others."

"Ah. And where would you go if you were given a choice? I've always wanted to see Africa."

William considered her question. He looked as if he'd momentarily forgotten he didn't like Rose, and she was pleased to have stumbled upon one of his interests. A body could be around Ferris for a second or two and know what he enjoyed. William was another matter entirely. He had to know and trust one before he honored one with any of his secrets.

"I'd like to go to India and see the maharajas and the tigers and the fakirs."

"That would be interesting, indeed. Have you read Mr. Rudyard Kipling's poems?"

William nodded. "And my da read me some of the stories out of *Plain Tales From the Hills*."

"Really?" Rose was impressed. She was surprised that a boy William's age could understand some of those stories, as they weren't intended for children. Then she chided herself. She'd been expected to think and act like an adult since she was younger than William, up to and including trying to rescue her father from ruin. Why should she expect less of this poor, lonely child who'd lost his mother, as Rose had lost hers, at far too early an age. "And did you like them?"

"Aye. But I liked 'Gunga Din' better."

Rose smiled. Of course, a young lad with a romantic streak would adore "Gunga Din." "I've always loved that one, too."

William glanced up at her and surprised Rose by asking, "Why do you want to go to Africa?"

Rose thought for a minute. "I guess it's the animals. The elephants and lions and antelopes and so forth. I'd love to see a herd of zebras running across the plains." She laid the tip of her finger on the globe in the middle of Africa. "And see here? So much of it remains a mystery to us. Only the animals and natives who live in these places know what it's like in there. Can you imagine, William? So much of the earth is left for us to discover. I should think it would be exciting to be an explorer."

He nodded thoughtfully. "But you're a lady." He didn't sound disparaging.

Rose understood. "Yes, I am. And you're a boy. And, therefore, both of us are considered unfit by popular standards to go exploring and adventuring."

"Aye."

"But at least we have books written by people who are neither too young nor too female to explore for us. And we can read about their exploits in the comforts of our homes and not have to suffer through the terrible deprivations some of them experienced."

"That's true." William sounded as if he was struck by the wisdom of her observation.

"I have several books at home in New York that you might be interested in, William. There's one by a Mr.

Doughty—at least I think that's his name—that tells all about his pilgrimage to Mecca."

William's eyes got big. "Oh, you mean he disguised himself? Like Sir Richard Burton?"

"Indeed, he did."

"My word. A fellow can get killed doing that, if the Arabs catch him at it."

"So I understand. His accent must have been much better than mine is when I speak French. I fear I'd be caught in an instant if I tried to pass myself off as a French-woman."

William actually laughed.

Rose felt a sense of elation all out of proportion to the small victory she had scored in the conquest of William O'Banyon's heart. She wished they could remain at the globe, chatting together, for an hour or two. Like most of her wishes recently, however, this one was destined to re-main unfulfilled. Not more than a minute later, Cullen's butler came into the room to announce that dinner was served.

When she turned, she saw that Ferris had gravitated to Kate, and that he and she seemed to be chatting. She silently blessed the friendly little boy for putting the smile back on Kate's face.

"May I accompany you to the dining room, Miss Larkin?"

She looked down at the serious question, put to her in accents so similar to those of his father that they took Rose aback, and smiled at William. "Thank you, William. I should be pleased to have you escort me to dinner."

Cullen caught her eye as they left the room, and she was surprised that he didn't return her smile. She thought she'd performed yeoman's service in getting on William's good side. She wondered why Cullen wasn't happy about it.

The notion that he might well not appreciate his mis-tress getting close to his children froze her heart.

But she wouldn't waver. She'd made a decision as she'd lain on her bed, trying to minimize the effect of all the tears she'd shed that afternoon. She was going to confess to being a fraud, and she was going to do it tonight, after dinner. She was going to confess her love to him, and to tell him that, although she would never require that he marry her, she'd accept him if he wanted her. She didn't expect that he would, in spite of the warmth she'd detected in his demeanor of late.

And then Cullen could toss her out like an old boot—she was well enough to travel now—or he could offer her a permanent place in his life. She feared she knew which one he'd choose.

The meal passed pleasantly enough. Kate seemed more cheerful, thanks to the valiant efforts of Ferris. Rose blessed the sweet-tempered boy. She glanced at Cullen several times, but he'd removed himself from them, emotionally. He appeared as remote as the sun and the stars as he presided over the meal. Oh, he talked, and he answered questions if they were asked, but his mind was elsewhere.

Rose almost lost heart and canceled her plans to talk to him but caught herself and steeled her nerve. As she and Kate got up, preparatory to removing themselves from the table, leaving the men—that is Cullen and his young sons—to whatever it was that gentlemen did after dinner, Rose softly reminded Cullen that she'd like to speak to him.

"Yes, yes," he told her. "We'll be along presently."

Cold. His answer had been very cold and very unlike the Cullen O'Banyon she'd grown to love.

Perhaps she *should* just leave. That would spare them all these decisions that her foolishness had forced them to make. She wished she could turn back time and start this mad adventure all over again. She'd never agree to Kate's scheme if she had it to do over. Even if she had to get a job selling silk stockings to rich women at a department store. At least that would have been honest work.

Kate drifted toward the sofa with the tasseled pillows as soon as they entered the parlor. Rose asked, "Would you care for a book, Kate? Or anything? I'll be happy to fetch your knitting."

Her aunt looked up at her distractedly, her mind obviously elsewhere. "No thank you, dear. I'll just sit and think for awhile."

Oh, dear. This boded ill. It was when Kate sat and thought that she came up with her odd fancies. Rose hoped to distract her. "You know, Kate, I've been thinking about what to do when we return to New York."

Kate's head whipped around and she stared at Rose. "Whatever do you mean, Rose, when we return to New York?"

Rose shrugged. "I suppose I shall have to seek employment. I think it would be a good idea to take a course in typewriting." She was horrified when Kate's lower lip began to tremble and she reached into her pocket to withdraw a handkerchief.

"Oh, Rose! No!"

"What do you mean no? Aren't we going to return to New York?"

Kate answered with a moan.

Rose rushed over to her, sat on the sofa beside her, and patted her on the back. "Kate, please, what's the matter? Didn't we discuss all of this earlier today? I'm sure we shall be quite happy in New York. And typewriting sounds like a much more pleasant way for me to earn my keep than working in a factory."

This time Kate wailed.

Cullen and the boys entered the room and stopped dead at the threshold.

"Whatever is the matter?" Cullen asked, concern and surprise evident in his voice.

William looked startled. Ferris stood rigid, and seemed frightened.

"Oh, dear," Rose murmured. "I don't know what's the matter, truly. Kate just seems to have dissolved into tears."

"It's all my fault," Kate choked out between sobs. "And now everybody will hate me!"

She leaped to her feet, shocking Rose, whose arms were thrust suddenly aside. Rose cried, "Kate!"

Kate cried back, "No! It's all my fault, and I'm so awfully sorry." She turned to Cullen, her face a mask of misery. "Oh, Mr. O'Banyon, please don't hate me!" And she raced out of the room as if all the demons in Ireland were chasing her.

Rose blinked after her and stood on shaky legs. She was beginning to fear for her aunt's sanity. "I'd better go after her and see what's the matter."

Cullen was at her side in an instant. "No, Rose. Let her deal with her emotions by herself this time. We need to talk. You asked to speak to me after dinner, remember?"

"Yes, but—"

"Let's talk *now*, Rose."

He sounded serious, and Rose didn't know what to make of him. She could only stare at him as he turned and said to his sons, "William and Ferris, will one of you please go see if Mrs. Flanagan needs anything."

The boys looked at each other. Ferris said softly, "I'll go," and William shrugged, giving him leave.

"Fine," said Cullen. "William, will you please go upstairs or outside for awhile. Miss Larkin and I have a few things to discuss."

Without a word, William turned and left the room on Ferris's heels.

Cullen went over to the door, looked to see if he could anticipate any more interruptions, and closed the door.

Rose was uncertain in the face of Cullen's odd mood. His manner was still cold and rather remote. She'd never seen him thus, and it unnerved her.

"Please sit down, Rose," Cullen said with icy politeness. "And tell me what you want to say."

Oh, dear. She'd known this was going to be difficult. She hadn't expected that it would be *this* difficult. Before dinner, she'd anticipated confessing her many sins to the warmhearted, kindly Cullen O'Banyon she'd believed existed in his body. This present Cullen O'Banyon was a different person.

"Well, ah—" She stopped and took a deep breath.

Cullen lifted a dark eyebrow and said, "Yes?"

She shut her eyes for a second and prayed silently for

strength. After folding her hands in her lap—she was afraid they would tremble—she blurted out, "I'm a fraud."

Cullen looked at her blankly and didn't speak. His eyebrow lowered, though, which Rose appreciated. He looked so quelling with his eyebrow up like that. She took another breath.

"I'm not at all worldly. I don't want to be an adventuress. I never did. I was an idiot to believe I could do such a thing as sell myself to various men at various times, like a . . . a . . . prostitute or something."

She could feel the heat creep into her face. She was unused to saying such shocking things. On the other hand, she'd been doing shocking things with Cullen for weeks now, so she ought to be able to live through this.

"I'm not sure I understand you, Rose."

His voice still sounded as cold as ice. Rose felt a lump like a boulder lodge in her throat and tried to swallow it, but the pain was so great she had little success. She wouldn't cry, though. Crying was weak and could be construed as a coy and manipulative ploy to soften Cullen's heart. Rose had sunk pretty low in her own estimation, but she refused to sink that low.

To help her through this ordeal, she lifted her chin and tried to appear proud. Any pride, even assumed, would help at this point. "You were right about me, Cullen. I'm a fool to think I want to be an adventuress. You've been kinder to me than I deserve. I thank you for your help and hospitality. I probably would have died without you." She tried to swallow again and furiously blinked back tears. "And I know you don't want a woman like me cluttering up your life any longer than need be. I'm feeling much better now, and—"

"And you're going to leave, is that it?"

Rose's mouth shut with a snap. He sounded enraged, and she didn't understand. She said uncertainly, "I, ah, Kate and I will leave as soon as may be."

"I see."

She didn't understand this. He should be happy to see

the last of her. "That is to say, we'll leave as soon as we can."

He was silent. Rose fancied she could feel waves of hot fury emanating from him, and she still didn't understand. Because she feared she'd burst into tears any second, she put a clamp on her misery and stood, still holding her hands together. She had to clear her throat before she could speak.

"So, I wanted to tell you how very much I thank you, Cullen. You've been wonderful. So have William and Ferris. I apologize for creating turmoil for you and your sons because none of you deserve such as I. And . . . and . . . and I wish I could repay you. I *will* repay you. Somehow. Someday."

This was going nowhere. Rose stammered, "So—so— thank you. I'm sorry."

He was still as if struck from stone, and still radiating rage. She thought she might burn to a crisp if he kept looking at her like that, so she took a step toward the door. She uttered a tiny shriek when he jumped up from his chair.

"*Damnation!* So you're going to leave me, are you? Just like that. You've had your fun and you're going away again, is that it?"

Flabbergasted, Rose gaped at him. "I . . . I . . ." She didn't have a clue what to say.

He stomped over to her and took her by the shoulders. "You waltz into my life, believing me to be some kind of carefree rakehell. You make me into something I've never been, never will be, never wanted to be. You make my sons love you. You rip my old life up and throw it to the four winds. You ruin my sanity and tear my peace of mind to ribbons, and now you're going to trample my heart in the mud and be on your jolly way. *What kind of woman are you?*"

"I . . . I . . ."

"Damnation, Rose Larkin, the only thing I ever wanted was to love you. I wanted to take you into my life and make you my wife. When you trip merrily away from me on your carefree little adventure, you're going to leave my heart and soul in shreds. Does that make you happy? Was that your goal? If it was, you succeeded beyond your wildest expectations, believe me."

Good heavens. "No. No, Cullen, I—I was a benighted idiot for falling in with Kate's scheme, just as you told me I was."

"Damnation, I *love* you!"

And he drew her to his chest and kissed her until she was sure she was going to faint.

Twenty

Rose couldn't believe her ears. She would have asked for an explanation, but his mouth was crushing hers at the moment.

Had he said he loved her? Had he honestly said that? Had he said he wanted her to be his wife? His *wife*?

This was incredible. She couldn't stand the suspense a second longer, and struggled out of his passionate embrace. "Cullen, stop it!"

"What?" he bellowed, still in the grip of fury. "So you can leave me now, Rose?"

"No."

"No? But that is what you just said you were going to do! Which is it, Rose? I need to know! What do you want out of life and stop lying to me!"

"I'm not lying to you! I love you! The only thing I want in life at this moment is to marry you and stay here with you forever! Stop yelling at me!"

Cullen quit shouting. His mouth opened slightly, and his eyes took on a glazed quality. He tried to say something, failed, swallowed, and tried again. "I beg your pardon?"

Rose lost the battle with her tears. She felt them sliding down her cheeks, but she couldn't wipe them away because Cullen still held her. "I've been in love with you for weeks. I asked you to make love to me because I wanted you to love me. It was . . . it was a stupid, heedless thing to do, and I know it. No man will marry a woman as loose and immoral as I've been."

"Loose? Immoral?"

She nodded unhappily. "Oh, I was so stupid! I'm not cut out for the life Kate wanted me to lead. Even *Kate* knows it by this time. I tried, though. I tried very hard. I've always tried so hard to do what other people wanted me to do that I—" She sucked in a breath and told herself to stop whining. This predicament was nobody's fault but her own.

Cullen's clasp loosened, and he licked his lips. "Wait a minute, Rose. I'm confused. Will you please repeat what you just said?"

"About being stupid?" She blinked through her tears and beheld his beloved face blearily.

"No. The other part. The part about being in love with me."

She blinked. "Well, of course, I'm in love with you. What woman wouldn't be? You're the kindest, dearest, most handsome, most wonderful man I've ever met in my life. You're not at all like my father and his friends. You're honorable and good and . . . and you have two beautiful sons. And the most wonderful horse farm in the world, and I never want to leave it. And . . . and . . . and . . ." She was almost out of breath and beginning to cry again. With one last push, she got out, "And I love William and Ferris, too!" Then she collapsed into Cullen's arms and sobbed.

He couldn't believe what she'd just told him. She loved him. *She* loved *him*? Reckless Rose Larkin loved stuffy Cullen O'Banyon? And she loved his children? And she never wanted to leave his farm?

Very carefully, he led Rose to the sofa and guided her to sit. He sat next to her and held her in his arms while she cried weeks worth of unhappiness onto his old dinner jacket. This was a very unsettling circumstance. He was almost afraid to believe she actually wanted to stay here with him. To be his wife.

If he was wrong and he'd misunderstood her, it would kill him to discover the truth.

For several minutes, Rose was beyond speech. Cullen kept his arms around her, and he kept checking to see if she was slowing down. After a little while, he perceived a lessening of her grief and cleared his throat.

"Ah . . . Rose?"

She uttered something that sounded like, "Mgrph."

"Um, I think we'd better talk a little bit longer. I'm not sure I understood what you were telling me."

She sniffled some more, wiped her eyes on his shoulder, and sat back. As she fished in her pocket for a handkerchief, she said thickly, "What? What don't you understand?"

"Um, did you say you wanted to remain here with me? On the farm?"

"Yes." She found the hankie, wiped her cheeks, and blew her nose. She sounded as defiant as a woman who'd just been on a crying spree could sound.

He licked his lips again. "And, ah, you don't want to go roving anymore?"

She made a helpless gesture with the hand holding the handkerchief. "I *never* wanted to go roving. It was all Kate's idea, and I was too stupid to refuse her."

"And, ah, if you were to become my wife, you wouldn't long for adventure and excitement every time we were together?"

"Good heavens, no. The thought of being with other men makes me positively sick." She shuddered and sniffed some more as tears dripped from her chin and she tried to catch them with her hankie.

"I see." The next part was the trickiest. If she gave him the wrong answer, he'd probably die here and now. "And, ah, did you mention whether or not you'd be willing to marry me?"

Her eyes, swimming in leftover tears, goggled at him. "Would I be *willing* to marry you? I'd give everything I have and ever will have to be your wife!"

"Good God."

Rose mopped more tears and eyed him as if she didn't quite trust what was going on. "What do you mean, *good God?* What does that mean?"

For a moment, Cullen was too overcome to speak. Then he soared up from the sofa, grabbed Rose in his arms, and spun her around until she shrieked. He didn't know if she was shrieking in joy or terror, but he didn't care.

There was a panicked booming at the door, and Cullen's estate agent, Ben MacNeill called out, "Cullen! Who screamed? Did somebody get hurt?"

The butler, Charles, called, "Mr. O'Banyon? I say, Mr. O'Banyon?"

Kate's voice wavered through the keyhole. "Rose! Rose! What's wrong?"

The next voice belonged to William. "Da? Is something the matter?"

"What's Miss Larkin crying for?" Ferris asked. He sounded quite distressed.

Still holding Rose, Cullen bounded to the door, threw the bolt, and whirled back into the room, Rose clutching his shoulders like a barnacle clinging to a rock.

The five people who'd been piled up beyond the closed door stumbled into the room. Cullen stopped dancing and turned to face them. He and Rose must have made quite a spectacle, because none of the five spoke. They stood still and goggled at the lovers.

The first person to catch an inkling of what had happened was Ferris. For a moment he stared, wide-eyed, and then his frightened expression eased. He smiled at his father.

Cullen nudged Rose, who had been hiding her eyes against his coat. "Rose? Turn around and say hello to your new sons."

"Sons?" William, who had seemed dreadfully worried, gaped incredulously.

Kate hauled in a bucket of air and let it out in a gasp. "Oh!"

Charles blinked, obviously unsure about what a well-trained butler was supposed to do in these trying circumstances.

At last someone moved. Ben MacNeill lurched forward as if someone had shoved him out of his trance, and a broad smile lit his face. "I say, Cullen, this is the best news I've had in years. Congratulations!"

In order to shake the hand Ben was holding out to him, Cullen had to set Rose gently on the carpet, but he didn't let go of her. Never again would he let go of her.

As for Rose, she was very embarrassed. Not only was her face showing the ravages of a most unladylike crying spree, but, she was sure, her attire must be all wrinkled. She'd never been picked up and whirled around like that. It had been perfectly wonderful.

Rose Larkin became Mrs. Cullen O'Banyon on the fifth day of September in the little church in the village supported by Cullen's horse farm. The entire community shared in the couple's happiness. It was about time, said they, that Cullen took a bride. Not only did he need the comfort of a settled home life, but his boys desperately needed a mother.

And if the girl was an American, and if she was young, so much the better. So many of their fellow countrymen had gone the other way, it was a pleasure to turn the tables. Besides, that nice Mrs. Flanagan was a good Irish lass come home again. And about time, too.

Rose sent for Bridget O'Doyle to serve as her own personal lady's maid—although she wasn't quite sure what to do with one—thus raising her status to that of a saint in the O'Doyles' neighborhood.

In time for their second Christmas together, Cullen fulfilled his promise to build a chapel at the farm and Rose presented him with a bouncing baby girl. They named the baby Katherine Rose.

William, who had come to the conclusion that life was happier with a mother, and Ferris, who hadn't had to learn that particular lesson, were ecstatic. Kate was overjoyed.

Cullen very nearly fainted dead away from relief when the nurse told him Rose and the baby were fine.

According to the village folk, that was the happiest Christmas their little community had ever experienced. The Mass said in dedication of the chapel was expanded to include the baptism of little Katherine Rose, who cried lustily through the entire ceremony.

The village folks went home afterwards, happily assuring one another that a child with such a good set of lungs boded well for the future of the O'Banyon family.

They were right.

TIME PASSAGES

SEDUCTION ROMANCE

*Prepare to be seduced…by the sexy
new romance series from Jove!*

**Brand-new, full-length, one-night-stand-alone
novels featuring the most seductive heroes in the
history of love….**

☐ A HINT OF HEATHER
by Rebecca Hagan Lee   0-515-12905-4
☐ A ROGUE'S PLEASURE
by Hope Tarr   0-515-12951-8
☐ MY LORD PIRATE (1/01)
by Laura Renken   0-515-12984-4

All books $5.99